THE BEARS
AND
THE BEES

THE BEARS AND THE BEES

Icalos

Podium

THE BEARS
AND
THE BEES

CONSEQUENCES

Ruckanos, the tower lord's son, stumbled out of the tower, wincing as pain shot through every inch of his body. His lord father had been ruling for several lifetimes before Ruckanos had ever been born. In that time, he had learned precisely how much damage a human body could take and survive. Knowledge that had been applied to Ruckanos most thoroughly.

A tower guard behind him shoved his back, sending a fresh wave of pain surging through him.

"Come on, move it!"

Ruckanos knew better than to glower or retort to the man's barking. Once upon a time, even the mightiest of the tower guards would grovel at his feet. Now, they would not intervene if even the lowliest peasant insulted him.

And Ruckanos knew why. Oh, he had been very thoroughly and repeatedly instructed as to exactly what he had done. Firstly, his frivolous, unnecessary, and preemptive celebrations had cost him his tower. The knowledge that he had lost his chance at the power, authority, wealth, long life, and blessing of the gods that had all been within his grasp was terrible enough. But on top of all the humiliation and loss of clout that came with this egregious failure, he had then been very much made aware that he had cost his lord father an extra seat at the Conclave. He was even informed that the High Council itself was getting involved. That rumor proved itself to be true when a censor arrived at his father's tower to interrogate him.

And he had been told, in no uncertain terms, that all his current pain was a mercy compared to what he deserved. The power a Tower of the Gods could offer *had* to be utilized responsibly. If it were not, there was no guarantee that the wrath of the gods would not once again fall upon the world. And if humanity failed once again, even after receiving the Blessing of the Towers, would the gods deign to show mercy a second time?

A tower that had not been bound and placed by the augurs was therefore out of the censors' reach. It could not be brought into the Conclave. It could not be monitored. It could not be dealt with, should the worst come to pass. And now, nobody knew where his tower had gone . . . or who was now in charge of it. Ruckanos had created an existential threat to all of humanity that the tower lords could do *nothing* about at present.

And to top it all off, his lord father had been surprisingly upset about his handling of the rabble. Apparently, putting the peasants to the sword was *not* what the lord had meant when he instructed his son to handle it "personally." Relocation was far less wasteful and drew less attention. And . . . it turned out that the small little village Ruckanos had seen no value in was the source of that new mead that had become his lord father's favorite recently. His lord father had been just about to search out the beekeeper responsible and induct them into his tower servants to run his personal apiary.

Ruckanos didn't think it possible, but his lord father had grown even *more* displeased when he discovered exactly which village Ruckanos had burned, and when he had learned there were no survivors. Even the bees of the local apiary had abandoned their hives, so he could not even take possession of them, much less recruit their keeper.

With all of this in mind, Ruckanos expected nothing but death. A slow, excruciating death that took as long as his lord father and the High Council deemed justified.

So, it was something of a surprise that he was now being led outside. The pair of guards behind him pushed him through the keep that surrounded his lord father's tower. He was led down a cramped stairwell and brought to . . . a bathroom? Ruckanos couldn't help but blink as servants stripped him of the rags upon his body and washed him up. A healer came and cast his magic, restoring just enough of Ruckanos's injuries that they would no longer impact his function. Not so much that every movement wouldn't ache, however.

Ruckanos gulped, but decided it was worth risking a question.

"W-What's going on?"

"Quiet."

Well, he hadn't been struck for daring to open his mouth, so he'd consider that an improvement. His questions only increased, however, when he was brought to the armory. He was equipped with some armor, a traveling cloak, a lance, and a sword, all lightly enchanted. Trash compared to the treasures he had once wielded, but items that were still powerful, functional, and the envy of all lesser soldiers. Gear that a tower guard would still find acceptable.

He was then led to a large, open courtyard within the keep, just outside of the tower itself. He froze and blinked until the tower guard behind him shoved him once again. Standing in the courtyard were all of his former personal guards, along with their captain, from his father's tower guard. The augur who had accompanied them to the village was present as well.

Behind them, a squadron of wyverns lay on the ground. Wyvern-tenders were brushing and feeding them as servants packed the large saddlebags tied to them. An official stepped forward and opened a scroll.

"By the decree of the High Council, a Grand Subjugation has been declared. The High Council calls upon all tower lords to join in this grand mission, to seek out and strike down the enemies of the gods wherever they may lurk, and to bring the lost to safety and blessing. Let the sins of the past be atoned for, the wicked brought to justice, and the world purified and reclaimed."

A tower guard standing next to the official saluted and stepped forward.

"The lord of the Starami Tower commits to this effort his own son, Ruckanos, who will personally lead this vanguard."

Ruckanos's heart fell. All his questions had now been answered. The tower lords were aware that not every tower that existed belonged to the Conclave. Single towers, pockets of towers, and even entire nations had been located over time as the Hunger had been driven back. Whenever they were discovered, they had brought into the Conclave . . . or dealt with.

But it was not enough to simply wait for them to appear as the borders of the Conclave slowly expanded. Who knew what a malicious individual could do with a Tower of the Gods in places unseen? Neither the Conclave, nor the High Council, nor the censors could let such a situation stand. The grace of the gods, and therefore the fate of the world, would depend upon it.

And so came the Grand Subjugation. Each tower lord would contribute a portion of their forces to strike out into the unknown. The selected explorers would soar above the Hunger in the skies or take to the Underway below and search the world for rogue towers. Now that a tower had been specifically *lost*, it was only natural a Grand Subjugation would be arranged.

The issue was, the majority of all forces sent out on a Grand Subjugation would never be seen again, especially those in the scouting vanguard. Neither flying high in the sky nor crawling underground were surefire ways to evade the Hunger. The Hunger might creep down into their path, flying and digging shades could assault them en route, and worse things could occur as the concentration of the Hunger rose.

Even if the scouts survived the Hunger's active attempts to consume them, there was no guarantee they would find a safe place to land when their mounts grew exhausted. And even if they did find a safe place to land, there was no guarantee they would find any supplies before what they carried with them ran out. And if all that didn't kill them, at the end of the journey they would find a tower lord, with all the power a tower could grant them, who did not acknowledge the authority of the Conclave. Those rulers of Towers that were merely misguided would be corrected. Those rulers of Towers with evil intent, especially the subhumans, were to be subjugated at all costs. Said rulers would, therefore, likely object violently to the presence of the scouts when they attempted to probe their defenses and decipher their nature.

Ruckanos understood the intention of this Grand Subjugation all too well. He, and everyone who had been with him that fateful day, was being sent to die. Thanks to his failure, every tower lord would now send people to die, but Ruckanos knew he would be the only tower lord's child in the first wave, the one with the highest casualty rate. The wayward tower had to be relocated, no matter how many lives would be lost in the process. His lord father and the High Council intended for his to be the first.

Ruckanos walked silently toward the wyverns. The former captain of his guard saluted, though his eyes held no life. The augur had a frown on his face. Ruckanos gave them a nod as he mounted his wyvern.

"As my lord father and the High Council commands."

But as the wyverns started to take off, a small fire sparked in the depths of Ruckanos's heart. He realized that, even though he was being sent into certain death, he had gained a small chance. He was no longer doomed to die in the depths of his lord father's tower, or at the hands of a censor. No, he had a chance. A small, minuscule chance, but one that at least existed.

If he managed to survive . . .

If he managed to pass over the Hunger . . .

If he managed to find a rogue tower . . .

And if he managed to bring it to heel . . .

Ruckanos's eyes narrowed. He was about to face the most difficult and perilous task of his life . . . but maybe, just maybe, his story wasn't over yet.

CHAPTER ONE

THE UN-BEE-LIEVABLE GRACE OF THE KING

Belissar had just received a mission from the God of Bees to build beehouses . . . but he did not get started immediately. Beekeeping may have been his passion, but commanding a tower was now his duty. He had stopped running purifications after the expansion in order to let the soldier bee army recover, but it had been a while at this point, so he'd need to resume those soon. He rubbed his chin and frowned. With the soldier bee army taking casualties so recently, he still wasn't sure if they were ready.

But then he had a thought. *Why not just ask them?* He had all the flower meadow queens with him right now, so he might as well hear it from them. He took a moment to think of how to phrase the question in a way that wouldn't just result in the usual "Whatever King chooses!" responses.

"So, I have a question. How is the soldier bee army doing?"

The queens all went completely still at that, causing Belissar's heart to race. That reaction was not what he had expected.

"Um, I mean, you lost a lot of bees lately, right? Is the army, um, recovering well?"

The bees remained still, but eventually the largest queen began to dance. Slowly, ever so slowly, barely enough for the tower's translation power to recognize it as communication.

"Army . . . okay. Losses . . . recovered."

Belissar gulped at her tone but took a deep breath to try and calm himself. The queen was clearly hesitant to talk about this, and Belissar wasn't sure why. He wanted to ask her, but given how reluctant she seemed, he didn't feel comfortable pushing further. He would just have to make a decision based on what she had already said and what he already knew. The soldier bee army training in the skies of the field beyond still painted a formidable sight to him, at least. So, if the queen confirmed they had recovered, then there would be no reason not to resume purifications, right? Belissar figured if the worst came to worst, they could just rely on the pit trap strategy again . . . assuming they would go back to getting the mini-wolf type shades.

"Okay, um, if there's no problem, I'm thinking of facing another minor purification tonight. Um, hopefully, one of the easy ones from before. So, um, let me know if there's anything we need to do first, but otherwise, um, get ready for later?"

The queens froze once again. Belissar was about to rescind the order when they exploded into motion. Belissar's eyes spun around as all the bees zipped about him, but the tower's magic barely managed to catch a few of their dances to translate. It seemed they were flying salute dances as quickly as they could.

Belissar was altogether confused at this point but decided to take the dances as a good sign. With that issue resolved, he moved on to begin preparing a new campfire site in the orchard and double-checking the defenses. Once that was settled, he'd move to get started on the new beehouse. Purifications had delayed it long enough as it was.

The Firstborn stood in a daze as her flower meadow compatriots continued dancing their salutes. And, unusually, the Conduit remained even after the King walked off. She landed by the Firstborn and began a gentle dance.

"See? King still trusts! Wants Second First of First do well! Still cares! Like Niobee said, King is best king!"

The Firstborn barely managed to acknowledge her. Satisfied, the Conduit flew off to rejoin him, leaving the flower meadow queens with their thoughts. After her abject failure in the latest purification, the Firstborn had been fully prepared for exile or death. She knew the King was unlikely to demand such things, but her instincts prepared her regardless.

Neither consequence had occurred. That was not a complete surprise, given the benevolent actions of the King thus far, but the Firstborn had expected at least *some* repercussions. Some sort of censure, or a demotion from her post, in favor of one of the other flower meadow queens or maybe even the First of the Fifth, should she have interest in the job. Or, alternatively, a reduction of her resources, or an increase in oversight. Perhaps the King or the Conduit would give her orders from now on. At the very least, the Firstborn expected the King to admonish her and to address her shortcomings.

But again, none of that had occurred. No. Instead, the King had called her to inform her that he was building her a palace by his own hand, as he had done for the most productive queens of the apiary. And he was not just building her a palace like those. He was making her something larger and grander, a new design he had not built before. Not only that, but he *consulted her directly*. He asked her and her comrades what they would want out of a home. He valued their thoughts and their desires, as small and limited as they were compared to his own wisdom.

He was granting them the grandest reward immediately after their greatest failure. The Conduit had told them the King loved all bees, regardless of their success or failure, but only now did the Firstborn understand what she meant. The Firstborn truly could not comprehend the depths of the King's favor for even the least of his bees. But perhaps that was to be expected of the King, who suffered not even a crippled soldier to die when he was able to save her.

But even his unfathomable gift was not the greatest surprise of the day. When the King asked of the state of her army, the Firstborn thought the moment of her punishment had finally come. She and all her compatriots had gone silent in shame. What could the state of the army be but abysmal? Yes, the queens had anticipated casualties and preemptively laid a new generation of soldier eggs, so the losses had been recovered almost immediately. But the army at its peak had failed utterly to stop the enemy. The army she had been so proud of had been revealed as flawed and incapable of its fundamental purpose. So, how was such an army doing? The answer could not be anything good.

And then, once again, the King had defied all of her expectations. He had specifically asked about the casualties. The Firstborn had given an answer, and then the King made the declaration that rocked them all to the core.

He was starting up the purifications again. And he asked *them* to be ready. Not only had the King forgiven them for their failures, but he was still expecting them to continue their duties. He was not replacing them or moving them to other roles. He was not reducing their resources or taking personal command over their hives. He still trusted them to defend the hive of hives, even after their failures.

As the Conduit had assured her, the King was far more forgiving than any queen the Firstborn had ever known. Even she herself would not have let one of her children continue in a role they had failed at so egregiously. They would have been reassigned, if not exiled outright. Instead, the King was giving them another chance.

The Firstborn leapt into action, her wings beating as fast as they could as she shot into the air. She would not let this chance go to waste. She would not let her King down again. So, she quickly conferred with the other queens to explain what she planned to do. They all immediately agreed and raced off into the skies above. Soon, they arrived at the place where their joint army trained. The soldier bees quickly ceased their maneuvers and gathered up before their queens, the mere sight of their mothers outside of the hives pulling their attention.

The Firstborn made the declaration.

"King giving another chance. We battle again today."

The army nearly dropped out of the sky in surprise as the soldiers' wings halted at the declaration. But the Firstborn gave them no chance to recover, as limited as her time was.

"Queens will fight too, today. Will command."

At that, some of the soldier bees fell so far they landed upon the ground, and then the objections began. But the Firstborn would have none of it.

"Not all. Today, me alone. Other queens stay safe. Our job to raise army. If did well, won't be hurt. If did poorly, another will replace. But no matter what, *cannot* fail again. Will not put King in danger again. Hive of hives bigger than one."

The soldiers ceased all dancing, hovering or standing in place. The soldiers of the other hives looked to their queens, every last one of whom danced their assent and commanded their soldiers to follow the Firstborn's lead for today's battle. This was the resolution of the Firstborn, as well as the result of her assessment of their failures. Their army was deadly and disciplined . . . but it was slow to adapt. They trialed new tactics in response to their failures, but only ever *after* the fact. That was no longer sufficient. The soldier bees, as strong as they were, were still limited by their own instincts. When they saw the enemy ahead, they lost most of their thoughts save to defeat it. They had trouble adjusting to anything that occurred until they experienced it directly.

The Firstborn had identified a potential solution from the past, ironically from the queens who had perished altogether. The queens of the First Spawner's First Dynasty that came before her had led from the front. Thanks to that, the Third Queen of the First Spawner's First Dynasty, the first of her line, had pioneered the rotating squad attack that was now the cornerstone of the army's tactics. Monster bee queens had more intelligence and flexibility than the average soldier or worker and were not as beholden to their instincts. Beyond that, they also had an innate ability to command their children through the links in their mana. Orders that came from a soldier's queen would be received and executed far more quickly than those from a fellow soldier.

The Firstborn had experienced all of this herself during the latest purification. In the darkest moment, she had confronted the shade directly alongside her workers in a desperate final stand. And when the shade had attempted to burn them all with its lightning, her greater sensitivity to mana had caught wind of it, her experience had identified the potential threat, her flexibility had suppressed her instinct to attack the enemy without cease, and her abilities as the queen had allowed her to pass her command to the workers in time. As a result, she and all of her workers had managed to evade the enemy's attack, something the entire soldier bee army had failed to do.

The Firstborn was therefore convinced that the presence of a queen on the battlefield could increase the flexibility and speed of the army. Perhaps they could adjust to the enemy before the worst occurred. And, if nothing else, witnessing the fighting with her own eyes might inform her how better to prepare the army in the future. Above all, the Firstborn needed to take responsibility for her own failure, and see the job done.

The soldiers were clearly unhappy that a queen would be exposed to harm, but they reluctantly agreed. Of course, a queen attempting to take command without practice would be a recipe for disaster, so the Firstborn joined the soldiers' training for the rest of the day. The other queens returned to their hives to continue their normal work. The Firstborn had proposed to rotate which queen commanded the army each day, so that each would have a chance to witness the battlefield for herself. When it was not their turn, the other queens would focus on growing their hives—as a queen must. She would simply be the first to try her wings on the battlefield.

And so, the Firstborn took command of the army. She only watched at first, familiarizing herself with the way the soldiers operated. And all the while, she thought of what she might do against the enemies they had faced . . . or against enemies they had not. This was her second chance, and she would do any and everything she could not to fail again.

CHAPTER TWO

IMAGINATIVE STRATE-BEES

After making a campfire site and confirming all the defenses were in place, Belissar returned to the apiary to retrieve his woodcutting tools, then walked down to the orchard. He went ahead and created a wood tree resource node. A spot on the ground began to glow. The glowing light then rose into the air and began to take shape. Suddenly, a fully grown poplar tree appeared in front of Belissar. It was relatively short, only a bit taller than himself, and just thick enough to be useful. At this point, he had expected such a feat from the tower, so he immediately got to work without much thought.

He stepped forward and reached out for the tree, which was still glowing slightly like the other resource node plants, signifying it was ready for harvesting. Belissar wondered if it might somehow pop out of the ground, but the tree didn't respond to his touch. It seemed the tower wouldn't assist him to that extent. Belissar shrugged and hefted his axe to do things the normal way.

The tree grew a bit brighter as he swung the axe toward it. Belissar blinked as he felt mana flash, and then his axe cut *much* deeper into the tree than he had anticipated. He moved to the other side to continue his work, but he barely needed to bother. It took all of three swings for the tree to fall.

Unfortunately for him, fall was all it did. The tree still remained in a solid piece, with the branches still attached, and the wood still wet, as far as he could tell.

Belissar sighed, and then got to work. He guessed he would be making a simple log house. In that case, he might need a few more wood nodes. He'd see how quickly he could process each tree before deciding to create any more.

Belissar worked at it until it was time for the next purification. He wiped the sweat off his brow and then turned to Niobee.

"Hey, Niobee, can you let the flower meadow queens know it's just about time? I'm going to go get the fire started, and then we'll begin."

"Okay!"

As Niobee flew off, Belissar returned to the apiary. He grabbed his firebow and some of the driest firewood, then found the apiary soldier bees and asked them to come with him. They gathered their torches, hooked themselves onto their ropes, and then flew after him with their cargo in tow.

It didn't take long for him to arrive at the end of the orchard, and soon he had a fire going there. The apiary soldiers took up positions by the fire and handed Belissar one of the torches.

"Thank you," he said, and the soldiers saluted in reply.

Belissar used his tower sight to check in on the flower meadow. He found the soldier bee army prepared and ready, with even one of the queens at its head. Belissar paused a bit at that but shook his head. The bees knew what they were doing and valued their queens even more than he did, so if a queen felt it was worth the risk to participate in the battle, he wouldn't complain.

He sent all the bees a message asking if they were ready, and was treated to the sight of the entire soldier bee army performing a salute dance in sync. He took a deep breath and went to activate the purification.

Please select a purification strength:
- Minor (Cooldown: 16 hours)
- Minor+ (Cooldown: 24 hours)

Belissar blinked. That was certainly new. He could apparently now select the strength of the ongoing purifications? And the cooldown of the minor purifications had gone down to less than a day. He could also now conduct a minor+ purification with the regular one-day cooldown.

Belissar rubbed his chin and furrowed his brow. If he had to guess, the change was probably because his tower had grown? Well, that would make sense. The area the tower was purifying had increased, so it probably had to deal with more Hunger than before. It would be natural for the purifications to increase in strength and frequency too, right?

Belissar shrugged. The mysteries of the tower's function were beyond him. And so too was the minor+ purification. Last time, that plus sign had meant two small wolf-shades, but Belissar did not want to test it today. The bees hadn't had a chance to prepare themselves for that, and it would take some time before the new monsters, rooms, and perks Belissar had selected would have an impact. He figured he would at least wait for some sprayers to grow before attempting anything tougher.

So, for today, the choices were irrelevant. He would go with the usual minor purification, and simply note that with the faster cooldown, he could start it earlier tomorrow if he wanted to. He made his choice, then shivered as he felt the chill of the Hunger. Once again, a wolf-shade appeared to test his tower's defenses.

The Firstborn flew toward the tower entrance and began arranging her army. This was it. The first battle she would be leading directly. It was to be a minor skirmish, but that was no comfort. Even a minor skirmish could result in accidental casualties, which would be unacceptable, since nothing short of a perfect victory was expected in such an engagement. If the Firstborn made a mistake, she could end up making the army perform worse and take damage when it was not supposed to. There were thus stricter expectations during a minor purification than in a battle with higher or unknown stakes.

But the Firstborn was resolved, and she believed in her soldiers. If all else failed, she would leave to them the task they had accomplished time and time again. It was her own efforts that were at risk here. If she could not bring about victory in such small and proven conditions, she could not possibly do so when all was on the line. So, she set about her task with all the effort she could muster.

The Firstborn moved her own children into position while keeping the rest of the soldier bee army further back. Part of this was practical reality. Her mana link only extended to her own children, and so the benefits of her command only applied to them. When she commanded the armies of her compatriots, her orders were received no quicker than those of the soldiers themselves.

But keeping the army back was also an intentional decision by the Firstborn. The instinct of the bees was to swarm their opponent with overwhelming force, bringing down beasts thousands of times their size with thousands of stings in turn. The latest purification, however, had revealed the weakness of this approach. The entire soldier bee army had deployed to encircle the shade; as a result, once the shade had escaped that encirclement, it had escaped the entire army, and there were no soldiers left to bar its path.

The soldiers had partially learned this lesson in the first minor purification and had adopted encirclement formations for that very reason, but the Firstborn now realized they needed to apply the principle on a larger scale. She was not only going to hold back some soldiers from the immediate attack, but hold back entire hives' worth of them, separated completely from the battle. A second army that could start a new fight should the first one fail, or fall back to defend the hives and the King before an escaping enemy arrived. Since the second army would not be actively engaged in the fight, the lesser speed of the Firstborn's commands to them would not be an issue. And if they needed to fall back to the hives, their own queens could assume command of them.

That was the idea, at least. The soldiers were uncomfortable at the idea of holding back the majority of their strength. The Firstborn could not claim she was entirely confident in the plan either. But . . . her soldiers had engaged the enemy in rotating squads already, so she believed reducing their numbers wouldn't reduce their overall effectiveness. And, ultimately, they had failed once already with the old way of doing things. Even the most hesitant soldier could agree that *something* needed to change.

And now came the moment of truth. The dark power held back by the might of the King coalesced once again. Once more, an invader blackened the land of the King with its foul presence. The Firstborn gave the command and her soldiers engaged. All around her, the reserve soldiers began to sway in the air, continuously extending and retracting their stingers. The Firstborn didn't need a familial mana link to them to understand their current feelings, but she held her ground.

Again and again, squads of her soldiers dove down upon the shade. However, their encirclement was noticeably lighter than usual, the natural consequence of holding back most of the army. The shade made a run for it, attempting to break out and fight on the move.

But the Firstborn saw it tense and identified its intentions. She immediately commanded her forces in response. And so, when it suddenly began sprinting, the soldiers did not panic but simply matched its movement with disciplined flight. They responded instantly to their queen's command, although they as individuals had not yet noticed the shade's latest move. Even soldier bees flying away after an attack run, unable to see the shade at all, now knew where to fly.

As a result, the encirclement moved in perfect sync with the shade. No matter how many sudden stops, twists, or turns it attempted, the bees kept pace. Squads continued their attack runs all the while, their stings mounting up on the shade. Soon, it began to slow down. Not long after that, it fell to the ground, and then faded away completely.

The Firstborn stared for a moment before her wings began to slow and she gently descended from the air. They had won. Her plan had worked. She had held back the majority of the army, and still they'd succeeded . . . and without a single sacrifice.

She quietly landed on the ground as the soldiers began to dance and celebrate. There could be hope for her hive yet.

THE BURDENS OF COMMAND

The next morning, the First Queen of the Second Spawner's First Dynasty, the first of her line, did not proceed to laying eggs as usual. Instead, she made her way *outside* of her hive and flew up into the sky. There, she found the joint soldier bee army waiting for her. Yes, *waiting*. Not immediately conducting their practice runs and training, as they normally would.

She would admit she had doubts about the Firstborn's idea. She knew that the Firstborn was correct about the benefits of having a queen on the field, yet she also knew that said benefits came at great cost. Even one day of a queen not laying eggs would impact the future growth of a hive, all the more so for the flower meadow queens who already operated at the edge of sustainability.

And even putting aside that, the very benefits of a queen commanding the soldier bees *also* applied to the operation of the hive. A queen's presence boosted efficiency all around, identifying inefficiencies such as traffic jams within the hive, over- or under-allocation of workers to specific tasks, or changes in the honey-making process due to climate, temperature, nectar source, or any number of other factors.

So, time spent commanding the soldier bees meant time that her hive would run less efficiently than normal, with no one around to identify and resolve issues. Her workers would be left on their own.

But, ultimately, the First of the Second could not object, not after the failure of their army. The Firstborn had come up with an idea to address their demonstrated weaknesses, which was more than she herself could say, so here she was, ready to take her agreed-upon turn at command. Without many ideas of her own, she simply followed the Firstborn's proposals.

She separated some of her own hive's soldiers into a smaller force and set the others as a reserve force, then set about practicing as the Firstborn had, making her hive practice attack runs while she moved the reserve force around.

Only half an hour later, her antennas were twitching and she was constantly shaking. This . . . was not going well. Oh, she found she could command her soldiers as easily as her workers, and they were performing marvelously. But not so with the rest of the army. As the Firstborn had reminded them during yesterday's celebrations, a queen's command did not extend beyond the reach of her children. Her orders had to be passed through the rest of the army one bee at a time, which led to delays in execution. Anytime she wanted to conduct quick movements in succession, the soldiers closest to her would respond immediately, but the ones further away would continue on with the previous order. The soldiers slowed down to avoid collisions, or else started to separate from one another as the distant soldiers continued on in the wrong direction. She was having to slow down and wait before issuing new commands, an inefficient use of her time on a task that was already dropping the efficiency of her hive.

She couldn't help but be a little frustrated at this. How could this be more beneficial than using the day to manage her hive? And she would have to do this on a regular basis? But she was a bee, and this was her assigned task for the day, so she would not abandon it no matter how frustrating or inefficient it seemed. She paused the exercise and told the soldiers to return to normal training for now. Since the command situation was not acceptable to her, she needed to think on how she could improve it . . .

Another agonizing half hour passed before she came up with anything. She gathered up the bees and separated her hive and the reserve force once again. This time, though, she sent several of her own soldiers into the reserve force, splitting up the force into sections and assigning one of her own soldiers to each one. She tasked each of these soldiers with passing her commands to their respective groups, while informing the other hives' soldiers to pay attention to hers.

She then, reluctantly, took command once again. She ordered the reserve force to fly forward, then suddenly turn to the right. Her soldiers received her command immediately and began passing it along without delay. The whole formation turned with only a minimal gap in time, and with significantly less collisions.

The First of the Second noted the improvements and began the exercises in earnest, conducting as many maneuvers she could think of. Even with the command delay, splitting the reserve force into several groups appeared to have other benefits. Since they were not all in one solid mass, the group did not get as easily tangled when the bees closer to her responded more quickly than those at the edge, which cut down on the chaos from earlier.

There was still a lag in the execution of her commands that grated on her, but it was *significantly* better than before. It was a start, at least. And it meant she could get comfortable enough with commanding to take on the intruder coming later today. That, ultimately, was the most important priority. That was the duty and purpose of the First of the Second, of every bee within the flower meadow. That, at least, *all* the flower meadow queens agreed upon. Not one intruder would ever make it past them again until every effort and breath they had was spent.

Back in the First of the Second's hive, the disaster she had foreseen was coming to pass. Well, ultimately the hive was still functioning, unlike her worst fears, but all was not well. A group of foragers dropping off nectar tried to enter the same area as a group just about to leave. The two groups ran into each other and had to confer and decide who would move out of the way. Then, once the arriving group was able to enter the area, they found all the cells already full and being processed. They had to leave and then search the hive for a vacant area . . . only to be told by a group on brood-tending duty that the first such area they found was slated for the queen to lay more eggs later, and so sending them to search once more.

Individually, none of these incidents took very long, just a few seconds for most of them. But all together, those seconds added up. This was especially true for a hive that always operated under the command of their queen. Where once they used to just receive and immediately execute commands from their queen, now they had to identify and solve issues on their own, which led to further hesitation whenever an obstacle was encountered. And all of this was compounded by a general sense of unease and anxiety due to the queen being absent . . . and potentially exposed to danger.

As the day moved along, the drop in efficiency became noticeable to the entire hive. The workers started to grow agitated and began moving hastily to pick up the slack. But without the queen to allocate the effort effectively, moving hastily was not enough, and so the inefficiency only grew.

It was then that the hive received visitors. A small handful of foragers from the Fourth of the Seventh's hive landed at their entrance to rest their wings and exchange news. At first, the workers of the First of the Second's hive had been wary of the intruders, but the newcomers had received permission from the Firstborn to operate in the flower meadow, and the exchange of information from the apiary proved useful to the queen, so the workers soon considered this just another task.

Without the queen to assign workers to greet them, however, it took a moment before some of the First of the Second's workers acknowledged the waiting bees, which the newcomers took note of.

"Problem with hive?"

The greeting worker couldn't help but begin a frustrated dance.

"Queen gone, hive not working well."

The newcomers burst into motion.

"What?! Queen gone?!"

The greeting worker paused before realizing her mistake.

"Queen okay, with soldiers. But not here, hard to work without."

The newcomers stopped their dance.

"Oh, good! Really? Work without queen all the time, not too hard."

The greeting worker nearly lunged at them.

"You . . . work without queen?! Know how?!"

The newcomers simply confirmed.

"Yes!"

The greeting worker nearly tripped over her own legs in her haste to dance.

"How?! Please tell!"

The Fourth of the Seventh's workers backed up a bit at the aggression, but in the name of exchanging information to bring back to their own curious queen they went ahead and explained how things worked in their hive. Specifically, they focused on how their hive had organized itself when their queen had to, or wanted to, fly off and handle a task outside. A single worker would take up the queen's tasks of keeping track of the state of the hive as a whole and issuing commands to the other workers. Tasks said worker continued to do . . . even when their queen was present . . .

The greeting worker was completely still as she stared at them, before she raced back into her hive to spread what she had learned. The newcomers, now left alone, glanced at one other.

"So, no news?"

"First of Second not at home, working with army? That news?"

"Yes, guess so. Let's go!"

And so the newcomers flew off, as word of their hive's unique organization spread throughout the First of the Second's workers . . .

CHAPTER THREE

DISTRACTING, OR BEE-NEFICIAL?

The minor purification went off without a hitch, the bees handling it as they had many times before. Belissar was curious when they arranged themselves differently but figured that was the influence of a queen joining the battle. Regardless, everything went according to expectations. Belissar got the usual minor choices and added another ten mana to his max. He wasn't planning another expansion for a while, but it could be useful to start working on the mana beforehand. More mana never hurt. Belissar threw a celebration for the bees and then turned in for the night.

The next morning, Belissar walked over to the orchard and found the wood tree had completely regrown during the night. He chopped it down, then started to remove the branches. He was just finishing up when something caught his attention. A shift in the tower's mana.

He turned his sight to the area in question, which turned out to be the entrance. A group of bear folk, including Chief Rohsuak, had entered the dungeon.

"Oh. Right."

Belissar had sort of forgotten about them, but it had been a day or two since the purification, so it was just about time for them to return. Belissar sighed and wiped some of the sweat off his brow. He didn't want to put off the beehouse work, but he *did* want to keep learning magic. Making magic honey that could help bees heal themselves was great, but there was a bit of a gap between that and the massive fireball Chief Rohsuak had displayed.

Belissar walked through the flower meadow to the tower entrance. Chief Rohsuak smiled at his approach.

"Hello, Sacred Den Master. I hope we're not intruding."

Belissar shook his head. "It's fine."

The chief smiled at him and waved to Metsaitti and his hunter group. "Thank you. Would you mind if our hunters resumed their challenges?"

Belissar slowly nodded. "That, um, should be fine. Just don't disturb the bees."

Belissar made a point to glare at them at that. The hunters all nodded vigorously, and then the group departed. Belissar turned back to Chief Rohsuak . . . and the young woman who remained with her. He thought he had seen her in an earlier group, but he didn't remember exactly.

"Um, so, should we start with the magic lessons, then?"

Chief Rohsuak gave a bit of a smirk. "About that . . . I have to admit, you have already completed your studies, Sacred Den Master."

Belissar gaped at her. "Huh?"

Chief Rohsuak nodded. "The magic that you and I possess is not so much of a school to be studied as an innate blessing that we have received from our respective gods. All you needed to learn was how to sense and manipulate your mana. And I have to say, you picked that up marvelously quickly. You have a talent for this."

Belissar squirmed a bit at that. "Oh, um . . . but I can't do big fireballs like you? Surely there's more you can teach me?"

Chief Rohsuak shook her head. "From now on, your blessing and your patron god will guide you in the development of your magic as you continue to use it. Our patrons are quite a bit different, so while I am willing to share my experiences, I do not expect you would learn much from them. My best recommendation would be to use your magic often and in as many ways as you can think of, as well as to reflect upon your patron's domain." She glanced up at the soldier bees flying overhead. "Though I don't imagine that will be a problem for you."

Belissar frowned at that. But before he got caught up in his thoughts, Chief Rohsuak motioned and the young woman stepped forward.

"However . . . I suspect there's more than one mystic art you may wish to learn. Allow me to introduce Juosiutik."

Juosiutik gave him a nod. "Nice to meet you, Sacred Den Master."

Belissar glanced at her. "Oh, um, nice to meet you."

Chief Rohsuak nodded. "Juosiutik here is our herbalist and potion-maker. You may remember her from when she offered tribute at your patron's shrine; she, too, is seeking a blessing from your patron. She is also most interested in your den's products."

Juosiutik leaned in and stared at him without blinking. "*Especially* the honey and the mana flowers."

Belissar took a step back and gulped. The soldier bees flew a bit closer, arranging themselves to be ready for an attack run if needed. Chief Rohsuak placed a hand on Juosiutik's shoulder. The young woman jumped a bit before glancing around sheepishly at the bees. Chief Rohsuak gave Belissar a reassuring smile.

"What we're proposing is that Juosiutik could introduce you to the art of potion-making in exchange for some of your products. Juosiutik tells me your bees' honey has great potential, so perhaps a collaboration could benefit you both?"

Belissar rubbed his chin and started to think. So . . . his magic lessons with Chief Rohsuak were done? That was unexpected. And he could keep learning magic on his own by just using it a bunch? With all the supposed dangers and complexity of magic he had been told about before, he'd figured it would be more complicated than that. Just another one of the tower lords' lies, he guessed. On the other hand, he *was* a dungeon master blessed by a god, so maybe magic was only easy for him. Now that he knew the feeling of mana, he couldn't remember ever feeling something like that in his life beforehand. If it weren't for the tower, who knew how hard it might have been for him to sense and move the mana?

But that was beside the point for now. The point was, his lessons with Chief Rohsuak were done, but this Juosiutik was offering to start new lessons—about potion-making. Another magical field Belissar had vaguely heard of and been warned against, though at this point he was leaning toward completely disregarding any warnings from his past. How many of them had proven to be even remotely true?

. . . Well, the warnings about the Hunger had turned out to be all too accurate, so there was that.

So, would it be worthwhile for him to trade resources and time to learn potion-making? Belissar looked at his hand and felt the mana flowing through it. The answer to that was a resounding yes, even with what little Belissar knew of real potions. He had seen the growth of his bees accelerate thanks to the mana flowers. He had seen basic herbs turned into healing honey and poisonous flowers turned into a weapon that could affect a shade of the Hunger. He had seen brand-new types of bees he could never have imagined taking on the attributes of those honeys. He had saved the wounded soldier with the magic honey he managed to produce.

If he could develop those resources into actual potions, who knew what might be possible? Maybe he could make healing potions that could fully restore a crippled soldier's wings. Maybe he could make poisons that would not only intoxicate but suffocate a shade of the Hunger without putting his bees at risk. Maybe he could make magical honey that would promote the growth of his bees even further.

One thing both the folk stories and the tower lords' warnings agreed upon was this: potions *were* magic, for better or for worse. Having access to that magic would give him new and potentially powerful options both to grow his bees and to defeat shades. Those options were precisely what he needed to protect his tower and his bees from whatever the future might hold.

But still, he hesitated.

"Um, Sacred Den Master . . . ?" Chief Rohsuak prompted.

Belissar jumped a bit, realizing he had gone silent for a while and both women were now staring at him. "So, um, I *am* interested in your potions, but . . . I'm starting work on a project for the sacred den right now. If our original lessons are over, I would like to focus on that project for now."

Yes, as helpful as learning the mystic arts might be, Belissar had put off building beehouses long enough, and he didn't want any more delays. If he had the chance to spend more time on the bees, he would take it.

Juosiutik's eyes widened. "Y-You can't, I need those . . . !" She cleared her throat. "Ahem, I think you, uh, shouldn't be too hasty in your decision, Sacred Den Master. Perhaps we could help you with whatever you're working on, and then you would have time to fit in a few lessons, right? Right?!"

Belissar took another step back at the sudden assault. "Oh, um, maybe? Do you have any building materials? Clay, sealants, adhesives? Dry wood?"

Chief Rohsuak's smile grew bright. "Actually, we could help you with that."

Belissar's eyes widened for a second, and then he started to grin. New materials that would let him upgrade the quality of the beehouses, *plus* learning magic potions in the mix? Now that was a deal worth taking.

"In that case, let's discuss the price?"

Juosiutik smiled as wide as she could while Chief Rohsuak chuckled.

CHAPTER FOUR

BEE-COME A POTIONMAKER?

Belissar and Chief Rohsuak hammered out the details. Belissar described the structures he was looking to build and the kind of materials he would need, while Chief Rohsuak confirmed or denied what they could supply.

Belissar had experience with home projects by necessity, but he was no master architect, so his needs were fairly basic. While the bear folks' previously nomadic lifestyle restricted what they had immediately available, they were at least familiar with anything known to Belissar, so the talk went smoothly. Once Chief Rohsuak had a good idea of what Belissar needed, she left to arrange things, at which point Juosiutik took over.

"Okay, shall we get started, then?"

Belissar thought for a second. He *could* spend the time cutting down more trees, but Chief Rohsuak had specifically stated they could provide dry wood, so he didn't really need to do that anymore. He could afford to spend some time today on a lesson.

"Yes, that should be fine."

Juosiutik nodded. "Okay, first of all, how much do you know about herbology and potions?"

Belissar shrugged. "Um, not much? I know some basic remedies and stuff, but I don't know anything about potions."

Juosiutik tried to hold back a frown at that. "I . . . see." She took a deep breath. "Okay, let's start at the beginning, then. Potions are *not* simple medicines, unlike what the hunters will tell you. If I had to put it simply, they're like medicines, but *more*. You have to learn regular medicine-making, and *then* add a whole extra layer of complexity on top of it."

Belissar gulped. "That, um, sounds pretty complicated. Um, what's the extra layer then?"

Juosiutik nodded. "It is very complicated. Okay, so, the basics. For a potion to be a potion and not just a medicine, you have to imbue it with mana. First, you need a source of mana. Either you have to add it yourself or you have to find some material that possesses it. Then, you imbue it into your ingredients. But mana isn't like any other ingredient. You can't just mash it together in a pot and expect it to work. Mana interacts differently with every different object—plants and ingredients included. Some plants that make powerful medicines normally don't interact with mana at all and are useless for potion-making. Other plants that are otherwise mere weeds have a powerful resonance with mana that make them ideal ingredients. And then, just having the mana and the ingredients present isn't enough. Every method of processing the potion, from mashing to drying to boiling, will affect the mana as well, and you need to account for that. Sometimes, you need to add ingredients and processes that are entirely unrelated to plants or herbology just to get the mana to develop properly. And mana has different types as well, so all of this will change depending on the source of mana in question."

Belissar's eyes were spinning at this point. "That, um, uhhhh . . . I'm sorry, that's a bit much. I don't really understand, I think?"

Juosiutik caught herself. "Oh, um, sorry. Maybe a practical demonstration might help? You have more of those herbs Metsaitti's group brought back from here, right?"

Belissar nodded and Juosiutik smiled. "Could you bring some, then? I could make a potion and explain what I'm doing, and maybe that would help? Oh, um, and since we'll be using both yours and my materials, would it be alright if we split the potions?"

Belissar nodded at that. "Okay, I'll go get some, then."

And with that, he made a trip to the healing herb patch by the flower meadow hives. There was a closer patch, but that was for Metsaitti's group to gather from, so Belissar figured he'd leave that one to them. Assuming his bees didn't need the flowers he was about to gather.

But they did not. The healing herb patch had more flowers than the glowing ones he could harvest, so grabbing those would not prevent the bees from continuing their foraging. Belissar was able to get what he needed without issue.

When he returned back to the tower's entrance, Juosiutik had set up a mat on the ground and put on some leather gloves. On top of it, she laid out a knife, a stone pestle and mortar, a water pouch, a small pot, and a radish of some sort. Belissar walked over to her and handed over the herbs. Juosiutik nodded as she took them and laid them down.

"Thanks. Why don't you have a seat? I'll get started, then."

Belissar nodded and sat in front of her. Juosiutik grabbed the radish. It was bright red with a bit of orange.

"I'm going to stay pretty basic, this time. Just the herbs you brought, and this fire root."

Belissar's eyes widened. "Fire root?"

Juosiutik nodded. "A root with a bunch of Fire mana inside of it. They're normally pretty rare, but the chief can sense sources of Fire mana, so we have a surprising amount of them. They'll catch fire if you pass a bit of mana into them. We use them to start fires and stuff. I'm going to use it here for both heat and mana. The heat will be for boiling, while the Fire mana will adjust the effects of the herbs and imbue the potion with mana."

Belissar rubbed his chin. "I . . . see?"

Juosiutik shrugged. "It's fine if you don't get it now, you'll see as I process it." She began to shave off a bit of the root with the knife. "Too much Fire mana will overwhelm the herbs' healing properties . . . or it will just burn off all the water and set the mix on fire."

Belissar gulped. "Um, how do you know how much is too much?"

Juosiutik gave him a serious look. "Practice."

Belissar started at that. "But . . . wouldn't you get burned?"

Juosiutik's gaze didn't waver. "Yes."

Belissar gulped again as Juosiutik's expression softened. "Well, for this, you can just learn it from me, so pay attention to how much I use. It's just . . . we lost our last potion-maker before I could learn everything I needed to, so I've had to figure a lot of things out myself."

Belissar let out a sigh of relief. He would much prefer to be informed what would catch fire *before* it actually did. Then he thought a moment longer and caught the rest of what Juosiutik had just said. Losing people and having to figure things out for yourself was something that sounded familiar to him.

"Um, sorry for your loss. Do you, um, want to talk about it?"

Juosiutik shook her head and immediately moved to grab the healing herbs and the mortar and pestle. "No."

Belissar nodded and said no more as Juosiutik put the herbs into the mortar. He caught little flashes of mana as she started to crush them up.

"Dumping mana directly into the ingredients while grinding is about the simplest way to go about it, but in this case it will work. These herbs you grow are *very* receptive to mana, and from what I've seen so far the mana easily resonates with their healing properties. They're very easy to work with. Normally, you'd need to be more careful about how you do this. In this case, though, I can just imbue them directly."

Belissar smiled slightly at that. He already knew his tower could do amazing things, and the more he learned, the more incredible its feats became. Apparently its power also extended to potion-making. Once Juosiutik was finished, she filled the pot with some water and poured the mashed herbs in, followed by the fire root shavings.

"Normally, I'd have to be more careful about this too. I'd have to add the fire root first and watch for a precise moment in the boiling process to add the other ingredients to ensure they aren't exposed to the Fire mana for either too long or too short, and that the temperature doesn't end up affecting the mundane properties either. But"—she furrowed her brow at the mixture—"these herbs are abnormally cooperative. Their healing properties don't go away even if I boil them from the start. I've boiled them down to almost nothing and they *still* worked. And as long as there's not so much Fire mana that they get entirely overwhelmed, I can expose them to it for as long as I like without them losing the healing effect. It's almost unfair how easy it is to work with them!"

The water began to bubble even without further input. Juosiutik motioned to it as Belissar's eyes widened.

"As you can see, even the mana I imbued into the herbs is enough to activate the fire root. Which is, again, why I'd *normally* have to be really careful about when, how, and in what order I added all this. But you can at least see that the mana in one ingredient can clearly impact the mana in the other, and if you're using ingredients that are harder to work with, you have to pay attention to that sort of thing."

Belissar nodded as he stared at the pot. Juosiutik mixed it a bit until the liquid began to glow with a soft greenish-blue light. She then took out a small, empty water pouch, stretched a cloth over the water pouch's opening, and held it to Belissar.

"Could you hold this open for me? Make sure to keep the cloth over the entrance."

Belissar nodded and held the pouch as Juosiutik carefully poured the contents of the pot into it. The cloth acted as a sieve, catching the debris from the herbs and the fire root. Once she was done, Juosiutik put down the pot, took the pouch from Belissar, and tied it shut.

"Let it sit for about an hour, and there you have it. A functional healing potion, a minor one at least. The Fire mana can cause or exacerbate fevers, so it can be helpful for some light illnesses, but it should be avoided if the patient already has a fever."

Belissar nodded in a daze. They . . . made a potion? One of those magical elixirs? Just like that? Well, maybe not *just* like that. There *had* been a lot of information involved, and Juosiutik did say doing it wrong could potentially set things on fire. Apparently the tower lords hadn't lied entirely about that part. But still, the process was far more . . . normal than Belissar had anticipated. He even thought he might be able to do something like that himself—assuming he knew what *not* to do to avoid setting the potion on fire. And speaking of which, Juosiutik nodded at him. "How about you give it a try?"

CHAPTER FIVE

PLEASE BEE CAREFUL

Belissar nodded. "Okay, I'll try . . ."

Honestly, the process didn't seem *that* different from mead-making, besides the mana and the burning roots. Under Juosiutik's watch, Belissar started mashing up some healing herbs and pouring his mana into it.

"Um, is it supposed to be glowing?"

Juosiutik frowned. "No, let me see."

She picked up the bowl. The herbs were glowing . . . or rather, *glistening* in the sunlight. If she looked closely, she could see a viscous, golden liquid leaking out of them. She narrowed her eyes.

"Why exactly did you put honey into the mix?"

Belissar tilted his head. "Huh?"

Juosiutik shoved the bowl in front of his face. "You heard me, honey got into the bowl somehow, and I definitely didn't put it there. Don't you remember what I said about this being a careful process? Adding random ingredients is a recipe for disaster!" She snatched the pestle from his hand.

Belissar held up his hands and shook his head. "I-I didn't, I swear!"

Juosiutik was about to object again when she heard buzzing. A squad of soldier bees flew down in between the two, while the rest of the bees began forming an encirclement around her. Belissar quickly began waving them off.

"Ah, no! It's all right, she wasn't going to hurt me . . ." Belissar suddenly stopped and glanced at her. "You, um, weren't going to hurt me, right?"

Juosiutik shook her head with all her might. Belissar turned back to the bees and nodded.

"Okay then, yep, it's alright."

The soldier bees swayed a bit in the air but slowly backed off again. Belissar rubbed the back of his head.

"Sorry about that."

Juosiutik shook her head. "No, I'm sorry. I know I get a bit . . . passionate about this stuff. There's, um, a lot of people in the tribe who don't get why I make a big fuss about 'minor' details in the process, so I may have overreacted."

She took a deep breath. "Still, it *is* an issue to add a new ingredient without warning. If you know how the honey got there, could you tell me?"

Belissar rubbed his chin, then suddenly smacked the bottom of his fist into his palm. "I think I got it. Um, this is what happens when I move my mana outside of my body . . ."

Belissar held out his hand and willed his mana to leave. It formed into a honeycomb pattern made of light and then converted into honey. Juosiutik's eyes went as wide as they could go.

"You . . . can make honey? Mana honey, even?"

Belissar slowly nodded. Juosiutik stared at him for a moment before she suddenly began mashing the herbs in the bowl as hard as she could.

"That's amazing! You have an endless source of an ingredient that I believe has incredible potential! Honey already has incredible medicinal and preservation properties, so what would happen if we imbued it with mana and then mixed it with other ingredients? I think this could become a revolution in potion-making! At the very least, it should dramatically increase the lifespan of a given potion, and I'm certain it will improve the medicinal effectiveness as well! Look, even now the mixture is soaking up my mana like a sponge! I don't know for sure, but I think the mana in the honey and the herbs are resonating with each other. Now, let's see what kind of potion awaits!"

Belissar was left glancing about as Juosiutik sprang into motion. He was barely able to keep up with what she was saying as she spoke as fast as she could. The knife flashed as she quickly shaved off a bit of fire root, and water sloshed precariously as she dumped it into the pot. Juosiutik had scarcely dropped the fire root in before she poured in the honeyed mash.

The pot immediately burst into a column of fire. Juosiutik's smile slowly faded. "Ah, oops?"

Chief Rohsuak watched as her people cleared a bit of the forest around their camp. They removed the branches and stripped the bark off the trees before carrying each processed log in front of her. She smiled and laid her hand upon the one in front of her now. She channeled just a bit of her Fire mana and the log began to heat up. Steam rose from the top and bottom as the water burned off in response.

This was the technique that allowed her people to continue woodworking and fueling fires as they traveled underground. Chief Rohsuak could dry wood even in a damp cave with no sunlight, using roots instead of branches or trunks. Though, the process was not an easy one. Too little mana and the process would take too long, risking burning the wood from long exposure to the Fire attribute. Too much and the whole thing would burst into flames. And the amount of mana necessary was different for each piece of wood, as each had different properties and carried different amounts of water. There was a person or two who could produce Fire mana in the tribe besides her, but she was the only one with the Blessing of Fire as well as the experience needed to fine-tune her mana with the requisite precision. She had tried to teach the others, but it was very slow going without the Blessing of Fire, maybe even impossible. At the very least, it would be years before any of them reached that level.

It had been one of her main concerns for the future. Chief Rohsuak was no longer young, so the tribe should not depend on feats only she could manage for their survival. But, fortunately, they had found a home before age claimed her. They could dry wood for fire-making and woodworking the normal way now, so her method had dropped from crucial to merely convenient. Chief Rohsuak used her abilities for the first round of lumber, giving her people immediate access to dry wood. With that, they could begin building homes for the first time since before she became chief. Once the basics were set up, she could take a step back and wean them off of her powers.

And, perhaps more importantly, they could now trade construction-ready wood to any other parties who might require such materials. She started to grin at that thought before shaking her head. This process had been a joint effort by her people, therefore the rewards of this trade must be for the community. And since she already had some honey of her own, she *definitely* could not justify taking any from the community's share.

She figured she'd better start rationing her personal store . . .

Juosiutik was staring at the ground. "I'm sorry."

Belissar waved his hands about. "No, um, it's . . . not really okay, but, um, no one got hurt, so no harm done?"

Juosiutik didn't move. "I'm really sorry."

Belissar shook his head. "It's, um, fine . . . since nothing else caught fire this time, at least . . ."

Juosiutik still didn't budge. "The chief keeps telling me I need to calm down. But I never learn. I absolutely should have expected that mana honey would resonate with fire root. That should have been obvious. But no. I went and acted stupidly. After lecturing you on the complexities and dangers of potion-making, too."

Belissar heaved a sigh and shook his head. But, well, this seemed to be a thing for the girl, and he didn't know what else to say to her, so he figured he'd just let her recover on her own. They and the bees watching them had all panicked when the fire broke out, but fortunately the blaze was contained within the pot. Still, if the flowers had caught fire, the whole flower meadow might have burned down, and quickly, so it was quite concerning. Belissar . . . might not have been so understanding if the flower meadow hives had been threatened by such a mistake. And speaking of the bees, he again had to reassure them that Juosiutik was not intending to harm him—after which they began looking for shades, having associated lightning fires with incoming purifications.

It got Belissar thinking. Fire had been his ally thus far, but would that always be the case? A brush fire could race across an open field like the flower meadow with surprising speed, so even a small fire could quickly burn the whole thing down. In that regard, Belissar had been a bit careless with his fire pit plans, and it had been *extremely* fortunate he had never tripped while carrying a torch. It would be a good idea to think about digging a fire ditch or something, at least around the hives, the memorial, and the shrine of bees. He or the bees might drop a torch, the bear people might do something with fire accidentally . . . or a shade might show up with black flames or something like that. It was a vulnerability he should prepare for . . . particularly since his tower lacked water sources at the moment.

But all those thoughts also brought something else to mind. Belissar turned to Juosiutik.

"Hey, you wouldn't happen to have extras of that fire root, would you?"

Juosiutik stopped mumbling to herself for a moment. "Huh? Um, well, yes, but they're kind of important. It's hard to start fires underground, you know?"

Belissar tilted his head. "But, um, aren't you moving into the purified area? So, you aren't living underground anymore?"

Juosiutik looked at him for a moment before tilting her own head. "That's, um, right?"

Belissar nodded. "In that case, I'd like to trade for some."

Juosiutik crossed her arms and nodded. "Well . . . I'd need to check with the chief, but . . . what did you have in mind?"

Belissar rubbed his chin. "How about a tray of mana honey—Wait, where are you going?!"

Juosiutik ran from the tower immediately, shouting for Chief Rohsuak. Belissar shook his head. Well, it *would* be a good thing to get it done as soon as possible. If he had access to these fire roots that would apparently burst into violent flames on contact with mana honey, then he wouldn't need to start fires at all. He could just drop a few shavings into a pit trap and watch them light up. That would minimize the risk of accidentally burning the flower meadow down until he could get some safety measures in place.

There was just one problem. Belissar crossed his arms as he looked at the pot and other materials still spread out across the ground.

"Um, should I just watch this stuff until she gets back?"

BEE AND THUNDER

The wounded soldier stood at the entrance to the memorial beehouse. She danced a salute as a squad of workers from her queen arrived, carrying with them precious honey. The wounded soldier then danced directions, and the workers dispersed. Other wounded soldiers stood at various points around the memorial. Some crawled on or around the beehouse, ensuring it was clear of debris and rot. Others kept watch from atop of the pillars. The wounded soldier kept track of them and directed the workers toward her injured comrades, ensuring each of them ate their fill before she, too, partook in the gift from her queen.

Some of them had been reticent to use their hive's resources as soldiers who could no longer fly with the army, as she had once been. So, she had simply refused to eat until they did. They were still reluctant but, given the King's interest in her and her contributions to the latest battle, none of them were willing to threaten her health by sacrificing their own. The wounded bees all settled into an uneasy compromise, allowing the workers to instruct them how much to eat. The workers fed them more than any of the wounded were comfortable taking, but that was the price they paid for arguing.

And now, with that task dealt with, the wounded soldier turned to her own personal quest. When she had first received a pair of lightning wings in place of her missing half, she had been ecstatic. She'd danced and she danced as she thought that now, finally, she could return to her comrades in the skies. She could once again join the fight to defend the hive from the very start, not only in desperate final stands.

Unfortunately, reality was not so kind. The lightning may have taken the shape of wings, but it did not perform their function. She could move them like her old wings, but they did not move the air around her. They did not generate lift and they could not bear her weight. She was still trapped on the ground.

Her disappointment had been immeasurable. But she was a bee, and it would take more than a bit of crushing despair to keep her from whatever work she could perform. She continued to experiment with the lightning wings and the lightning itself, which continued to flow through her body. And soon, she'd come up with another idea. Something else she could do with these wings that might allow her to further contribute to the hive.

She recalled what the King had done to save her life, how he had moved the mana beyond his body. As a monster bee, she already had an instinctual ability to manipulate her mana. She could concentrate it in her wings for a burst of speed, in her chitin for improved resilience, or, most commonly, in her stinger for greater damage. But all of these uses had ultimately been within her own body; she had never manipulated mana outside of herself as the King had.

Until now, that was. Now, her mana was automatically flowing outside of her body, in a way. The mana generating the lightning that now took the place of her missing wings had not truly left her body. It remained connected to the flows of mana within the rest of her body and it acted, for all intents and purposes, as if it were within the missing part. And yet . . . it was, in fact, outside of her body, but still under her control.

She thought that maybe, just maybe, she might be able to do something with that. She would never presume that she might match the wisdom and power of the King, but to follow his example was only natural. She remembered, very viscerally, what the enemy had done with the power of lightning. If she could replicate even a small fraction of that with the lightning coursing through her, then perhaps she would not need to fly to rejoin the fight.

She tried once again to take control of the lightning. The lightning in the wings resisted her, holding to its shape even more strongly than the mana in the rest of her body, so she tried with the lightning inside her body instead. Like with her mana before her injury, she had some ability to move and concentrate it on different parts. And yet, it largely refused to leave her body. She could eject it through her stinger, but that simply infused her venom with the mana. It was not the external manipulation the King had displayed.

But with the other wounded soldiers now helping her maintain the memorial, she now had time aplenty. So, she tried. And she tried. She tried and tried again and again. She tried all sorts of different ways to manipulate the mana and the lightning. She could already move the lightning wings as easily as her original pair, so she knew there *had* to be a way to do this!

She thought back to when she had to take control of the shade's lightning in her body and used that as a basis. She rubbed her legs and wings and hairs together to generate tiny lightnings, and then reached out with her mana and her lightning wings to try and exert some control over them. She found with the lightning wings it was far, far easier to generate the tiny lightnings than before; she could even make sparks appear across her body by adjusting the amount of mana flowing through the wings. Soon, she was able to make them appear and dance between her normal wings and her lightning wings at will.

These newly generated lightnings however, were simply dancing between her wings, her body, and her hairs, and not doing anything particularly useful. She hoped for something more, so she attempted to exert control of the generated lightning by passing her mana through it. Fortunately, this worked fairly easily, with the mana pulling the generated lightning dancing around her body into her lightning wings, joining that circuit.

And then came the hard part. All she had done so far was boost the amount of lightning in her wings and her body, now she had to try and actually do something with it. Currently, all the lightning and mana within her was just another automatic flow, a part of her body that was not part of her body. Now, she would attempt to adjust that flow consciously.

She could redirect mana and lightning when they first left her body, but that simply caused them to sputter out in another direction, unable to complete their path. So, she tried another angle. She tried manipulating the lightning wings themselves, where lightning was already flowing outside of her body but also maintaining a coherent shape. She slowly moved the crackling wings, also adjusting the mana within them. And the flow of mana and lightning between her wings stretched out, gradually changing its path to reach its new destination.

She repeated the process, paying extra attention to the movement of her mana as it traveled along the adjusted path. Then she repeated it again, and again, and again. Finally, she gave it a try herself. She returned her lightning wings and the mana flowing through them to their original position but tried to make the mana flow along the adjusted path herself.

She tried . . . and failed. So, she tried again, and failed again. Over and over, she tried. Over and over, she failed. But she kept at it. And if there was one thing she had too much of these days, it was time.

And eventually, her persistence paid off. The flow of mana elongated and curved ever so slightly. Had she truly manipulated a flow of mana outside of her body? She couldn't believe it at first, so she tried again . . . and succeeded again. She did it a third time. And then a fourth. She started to push a bit, making the curve a bit more apparent so she could be really sure she was actually changing it. And it moved according to her will.

She paused for a moment, and then burst out dancing, drawing the attention of the other wounded soldiers around her. She had done it. She had taken a step. A tiny step, to be sure, but a step. She knew now that it was *possible*. That if she kept at it, she could actually succeed at this. She could actually do something with this lightning.

She could be of greater use to the hive. She could justify at least some of the attention the King had lavished upon her. Perhaps, one day, she could even rejoin the fight.

She doubled her efforts. Now that she had determined a way to manipulate the mana, her progress accelerated. She pushed to see how far she could elongate and curve the flow, moving it a bit further with each attempt. Soon, she could make a separate circle of lightning on the edge of her wings, the lightning looping in a second circuit before rejoining the first. And that meant . . . she could begin forming shapes with it, like the King had.

It would take time, but she had plenty of that and would spare none of it. For now, rejoining her sisters in battle was no longer just a dream. And her wounded comrades around her watched her with great interest . . .

CHAPTER SIX

A FIER-BEE TRADE

An embarrassed Juosiutik returned a bit later, shuffling into the tower as she realized she had left Belissar and all of her gear behind without a word. But she also returned with a small clay pot full of fire roots.

"Um, hi. S-Sorry about that, I, um, got a bit excited. I-I got permission from the chief, though! I can trade this for some of the honey!"

Belissar smiled and was about to agree when he had a thought and tilted his head. "Good, but um, is there anything I should know about those fire roots?"

Juosiutik nodded. "Fire roots are useful for starting fires and a bit of potion-making, but that's pretty much it. You definitely can't eat them. To be honest, mana flowers are *way* more useful and can do all sorts of things in the right hands. And mana honey . . . well I've never dealt with it before, but if you can eat it safely, that alone would make it incredible. It's practically a potion on its own, and who knows what else we might be able to do with it?"

Juosiutik fidgeted, looking a bit uncomfortable. "Honestly, fire roots aren't worth anywhere near as much as either your mana flowers or mana honey should be. But, um, if you're okay with it and really want the fire roots, maybe it's okay? If you want, you could count it as part of the payment for the teaching?"

Belissar blinked and then started to rub his chin. This was . . . weird. He'd always had people telling him how crappy his stuff was and how it was barely worth what they were giving him in exchange. He still wasn't used to being told his stuff was *too* valuable, so he didn't really know how to address the situation. Eventually he shrugged.

Well, the bear folk weren't going to deceive him by telling him his stuff was too valuable, right? Besides, he already knew the fire roots would be useful, and he had mana honey trays galore thanks to the apiary, so as far as he was concerned it was a valuable trade. Heck, he still had another room slot, so he could always add a second apiary if he felt he needed more.

So, he nodded his head. "Um, as long as there's at least five or more, I'm fine with that. Is one honey tray enough?"

Juosiutik nearly leapt at him. "YES!"

Belissar took a step back. "Um, right, well, I'll go get that, then."

Juosiutik nodded as fast as she could. "I'll be waiting!"

Belissar went back to his stockpile in the apiary and came back to make the exchange. Juosiutik nearly ran out of the tower again before Belissar reminded her of her stuff on the ground. With a flushed face, she rushed to pack it all back up before running out again. Belissar shrugged.

"Guess the lesson's over for today?"

He looked inside the pot, where a dozen fire roots rested. He picked one up and smiled.

Absorb Flame Radish Root? Samples 0/10

He frowned a bit. The message had appeared as he had hoped, though the sample number was twice as big as he'd expected. Also, the name apparently wasn't actually fire root? But he shrugged.

"Thank goodness she gave me a dozen . . ."

He went ahead and absorbed the necessary number.

Flame Radish Root absorbed.
Sufficient samples gathered. Flame Radish now available.
*Current applications: Flower Meadow, Apiary**

(=Resource Node only)*

Belissar blinked and then began to smile. He had been steeling himself for the fire root—or flame radish, apparently—to not be available in any of his rooms, like all those cave plants. It was something the bear people found underground, so surely it would need a similar environment to grow. At the very least, he didn't think something fire-related would go with flowers or fruit trees. But apparently it did. He guessed the rest of the flame radish must grow above ground and make flowers? He shrugged again.

"Guess we'll find out!" he said aloud.

Not only were the flame radishes useful in and of themselves, but if they had flowers, too . . . then that meant his bees could gather from them as well! All in all, he didn't really know what Chief Rohsuak was talking about. In his opinion, this was an excellent trade.

But first, he figured he should carefully store the pot with the remaining two flame radishes somewhere nice, safe, non-flammable, and far away from any mana honey . . .

Belissar ended up putting the pot in the apiary campfire pit. It was surrounded by dirt and far from any hives, so it was the safest place for something that could combust. He figured, as well, that he wouldn't need to start fires there specifically, both due to having flame radishes now as well as the fact that the apiary was now far away from where the fires would be needed.

And just in time, as the cooldown on the minor purification was just coming to an end. Belissar had informed the bees of the faster cooldown yesterday, so the soldier bee army was already getting ready. Belissar considered testing the flame radishes now. He grabbed his knife and cut a small piece from one of the remaining radishes, then walked to the nearest fire pit. It was already set up with honey and kindling, so all he needed to do was toss the piece inside . . . and run away the moment he did.

But, contrary to his expectations, there was not a gigantic spout of flame from the pit, just a bit of smoke that gradually increased. He started creeping toward it before remembering his tower sight and then took a look from a safe distance.

The flame radish piece had caught fire and was lighting the rest of the pit's fuel, but not as dramatically as what had happened in Juosiutik's pot. Belissar rubbed his chin at that.

Maybe it was because the honey in the potion had come directly from his mana? Or maybe it was the age of the mana honey. This pit *had* been set up a while ago. Did mana honey lose its mana over time? That . . . was actually something he should figure out.

In any case, he had now confirmed the flame radish would light the pits about as well as a torch, though not as dramatically as he had expected. He considered trying it out sometime in place of a torch . . . but he wasn't sure if the root was safest for the bees to touch. It seemed safe enough for him to handle, but maybe he should make some sort of bag for the bees to carry it? That would take time, though, so he shrugged and figured he would use the regular torches today, and experiment when he had more time.

There had already been one accidental fire today, after all, and he had recently become aware of just how flammable his tower might be . . .

The First of the Second lined up her forces, utilizing the same formation as the Firstborn had the day before. She was swaying in the air, moving this way and that. One part of the reserve formation seemed a little low, so she ordered them to gain altitude. Another part was too far forward, so she pulled them back. But then they flew too far back, and she had to send them forward again. She spent the next half hour making constant minor adjustments to the formation.

She couldn't help it. This was her first time facing a foe directly, and she had not been confident taking command in the first place. And now, there was no more time to prepare. The enemy had arrived.

She trembled in the air. The enemy appeared far larger and more vicious than she remembered. But she still gave the command. She knew that her army and the armies of her fellow queens had dealt with such foes before, and with ease. It was only she who was unprepared for this.

Despite her misgivings, her soldiers immediately leapt into action, executing her plan. A squad of her bees dove down and stung the shade, catching its attention, and then slowly flew away from it. It chased after them and then fell right into the first pit trap.

The First of the Second had kept things simple and proceeded with one of the older plans. She did not feel ready to command the battle directly as the Firstborn had. Her hive, and all the hives of the flower meadow, had taken casualties recently. They had recovered, but it had taken a notable expenditure of their honey reserves to do so, and the First of the Second knew they were supposed to be stockpiling for a new generation of queens. As such, she felt that casualties today would be unacceptable, and so she would not risk them on experimental commands unless she was fully confident in success—which, due to her own unpreparedness, she was not.

Fortunately, though, the plans of the King were proven and effective. The shade was trapped in the pit. She gave the command to the soldier bees from the apiary that were carrying one of the King's fire sticks, and they made the run. Their aim was true and the pit went up in flames, taking the shade with it.

The queen nearly fell from the sky in relief as she realized the battle was won, and her day of command was finally over.

By now, that relief had faded entirely, as she slowly flew toward her hive. The post-battle celebrations had been nice. She would admit she'd enjoyed the praise of the Firstborn as she was extolled for her innovations in command. But now came time to face the consequences of the day. Now, she had to see what had become of her hive in her absence. She steeled herself and stepped inside.

She found her workers gathered into sections, with a single worker at the head of each. The single workers motioned and then the whole hive saluted as one. She nearly took a step back.

The workers then began to report. The efficiency drop had not been nearly as bad as she'd feared, and this had been due to the aid of the Fourth of the Seventh's workers. They had explained to her hive a system by which the workers could carry on their duties in their queen's absence with minimal loss in efficiency . . . one that closely resembled the system she herself had implemented for the army. It was quite simple, in retrospect. Simply tasking a few of the workers with identifying inefficiencies and keeping things running would result in only the loss of those workers' outputs, a minor trade-off to avoid the wider issues that would impact the hive as a whole.

Her workers then stood still before her, their antennas drooping as they awaited her verdict. She danced . . . her approval. In fact, she could not have been more proud of them. They had done for her hive what she had done for the army, and done so without the need for her to instruct it. They had kept the hive running and avoided the outcome she'd feared. They had done what she would have wanted them to, all on their own.

The workers began to dance happily, and the First of the Second could not help but join them. She had feared today would be a day of disaster, but thanks to both her efforts and those of her workers, it had become a day of triumph.

CHAPTER SEVEN

APOLO-BEES

The next day, Chief Rohsuak arrived with a large group of the bear folk, including Juosiutik. The young potion-maker was standing next to the chief and staring at the ground with a frown on her face. Belissar wasn't paying attention to that, though, but rather to the other bear folk carrying stacks of lumber.

"What . . . is this?"

Chief Rohsuak gave him a smile. "Dry wood for construction, as you requested, Sacred Den Master."

Belissar's eyes widened and he motioned toward the wood. Chief Rohsuak nodded and he walked over to the nearest plank. He touched it with his hand. It was completely dry.

"How is this possible?"

Chief Rohsuak smirked slightly and raised a finger. A small lick of fire appeared on top of it. "A god's blessing has many uses."

Belissar just nodded blankly.

"Do you have somewhere you want us to put this?" Chief Rohsuak asked.

Belissar started a bit and then rubbed his chin. At first, he was going to say anywhere was fine . . . but then he thought of carrying all that wood across the room by himself. And, well, she *was* asking him where to put it.

"Oh, um, further in, by the end of this room, if it's not too much trouble, please."

Chief Rohsuak's expression turned serious. "In that case, could we request your assistance with the shades? We will be vulnerable while carrying the wood."

Belissar nodded. "Oh, um, that makes sense. Hang on a second."

He turned to Niobee flying behind him and the soldier bees watching over him. "Could you gather the others and ask them if they can help guard the bear people?"

"Okay!"

He turned back to Chief Rohsuak. "They're on their way."

Chief Rohsuak smiled at him. "Thank you. Now, since we have some time." She motioned to Juosiutik, who flinched and then took a step forward.

"Um, I'm sorry, Sacred Den Master."

Belissar tilted his head. "Um, what for?"

Juosiutik's face scrunched up. "For, um, almost setting you and your den on fire . . . and, um, being a bit rude . . . and, um, getting a bit excited and running off . . . twice . . ."

Belissar felt . . . itchy, for lack of a better word. She was apologizing to him? He had no idea how to respond to that. He hadn't heard an apology since . . .

"I'm . . . sorry, Belissar. Please . . . live on . . . be happy . . ."

He shook his head and tried to calm his beating heart, glancing away from the bear people.

"It's, um, fine. Just . . . be careful with the fire, please."

Juosiutik nodded slowly. "Um . . . do you want to continue the lessons? I, um, understand if not. I'll, uh . . ."

The words caught in her throat, but Chief Rohsuak put a firm hand on her shoulder. Juosiutik sighed and continued, her face twisting in anguish.

"I'll . . . return . . . the honey . . . if so."

Belissar shook his head, just wanting this conversation to be over already. "It's fine. I still want to learn about potions."

Juosiutik's eyes widened and then her face broke out into a bright smile. Chief Rohsuak shook her head and chuckled. And then, fortunately, the full soldier bee army arrived, with Niobee leading one of the flower meadow queens to Belissar. Belissar quickly turned to them and smiled as the queen danced a salute to him. Right on time!

"We'll need to protect them from the remnants . . . um, little shades that will appear around them. Can you do that?"

The queen and the soldiers saluted in unison and then began assembling around the bear people. The bear people eyed them warily, but Chief Rohsuak just waved them off. Soon, the group was on their way.

Another mini shade appeared . . . and was immediately set upon by a dozen soldier bees. It barely had time to cry out in pain before the soldier bees retreated and another dozen took their place, plunging their stingers deep into the shade. With the second wave, the shade fell to the ground and burst into mist.

The lumber carriers slowed down as they stared at the spectacle. The hunters guarding them were gaping with their jaws dropped. Even Juosiutik couldn't tear her eyes from it. Chief Rohsuak glanced at Metsaitti. They both smirked and shook their heads. If their people were impressed by this much, then it truly had been too long since they had challenged a sacred den.

Their period of sojourn had been no pleasant journey, and everyone in her tribe had seen their share of hardship. But in many ways, they were still like cubs. They had been so focused on their own experiences that they were surprised by anything different. Like the sacred den master.

Chief Rohsuak nodded to herself. This experience was good for her people. She knew that the den master did not present the most imposing figure, and that many of her people had been deceived by his timid demeanor. He simply did not act with the same confidence most of them possessed on account of the dangers they had faced and overcome, which led them to assume he had not experienced anything like they had . . . or that he lacked the capabilities they did.

So, it was quite a shock for them to watch him command the soldier bee army. The bees were an impressive sight even just hovering around, but that was nothing compared to watching them in action. The soldier bees were gigantic for bees, but they were ultimately still small, and Chief Rohsuak figured most of her people probably hadn't thought much of them individually.

That was no longer the case. The bees attacked instantly, without fear or hesitation, and they flew at surprising speeds that many of her people had trouble keeping track of. Their stingers stabbed as deep as any spear tip. They tore apart shades in mere seconds, the same shades that the hunters trained by Metsaitti had to approach with caution. And the bees were using barely a fraction of their numbers . . .

Chief Rohsuak imagined that everyone here would now understand the need to treat the sacred den master with respect. Which was why she'd insisted that Juosiutik apologize and offer to return the honey she had received. She knew the bear woman got carried away when it came to potion-making, but the chief was still aghast when she heard how the first lesson had gone. The sacred den master was *not* another arrogant young hunter who didn't take Juosiutik's instructions seriously. So, to hear what sort of tone Juosiutik had initially taken with him had been a shock for the chief. And then to hear that she had gone and set *another* potion mix on fire right in the sacred den . . . and then that she had run off and left him behind . . .

She put her hand on Juosiutik's shoulder and whispered into her ear. "Understand now?"

Juosiutik slowly nodded and paled slightly as she watched another shade vanish under a swarm of black and yellow. Chief Rohsuak nodded in approval. The good news was that they had confirmed the sacred den master to be generally good-natured, as he was not at all angry. In fact, he seemed entirely confused that there was any reason for him to be angry at all. But that didn't mean Chief Rohsuak could let up on Juosiutik, or any of her tribe. The last thing she wanted was for them to get overly comfortable, and then to cross a line they didn't realize the sacred den master had. Even this timid and cooperative young man could bring ruin upon them if he so chose, and nobody save Chief Rohsuak herself would have a chance of stopping it.

Chief Rohsuak watched the bees more closely. How they moved not as individuals, but in small groups. How they each moved in coordination, staying out of each other's way as they rotated in and out of the fight. How the big bee at the center of the swarm would dance and then the entire force would shift immediately.

If she was brutally honest with herself, she was not certain she would be able to face this swarm alone, not even with her mighty blessing. Maybe if she was in her prime, but at this point she wasn't getting any younger. As of now, she had the power to destroy a swarm if it came at her all at once, but these bees seemed smarter than that. Intelligent, organized even. If they spread out and coordinated to come at her a few at a time . . . well, her endurance wasn't what it used to be. She thanked the gods they had found a forgiving and non-aggressive sacred den master, and she resolved to keep her people as respectful as his power deserved, no matter how surprised the young bear folk might be that such an unassuming person could wield such power.

But the surprise wasn't over. Gasps rang out among the group as they neared the wall of trees at the end of the room. There was a second shrine identical to the one by the entrance. Next to the shrine was some sort of monument, with engraved pillars surrounding a beehouse. But that was not what her people were focusing on. No, they were exclaiming at the row of hives and the countless bees streaming to and from them. As well as the patches of flowers they were flying to.

Juosiutik cried out. "Chief! That's . . . that's . . ."

Chief Rohsuak nodded. "Mana flowers."

It was not just the one or two flowers Metsaitti's group had encountered. It was an entire patch of them, their joint glow visible even in the light of the sun. And they were absolutely surrounded by bees, with long lines of workers extending from each flower, each waiting their turn.

Juosiutik was twitching. She kept glancing between the flowers and the soldier bees above, smiling and frowning in turn. Chief Rohsuak chuckled. This trip was proving more and more useful. Her people could now see both the honey and the sting this sacred den possessed.

"Um, if you could just leave the wood over there, that would be good," said the sacred den master.

Chief Rohsuak agreed and instructed her people as the den master asked.

He then turned to her and Juosiutik. "Um, maybe you could give me some time before the next lessons? I want to get started on this . . . and, um, maybe also prepare a safe spot for the lessons."

Juosiutik jumped and quickly began nodding repeatedly. "Yes! Whatever you want!"

The den master looked confused. "Um, thanks."

Chief Rohsuak rubbed her chin as she watched the exchange. She felt more and more that they had a unique opportunity with this den master here . . . so long as they remembered to respect him. And after today, she hoped they would do just that.

CHAPTER EIGHT

A HOT AND BEE-UTIFUL NEW FLOWER!

Belissar had the bear folk stack the wood near the flower meadow queens. He then went and got some trays of mana honey to give to them in exchange. Chief Rohsuak wanted to refuse, but Belissar convinced her to take enough to share with the laborers. After that, he and the soldier bees escorted the bear folk back out of the tower, and then he finally made his way to the end of the flower meadow where the wood pile now waited.

Well, it had taken a bit longer than Belissar hoped, but the bear people and their awkward conversations were finally gone. And that meant he could get started on his projects! He had a nice stockpile of fully dry wood now, so he could make a higher quality home than he had planned.

But first things came first. He wanted to dig a ditch around the hives, the shrine of bees, and the memorial to ensure they wouldn't be at risk if the flower meadow ever caught on fire. He would also dig another, circular ditch nearby to create a safe place to plant some flame radishes. He didn't know if the whole plant would be as flammable as its roots, but he figured it would be best not to take any chances.

He then, of course, realized that he should have asked if the bear people had any shovels or digging tools. They came from an underground tunnel, so they had to, right? That would be a *lot* easier than trying to dig by hand, or with the knives, saw, and axe he had available. But at the same time, Belissar didn't want to go running off after them immediately after they had left. Plus . . . he was *just* calming down from their last interaction.

Ultimately, Belissar decided he would leave that until tomorrow and see what he could do with what he had now. He also figured he should see if the tower had anything he could use to help with the process. And it turned out it did, now that he managed to remember it. He could clear small areas of the flower meadow and the apiary of flowers, which was how he'd prepared the campfire sites in the first place. And if he thought about it, the flame radishes didn't specifically *need* a ditch in the ground, they just needed an area clear of anything flammable. So, Belissar cleared a small area near the other flower meadow resource patches.

It was one thing to watch the tower magically grow plants, but it disturbed Belissar slightly to watch them now disappear, receding back as if they were growing in reverse. He shook his head and continued on with his task.

> *Available Resource Plants for Flower Meadow:*
> *- Basic Healing Herbs (Mana Upkeep: 3 per node)*
> *- Basic Poisonous Flowers (Mana Upkeep: 3 per node)*
> *- Basic Textile Flowers (Mana Upkeep: 3 per node)*
> *- Mana Flower (Mana Upkeep: 5 per node)*
> *- Flame Radish (Mana Upkeep: 10 per node)*

Belissar paused at that. That was . . . quite expensive. The most expensive resource plant to date. The same upkeep as a monster bee queen spawner after the Blessing of Bees discount. The full amount of extra mana he could gain from a minor purification. More expensive than the flower meadow room itself.

But then he shrugged and selected it anyway. He had the extra mana to afford it, the flame roots would be useful, and new flowers could mean new honeys, new bees, or even new plants, depending on if it worked with cross-pollination. He was curious as to why the flame radish was more expensive than a mana flower, given what Juosiutik had told him about their relative value, but he didn't know enough to guess, so he moved on.

A short, ground-level plant popped out of the ground. Four-petaled flowers grew out of it that transitioned from yellow-orange at their center to bright red at the edges. Belissar slowly and carefully approached the new plant. He could feel a small amount of heat radiating from it, just enough to warm the surrounding area slightly. He narrowed his eyes as he watched the plant, feeling the mana of the tower flowing through it.

But ultimately neither the new plants nor the area around it caught fire, even with the tower's mana flowing all around it. It *seemed* like it would be fine, for now. Belissar took a deep breath and then turned to the bees that were starting to investigate.

"Um, be careful with this one. It might catch fire, especially if it touches mana honey or has mana pass through it. It, um, might also be dangerous to drink. Juosiutik said humans . . . or bear people can't eat it. I'm not sure if that applies to bees too."

The worker bees danced salutes and then began a different dance to pass his message to their newly arriving sisters. Some of them flew back to relay the message to their hives. Belissar took another deep breath. Well, he didn't know how these plants would interact with his bees, but he figured the bees would know best. They could drink nectar from the poisonous flowers without any problem, so maybe it would be the same here? He couldn't help but worry, but he trusted the bees to know flowers.

"Niobee will check!"

It turned out there was a bee particularly sensitive to his worries who flew straight toward the flower.

"Hey, wait . . ."

But Niobee moved faster than him and hovered over one of the flowers. She extended her proboscis and drank some nectar from it. Belissar frowned, but then he remembered that Niobee could apparently return from death, so if any bee was going to test the possibly flammable flowers, she was the best. Even though Belissar absolutely did *not* want to see her get hurt.

And so, he paced and sweated as Niobee drank. He gulped as she slowly flew back over.

"Well . . . are you okay?"

Niobee started dancing slowly. "Nectar is hot . . . but okay! Not hurt!"

Belissar released his breath as the worker bees slowly began to approach the new flowers. He watched as they, too, landed on the flowers and began to drink the nectar. Each of them paused as they first tasted the nectar, but then they continued on with no ill effect. When the first round of workers took off and flew back toward their hives, Belissar finally tore his eyes away from the flower and started to move. By all accounts, it seemed safe, and at this point was out of his hands. So, he decided to prepare another of these flowers for the apiary as well . . .

The First of the Fifth could not help but dance as she heard the reports. The King had prepared an entirely new type of flower specifically for her and had even gone out of his way to advise her workers on its unique properties!

She knew now she was on the right path, even though the implementation of the King's new gathering method was going . . . slowly. Or more specifically, the implementation had occurred immediately, but had not produced any results as of yet. As she had predicted, the blending of different nectar sources was not improving the quality of the honey, and it was making quality control more difficult. She could not currently see any advantage over her prior methods. Regardless, she would never question the wisdom of the King, so she had decided to be patient. The King himself had informed her of this method. So there had to be a reason behind it. And the King was larger, grander, and . . . *more* than any bee, so she knew it was possible he was looking at a timeframe beyond what she could comprehend.

Still, it was encouraging to receive such a boon from the King, a clear sign that he was still pleased with her. It gave her confidence that she was not wrong in her implementation of his will, even if it had not produced results yet. It also gave confirmation that she was correct to choose this aspect to focus on and let her daughter handle the new room and its new plants.

Speaking of which, she wondered how her daughter was doing. Now that she thought of it, she had not checked in with her in a while. Preparing the surplus healing honey for the latest battle had taken most of her focus. Her daughter had finished moving away during that period and she had not received any reports since. She assumed, though, that no news was a sign of success, especially since the Fourth of the Seventh had been assisting her daughter, and so had not made checking on her daughter a priority. Since the Fourth of the Seventh was presumably still setting up her own hive after the move, her workers were not yet revisiting the apiary, so all news outside of the apiary was slow in coming these days.

But that was fine. The First of the Fifth assumed her daughter would alert her if there were any crises that needed to be addressed, so she believed no news was good news. The Fourth of the Seventh would surely reestablish contact in time, and alert her if there was anything she needed to know. And beyond that . . . well, the First of the Fifth was not concerned with any of the bees further away than the Fourth of the Seventh, those failures of the flower meadow who had put the King himself in danger. It was only natural that they had been moved further away from his abode. The First of the Fifth would follow the King's lead and have nothing to do with them.

So, no, there was nothing going on out there that she needed to concern herself with. She would wait patiently for the Fourth of the Seventh to inform her about her daughter's progress, and focus on her task in the meantime. She knew that the new gathering method would surely pay off in time, and now she had a new flower to focus on, new resources with which to propel herself further and further. Surely, all was going her way . . .

THE KING'S REWARDS

The First of the Fifth's First Daughter laid the last egg her current mana would permit. She gave her workers some space to tend to the new egg. Now that she needed to wait for her mana to return, she took a moment to observe her hive. Or rather, *their* hive.

When the Fourth of the Seventh's workers offered to assist her with building her hive in the first place, she had worked up her courage and proposed to build one joint hive. Since they were working together anyway, it didn't make sense to do the same job twice, she thought. And, on a more selfish note, if their hives were joined together she would have more opportunities to repay the Fourth of the Seventh for all she had done.

She recalled trembling as she had approached the Fourth of the Seventh with her unthinkable idea. What queen would share a hive with another? There were bees that did that . . . the cuckoo bees. Those evil scourges that refused to produce anything of value and stole the work of others. She had prepared a full dance routine to explain her reasoning, and how her intentions were purely to improve the efficiency of both their hives. How she would never, under any circumstances, even think of exploiting the Fourth of the Seventh's efforts, and how she fully intended to contribute back in excess of what she had received.

But, when she first asked the question, the Fourth of the Seventh cut her off and said . . .

"Okay!"

And now they were working together. She and her mighty savior. In a grove filled with mana flowers and protected by vast chasms, built specifically for them by the *King himself.* A clear sign of his favor, one that would surely please her mother greatly once she was ready to report on their progress. The First Daughter also admitted the King's favor made her feel quite happy in and of itself, and now understood why her mother sought it so.

She watched as her workers returned with nectar brimming with mana . . .
including workers from the generation she'd once feared she would lose. Instead,
they were now the most numerous and energetic of her laborers yet. And it was
all thanks to the Fourth of the Seventh.

Speaking of which, one of the Fourth of the Seventh's workers now approached
her. The same one who had approached her from the start and coordinated their
hives' efforts. The First Daughter and the worker greeted one another. And then . . .
the worker paused. She seemed hesitant to start her next dance. The First Daughter
crawled forward and gently brushed an antenna against the worker. Their mana
and pheromones had clashed at first, but at this point the hives had started to
acclimate to each other. They knew they did not belong to the same brood, and
yet they were not strangers or rivals. So, the worker relaxed and slowly began to
dance.

"Other queen . . . have request. Hives stabilizing, move complete. Queen had
plan before move, wanted to use soldiers and copy King. Can let her start again?
Might have less workers, honey from us . . ."

The First Daughter froze, and then immediately began to dance. She was
surprised by the request, but once she realized what was being asked, she did not
waste even a single moment thinking about it.

"Yes! Of course! My hive, growing well. Don't need extra help. Can give help
instead. Will give help!"

The moment she could begin repaying her savior had arrived sooner than she
had ever imagined. The worker began a dance of gratitude and apology, and then
the queen and the worker began to plan their future honey production and
expenditures . . .

The Firstborn stood in her hive, watching a large, waxed-over cell. So far, her plan
had been successful. Under her own command, the army had managed to handle
a shade even while keeping the majority of the army in reserve. The First of the
Second had pioneered a new command structure for the army and introduced
them all to the Fourth of the Seventh's organization for hive management in a
queen's absence, both of which eased the obstacles that had arisen. The next queen
to take command thus settled in well, familiarizing herself with the situation even
faster than either the Firstborn herself or the First of the Second had. The Firstborn
now had faith their army would be far more adaptable to the next unforeseen
challenge.

But this was only the beginning. They had grown more flexible, but they had
not grown *stronger*. That . . . was about to change. As she watched, two mandibles pierced through the wax cover from within the cell. Medicinal workers moved
to assist and began pulling open the wax. Soon, there was a hole large enough for
the cell's occupant to crawl out.

A new maddening soldier emerged. She appeared a bit smaller than normal, save for her abdomen, and she lacked a stinger entirely, with a small nozzle taking its place. She shook herself, buzzed her wings, and then turned to the Firstborn, dancing her salute. The Firstborn brushed her antennas and then instructed her to join the army. The Firstborn then turned to the next two cells as their occupants also began to break through.

The first soldier bee sprayers had arrived. A brand-new addition to the army, created by the King himself. An addition that would not simply improve the army but introduce an entirely new element to it. The Firstborn wanted nothing more than to follow the sprayer out into the field and see her in action. To see how strong their army would now become.

But she didn't. Instead, she left the soldier cells and began laying more worker eggs. She'd already organized her hive into sections with different roles and appointed individual workers as the leaders of these sections, in accordance with the First of the Second and the Fourth of the Seventh's methods. She now double-checked the routes of the foragers, the processors, and the brood tenders to resolve any unbalanced allocations of workers, traffic jams, and other such inefficiencies.

She'd had her turn in command, and now it was her duty to manage her hive. In fact, she needed to put in even greater effort so that her hive would continue to grow when she took command of the army once again. The more efficiently her hive ran, the more sprayers they could introduce. Seeing the sprayers in action and determining how they would fit into the army was the job of today's commanding queen.

That was what it meant to be the hive of hives. Each had their role, each had their duty, and all needed to work equally diligently at whatever task they had. The Firstborn would strive no less at laying eggs and managing the efforts of her workers than she did at commanding soldiers and fighting shades. The army was counting on her to do both with equal fervor.

And now that the King's battle had been won, and the first sprayers had started to evolve, it was time to revisit raising new queens and expanding the army overall. The King also had created new lands and new flowers, all of which needed new workers. So, she would need much honey in the near future, and many more workers to produce it . . .

The First of the Fifth's workers moved in coordinated groups, one of which split into three separate squads. The first two squads visited the mana flower patch and the healing herb patch respectively, gathering the first and freshest of the nectar for the pure honey batches. The third squad visited both flower patches in turn, blending nectar and pollen together for the mixed batches.

And this time . . . as they flew from the mana flowers and landed on the healing herbs, some of the initial pollen they had gathered got left behind. This was intentional, done in accordance with the new instructions they had received. Once each worker landed on a certain healing herb, they rubbed their wings and legs together to scrape a bit of the pollen off, even adjusting the tiny-lightnings on their bodies so that the pollen wouldn't stick to them. And then they flew off to return their resources to their queen and hive.

The pollen from the mana flowers pulsed faintly with a subtle glow from the mana still contained within it. This glow then entered into the center of the healing herb flower, which began to close. The flower quickly wilted . . . and a faintly glowing seed dropped from its head into the patch.

The next day, the First of the Fifth's workers would pause as they arrived at the healing herb patch. A new flower had appeared, reminiscent of the other healing herbs, but glowing with a soft, blue-green light . . .

The First of the Fifth was beside herself, dancing about in a rapid, meaningless dance over the cells filled with the latest batch of nectar . . . something that was entirely new.

For this was beyond anything she had ever imagined. The instincts granted to her by the King were not for the sake of producing excellent honey, which explained why she couldn't bring the quality of the blended batches up to standard. No, they were for something else. Something so much more. An entirely new flower had grown from her workers' efforts.

She tasted the nectar herself. It *started* in a similar state as *finished* healing herb honey, infused with mana that resonated with and elevated the medicinal compounds within. The mana in this new nectar not only elevated but adjusted those compounds at a fundamental level, granting them greater effects than could be achieved in a mundane plant. This nectar could be processed into healing herb honey through basic concentration and evaporation, with no need for her workers to imbue it with their mana at all. And if they did so anyway, running through the process with the maximum effort and precision the First of the Fifth always strove to achieve? The result could be the First of the Fifth's greatest achievement yet.

She and the King had now collaborated not merely to produce new honeys from new flowers; they had changed the very landscape itself, bringing to life a new and powerful flower never before seen in his lands. The King and her hive, working together, had done this.

And what was more . . . who was to say this would be the last such achievement? There were the poison flowers, and new flowers that radiated heat. There were also those useless flowers in the flower meadow, though the First of the Fifth didn't see much hope there. And there was an entirely new room filled

with fruiting trees. What other new flowers could result if her workers continued to pass between them?

The First of the Fifth's mind raced as she considered how to prioritize her
efforts. She would need to have the mixed foragers passing between as many
different flowers as they could. At the same time, she now had multiple new
flowers to produce honey from, honey that she would then need to refine and
iterate upon until it reached a quality suitable to serve to the King. She just had
so much to do.

It was at this moment she received word that contact had been reestablished
with the Fourth of the Seventh's and her daughter's workers.

FAILURE

Despite all that she currently had to do, the First of the Fifth found herself standing still at the front of her hive. Dancing in front of her were several workers from her daughter, giving her a report on recent affairs. First of the Fifth was confused, confused to the point that she was now standing here to confirm and clarify the report in person.

The start of the report had gone well, beyond the First of the Fifth's wildest expectations. Not only had her daughter successfully made the move, but the *King himself* had built a perfect place for her to construct her new hive, well-defended and stocked to the brim with resources. The King was directly supporting her efforts. It took a while before the First of the Fifth was cognizant enough to receive the rest of the report. Which only made the next piece of news all the more confusing.

"My daughter . . . formed joint hive? With Fourth of Seventh?"

The workers danced the affirmative. The First of the Fifth did not consider for a moment if they had told the truth, for anything else was unthinkable. Besides, these workers, being the children of her own child, were still partially under the effects of her ability to command her own offspring. They replied to her questions as honestly and thoroughly as her own workers would. So, there was no mistake in the report itself.

". . . Why?"

Try as she might, the First of the Fifth couldn't see any rationale for this turn of events. Coordinating and cooperating with the Fourth of the Seventh was one thing. Forming a *joint hive* with her was something else entirely. That was a measure that could be taken . . . but only ever by related queens, and only under the most extreme of circumstances. Mixing workers and broods and honey with an unrelated queen could only produce inefficiency and dilute her offspring's achievements. How would her daughter possibly achieve the rigorous quality control to produce accept-ably good honey if she wasn't even in command of all the workers in the hive?

The First of the Fifth knew that the Fourth of the Seventh had been surpris-ingly cooperative and subservient, but she could not believe that could extend as far as the Fourth of the Seventh subordinating her own hive to another, especially a bee far younger and smaller than she. Nor could she imagine her own flesh and blood subordinating herself to the Fourth of the Seventh, one of the least of the apiary queens. How had these events come about?

"Hive was running out of honey, not enough to move and raise next genera-tion. Fourth of Seventh offered help. Hives worked together, built together for better efficiency."

The First of the Fifth froze solid. Her daughter . . . had run out of honey? How was that possible?

The First of the Fifth thought back to her daughter and all that she knew of her affairs. She started to tremble. She had ordered her daughter to operate on the very edge of sustainability in order to achieve maximally rapid growth—which had only been a reasonable command because she herself would provide the extra resources to ensure her daughter's hive did not collapse. She wanted her daughter to grow greater than the other apiary queens, after all, which would take even greater efforts since she did not possess one of the King's magical palaces.

And then, she had withdrawn those extra resources in order to support the King's great battle. And . . . she had not commanded her daughter to act any differently as a result. If she was like any of her other offspring, her daughter would have continued to execute her commands without question. She would have con-tinued to operate at the absolute limits of her honey production, possibly beyond. So she would not have had any reserves when the First of the Fifth commanded her to move. And if she tried to move immediately, without those reserves . . .

The First of the Fifth's wings buzzed as she began to pace about rapidly. This was a disaster of her own making. She had not paid sufficient attention to her daughter, treating her like just another worker. And because of that, she had placed her daughter in a desperate situation, where the child had no choice but to accept aid from an unrelated queen in order to fulfill her commands. The First of the Fifth had spread her attention too thinly, and her daughter had suffered as a result. When she thought about what her daughter would have been forced to do had it not been for the Fourth of the Seventh . . .

A joint hive with an unrelated queen was the *best* outcome of all this, even if it were the scenario where her daughter was now subordinated to the Fourth of the Seventh's rule. In the worst case, her own daughter's hive could have collapsed. She could have been responsible for the first failure among all the hives of the King that resulted purely from their own mistakes, without even the interference of an external invader.

The report continued. The workers described the current situation of the joint hives and the new room they found themselves in. The First of the Fifth could hardly pay attention, but at the very least she was relieved the joint hive was now doing well. No thanks to her, but at least her daughter was not starving. It was a heavy blow, but far lighter than it could have been.

She thought that was the end of it, but the workers had more to report. The Fourth of the Seventh's workers had also reestablished contact with the flower meadow and had passed on news from there, as they had done before. So, for the first time since the King's battle, the First of the Fifth received news of the flower meadow and its queens.

She froze even her anxious pacing as the meaning of the workers' latest dances reached her mind.

"King . . . building palace . . . for flower meadow?"

The workers danced the affirmative.

". . . Consulted with Second First of First on it?"

The workers again danced the affirmative.

"Received new flowers? Still commanding army?"

The workers danced the affirmative yet again. The First of the Fifth turned around and walked back into her hive in complete silence. The Second First of the First, who in her opinion no longer deserved the title of Firstborn, had failed egregiously, and put the King himself at risk. She deserved no less than exile. It was only by the King's boundless grace that she was permitted to endure. But it had been clear that she had lost any favor she had with the King, evidenced by the fact that he had pushed her away from his abode, separating them with an entirely new room. And it went without saying that she could not be trusted to command his defenses any longer. The First of the Fifth had even been prepared for the King to ask *her* to arrange things in the Second First of the First's stead, but if not her, then someone else. Such was the natural outcome for total failure, the natural fate of one who had lost the King's favor. Or so the First of the Fifth had believed.

But, apparently, she could not have been more wrong. The King had not cast the Second First of the First out, nor had he replaced her as his defender. No . . . he had treated her with *greater* favor than before she had failed! He continued to trust her with the defense. He granted her new resources and a new type of bee with which to fight. And now he intended to construct for her a palace, which had previously been an honor restricted to the Fallen Dynasty and the apiary queens alone. And not only that, but he had consulted with the flower meadow queens on the palace. He had taken their meager opinions and desires into account. He had not done that much even for the First of the Fifth. Measured by the rewards alone . . . he would be showing *greater* favor to the Second First of the First than to the First of the Fifth.

It made absolutely no sense. There was no way she could justify it in a manner she could understand or accept. How could the Second First of the First possibly have gained that much favor after such an egregious and critical failure? How could she have surpassed the First of the Fifth after placing the King himself in harm's way? Why did the King lavish rewards upon her so?

The First of the Fifth could not help but let the doubts creep into her mind. What if these rewards were *not* a sign of the King's favor? But if that were true . . . then none of the First of the Fifth's own rewards could be considered a sign of his favor either. Which might mean she had misread the King's actions and intentions entirely. Forget knowing him better than all, she might not know him *at all*.

Previously, she might have been able to put such doubts aside, confident in her own achievements and her own observations of the King. But now? His treatment of the Second First of the First was conclusive proof that his thoughts were different from hers, for his actions were completely opposite of anything she would have ever expected. And worse, she could no longer claim to be the greatest of queens. Her failures with her own daughter had revealed that her own plans and methods were flawed. She, the queen producing the most and greatest honey of all, had nearly driven her own offspring to *starvation*. She had failed in her area of expertise, her primary task and the one she considered most important. A failure on par with the Second First of the First's own . . . or possibly even worse, since no external force had played any part in it.

And then . . . it got worse. She had a thought. If the King's boons were not a reward for his favor, then what was their purpose? The Second First of the First had received them *after* a failure. In that case, was it possible that the King was not rewarding the best of his bees, but trying to bring those who were failing up to standard? The Second First of the First's case would indicate so. And then there was her daughter, who had received a perfect location for the hive from the King when she had been so desperate that she had to join with another queen. The evidence only grew.

And if that were true, then what of all the boons granted to the First of the Fifth? What if they were not a sign she was the most favored . . . but *the very opposite*? A sign that she had *never* been trusted like the Second First of the First had been?

The next thing she knew, she was flying through the air as fast as she could. Away from her hive, away from her daughter's workers, away from . . . everything.

Niobee flew in front of Belissar and began to dance.

"King, need to do something! Is okay? Will be back soon!"

Belissar tilted his head but nodded immediately with a smile.

"Yeah, that's fine. See you soon."

"Thanks! Will be back!"

And with that, Niobee flew off.

THE TRULY FAVORED

The First of the Fifth flew and she flew. Her workers followed after her, but she commanded them to leave her alone. Her mind raced. What should she do? How could she find the answer to these questions, these doubts? And how could she go on if they were true? If she were not the most favored . . . but the *least*? If she were completely wrong about the King and knew nothing of him at all?!

She sped through the air until she reached the end of the apiary, where the shrine was. She could go no further from here, and her wings ached. She slowly landed on the ground and began walking around in circles.

Just what should she do?!

It was then that a shadow passed over her. A large bee landed in front of her. The First of the Fifth nearly stumbled over herself as she tried to dance.

"No! I-I told you to leave me alone!"

"Didn't tell me, though?"

The First of the Fifth took a closer look and then suddenly took a step back. She was not dancing to one of her own workers or soldiers.

"T-The Conduit . . ."

The Conduit danced before her. "First of Fifth okay?"

The First of the Fifth froze and nearly flew off again. But then, she paused. The Conduit was her greatest rival, or so she'd once thought. The only other bee who could possibly claim to know the King as well as she did, or to be as favored as she was. She therefore minimized her interactions with the Conduit, for she did not wish to reveal her hand to the one she needed to defeat.

But now? Now . . . she realized if there was *any* bee that knew the mind of the King . . . if there was any bee who could answer her questions and doubts . . . it was the Conduit. She reached out to the only hope she had left. She lowered her head as she slowly began to dance.

"Conduit . . . does the King favor us?"

The Conduit began a confused dance. "Um, yes?"

The weight began to lift from the First of the Fifth's wings, but she could not allow herself to hope just yet.

"T-Then . . . are we the *most* favored?"

The Conduit rubbed her antennas and then began to dance. "Most? Like, more than others?"

The First of the Fifth could barely bring herself to confirm. "Y-Yes . . ."

"Um, no?"

The First of the Fifth collapsed on the ground, more confused than ever. And then she got up and began to dance. She had to figure out what was going on.

"Conduit . . . why does King give rewards? Why did he give us palaces? Why is he giving Second First of . . . the Firstborn a palace? Why did he help my daughter? Why . . ."

She paused before asking why he rewarded her, for she was not certain she could handle the answer. And once she paused, the Conduit began her dance with no hesitation.

"Easy! King loves bees!"

The First of the Fifth paused again. She repeated the Conduit's dance back to her far more slowly. "King . . . loves bees?"

"Yes!"

The Conduit began an animated dance. "King loved bees before was king! Made hives for old queen! Safe and warm! Protected us from bears! Saved me from spider! And not just old queen! Also helped other bees! King loves all bees!"

The First of the Fifth fixed her eyes upon the Conduit. "King loves . . . all bees?"

The Conduit continued. "Yes! Even evil hives that wanted old queen's flowers! That's why Queen of All Bees likes! That's why Niobee likes!"

The First of the Fifth fell still as she pondered the Conduit's words. Only after a few silent minutes did she begin to dance. "So . . . King . . . loves bees?"

"Yes!"

Thus began a quick exchange of dances.

"All bees?"

"Yes!"

"All as much as each other?"

"Yes!"

"Even Firstborn . . . after she failed?"

"Yes!"

"Even . . . me?"

"Yes!"

The First of the Fifth fell still again. So . . . she *had* been wrong after all. The King did not favor her above all others. His gifts to her were not, in fact, a sign of his special favor for her. But . . . she hadn't been entirely wrong. The King did not hand out assistance to her because she was the least favored, either. The King gave her gifts because . . . he loved her? So she *was* favored, just not in the way she imagined, and not any more than the other bees. Rather, the King favored them all and gave them gifts because of that. In that manner, the gifts *were* a sign of his favor. His equal favor.

"King . . . doesn't favor best or most productive bees? King . . . favors all bees?"

"Yes!"

The First of the Fifth thought back upon the King. She saw him raising up huge patches of the most valuable flowers by his home.

"Go ahead, I made it for you all."

She recalled him after the great battle, when his first thought was not to celebrate with honey, or to chastise the Firstborn for her failures. No, what he had done was race to a wounded soldier at the end of her life, one who had already been crippled and rendered useless. He gave of his own mana to save her life, she who had no further value to her hive whatsoever. She who had already fulfilled her purpose and could do no more.

The First of the Fifth recalled the moment she had been born. She'd known nothing at the time save that she had been born to serve the King and protect his home. She flew to him to pay her respects.

At the time he had been inspecting a palace. A palace that would magically boost the productivity of any hive that dwelt within, propelling them to guaranteed greatness. For a newly born queen, such a hive was little more than a dream. She could not help but feel drawn to it, even though it surely must have been reserved for only the mightiest of his servants. So, she tried to put it out of her mind as she greeted her master.

"What do you think? I'm sorry they aren't the nicest but . . . do you want to use them?"

She had frozen at that moment. His first words to her had been to offer her that dream of a palace. She quickly saluted and flew into the hive, for it couldn't have been real. But it was. The palace, for all its wonders, was empty . . . and the King had just gifted it to her. She had not needed to build her own hive from scratch, gathering her own nectar and pollen to construct the cells in which to lay her very first eggs. No, she'd *started* with a hive that would already have been the envy of even a successful queen. And one that was the closest to the King's own abode.

She'd had no doubts in that moment that the King favored her over all others, a conviction that only grew as it turned out the King was not satisfied with even that wonder of a palace and had built her a new one with his own hands. But now that she looked back upon it . . . how foolish had she been. How could she, a newly born queen without a worker to her name, have earned the favor of the King? She had barely finished her very first salute before he offered the palace to her.

If she had been right about the King favoring the best and most productive bees above all others . . . then he would not have offered such a palace to her at all. Even if she was right about the existing queens being out of favor, surely he would have had her generation construct their own hives, and then rewarded the palaces only to the most productive of them?

But he had not done that. No, she must have received that palace . . . simply because the King loved all bees, her newly born self included. He had loved her before she had done anything worthy of his favor.

She thought back to other interactions with the King. He praised the other bees as much as she. He gifted the same flowers to the flower meadow and the apiary and in the same quantities. And he thanked and praised her most not when she gave honey to him, but when she gave honey to *the other bees*. The Conduit was right. The King did not favor one bee . . . he favored all bees. The First of the Fifth was not the most or least favored, she was simply favored.

All the pieces fell into place now. The First of the Fifth could not claim to be happy at this outcome, but at least the confusion and the doubts had cleared. She had completely misread the King, but now, she had what she hoped was a relatively accurate understanding of him.

She turned to the Conduit. The bee that had once been her greatest rival. The bee that had now come to help her and to clear her doubts. She slowly began to dance.

". . . Thank you. I . . . need to think. But . . . will be okay now. I think."

"Okay! Will go back to King now! Let Niobee know if need help!"

And with that, the Conduit immediately flew off. The First of the Fifth watched her. The Conduit did not spare another moment on her, not even to point out the First of the Fifth's mistakes or the Conduit's own superior understanding of the King, but rather immediately flew to be at his side. She truly was devoted.

The First of the Fifth looked up at the Shrine of the Godden, the Queen of All Bees. A soft light filled the statue. She slowly took to the air and made the journey back toward her hive.

She had a lot to think about.

CHAPTER NINE

O-BEE-OUS OUTCOMES!

The First of the Fifth gradually began to speed up as she flew back to her hive. Once she arrived, her workers swarmed around her. A thousand dances and a flood of pheromones asked what had happened and if she was okay, as nearly all her hive now gathered around her.

Soon, she began to dance. Her workers gave her room so that they all could watch.

"We . . . are not most favored hive."

Thousands of wings began to buzz as the workers processed her shocking statement, but the First of the Fifth continued before they could despair.

"But not because we failed. King . . . loves all bees. King favors all bees. Good hive or bad hive doesn't matter. He favors all."

The workers fell silent. All eyes fixed upon her, waiting for their queen. For she had already decided what to do.

"So . . . we will still be best hive! We will work hardest, make most and best honey! We will help King most! And we will be most loving! We will help other bees most too!"

Yes, the First of the Fifth had decided. She apparently could not earn the King's favor by putting herself above the others. So, she would grow closer to the King in another way. She would follow after his example and become his ideal bee! She, too, would love all bees. She would love them the most! She would be the most loving queen! And then she would be the queen closest to the King, practically his shadow! Maybe he'd even love her more for it!

She had once again found the path to his favor!

And so, the First of the Fifth returned to work. She reorganized the foragers and the honey makers, for she still would not compromise on the quality of her offerings to the King. But . . . she also arranged for something new. A portion of her workers would be sent to each of the hives of the apiary, as well as to her daughter. She would visit and learn more about each of the other queens around her. Never again would she let her daughter starve because of her own ignorance. Nor would she allow any of the King's bees to remain neglected, not anymore.

The apiary queens would be quite confused at the sudden visitors . . .

The First Queen of the Third Spawner's First Dynasty, the first of her line, watched as squads of new soldiers gathered up in the air. It was her turn to command, and she had intended to follow in the Firstborn and the First of the Second's examples. But, as the King would have it, it was the army itself that would change today. A brand-new type of soldier had appeared, and now it would be her job to integrate them into the army. For now, the First of the Third wanted to see what they could do, so she gathered them into their own squad and had them join the training. During the normal maneuvers, they flew a bit faster but otherwise weren't much different from any other soldiers.

But now would come the key moment. It was their turn in the attack rotation, and they dove down toward the bee who was acting as a target. But, curiously, they curled up and pointed their abdomens forward far earlier than the other soldiers, while they were still a ways away from the target.

And then . . . streams of liquid began to spray from their abdomens, quickly spreading out into cones of toxins that reached about a dozen soldier-bee-lengths away. The target bee quickly flew back, retreating from the sudden assault.

The First of the Third stared at the liquid as it splattered on the ground. She already knew from her instincts what these soldiers were capable of, but now she saw it in action for the first time. Her mind began to race. So, these soldiers could sting from a distance. She quickly began to dance to one of her soldiers.

"That range . . . same size as invader tail?"

"No, longer," the soldier replied.

"So . . . invader can't reach?"

The soldier paused for a moment before dancing.

"Claws, teeth, tail, no. Mist, yes."

The First of the Third pondered what this would mean as a second squad of sprayers started their attack run.

After getting the flame radishes set up, Belissar then cleared a ring of dirt around the flower meadow hives, the shrine, and the memorial. He would still need to dig a ditch for defensive purposes, but clearing the area of flowers would make that easier to do later, and it would also provide some protection against a sudden fire.

At this point though, the cooldown for minor purifications was almost complete. With the shorter cooldown, the purification was available earlier and earlier each day. Today, it was ready just around midday. For a brief moment, Belissar wondered if he should keep doing them whenever they were ready, or if he should stick to one a day at a common time. But for now, he shrugged and made his way over to where the soldier bee army was training. If they were ready, there was no point in delaying.

The queen in charge of the army flew down and saluted to him. Belissar nodded back. "Ready for a minor purification?"

The queen immediately danced her confirmation. Belissar nodded again. "Okay, I'll prepare and then start it up as soon as we're both ready, then."

While the soldier bee army redeployed to the tower entrance, Belissar made a quick trip back to the apiary campsite. There, he reached into the flame radish pot and pulled out one of the radishes. He carefully cut off a small piece, then paused for a moment before turning to Niobee, who was flying around him as normal.

"Hey, Niobee, could you help me test something? It, um, might hurt."

"Yes! Not problem!"

Belissar nodded and took a deep breath before holding out the flame radish piece. "Can you, um, try to pick this up? Be careful not to let any mana or honey touch it, or it might catch fire. And let me know right away if it hurts."

"Okay!"

Niobee flew over. She wrapped her hind legs around the flame radish sliver, using the hairs of her pollen baskets to help hold it in place. She then took off, hovering in the air.

"Can carry! Not hurt!"

Belissar exhaled his breath and nodded. "Okay, good. Could you gather the apiary soldiers, then? I'd like to show them this."

"Okay!"

A short while later, Belissar was standing in the orchard, just in front of the entrance to the flower meadow. The apiary soldiers hovered around him, one of them carrying a flame radish sliver. The soldier bee army, meanwhile, was assembled at the entrance to the tower.

"Okay, here we go," Belissar said.

He triggered the minor purification and once again a small wolf-shade coalesced at the entrance. A squad of bees dove down toward it . . . but pulled up long before they reached it. Belissar tilted his head at this, but soon realized what was going on. The squad was composed of sprayers, and they had just unleashed their toxic attack. The shade was coated in the venom, and it began to roar. It jumped and pounced and swung its tail, but the sprayers were far away and only needed to fly a little higher to remain entirely out of its reach. They didn't even have to break away after their attack.

They apparently needed a bit of time before they could attack again, but a second squad of sprayers took their place and attacked as well. This time, the shade jumped out of the way, and most of the toxic liquid splashed against the ground. The shade took a deep breath and then retaliated with its own black mist attack.

However, the sprayers had mostly evolved from former soldiers, and so they already knew what to do. They dispersed with practiced efficiency, and with the additional distance between them and the shade it was all too easy for them to evade the breath attack. The black mist dissipated into the air without touching a single bee.

The first squad was ready again. This time, one bee attacked on its own, causing the shade to dodge. The other bees of the squad then sprayed the shade once it was in motion and couldn't adjust its course. It roared as it was again doused in toxins. The second squad attempted this as well. This time, the shade didn't dodge the first attack, so the other bees went off course. It still took one attack's worth of toxins in the process, however.

At this point, the shade began to wobble. It had been doused with over a dozen soldier bees' worth of venom at this point, and many of the sprayers had evolved from maddening soldiers, so their venom had the same intoxicating effects. The shade stumbled and fell onto the ground, unable to evade any more of the attacks.

It did not take long before the shade dispersed entirely.

All hostiles defeated.
Purification successful.

Belissar blinked. That was easy. Well, to be fair, the regular soldier bees could handle a minor purification shade like that in the same way, but in this case the bees never even gave the shade a chance to attack them. He turned to the apiary soldier bee who carried the flame radish piece.

"Um, sorry, looks like we're not going to use that after all. Maybe next time?"

The soldier bees just saluted and then Belissar retrieved the flame radish slivers. As he did, he started to wonder.

He now had flame radishes that could set the pits ablaze far more easily than a torch. Sprayers that could take down a shade from a distance. And the bees themselves seemed better and better at this. Maybe it was time to consider the minor+ purifications?

AM-BEE-TIONS

Back in the bear people's camp, Juosiutik was currently staring at a bubbling pot, hung over a normal fire this time. Since the mana honey had a . . . potent reaction with fire root, she was processing this potion without it. She stirred the mixture and gently swirled her own mana into it.

"Hm . . . from what I can tell, it's resonating well." She narrowed her eyes at it. "Too well."

Juosiutik was currently testing the mana honey in some of her recipes to determine its exact effects. In this case, the healing herbs from the sacred den were a bit too forgiving in maintaining their properties, so she was using other ingredients gathered on their sojourns.

And yet, the infusion of mana into the potion and the resonance of the compounds within was going about as well as it would if she had used those healing herbs. The mana honey was resonating with it all and helping to smooth out clashes in the ingredients.

Juosiutik frowned. She would have to wait for the potion to settle, and for a good opportunity to actually test its effects, but from what she could tell . . . this would likely end up one of her strongest potions yet. Despite the fact that it required less than half the steps and efforts of those she had made before.

It was incredibly exciting, but for some reason also kind of irritating.

In the apiary, the Second Queen of the Sixth Spawner's First Dynasty, the first of her line, stared at the workers just outside of her palace.

"First of Fifth . . . letting me access a new flower?"

"Yes."

She stared at the workers for a moment longer before conducting a slow, guarded dance.

". . . Why?"

The worker bees repeated a dance from when they had first greeted her. "Queen says Second of Sixth not making enough honey, not good enough honey. Needs better nectar."

The Second of the Sixth put aside the insult. Such was par for the course for the arrogant First of the Fifth. More aggravating was that the First of the Fifth was within her rights to say so. Her hive did, in fact, produce the most and best quality honey, so few queens could argue should the First of the Fifth disparage their efforts. Still, the Second of the Sixth also knew that such words were beyond the point. The First of the Fifth cared little for the operation of other hives beyond her own, so that could not be the ultimate point of all this.

". . . What does First of Fifth want?"

Yes, the only reason the First of the Fifth addressed the other queens was when she needed something for her own plans. Unfortunately, she also controlled the most valuable of the apiary's resources, so the Second of the Sixth would have to at least entertain the idea. Just scraps from the First of the Fifth could be highly profitable to the other queens, even those fortunate enough to dwell in one of the King's magical palaces like the Second of the Sixth. She herself had obtained access to the medicinal flowers by raising a drone when the First of the Fifth wanted to raise a new queen, so she figured it was something like that.

"Nothing!"

The Second of the Sixth was taken aback. She spun around and brushed her antennas, then fluttered her wings.

"Nothing?"

"Yes."

The Second of the Sixth paused before she realized what was going on. This, too, had happened before. The First of the Fifth had once given free access to a flower patch to the Fourth of the Seventh, one of the younger queens who didn't have a magical palace of her own. That flower patch, upon investigation, had turned out to be located all the way in the flower meadow, and it was rumored to be of low quality. The First of the Fifth must have identified this new flower as low quality and was now "gifting" it to another queen in order to offload it without relinquishing her claim to all new resources. The Second of the Sixth, however, would not be so easily deceived.

Well, it was also true that the new flowers *had* benefited the Fourth of the Seventh in the end, as evidenced by her growth and her ability to move her hive and claim a new room, so the Second of the Sixth couldn't reject the offer out of hand.

". . . Thanks. Will send workers to check, see if hive needs new flowers. If not, can give to others."

"Okay, will let queen know. New flower in medicinal flower patch. Is glowing."

With that, the First of the Fifth's workers departed. The Second of the Sixth instructed her foragers to check out this new flower and report to her before foraging was arranged. Whatever the First of the Fifth's intentions with this, she would be ready.

It turned out, though, when her workers brought her a small sample of the new flower's nectar, that she had not been ready after all.

The Fourth of the Seventh zipped through the air, led by her scouts and flanked by her soldiers. She was going to the flower meadow! Herself! She had only been there during King's big post-battle banquets, and never had the chance to explore much!

When her workers had told her to go, she couldn't believe it. They . . . were letting their queen leave the hive? For a long trip to another room? But it turned out the First of the Fifth's First Daughter had offered to look after their joint hive in the meantime. The Fourth of the Seventh had spent a full fifteen minutes on a gratitude dance before her workers gently stopped her.

The First of the Fifth's First Daughter was a wonderful queen! Maybe even her favorite!

She soon entered the flower meadow, where wide open skies and a vast sea of flowers opened up before her. She simply paused and took in the sight for a minute before one of her soldiers started nudging her. She danced a quick hello to the wounded soldiers by the memorial. One of them was even playing with lightning! She would have to have her workers ask her about it later!

She then made her way past the flower meadow hives and toward the patches they gathered from. There, she saw a curious sight. One of the flower meadow queens was outside of her hive, flying around with the soldier bee army. She remembered her workers mentioning that!

The queen paused when she saw the Fourth of the Seventh and flew over.

"I'm First of Third, is my turn to command army today. Should go back to hive."

"I'm Fourth of Seventh! Hi! Wow, flower meadow queens command army?"

The First of the Third paused for a moment. "Fourth of Seventh? From apiary, right? What doing here?"

The Fourth of the Seventh spun happily in the air. "Gathering flowers!"

The First of the Third paused again before starting a slow dance. "Gathering . . . flowers? But . . . Fourth of Seventh is queen. What about hive?"

The Fourth of the Seventh sped up even more. "First of Fifth's First Daughter helping!"

The First of the Third was no less confused at the answer. "First of Fifth's Daughter? But . . . what about First of Fifth's First Daughter's hive?"

"Same hive! We share, built together!"

The First of the Third fell completely still, nearly dropping from the air as her wings stopped for a moment. Seeing that the conversation had concluded, the Fourth of the Seventh bade her farewell and continued on with her quest. Soon, she arrived at her destination: the flower patch her hive had foraged from ever since the First of the Fifth told her about it. And, for the first time, she saw the flowers that had provided her hive with much nectar. They had five bright blue petals with yellow centers, and sat on top of long, thin stalks. A few of them were glowing slightly.

"Okay! Let's try grab flowers!"

Her soldiers saluted and flew with her to the flowers. The Fourth of the Seventh knew the King gathered whole plants—flowers, stalks, and all—and so she was attempting to follow suit. Her scouts said he just pulled them right out of the ground, but his might was far beyond that of any bee's, so the Fourth of the Seventh didn't know if that would work for her. But she'd do her best to figure it out either way!

The scouts also said the King gathered the glowing ones and left the others alone, so the Fourth of the Seventh figured that was how he knew which ones were fully grown. So, she and her soldiers flew toward one of the glowing stalks. They all wrapped their legs around it as best they could.

"Okay, together!"

The Fourth of the Seventh then pulled with all her might, and her soldiers with her. They beat their wings as fast as they would go.

And then instantly flew out into the sky and started careening out of control. The entire plant had come right out of the ground with hardly any effort at all. They ended up crashing into the ground.

"Wow, was really easy!"

The Fourth of the Seventh danced at their success before she and her soldiers picked up the plant off the ground and began carrying it back to their hive. She could finally begin following in the King's footsteps!

Later, when the day came to a close and the flower meadow queens gathered to review the army command, the First of the Third shared some shocking news on how the Fourth of the Seventh and the First of the Fifth's daughter ran their hive . . .

BEE-COMING THE HIVE OF HIVES

The Firstborn was the first to arrive at the memorial, where the queens of the flower meadow gathered at the end of the day. They had agreed to confer with one another once each day so that the queen in command of the army could report to the others on what she had done and any changes she had made, as well as to confirm who would be in charge next. Soon, they all had arrived and formed a circle with the queen in command for the day, the First of the Third, in the center. She began to dance.

The First of the Third's report resulted in buzzing wings and twitching antennas. The Firstborn herself couldn't help rising in the air a bit. The sprayers had performed remarkably well in their first battle. The shade had hardly a chance to retaliate as they took it down, and not once had a single bee been in any real danger.

The Firstborn's mind wandered a bit. Would these sprayers have changed the outcome of the battle against the flying enemy? It certainly seemed possible. The shade's overwhelming speed might have been less of a hurdle to the sprayers, who could still have landed attacks even if they couldn't catch up to it. Bees attacking from a distance also would have had more time to evade the shade when it turned to assault them or when it unleashed its lightning attack.

On the other hand, the sprayers did not seem faster than the shade had been, so if they had all been deployed forward and the shade got past them, the outcome may have ended the same regardless. The shade may have taken a toxic spray or two, but would that have been enough to bring it down? It may have been weakened, but the Firstborn imagined it would still have come down to her and the wounded soldier.

Still, she had not yet seen the sprayers in action, so she could not say for sure. They should not neglect their current efforts just because they had a new type of soldier. The sprayers would do their job and do it well. It was the queen's role to put them in a position to succeed.

But the Firstborn put her wonderings aside, for the First of the Third indicated she had more to say.

"Also, met Fourth of Seventh, here in flower meadow . . ."

That alone stopped all the dancing and pondering and brought every queen's attention back to her, the Firstborn's included. The only time queens had moved between the rooms were major battles, the King's banquets, or when the First of the Fifth came to coordinate with her. So, the Firstborn knew that this news must be important. But even she could not anticipate the First of the Third's next dance.

"Has new way of organizing hive. Formed joint hive with First of Fifth's First Daughter. First of Fifth's Daughter watched joint hive while Fourth of Seventh visited flower meadow."

The Firstborn dropped a bit as her wings paused for a second. The Fourth of the Seventh . . . had formed a joint hive with another queen?

The Firstborn started to tremble. What an incredible idea. An incredible, amazing, and simple idea. While she and others talked about the hive of hives, the Fourth of the Seventh and the First of the Fifth's First Daughter had gone and *built* one. Not just as an idea, but as a practical reality. And what was more, no queen in the flower meadow could miss the implication this had for their current efforts. The First of the Second, in particular, began a slow dance . . .

"That . . . seems efficient. Two queens in one hive, if one queen leaves, other still commands. Workers not left on their own, still get half of eggs laid."

The Firstborn danced in agreement. It was, of course, something she had noticed after her day of command. Her hive *had* dropped in efficiency and honey production that particular day. The next day, the First of the Second had reported a countermeasure, also developed by the Fourth of the Seventh's hive, but this would go beyond even that. With a second queen, the drop in efficiency from one queen being absent would be minimal.

So . . . the idea would be remarkably beneficial to the flower meadow queens, whose command of the army took them away from their hives on a regular basis.

Well, the others who had not commanded yet seemed a bit uncomfortable at the idea, judging by the way they slowly swayed and spun about, but the Firstborn knew they would realize the benefits once they had their turn. Still, this would be a difficult idea to put into practice in the short term. None of them had built their hives with two queens in mind, so moving in together would be a process. Likewise, there was the question of which hives to expand and which hives to abandon. Forcing one queen to double her efforts and another queen to abandon hers would not be a good way to go about it.

But the Firstborn had an idea, again inspired by the Fourth of the Seventh, that would pair nicely with their existing plans. She flew forward a bit, signaling her desire to take the floor. The other queens danced their assent and the Firstborn flew to the center.

"Fourth of Seventh didn't join existing hive but took new queen under wing. How about . . . expand hives while raising new queens, then keep new queens in hives? We help set up, they help take care of hive when we lead army."

The flower meadow queens were already planning to expand their numbers but were finding it difficult to justify the expense. New queens would need to migrate out, find suitable locations, construct their hives, fill out their worker ranks, and absorb the requisite mana to grow. Then, and only then, could they begin to contribute soldiers to the army. With the King's battle and the casualties that had resulted, the weaknesses and flaws that battle had revealed, and then the new soldier types created that needed to be raised and integrated into the army, it was hard to set aside resources for any purpose other than strengthening the army, especially for the long period of time that would be necessary for the new hives to grow. The queens could help speed up the process by donating workers and honey but that, too, would be a drain on their immediate resources for a future payoff. It was something none of them felt like they could afford.

But the Fourth of the Seventh had revealed a simple solution. What if the new queens *didn't* have to migrate, scout locations, and build new hives? What if the flower meadow queens didn't have to wait for their children to match their growth before they could begin contributing to the fight? If they formed joint hives from the start, the new queens could start laying workers right away. They would immediately begin contributing to the joint hives, for even a small addition of extra workers would allow the older queens to devote more of their resources to soldiers. And, of course, there was the aforementioned benefit of having someone else around to watch the hive when it was a queen's turn to command the army.

The expense would be far easier to justify if the new queens would boost their hives directly, and from the start. The new queens would also grow more quickly, since they would receive resources directly from their mothers and so wouldn't need to keep as careful a balance as an early hive normally would. And once they had grown . . . Well, the flower meadow would then have twice as many queens that could raise soldiers and take command.

And, perhaps most of all, it would turn the hive of hives ideal into a reality. They would not merely pursue the King's vision, but they would each live it.

The rest of the queens paused and slowly began to dance as they considered the Firstborn's words.

"Joint hive . . . but if with daughter, then . . ."

". . . Could work. Would still need bigger hive, though."

"King is building palace, though? Will need new hive anyway?"

"That's . . . right. If that case . . . can do?"

The Firstborn danced once more.

"Then, in agreement? Start gathering honey for new queens?"

One by one, each of the queens danced their answer. The First of the Second went first and immediately agreed. The First of the Third followed, and then the rest of the queens confirmed their agreement. From there, each queen began to report the status of their hives and honey stockpiles. Together, they estimated how long it would take for each queen to be ready for a daughter, and discussed how they might share resources to balance out the process.

As the Firstborn watched the dances and danced in turn, she could not help but feel her wings beat faster. Here it was, queens of different lines and unrelated lineages working together. Sharing honey instead of fighting for flowers. Acting as one to build something greater than any of them could achieve alone. And all based on the example of two queens from another room entirely.

Individually, she might have failed utterly. But . . . this was exactly the sort of thing she needed to overcome her own limitations. She was not alone. She did not need to face her challenges on her own. Within the King's realm, no bee did.

The hive of hives was taking shape in more ways than one.

CHAPTER TEN

NEXT CHALLENGE TO BEE-T

When the next day began, Belissar made his way to the new flame radish node in the apiary. As with other resource plant nodes, a few of the flowers were glowing slightly. He pulled on one of these and the whole plant came out, including a brand-new, fully grown flame radish at the bottom. He very carefully took it over to the shrine of bees and, as he had and continued to do with all the products he gathered, placed the radish within the wax chest, watching very carefully for any sign of flames.

"Thank you again, for everything. I hope you like it."

The statue and chest glowed with light. When the light faded and Belissar opened up the chest, the flame radish was gone. He exhaled; the offering had gone well and with no unintentional fires.

With that, he continued on with his day. He gathered the remaining flame radishes and stored them in the pot he'd left in the apiary's campfire pit. He then gathered and offered some healing herbs, mana flowers, and honey trays to the shrine before storing the remainder. He didn't gather every resource in his tower every day, but more medicine was always good to have, the mana flowers were supposedly very useful and valuable, and the apiary bees were happy whenever he accepted honey from them, so he always gathered those three at the very least.

After that, Belissar considered his next move. The minor purification cooldown finished in the morning today, so he could start one right away. But he did not. Instead, he walked over to the flower meadow. He found the soldier bee army had already started their training, with one of the queens leading them. The queen in question flew over and saluted to him.

"Good morning!" Belissar greeted her. "Um . . ."

He took a minute to figure out how to word his question. "If two of the normal wolf-shades attacked, how would it go?"

The queen immediately began to dance, indicating that the army would bring it down. Belissar rubbed his chin. "And . . . how many bees would we lose?"

The queen paused for a moment before she turned around and began a dance facing the army. A few of the soldiers flew to her and saluted, then began their own dances. She turned back to Belissar.

"A few at most, none is possible."

Belissar nodded at that. "Got it. In that case . . . I'm going to delay the purification until the late afternoon, the time we were originally doing it. But . . . it's going to be a minor+, so a bit stronger than normal. Last time it was two of the wolf-shades . . . but, um, I think we might want to be ready for a surprise, just in case. Just letting you know so you have time to prepare."

The queen and the soldiers behind her immediately began salute dances. Then they flew off into the air. A wave of dances passed through the soldier bee army and then the training resumed at a noticeably faster pace. Belissar took a deep breath.

He was relatively sure that the bees would be able to handle it. They had handled a minor+ purification before and had grown stronger since then. But the tower had a habit of surprising them, with occasionally deadly results, so Belissar couldn't help but worry anytime they tried something different.

He forced his fears down as he watched the queen dance in the air and the soldier bees zip around in response. His bees were working as hard as they could to ensure such losses did not occur. What sort of dungeon master and beekeeper would he be if he didn't trust in their efforts? And, ultimately, he wanted to take the next step, if they could handle it. The previous expansion had brought with it an orchard that enticed the bees enough to move their entire hives there, sprayers who could bring down a wolf-shade with impunity, and cross-pollination that . . . well, he wasn't sure if that had resulted in anything yet. He put checking the different flowers and resource nodes on his mental to-do list. The point was, though, that they gained many new options when they took on more dangerous purifications. Those new options in turn helped them face those challenges more easily.

He had recently become aware of some new needs, in fact. He would have liked to practice making the potion Juosiutik had shown him, but he currently lacked a water source or suitable containers for both processing and storing liquids. He could potentially make some basic pots and bowls out of wood, or trade with the bear people for some, but he figured water was something he might want a tower option for. Not least of all because of the potential flammability of his tower; a river cutting through the flower meadow, for example, would go a long way in easing his concerns.

But, well, with a grand total of three minor purifications thus far, his current mana was only at three hundred and thirty, not nearly enough to consider another expansion purification even if he felt confident in facing another shade of that caliber. Likewise, while his dungeon points—or DP as the Tower normally called them—were growing nicely, he was still a ways off from affording any of the options in the DP store. Taking on a bit more challenge as the bees were able would open up new options that much sooner.

With the plan for the day set, Belissar then turned his mind to his other tasks. First of all, he needed to spend some time practicing his magic. Chief Rohsuak had said the best way for him to learn at this point was for him to use it, so it wouldn't do to slack. Well, right now all he could really do was make honey. He made another little honeycomb pattern out of mana and watched the honey pool in his hand. He furrowed his brow, then held up his hand.

"Niobee, want some honey? I, um, didn't think about what to do with it before I made it."

She flew in front of him and began to dance slowly. "King . . . giving honey? Honey he made?"

Belissar nodded. "Yep."

Niobee paused, swaying about in the air for a moment before she suddenly started zipping. "King . . . can make honey! And hives! And bees! King is best king! Definitely not useless drone! Niobee knew!"

Belissar started chuckling and smiled at her. "Well . . . I guess I can, in a way. So, do you want some? I already made it, so I'd appreciate it if you could help me with it."

"Okay!"

Belissar's grin grew as Niobee hovered in front of his hand and drank up the pool of honey in his palm. If it made Niobee this happy, then even this small bit of magic was something incredible.

After Niobee had drunk her fill, Belissar got to work on the flower meadow beehouse. He sawed the dry wood provided by the bear people into appropriately sized planks and cut grooves into them that would fit together. He then started laying out a foundation for the house, slotting the grooves together.

It . . . was a bit slow going. Belissar was no stranger to lifting heavy objects, but handling large pieces of wood like this alone was a bit much. Still, he was determined to see it through, however hard it was or however long it took. His bees deserved no less.

And before he knew it, it was about time for the purification. He put the last log into place and then rubbed his arms and back. The day was wearing on, and he needed to at least gather a flame radish, so he had to stop here. He heaved a sigh.

He really hoped it would go well today . . .

The First Queen of the Fourth Spawner's First Dynasty, the first of her line, flew through the ranks of her soldiers. She flew to the very front of the army, where her hive gathered at the entrance of the King's realm. Where the invader would soon arrive. She danced as her soldiers saluted.

"Everything ready?"

The designated leader soldier replied, "Everything ready, queen! Ready to fight!"

"Good."

She looked at the entrance for a while longer, the place that would soon become a battlefield. She slowly began to back up, keeping her eyes on the entrance for as long as she could before turning around and flying to take her place at the head of the reserve force.

Long had the First of the Fourth had her soldiers report to her of their deeds. Long had she watched them train against imaginary foes. Long had she listened to the stories told by the Conduit about the First Dynasty of the First Spawner and their courageous, if doomed, final stand. Long had she stood on the very top of her hive, straining her eyes to catch even the smallest glimpse of the battles in progress.

Sometimes, she wished she could join the army as it flew to the fight. But she knew her place. If not for her and her fellow queens, there would not *be* an army, so she did the next best thing and raised the mightiest soldiers she could.

She had burned with rage when their army was nearly defeated. But . . . she would admit that she had been ecstatic when the Firstborn proposed how to prevent such a thing from happening again. She, along with the other queens of the flower meadow, would now have the chance to lead from the front, like the courageous queens of the First Dynasty on their final stand. She had patiently waited her turn, even though she could hardly stand still these last three days as she watched the other queens fly with the army and listened to them recount tales of their battles.

Now, it was her turn. And her patience had granted her an unexpected reward. Today, on the day of her command, the King had acknowledged their growing might. He would once again entrust them with a battle of greater proportions, sending them against a more powerful foe than the daily invader. She would be the first to test her strength in such a battle.

It was with reluctance that she returned to the reserve force. She thought briefly of leading from the very front, with the soldiers of her own hive. But she knew better. Her wings were not as fast as a soldier's nor her stinger as long and sharp. To get any closer would be to needlessly place herself at risk. Besides, it was her duty to command the army as a whole, which meant she needed to be in a place where she could see the battle in its entirety.

But that was fine. She would still be watching the battle with her own eyes. She would be responsible for facing the enemy directly and bringing it to heel. The fate of all hives and the trust of the King hung upon her, and she would not let them down.

"Everybody ready?"

The voice of the King resounded through her very being, and she could have only one response. She danced the salute.

The time had come.

THE BIRD AND THE BEES

Okay, here we go."

The King gave his command. The First of the Fourth felt the entire world shift at his word. It filled her with heat and power, spurring her to action. And she knew why, as she felt a cold chill creeping toward her.

This was it. She fixed her eyes upon the entrance, not looking away for even a second. Something dark began to coalesce around the tower's entrance . . . *above* the ground. The First of the Fourth began dancing immediately, sending her meaning along her mana to her children at the front.

"Air attack!"

The King had warned her to be ready for anything, and the First of the Fourth had taken his words to heart. His wisdom was clear as the enemy immediately defied their expectations. But the soldiers and queens both had learned the lessons of their recent defeat well. They knew now it was possible for an enemy to appear higher up. The soldiers had trained and drilled for that exact occurrence, and with the First of the Fourth's quick command they now immediately reorganized for an aerial foe.

Some squads moved closer to the ground to prevent the enemy from flying beneath the army, while a group of sprayers moved into range above the incoming invader. The rest of the soldiers began to move as well. No longer did they hover in place, holding a static formation around the enemy. Instead, they began to zigzag through the air in constant movement, with random stops and dives and turns to prevent the enemy from tracking their trajectory. They would not wait for the enemy to strike but would begin their evasion before the attack approached.

A moment later, a screech rang through the First of the Fourth's body, far louder than she had anticipated from the stories. Her body trembled as her eyes beheld the enemy. A bird, much like the one that had broken through their army, now flapped in the air. It was far smaller than the original had been, comparable to the difference between the daily wolf-shades and the very first. But the First of the Fourth would not let its size fool her. She knew that this was a foe that could quickly escape her grasp if she made a single mistake.

She would not let it have the chance. The moment the shade appeared, the sprayers launched their attack, coating the bird in toxins. The shade screeched at them and flapped its wings, but the sprayers had already melted back into the swirling mass of bees and the shade lost track of them. A second sprayer squad jumped out of the mass and launched the next attack. The shade dodged out of the immediate path of the attack, though it still caught some drops of toxin as the sprays spread out.

The shade then shot into the formation of bees all around it, its sharp beak opened wide. But it had many targets to keep track of and the bees only had one. The bees it had aimed for had already adjusted their course. The bees heading toward it, on the other hand, spun around and thrust their stingers forward, plunging them into the shade's back. The shade screeched and snapped at them, but they had already retreated a safe distance away. The shade flapped its wings and surged toward these latest attackers, but they had dropped down and evaded its wrath once more.

The battle continued in that fashion. The shade would fly forward, but each time the bees' random and shifting motions kept it from overtaking them with its speed. It seemed as though the army's plan would work. But the First of the Fourth kept her eyes on the shade and noticed a problem. The shade kept flying in the same direction, and the bees kept shifting their formation to keep it contained. But the bees were still ultimately slower than the shade, and flew even slower on account of their evasive maneuvers. The number of bees ahead of the shade was growing smaller as the other side of the formation fell behind. The queen ordered the soldiers in the back to abandon random evasion and prioritize speed, but it would still take time for them to catch up.

And then came a mistake. Lightning began to crackle around the shade. The First of the Fourth and her soldiers had been on the lookout for that and immediately evaded. A small cone of lightning erupted from the shade's beak and struck nothing but air. However, the formation around the shade had already grown light enough that the sudden retreat left a clear gap. The shade's glowing red eyes narrowed and it flapped its wings, rushing toward that gap.

The bees reacted immediately. A squad of soldiers dove toward it while a squad of nearby sprayers unleashed their attack. But the two squads had not coordinated, and the soldiers passed right in front of the sprayers. They were doused by the toxic spray, which thus did not hit the shade. The soldiers themselves had a bit of resistance to the toxins, so they weren't in immediate danger, but the sudden spray threw them off course and drenched their wings, slowing their flight. As a result, neither the soldiers nor the spray reached the shade before it had escaped the formation entirely.

Once again, the shade was free and clear to head toward the hives and the King waiting beyond.

Or was it? As the shade flew forward, another hive's worth of soldiers took up positions ahead of it. The shade veered to the side, but a second hive was already moving there. It stopped and flew straight up, but it could see a third hive already climbing and now turning to dive toward it. Yet another hive plugged the other flank while the soldiers the shade had just escaped came up from behind.

The First of the Fourth was *not* about to let their army fail in the same way as before. As the first formation had started to thin out, she'd ordered the reserve forces to move. She had built the same containment strategy on a much larger scale, forming new containment formations in every direction the shade could go. It could not move without a new hive wrapping around it.

The First of the Fourth had to admit she had questioned the Firstborn's organization of the army. If their army had proven too weak to bring the enemy down before it could escape, how would making the force fighting the enemy *weaker* help things? But now she could see the benefit. With the majority of the army *not* engaged in the fight, the queen had substantial forces to move as she saw fit, and so she could easily set a trap for the shade when it escaped the first formation.

The shade glanced around but found no gaps to exploit. It began to gather its lightning again, but the First of the Fourth moved first. She ordered the sprayer squads forward and had them attack. Toxins sprayed onto the shade from all directions. She held her soldiers in reserve for now, wary of the sprayers hitting their own side again. But the strategy was working. If the shade remained still, the sprayers would continue to bombard it. If it tried to break through, the soldiers would move to meet it.

It turned out the shade wouldn't attempt to break out at all. The shade squawked, but its voice was weak now. Lightning crackled across it but never gathered into another blow. The toxins and stings it had already received were taking hold even as the sprayers laid on more and more. It began to wobble . . . then to dip . . . and soon, its wings were not beating fast enough to keep it aloft. It plunged toward the ground.

The bees below cleared out of its path while dealing it additional stings along the way, but that was unnecessary. The shade was no longer even attempting to attack them. Black mist had begun to waft from its body, and it vanished into a fading cloud before it even hit the ground.

The First of the Fourth stared for a moment until she heard the King's mighty voice.

"Looks like you got it, great job everyone!"

She stood still and then burst into a dance, flying about as fast as she could. That . . . was amazing! Her first battle, and they had come out on top! The very enemy that had defeated them had now been vanquished, without once laying its beak upon even a single bee! She had prevailed against the dangers that the First Dynasty had flown against!

Well, not exactly. She had been there for the second purification and had seen the shade that had brought destruction to the First Dynasty. This shade could fly and move fast, but it did not match the sheer power that the first wolf-shade had brought, nor did it match the size of the bird-shade that had defeated them recently. But still, her first battle had been a victory, and the army had proven it could contain a flying invader.

It was a good start. And if the First of the Fourth had anything to say about it, it would only be the beginning.

CHAPTER ELEVEN

HOME BEE-VAMPING

Belissar's breath caught in his lungs as he saw another bird-shade appear. After the damage the previous one had done, he had *not* expected one of these to count as a minor+ purification. Fortunately, the bees had prepared for such an event and reacted well. The shade was immediately sprayed with toxins on appearance and quickly surrounded by a formation of constantly moving bees. It was then that Belissar noticed the shade was significantly smaller than the first one had been, and that its lightning attack was a lot more limited. He had another fright when the shade broke away from the bees, but it was then surrounded by a bee formation many times the size of the first.

His eyes widened as he watched the bird-shade vanish into mist. His eyes went even wider as he realized that not a single bee had fallen in the process. He soon broke out into a wide grin.

"Yes!"

His bees had grown remarkably in the handful of days since that first battle. And, perhaps even more relieving, Belissar had managed to correctly assess their growth and their readiness for a greater challenge. Even though he personally had not expected a small bird-shade, the bees had no trouble handling the situation.

And, of course, with victory came rewards.

Minor+ Purification completed!
*Please select a reward.**
- +75 DP
- +15 Max Mana
- Beehive (Rarity: Uncommon. Type: Bee, Resource, Monster Nest.)

*(*One or more choices upgraded due to Blessing of Bees)*

Belissar's grin grew. For once, he didn't need to wait until after the celebration to make his choice. He knew exactly what he was going to pick this time.

Beehive selected.
Beehive variation unlocked: Belissar's Beehouse.

Belissar nodded in satisfaction. He would have insisted on upgrading the beehives anyway, so he was pleased to learn the tower could build his versions right away. And now, all his bees could receive the honey production and brood growth benefits of the apiary's beehouses. Perhaps it wasn't the water source he had been thinking about, or something as dramatic as a new bee type, but anything that made his bees happy was an ideal choice for Belissar.

Plus, there was the fact that such a feature came from a minor+ purification, which he could perform every day and which his bees had just proved they could handle. Who knew what other options might be available from those rewards?

In any case, he was satisfied for now. It was time to bring out the honey for a victory celebration . . .

The next day, Belissar stepped out of the apiary farmhouse. He intended to get started placing beehives for each of his queens, but there was a bit of math to do first, which meant finding some dirt he could draw numbers on to keep track of it all. Which he now did. There had been nine apiary beehouses compared to thirty-two queens, four each from eight spawners, so there were quite a few who had gone without. He then took a look at the new feature . . .

Beehive

Type:	*Bee, Resource, Monster Nest*
Mana Upkeep:	*5 (2 with Blessing of Bees)*
Base Production Rate:	*1 honeycomb per 24 hours*
Available Variations:	*Belissar's Beehouse (100 DP per hive, 25 if manually constructed)*

Slight boost to monster bee growth rate.

That gave Belissar pause. He checked the information on the apiary.

Apiary

Type:	*Bee, Resource, Settlement*
Innate Features:	*Beehives*
Mana upkeep:	*10 (5 with Blessing of Bees)*

A farm dedicated to beekeeping. Comes with beehive nodes that produce honeycomb. If Bee type monsters are available, may settle in beehives for a slight boost in brood growth and beehive productivity.

Belissar had a free room where he could potentially add a second apiary as an alternative, so he was trying to figure out which would be better. An apiary cost five mana and provided nine beehives without any additional cost . . . save the DP required to upgrade them, but that was the same regardless. Making the beehives one by one, on the other hand, would require eighteen mana for the same number. There was a pretty clear mana advantage to using the apiary.

However, placing a second apiary would use up another room slot—his last available one, in fact. Room limits could be increased, but the option to do so seemed quite a bit rarer than options to increase mana, so might it be better to spend the extra mana? Instead of an apiary, he could add a second flower meadow or orchard. Notably, the apiary had enough flowers to support its beehouses and then some, but it still had less than the other two rooms, and he had already confirmed that some types of flowers the others had weren't available in the apiary. So, if he added one of the other room types and built the beehives himself, he might be able to support more queens than a dedicated apiary would.

There were other possibilities too. He could add a flower meadow or orchard to the very front of the dungeon that he *wouldn't* add any beehives to. That would give the soldier bee army a place to fight that didn't have any hives in harm's way . . . and it would also give the bear people a place to gather from without disrupting his bees. He was a bit loathe to add stuff that wasn't for his bees, but he had noticed them crossing rooms on their foraging trips, so the bees could still gather from the room even if their hives weren't located there.

And, of course, there was always the possibility of acquiring new room types somehow. Belissar checked and found it was possible to remove a room after the fact—the problem being that if any of his bees set up hives in a given room, he would not be willing to rip up their homes. So, if he placed another apiary, it would be there to stay. Any new rooms would then have to wait for more room slots.

All in all, there were too many possibilities for Belissar to handle, and his eyes were starting to spin. So, he decided he would just add the beehives one by one. He'd have to do that anyway for the flower meadow and orchard queens, and he could always just expand his mana reserves with the daily purifications. He'd just do it this way for now and keep the last room free in case he needed it for something else.

Beehive (1 mana with Blessing of Bees and Apiary Discount)

Belissar stared at the message for a moment and then slapped his forehead. Of course. *Of course* the beehives would also be cheaper to place in the apiary. He didn't even need a second apiary to get a discount on the hives, it seemed. Which, if he had thought to check, could have saved him a lot of this thinking and decision-making.

He sighed, shook his head, and then got to work. He shifted to his tower sight and a transparent beehive appeared in the apiary. He moved it toward the nearest queen without a beehouse . . . and then paused. He realized that if he just put the beehive next to the colony, the queen would have to move and rebuild all of her comb. He wondered if there was anything he could do.

Just to check, he tried moving the new beehive over the existing nest . . . and the transparent image didn't turn red. Instead, it seemed to wrap around the nest.

Belissar mentally nodded to himself. It was good that he had checked first. Well, he hesitated slightly as he worried whether this would impact the bees and their larvae inside. But when he had upgraded the occupied beehives into his bee-houses, the colony hadn't been negatively impacted, so he figured this shouldn't hurt them either. And so, he went ahead and confirmed the new feature.

The Third Queen of the Sixth Spawner's First Dynasty, the first of her line, fluttered her wings as she checked over the latest batch of honey. It was coming along nicely. Sure, it wasn't nearly as good as the First of the Fifth's, or any of the other nine apiary queens who were born before her, but she could say that it was her best.

She had been born just a few minutes too late to receive one of the magical palaces, and so she had been relegated to the outskirts of the apiary, far from the King's abode. She'd had to build her hive by herself, and her workers had to imbue the nectar of mundane flowers with mana by themselves. They, therefore, couldn't produce honey in the kind of quantity and quality that the other queens could, and her hive couldn't grow anywhere near as quickly. Soldiers, if she had been inclined to raise any, were just a dream, and she herself was still a similar size to her workers. It was a humble, but good and honest living. She might not have done much in comparison to her peers, but everything she had was achieved by her own efforts, and those of her children. She took pride in it, and that was the truth.

Still . . . there was some small part of her whispering on the edge of her mind. It asked . . . What if she had been born but a few minutes earlier? What if she had been one of the favored queens who had received magic palaces and flowers brimming with mana? What if her hive produced honey in such quantities that she could offer tribute to the King on a daily basis, receiving constant visits from him as a result?

What if it had been her? But she put such things aside. This was her lot in life, and all she could do was make the best with what she had. Maybe, one day, the King might see her efforts and—

She buzzed her wings and shook herself. Such thoughts did not aid in her work, and there was work aplenty for her to do. So, she tried to put her wondering aside and get back to it.

But at that moment, something changed. The air began to thrum with mana, causing all of her workers to pause. Her antennas twitched as she reacted to the swirls of power flowing all around her. The very walls of her hive began to glow, growing too bright for her to make out anything.

Then, slowly, the light began to die down. And the Third of the Sixth froze solid once she could see again.

Her hive was gone, or at least the hive she'd had before. Thick wooden walls like the trunk of a gigantic tree had replaced the exterior of her hive, granting her powerful protection against the outside world. Most incredibly of all, she could feel rivers of mana flowing through those walls, and even through the air itself. The mana flowed into her honeycomb, imbuing the nectar stored there as her workers might otherwise have needed to. It wrapped around her eggs and larvae, and they drank it up, accelerating their growth. The mana even condensed down in empty cells, where honey began to spontaneously drip from the walls.

Her mind couldn't process what had occurred. Her workers began to dance around her as they requested instructions.

And then, she felt the tremors as something huge approached her hive. She slowly turned around and crawled toward the entrance as a shadow fell over it. She peeked outside and confirmed the unthinkable suspicion that had crept into her mind. There, standing outside of what had once been her hive, was the King.

"Hey there. Sorry for doing this without warning you, but I hope it helps you. These hives aren't the best, but I'll build you a new one soon, so hopefully this is okay for now."

The Third of the Sixth began to tremble. The King . . . had gifted her a magic palace? Was going to make it *even better* later because he wasn't satisfied with it?

Her mind went blank as she began to dance. She had no idea what she said to the King. But what she remembered was this: The King had seen her. Had acknowledged her. Had gifted her with the same blessings the others had received. Now she could grow as powerful and productive as them. Now she could make vast quantities of excellent honey like them. Now she could offer tribute to the King without worry or shame.

And she would do just that.

CHAPTER TWELVE

THE SINCEREST FORM OF FLATTER-BEE

From there, Belissar visited each of the apiary queens without beehouses one by one, figuring after the first one he should give them a heads-up before transforming their hives. He couldn't help but grin as he remembered all of their happy dances. He might not have been happy with the basic beehive, but it seemed the queens absolutely were.

He was giving them the basics for now, as the upgrade to his version would be much cheaper if he built it himself. Plus, he liked the idea of building the beehouses by his own hand, and now that he had access to dry wood he could improve upon the design currently in use. That would have to wait though, as he wanted to keep working on the flower meadow beehouse first.

Speaking of which, he wondered how he was going to construct their home, since he was building a much different beehouse than usual. He hoped that he would get another potential upgrade for the beehives when he finished, but he couldn't be sure. Well, if it came to it, he could always build normal beehouses inside of the rooms of the bigger one, so he'd continue on as planned and see what happened.

Though, that brought him to the next question. He turned his attention to the orchard queens . . . and found they had joined their hives together into one big hive. Multiple queens in a single hive . . . Belissar had seen it once or twice in his life, but it was rare and had never lasted long. But well, the monster bee queens proved far more adaptive than his old bees had been, so he guessed they had figured something out. The problem was that the transparent beehive was currently turning red when he moved it over the joint hives. Maybe because they were too big? Or maybe because the hives were currently built in the branches of the groves, high above the ground? Belissar wasn't sure.

He returned from his tower sight to his body and rubbed his chin. It looked like he'd have to figure out something different for the orchard queens. Maybe if he built a bigger beehouse in the trees? Well, he'd set that as his next project, after finishing the flower meadow beehouse. Now that the new beehives had been placed, it was time to resume work on just that.

He walked down to the orchard and through to the flower meadow and surveyed the scene. He had the basic foundation of the beehouse set up, so now it was time to begin working on the frame. Eventually, he got some grooves cut in an appropriate beam. He struggled to stand it upright and managed to slot it into the corresponding groove on a floor beam. He took a step back, ready to stabilize it if it fell.

The beam remained upright, but it seemed a little unstable for his liking. He frowned and looked at the grooves. The pieces fit together, but not perfectly since his cuts were rough. He thus had to make the grooves a bit larger than necessary to ensure the beams would fit within them, leaving room for them to lean and sway about. He crossed his arms and thought.

If he had some nails . . . but he didn't. The bear people had some metal implements, but Chief Rohsuak had said they didn't have any nails, and that it would be some time before they started making any. If he had some glue, clay, or mortar maybe he could stabilize it a bit more . . .

Belissar glanced over at the beehives and remembered when Niobee had used some wax to reinforce his first rickety frames. He then stared at his hand.

"I wonder . . . I can make honey, right? What about wax and propolis?"

He crouched down and held his hand toward the groove. He stirred up his mana and formed the honeycomb pattern in the air . . . and then honey dripped onto the wood. He frowned.

This time he tried again, and really focused his thoughts on wax and propolis. He imagined the mana becoming sticky propolis sealing the gaps, then solidifying into wax. He thought of bees building their comb and sealing up their hives. A mana pattern began to form once more, but this one was different. Whereas the normal pattern featured bright lines outlining a hexagonal shape that was filled in by a dimmer glow, this time only the hexagonal lines formed, creating an empty honeycomb pattern inside. It then condensed down into a glowing ball of light that covered a bit of the space between the two pieces of wood.

Belissar grunted. His head started to pound and his arm started to burn, but he kept at it. Soon, the light died down. Belissar grinned as he saw the results.

In place of the ball of light was a piece of wax. He tried to push on it with a finger and found it was now sealed to both pieces of wood, with propolis helping to bind the places where the two pieces of wood touched directly. He then took a deep breath and attempted to repeat the process. It took a lot of pain and focus, but he was able to extend the wax by another piece. And another. And then another. He was sweating and had a massive headache, but with each attempt the pain grew just a little less.

"Niobee will help!"

Niobee landed on him and he could feel the warm flow of mana pass through his body from her. He grinned.

"Thanks, let's work together?"

"Yes!"

The two then kept at it until a seal formed over the intersection of the two beams and the upright beam was acceptably stable.

The wounded soldier, once again, was attempting to form her lightning magic into an actual shape. Her progress had slowed after her initial successes, unfortunately. She could now curve the stream into a loop . . . but bending it any further caused it to break, the looped parts interfering with each other and causing the whole thing to disperse.

She could tell at this point that the method wasn't working. A little loop of lightning was a far cry from the massive waves the enemy had used. At the same time, though, she wasn't sure what else she could try. If she just needed more practice with this method, she'd practice as much as she needed to, but if she had hit the limit, then she needed to try something else. Even mundane bees adapted that much.

It was then that the King arrived in the flower meadow. The wounded soldier dropped her practice to dance her salute as he passed by, then watched as he began his work on the grand palace he was building for the flower meadow queens near the memorial.

It was later in the day when she felt the pull of the mana of the realm. She turned to face the direction of its flow, and saw there the King kneeling by a large pillar of wood. The Conduit was dancing on his back and pulling the mana from all around her into the King. The King formed a honeycomb pattern out of mana before wax appeared out of thin air. The soldier had seen the honeycomb pattern before; it was what she was attempting to mimic in the first place.

The wounded soldier's wings buzzed. She had an idea. She stirred up her mana and began beating her wings, the lightning wings included. She formed another arc of lightning between her physical wings and her lightning ones, then rose to her feet . . . and started to dance.

If the mana would not leave her body to form a pattern, then why not use her body to form the pattern? Instead of trying to curve and twist the arc of lightning, she tried to extend it, leaving a trail behind her as she danced. She danced in a little hexagon before arriving back at her start. The trail vanished quickly, however, and it had faded by the time she arrived.

So, she tried again. She danced faster. She beat her wings harder, increasing the intensity of the lightning arc between them and causing the trail to remain just a bit longer. She pushed the arc further, extending the trail by just a bit more.

She danced and danced, speeding up as fast as she could go and then willed herself to go even faster than that. She pushed the lightning arc as far as it could go and beat her wings to build up as much lightning as she possibly could. The lightning crackled and lit up her surroundings as she zipped about.

And then, finally, the trail extended far enough and lasted long enough that she could catch it before it faded. The lightning touched and then connected back to the original arc between her wings.

The lightning crackled and began to glow even brighter. She stepped away . . . and found that the lightning remained, crackling in the shape of the hexagon she had danced. The crackling grew louder and the light brighter as the little hexagon began to shrink down until it formed a bright little speck of light. The wounded soldier couldn't tear her eyes away even though it began to hurt.

And then, the light receded. There, on the surface of the memorial beehouse, was a tiny drop of honey. A faint bit of tiny lightning zipped across its surface. The wounded soldier looked at it before breaking out into a dance of celebration.

She had done it. She, a crippled soldier, had *made honey*, a feat no soldier should have been capable of. And she had done so by replicating the very magic of the King himself. A single drop of honey wasn't exactly a lot, but it was a step. A small, but successful step. And now that she knew the path to take, the wounded soldier could begin stepping again and again until, one day, she could contribute to the hive as she once had.

One by one, wounded soldiers around the memorial came to see what was happening, and joined her in the celebratory dance.

A QUEEN'S DEBTS

The First of the Fifth flew through the air, flanked by the handful of soldiers she had raised. She beat her wings as fast as she could, willing herself to go faster. Every moment she was out of her hive was a moment she could not guarantee the absolute quality of her honey. She might now know that top-tier honey was not a path to the King's favor, but she still couldn't fathom offering anything less than her best to him.

But this trip was necessary. And it was something the First of the Fifth needed to do herself. She had left her instructions as best as she could and then set off. She had just finished flying through the apiary and through the empty rooms that now separated it from the rest of the King's domain.

Soon she arrived at the orchard. The sight of it caused her to slow for just a second. Towering trees rose above her, their canopies filled to the brim with massive fruits and colorful flowers. A land of great abundance. The First of the Fifth wondered what sort of honey was made with the nectar of such plants. How much water did it possess? What was its sugar and mana content? Did it possess any distinct flavors or compounds with magical resonance? But that was not the purpose of this trip. She set these thoughts out of her mind and continued on her way forward.

Eventually she reached the end of the room and turned to the side. There she saw a grove of tightly packed trees, so close their branches and canopies crossed together into one. She sensed more than saw the mana of the defensive chasms surrounding the trees, revealing the defenses the King had placed to protect them. Streams of bees flew to and from the grove, gathering nectar from the fruit trees beyond. Some of them noticed her approach and flew back toward their home, no doubt to inform their queen of her arrival.

She found a patch of glowing mana flowers at the center of the grove, where a single column of sunlight pierced through a small hole in the canopy above.

The hive itself was not on the ground, but high up in the canopy, built upon the intersection of the grove's branches. The First of the Fifth climbed until she arrived at the entrance. Her daughter stood there waiting, along with the Fourth of the Seventh. Her daughter danced a salute.

"Queen mother, welcome to home."

The slight twitching of her antennas and her wings indicated her nerves. The First of the Fifth, therefore, wasted no time with her task and began her dance. Her body tried to slow down, but she forced herself to go through with it.

"First Daughter . . . I'm sorry."

Her daughter ceased all movement, so she continued. "Didn't pay attention to you, put you in dangerous situation with foolish commands. My fault."

Her daughter stood still a moment longer before bursting into movement. She jerked and tripped over her steps in her haste.

"N-No, only wished to fulfill queen mother's command! Just . . . not as good as queen mother . . ."

The First of the Fifth stepped forward and touched her daughter's antennas with her own, stopping the young queen's frantic dancing.

"Queen's job to keep track of hive, ensure workers work hard, but don't damage selves. Queen's fault if they do. I didn't keep track of First Daughter before giving new command. First Daughter managed to succeed anyway. First Daughter did excellent work, struggles were because of commands. Very happy with success."

Her daughter swayed about. "Queen mother . . ."

The First of the Fifth took a step back and began a steady dance, holding herself to complete each step in turn, this time without any staggering or hesitation.

"That is why rescinding old commands. New command is this: Grow hive as First Daughter sees fit. First Daughter did well, overcame problems I created. First Daughter is wise enough to build own hive."

Her daughter ceased all motion once again. The First of the Fifth then turned to the other queen.

"Fourth of Seventh, I thank you for helping my daughter."

The Fourth of the Seventh danced about.

"You're welcome!"

The First of the Fifth then continued. "Will not forget. Wish to give something in return. Fourth of Seventh wants anything? Will give."

The Fourth of the Seventh paused. "No need? Already got lots from First of Fifth?"

But the First of the Fifth did not waver. "I insist. Want to help."

The Fourth of the Seventh paused, then began slowly walking around in a circle. After a few rotations, her eyes came to rest on the First of the Fifth's retinue. She then began to beat her wings and dance about.

"Oh! Soldiers can start visiting again? Want to talk more!"

The First of the Fifth paused. This time, she *did* waver. "You . . . want soldiers to come? Eat your honey, use your time?"

"Yes!"

The First of the Fifth fell still. This . . . was not the request she was anticipating. She was prepared to donate honey, grant access to flowers, or even offer the assistance of her workers. All the things she might have asked for had another queen owed her a debt. But instead, the Fourth of the Seventh was asking her for . . . the opportunity to feed her soldiers? The thing the First of the Fifth had taken from her as *payment* in the past?

The Fourth of the Seventh started to slow down as the First of the Fifth remained still. "Is . . . not okay?"

The First of the Fifth finally resumed her movement. "Is okay, but . . . want to ask. Why?"

The Fourth of the Seventh slowly danced her response. "Soldiers helped King weave stems! Trying to learn how, want to ask about soldiers' work."

The First of the Fifth wings began to buzz. Now that made more sense. The Fourth of the Seventh had apparently found value in the soldiers' visits that the First of the Fifth had not considered. She turned to look at her soldiers. Their antennas began to twitch under her gaze.

She realized that this request was appropriate. Beforehand, she might have assumed this was a ploy to usurp one of her own plans out from under her and gain the favor of the King. But the Fourth of the Seventh had assisted her daughter unprompted. Even if the Fourth of the Seventh did have ulterior motives in doing so, the value of whatever she might have gained from the First of the Fifth and her daughter would still have paled in comparison to her daughter's hive collapsing out of her own mistakes. And with her new knowledge of the King . . . the First of the Fifth somehow didn't believe that the Fourth of the Seventh had considered all that.

So, this was a chance for the First of the Fifth to both repay a debt *and* follow the example of the King. Besides, with the new room separating the apiary from the flower meadow, only the Fourth of the Seventh was in any position to do anything with the flowers the King had worked with.

The First of the Fifth began to dance her command.

"Soldiers, stay with the Fourth of the Seventh. Help her, consider her as queen until I give new command. Do whatever she asks."

The soldiers paused, glanced at each other, and then slowly gave their salutes. Meanwhile, the Fourth of the Seventh began rapidly spinning about. The First of the Fifth could barely make out a dance from the motions.

"This is amazing! Incredible! Thanks so much!"

The First of the Fifth's antennas twitched as she paused. Her dance was a bit unsteady. ". . . You're welcome? If that is all, will take my leave. First Daughter, don't hesitate if need help. That's command. Ask if need help."

Her daughter saluted, and then the First of the Fifth flew off. She considered the interactions as she made her way back home. There was always a chance the Fourth of the Seventh was putting on an act . . . but the First of the Fifth didn't believe so. The Fourth of the Seventh had made no moves or accomplishments of note before the First of the Fifth had reached out to her. The Fourth of the Seventh's workers were always deferential when encountering her own, and the Fourth of the Seventh herself had seemed subservient in their few direct interactions. That was why the First of the Fifth had chosen her when dumping the poor-quality flowers from the flower meadow.

Previously, the First of the Fifth had taken the Fourth of the Seventh's enthusiasm for the inferior flowers as a sign of her desperation. A queen with no hope of gaining any favor grasping at any slim chance for relevance, regardless of whatever disadvantageous conditions were attached to it. But now, now the First of the Fifth couldn't help but wonder if she had misread the Fourth of the Seventh as well. Was it possible that the Fourth of the Seventh had just never considered favor to begin with? That she had acted as she did because she had been legitimately happy to give and receive? That she had just chosen to help the First of the Fifth's daughter for no particular benefit at all? That she strove to help the bees around her as the King did?

Was it possible that this queen, who had barely had an opportunity to even see the King previously, better understood the King than she herself had? Was closer to the King than she? It bore consideration. For if that were true, then the First of the Fifth would have an example to take note of. She may have been mistaken before, but now she intended to be the closest to the King's ideals as she could be . . . and closer than any other, if she had anything to say about it.

In addition, this latest interaction had her feeling . . . strange. She was not sure why, or even what exactly it was that she felt. But she didn't think she necessarily disliked it . . .

CHAPTER THIRTEEN

PROPER-BEE RIGHTS

The day wore on and soon it was time for the next purification. Belissar once again prepared the flame radish slivers while the soldier bee army gathered by the entrance, this time positioned high in case of an aerial opponent. Belissar took a deep breath.

"Okay, here we go."

Minor+ purification attempt commencing.

He triggered the purification and once again the Hunger coalesced. However, this time it did not gather midair, but on the ground. The Hunger split in half, and two small wolf-shades appeared, just like the first minor+ purification. Belissar frowned.

The minor purifications had always been the same, but apparently the minor+ purifications could change day to day. And now, for only the second time ever, his bees faced more than one opponent.

The bees quickly reoriented themselves, a second sprayer squad diving to join the first as they started their attack. Both shades roared as they were greeted with toxic sprays coating their entire bodies. They retaliated with two breath attacks, but the sprayers had already retreated. When a third and fourth sprayer squad began their approach, the shades noticed and took off into a run. The sprayers broke off, but two squads of regular soldier bees dove in from the flanks. The two shades moved closer together and swung their tails to either side, warding off the soldier's attack.

But then, one of the shades yelped and vanished, falling into the first pit trap, where it was doused by the mad honey sticky trap. The other shade stopped and turned to look inside the pit. The third and fourth sprayer squads then pulled up and assaulted it.

The remaining shade yelped and launched another breath attack, but caught nothing. It glanced around at all the bees surrounding it. Then, just like when the bees had faced two shades for the first time, the second shade jumped down into the pit to regroup with the other and take shelter from the bees.

But unlike the first time this happened, Belissar and his bees were prepared. The apiary soldier bees were already on their way, grasping flame radish slivers with their hind legs, ready to handle the very situation that had prompted their training. They flew over the pit, just high enough to avoid any breath attacks, and released their slivers with practiced precision.

The slivers fell into the pit. Smoke and then small flames grew as the root reacted with the mana honey. Soon, a roaring fire filled the pit and black smoke climbed into the air. Smoke mixed with dissipating black mist.

All hostiles defeated.
Purification successful.

Belissar crossed his arms as he thought back to the first battle against two opponents. He cracked a small smile as he narrowed his eyes.

"That was for the soldiers."

Minor+ Purification completed!
Please select a reward:
- +75 DP
- +15 Max Mana
- Hidden Wax Cell (Rarity: Common. Type: Bee, Trap.)

This choice was fairly easy. Hidden wax cells appeared again, but Belissar didn't currently see the need for them. His bees didn't really hide much, and he was going to try and get a shovel from the bear people, so he could make something similar if he felt the bees needed it. He grabbed the extra mana, bringing his current total up to three hundred and forty-five, with eighty-six available for use. He nodded at that. His reserves were growing nicely, which was good given he was gaining more and more things to spend mana on.

And with that, the only thing left to do was to celebrate the victory. Belissar made his way over to the apiary to grab some honey trays . . . and was greeted with a surprise. He saw one of the apiary queens leading her workers as they carried honey toward the orchard and the flower meadow. He thought they only did that in special circumstances, though maybe a minor+ purification counted?

He smiled at the queen as she caught sight of him, and then he moved to gather some honey trays from his own stockpile.

The next morning, Belissar was in the flower meadow working on the beehouse when the bear people arrived at his dungeon once more. Metsaitti and his hunters were there, along with Chief Rohsuak and Juosiutik. Belissar finished up the beam he was working on, then walked over to the apiary and grabbed the flame radish pot before making his way over. The soldier bees, including the queen that was with them today, broke off their training and accompanied him as usual.

As Belissar approached the entrance, the bear people noticed him. Metsaitti inclined his head.

"Good morning, Sacred Den Master."

The other hunters glanced at one another and followed suit. Belissar shrank a bit at the attention.

"Oh, um, hi."

Belissar waited to see what they wanted, but they said no more and moved into the flower meadow. Belissar blinked, shrugged, and then turned to Chief Rohsuak and Juosiutik.

The chief smiled at him. "Good morning, Sacred Den Master."

Juosiutik was glancing all over, on the other hand. "G-Good morning."

Belissar waved his hand. "Hi. Did you need something?"

Chief Rohsuak shook her head. "Only to see if you wished to resume the potion lessons anytime soon."

Belissar thought to himself before replying. "Hm, that would be fine as long as I can keep working on my project. Maybe in the mornings?"

Juosiutik nodded repeatedly. "Yes, please!"

Chief Rohsuak chuckled. Belissar turned to her. "I, uh, also have a request? Do you have any shovels or other digging tools? I'd like to make a trade if so."

Chief Rohsuak hummed and rubbed her chin. "We do. Did you have something in mind?"

Belissar put the flame radish pot in front of them. "I do. I got some more flame radishes from the tower, so would that work?"

At first, Juosiutik's eyes widened and she smiled. "Flame radish? What's that?" Her face fell as she looked in the pot. "Oh, you meant the fire roots?"

Belissar blinked for a moment before realizing the cause of the confusion. He rubbed the back of his head as he spoke. "Ah, yeah, sorry. The tower called them flame radishes, so that's what I've been calling them."

Juosiutik turned to look at Chief Rohsuak, who shrugged in response. "We've never had much of an official name for them."

Juosiutik raised an eyebrow. "You're trading them back?" Then she froze. "Wait, did you say *more* fire roots . . . flame radishes?"

Belissar tilted his head. "Um, yes?"

Juosiutik leaned toward him. "As in . . . you grew these in your sacred den? Like the healing herbs the hunters gather?"

Belissar blinked. "Um, yes?"

Juosiutik began to step toward him before Chief Rohsuak placed a hand on her shoulder. Juosiutik stopped moving but kept her eyes on Belissar. "As in, you grew new ones in the few days since I gave them to you?"

Belissar nodded. "Yes?"

Juosiutik inhaled a large breath . . . until Chief Rohsuak tightened her grip and Juosiutik let it go. "Okay . . . um, may I see one of the new flame radishes?"

Belissar nodded and pulled one out of the pot, handing it over to her. Juosiutik looked over it with a furrowed brow. Chief Rohsuak also looked over her shoulder at it.

"It . . . appears entirely healthy from what I can tell but . . . Chief?"

Chief Rohsuak nodded. "Yes, I can feel the Fire mana within. This one should be more potent than average."

Juosiutik slowly turned her gaze back to Belissar. Something in her eyes made him take a step back subconsciously. "So . . . if we give you plants . . . you can grow more of them?"

Belissar gulped. "Um, it depends? But if the plant will grow in one of the rooms I have, then yes?"

Juosiutik tensed and tried to step forward, but Chief Rohsuak's grip was firm and Juosiutik turned back to look at her. The chief just had one of her eyebrows raised. Juosiutik turned back to Belissar and lowered her head.

"Sacred Den Master, if I give you whatever plants I have, would you be willing to share what you produce with me? Maybe you could grow them by the front or by the healing herbs so the hunters can gather some?"

Belissar's eyes widened. "Oh, that would be great! And, sure, that sounds fair? Um, I should mention that the tower needs to absorb a certain amount before it can grow them . . . and again, I can't guarantee that any particular plant will grow in the rooms I have right now."

Juosiutik looked up to him, her eyes narrowed. "How many do you need?"

Belissar gulped and took another step back. "Um, it depends. It changes for each plant and how whole the pieces are, so I, um, won't know until I hold the specific plant."

Juosiutik began to tremble. She took a deep breath and turned back to Chief Rohsuak, pleading with her eyes.

"Chief . . ."

Chief Rohsuak chuckled and shook her head. "The sacred den master has already agreed."

The chief had barely eased her grip before Juosiutik vanished, sprinting out of the tower and back toward the bear people's camp. Chief Rohsuak sighed, though there was still a smile on her face as she turned to Belissar.

"Thank you for your patience, Sacred Den Master. I know Juosiutik can get a bit . . . passionate."

Belissar shook his head. "It's fine . . . as long as she doesn't set the tower on fire. And, um, this deal is pretty good for me."

Chief Rohsuak rubbed her chin. "I see. In that case, would you be open to extending the deal to other plants besides Juosiutik's herbs? Something more mundane, like food crops or trees?"

Belissar nodded. "Sure, that'd be great. Anything with flowers, especially."

Chief Rohsuak smiled and nodded back. "Wonderful, I'll see to it then. Would one third of our harvested material suffice as tribute?"

Belissar blinked. "Tribute?"

Chief Rohsuak nodded. "We will be imposing upon your den for resources. It is only natural to offer some back, is it not?"

Belissar tilted his head. "Um, I thought that was in exchange for giving me the stuff in the first place?"

Chief Rohsuak rubbed her chin. "Perhaps, but that's a one-time benefit. We would like to continue gathering into the future if you are willing, so a more permanent compensation would be natural, right?"

Belissar frowned. "Is that so? But . . . it's the tower growing it, right?"

The only thing he knew of tribute was that the tower lords had demanded it of him and his village. He had done a good job putting them out of his mind recently, so he didn't particularly like the reminder.

Chief Rohsuak shook her head. "It is your sacred den, and you are the one growing the plants, by our request even. You should receive your portion from each harvest of your own land."

Belissar furrowed his brow. "That's . . . right?"

He guessed that was true. It wasn't like before, where the tower lords had taken stuff from land outside the tower. Instead, the bear folk were coming into the tower to gather stuff from it. And he *was* the master of this tower, and he *did* use up some of his total mana on the resource nodes. So, if he was going to share, he guessed it did make sense to get something back for it. Especially since the new plants would be placed further away from the hives, making it harder for the bees to gather from. The bear people would even be taking away some of the flowers that bees could otherwise gather from. Flowers that would grow back on a daily basis, but the point still stood! When Belissar thought of it that way . . .

He narrowed his eyes and nodded quickly. "Yes, that's right. One third seems like a lot, though. How about one tenth for me, and you give one tenth to the

God of Bees? And you still can't hurt the bees when you gather, okay? If you have anything you can give them too, then please share."

Chief Rohsuak's smile grew. "Very well. One tenth to you, one tenth to the God of Bees, and offerings to the bees themselves, as well as care not to disrupt them. Is that acceptable?"

Belissar nodded and Chief Rohsuak continued. "Good, then I will make the arrangements. Thank you, Sacred Den Master."

TO INFINITY . . . AND BEE-YOND!

The Second Queen of the Second Spawner's First Dynasty, the first of her line, was about to take her turn at command when she caught sight of the King. The Conduit then came to her.

"King greeting others, come watch?"

The Second of the Second danced her salute and gave orders to the army. They formed up around her as she flew over to the King. She did not like the outsiders. They were from the Beyond, where death and destruction came from. They were not born of the King, nor did they follow after his commands. They could not be trusted.

And worse, something about them rubbed the Second of the Second the wrong way. Their appearance set her on guard, stirring up instincts inherited from her mundane ancestors. They warned her of snouts and claws that could shatter the walls of hives, and of fur so thick stingers couldn't pierce it. A monster so large and powerful an entire colony would be helpless before it as it consumed their winter stores and their young.

Fortunately, the King's hives were not so weak, and these outsiders not so strong . . . for the most part. They were not as large as her instinctual warnings seemed to imply, and they had numerous gaps in their fur that could be targeted. Even if they hadn't had those weak spots, the King's hives were defended by soldiers far larger than any mundane bee—and with equally larger stingers. She was confident the army could handle most of them. There *was* the one who could apparently create flames as large as the King's fire chasms who would be a threat, but the Second of the Second believed the army could bring her down with acceptable losses if they needed to.

Still, she treated them with wariness, particularly as the King began to speak with them. There was one who was particularly aggressive toward him, and it was only the King's command that stayed the army's hand. She did not know why the

King exposed himself to such dangerous beings. They could not even speak! The sounds from their mouths lacked the warm mana of the King and so could not convey any sort of meaning.

The King, though, seemed to understand such things, so great was his wisdom and insight. So, as always, the Second of the Second deferred to him, though she still kept an eye out for danger. She could at least understand the King's responses, and so gathered that some sort of conversation was occurring.

"Sure, that'd be great. Anything with flowers, especially."

The Second of the Second flew a bit closer. From what she could gather, the conversation had turned to some sort of exchange . . . involving flowers? She thought for a moment. Her soldiers' reports on the aggressive one had mentioned that at one point the King had traded an entire tray of honey for a rock with a hole in it that apparently held plants of some sort. Around the same time as that report, the King had raised a new type of flower.

Suddenly, she understood. These outsiders could provide new flowers. That would explain why the King was willing to expose himself to their threat. And it made sense. It had been in the Beyond where her scouts and those of her fellow flower meadow queens had located mana flowers, which the King subsequently spread throughout his domain.

Then, the Second of the Second froze. She realized . . . they had made a mistake. And she would need to report it as soon as possible. Fortunately, the outsiders soon left and the King returned to the new palace he was building, so the Second of the Second was able to return to the hives. She immediately called for a meeting of the queens.

Every queen of the flower meadow, the Firstborn included, stood completely still after the Second of the Second's emergency report. In the Firstborn's opinion, the Second of the Second had been right to call them. They had made a massive oversight.

In the early days of the Second Dynasty, before the first soldier was born, the flower meadow queens had sent scouts and foragers to the Beyond. The resources of the flower meadow had been growing thin at that point, and they needed more if they wished to raise an army. It was then that they discovered the mana flowers. That, in hindsight, may have been the most important achievement they had ever made.

And yet, after such a massive success, they had *stopped* their scouting, almost entirely. Once the King spread mana flowers throughout his domain, the queens had an abundance of riches right in their immediate surroundings. They could support their entire army on the bounty of those flowers alone, not to mention the additional flowers the King also raised after that. They, therefore, turned all of their attention to the growth of their hives and the army. All their workers were pulled back to focus on the highest-priority flowers.

At that point, it seemed to them that expeditions to the Beyond were no longer necessary, and no longer worth the risk. A handful of scouts still held the perimeter of the King's domain and kept an eye on the outsiders at the King's behest, but aside from that the flower meadow queens had largely stopped operating in the Beyond. They certainly weren't foraging from the flowers there, nor were they searching for any more.

But, if what the Second of the Second reported was correct, that had been a mistake. There were still more riches to be discovered in the Beyond. The King had raised a new flower, one that also contained potent mana within its nectar, due to his dealings with the outsiders. A flower that they had brought from the Beyond. And, because they had stopped their own scouting, the King had been forced to act on his own. He had exposed himself to the threat of the outsiders because the flower meadow hives had failed in this duty.

That could not be permitted to continue. And yet, none of the flower meadow queens made a move to dance, looking at one another in silence. The Firstborn knew they were all doing the same calculations as she . . . and they would all come to the same conclusion. The flower meadow queens had to continue to strengthen their army, to raise more soldiers and more of the new sprayers in anticipation of the greater challenges the King now permitted them to face. They had to prepare to move their hives once the King finished his grand construction. And they had to stock up enough mana-rich honey to raise queens and drones for their own expansion plan.

Foraging missions to the Beyond had stopped because they were far less efficient than trips to the local mana flowers. Any workers they devoted to scouting would have to be written off in terms of honey production. Sending soldiers to scout, on the other hand, wasn't effective. Their senses weren't as attuned to flowers as those of the workers, and they had trouble gathering nectar as well. Their search wouldn't be as thorough. Not to mention that any soldiers sent would have less time to train compared to their peers.

Something would have to give if the queens wanted to resume this duty, and the duty needed to be resumed. But they did not know which of their tasks they could afford to pause. The army was their primary purpose, necessary for the protection and growth of the hive of hives. The King himself was building their new home, and they would not waste his efforts by remaining unprepared for its completion. The expansion plan had already been delayed several times at this point, and the sooner they started it, the more time the new queens would have to grow. It was urgent that they follow through on it as soon as they could. So . . . what should they do?

It was at that moment that they had a visitor.

"Hi! What queens doing?"

The Firstborn and her peers turned to see another queen flying into the flower meadow. The Fourth of the Seventh had stopped by once again, making her own foraging trip to the flower patch with her workers and soldiers. The other queens turned to the Firstborn, so she took it upon herself to respond.

"Meeting. Have . . . problem."

"Problem? What problem? Can help?"

The Firstborn considered that. She wasn't sure if the Fourth of the Seventh could help . . . but the hive of hives extended beyond just the flower meadow, so she figured she might as well let the Fourth of the Seventh know what was going on. The Fourth of the Seventh had already provided several other solutions to issues they had faced, after all.

"Well . . ."

She had barely finished explaining the situation when the Fourth of the Seventh suddenly burst into a high-speed dance.

"I'LL DO IT! LET ME DO IT! WILL SEND WORKERS RIGHT AWAY!"

The Firstborn and the other flower meadow queens were stunned into motionlessness at the Fourth of the Seventh's sudden assault. Eventually, the Fourth of the Seventh's soldiers pulled her away and back to the orchard. The flower meadow queens glanced around at one another until the Firstborn began an unsteady dance.

"Guess . . . Fourth of Seventh will handle for now?"

CHAPTER FOURTEEN

BEE-HOLD THE SACRED DEN!

Belissar did a little bit more work on the flower meadow beehouse while he waited, and the bear people returned before long. Juosiutik rushed into the tower . . . at least, Belissar thought it was her. She had so many bags hanging off her that he could barely see anything save for the top of her head. After that came Chief Rohsuak and a few other bear people Belissar didn't recognize, each carrying a bag of some sort. Belissar made his way over, the bees following him as usual. Juosiutik popped out from behind her cargo, her eyes lighting up as she saw him approach.

"There you are! Let's get started!"

Chief Rohsuak chuckled and shook her head. "Juosiutik, I know you're excited, but perhaps we should let Leijaliuk go first?"

Juosiutik frowned and sat down silently, not taking her eyes off Belissar. Chief Rohsuak shook her head and then stepped forward with a middle-aged bear woman.

"Hello, Sacred Den Master. May I introduce Leijaliuk?"

Leijaliuk bowed her head. "I am honored to meet you, Sacred Den Master."

Belissar nodded back. "Um, nice to meet you."

She raised her head. Chief Rohsuak smiled. "Leijaliuk here is in charge of our food stores. She's here to show you what food crops we have."

Leijaliuk nodded and motioned to the other bear folk, who placed their bags on the ground and opened them up. Belissar glanced inside and saw an abundance of mushrooms, roots, and tubers, along with some seeds, nuts, and grains.

"At this point, most of our stockpiles are what we could gather underground. Do you have any good locations to plant these?"

Belissar shook his head. "Not yet, sorry. I still have those cave carrots and stuff you first brought, but I can't grow them just yet."

Leijaliuk raised an eyebrow slightly at the *yet*, but otherwise nodded her head. "I see. In that case, we do still have some seeds from our time on the surface. I am not certain of their viability, however, and we do not have many of them left. If you are not confident you can grow them, it may be wiser for us to try and plant them first."

Belissar rubbed his chin and then reached out his hand. "Could I hold them, please?"

Leijaliuk nodded and took some of the seeds, handing them over to him.

Absorb Rye seed? Current samples: 0/30
Absorb Oat seed? Current samples: 0/30
Absorb Cloudberry seed? Current samples: 0/30
Absorb Sweetvetch seed? Current samples: 0/30

Belissar hummed. "Um, so I need thirty of these to even try."

Leijaliuk furrowed her brow. "I see. The grains are one thing, but for the berry plants that's just about our entire remaining stock. How certain are you that they will grow?"

Belissar rubbed his chin as he thought about it. Rye and oats didn't make big flowers, and he couldn't recall seeing any bees visiting them. That would count against them being available in the flower meadow, and the orchard was mostly trees. Cloudberries and sweetvetch were not something he recognized by name, so he wasn't sure about those.

"These cloudberries and sweetvetch . . . What kind of plants are they? Would they have flowers similar to the ones in this field? Do they need any special conditions to grow?"

Leijaliuk slowly nodded. "Yes, they are flowering plants. They come from colder climates than this field seems, though."

Belissar nodded. "I'm pretty sure it will work, then. Maybe I can try with one and then see about the other?"

Leijaliuk frowned and turned to Chief Rohsuak, who shrugged. "We're pretty far south. I doubt they'll grow here if we try to plant them ourselves."

Leijaliuk took a deep breath as she turned back to Belissar. "Okay."

She rummaged through the bag, gathering up and counting out the cloudberry seeds and handing them to Belissar. Belissar took the first one and absorbed it. The bear people all paused and stared at his hand as the seed was covered in glowing light and then vanished. Juosiutik and Leijaliuk were staring particularly intently.

Cloudberry seed absorbed. Current samples: 1/30

Belissar gulped at all the eyes on him. "Um, I'll need some more."

Leijaliuk shook her head. "Right."

She continued handing him the cloudberry seeds until he had absorbed the needed thirty. Belissar held his breath as the message appeared before his eyes.

Cloudberry seed absorbed.
Sufficient samples gathered. Cloudberry now available.
Current applications: Flower Meadow, Apiary.

Belissar exhaled his breath and then smiled. "Looks like it worked."
Leijaliuk raised an eyebrow. "Truly? Could you show me, if you don't mind?"
Belissar nodded and brought up the relevant menu.

Available Resource Plants for Flower Meadow:
- Basic Healing Herbs (Mana Upkeep: 3 per node)
- Basic Poisonous Flowers (Mana Upkeep: 3 per node)
- Basic Textile Flowers (Mana Upkeep: 3 per node)
- Cloudberry Flowers (Mana Upkeep: 3 per node)
- Mana Flower (Mana Upkeep: 5 per node)
- Flame Radish (Mana Upkeep: 10 per node)

He could apparently also add cloudberries as a general flower type across the field, though that did cost one mana, unlike the other mundane flowers. In this case, however, he decided to stick with resource nodes, since the point was to let the bear people gather them. In that vein, he went ahead and formed a node right by the entrance, where it would be easy to access.

A small patch of the ground began to glow, and the bear peoples' eyes all widened. They began to gasp as new shoots pushed out of the ground and grew to full-sized plants in seconds. White, five-petaled flowers budded and bloomed, and then the tips of the petals turned red as berries of the same color formed in their centers. Leijaliuk slowly turned to Belissar with her eyes as wide as they could go.

". . . These flowers . . . Will they grow berries as quickly as that every time?"

Belissar shook his head. "Um, not that fast. But you see those ones that are glowing slightly? Those should regrow every day."

Leijaliuk stared, started to tremble, and then immediately crouched down and grabbed the bag, practically pushing it into Belissar's hands.

"Please try with all the rest, okay? And can you make more patches like this? If we can gather that many every day . . . we'll never have to worry about going hungry ever again."

Chief Rohsuak sighed and stepped forward, pulling Leijaliuk back by the shoulders. "Calm down, Leijaliuk. The bees are about to attack you."

Leijaliuk glanced back at Chief Rohsuak, then up into the air where the soldier bees had started to gather around her. "Oh, um, sorry about that."

Chief Rohsuak shook her head and turned to Juosiutik. "That's what you look like, by the way."

Juosiutik averted her gaze. Chief Rohsuak sighed and then chuckled. "I'm sorry, Sacred Den Master. Please have some patience with us, your sacred den is quite incredible."

Belissar nodded as he thought back to the first time he had seen the tower do these things. "Well . . . I can understand that."

Leijaliuk then, under Chief Rohsuak's strict gaze, calmly handed the other seeds to Belissar. In the end, sweetvetch was also compatible with the flower meadow and the apiary. Rye and oats, as Belissar had predicted, were not. Leijaliuk had a few other seeds but none in sufficient quantity, save for the subterranean plants that Belissar already knew wouldn't work out.

Belissar added a sweetvetch patch and then rubbed his chin. "How about a healing herb patch? I think I could move the one you gather from closer?"

Leijaliuk smiled. "Anything you have would be much appreciated."

Belissar had no issues moving the healing herb patch by the entrance, and then he rubbed his chin again. "How about flax? I have that too. It, um, comes unprocessed, so you'd have to deal with that yourself."

Leijaliuk's eyes widened a bit and then she began nodding quickly. "Ah, yes! That would be really helpful!"

Belissar created a textile flower node. "Oh, there are apple and wood trees too, but they don't work in this room. There's another room further in, past the other shrine of bees you delivered the wood to. It should be fine if you gather from those trees too, just don't disturb the bees there."

Leijaliuk's eyes started to sparkle, but then she frowned and turned to Chief Rohsuak. "That would also help, but we would have to challenge the sacred den to reach it, right?"

Chief Rohsuak nodded. "This is excellent for now, and we currently don't lack wood. If we need something like that and the den master agrees, we could arrange a group with escorts."

Belissar nodded back. "Yep, as long as you don't disturb the bees."

Chief Rohsuak smiled. "Of course."

Leijaliuk took the other bear people back with her, intending to drop off the leftover seeds and then arrange a first foraging trip. Meanwhile, Juosiutik was staring at Chief Rohsuak with all her might, pleading with her eyes. Chief Rohsuak sighed and motioned to her.

"Yes, Juosiutik, it's your turn. Just pay attention to the den master and try not to make him uncomfortable, okay?"

Belissar decided not to mention he was already uncomfortable. But he was acquiring new flowers for his bees, and that was worth any discomfort. He still couldn't help a slight shiver as he watched Juosiutik approach with a wide grin on her face and a dangerous glint in her eyes.

CHAPTER FIFTEEN

FRIEND-BEE EXCHANGES

Juosiutik waddled over to Belissar and then plopped down on the ground, offloading her bags. She immediately began to rummage through one.

"So, to confirm based on what you said to Leijaliuk, you're currently limited to flowering plants and trees, right? Any possibility that will change?"

Belissar nodded. "Yeah, I can get more rooms eventually but . . . it'll take a while."

Juosiutik stopped and rubbed her chin. "Hm, I see. That does limit us a bit, but we should still have a good spread. Let's see, how about this?"

Juosiutik removed a seed from one of her bags and handed it over to Belissar. He dutifully took it and read the message.

Absorb Sleepy Chamomile seed? Current samples: 0/50

"Hm, I'd need fifty of those."

Juosiutik frowned. "I saved up some for when we had a chance to plant surface plants again, but I'm not sure I have that many . . ."

Belissar hummed a bit before his eyes widened slightly. "Ah, you know it doesn't need to be seeds right? From what I've seen, it actually takes less if you have the full plant."

Juosiutik nodded and pulled out a dried chamomile flower. "Here, what about this?"

Absorb Sleepy Chamomile? Current samples: 0/5

Belissar nodded. "Yes, I'd only need five of those."

Juosiutik crossed her arms and hummed. "How about a combination? Could you use both seeds and plants?"

Belissar tilted his head. "Um . . . I'm not sure."

Juosiutik furrowed her brow. "Hm . . . why don't you try with that plant and then check again?"

Belissar nodded and absorbed the dried flower. He then looked at the seed and checked its information.

Absorb Sleepy Chamomile seed? Current samples: 10/50

His eyes widened a bit. "Ah, yeah, that worked. Looks like that counted as ten seeds."

Juosiutik began to grin. "We should be able to make this work, then. Here."

She handed to him two more dried sleepy chamomile flowers and a handful of seeds. Belissar absorbed them all as they came. Juosiutik stared at him and held her breath.

Sleepy Chamomile seed absorbed.
Sufficient samples gathered. Sleepy Chamomile now available.
Current applications: Flower Meadow, Apiary.

Belissar smiled. "It worked."

Juosiutik let out a shout, her ears waggling about as she pumped her fists. "YES!"

She then suddenly piped down and glanced around at the bees. "Um, sorry. It's just . . . we've been scrounging and scraping for a while now. Having a consistent source of ingredients is going to do wonders for our stockpiles. And it'll let me experiment more, get my skills up to par."

Belissar smiled and shook his head. "It's alright. It's exciting for me too."

He held out his hand and Niobee, flying around him as always, came and landed on it. "New flowers make the bees happy. They can make new types of honey with them, or even new types of bees altogether. It's pretty exciting for me too."

Juosiutik froze and went completely silent. She slowly turned her head to look at Belissar. "Did you say . . . new types of honey?"

Belissar nodded. "Yes."

Juosiutik began to lean in before she caught herself and shook her head. "Later. Tell me more about that later, okay? For now, let's continue."

Belissar grinned and nodded.

Gelatinous Heather seed absorbed.
Sufficient samples gathered. Gelatinous Flower now available.
Current applications: Flower Meadow, Apiary.

Snakebane seed absorbed.
Sufficient samples gathered. Snakebane now available.
Current applications: Flower Meadow, Apiary.

Burrowing Stonecrop seed absorbed.
Sufficient samples gathered. Burrowing Stonecrop now available.
No current applications.

Juosiutik had been excited when she packed, but it turned out most of her current stockpile was subterranean in nature, or else too limited to risk Belissar not being able to grow it. They tried a flower she'd found underground anyway, but agreed to hold off on the rest when it turned out Belissar couldn't make a node for it in any of his current rooms. Still, Juosiutik was practically squealing as the nodes for the new plants appeared.

At that point, Leijaliuk returned with a bunch more bear people. "Sacred Den Master, could I request a few more nodes? Perhaps two more sweetvetch, one more cloudberry, and one more flax?"

Belissar rubbed his chin and checked over his mana.

Mana: 77/345

He crossed his arms. His mana was starting to dip a bit low . . . and he also needed to replicate all these nodes in the flower meadow and apiary for his bees. On the other hand, he wasn't using the mana for anything else right this second, and he could get more from the purifications.

"I . . . think that should work, but you'll need to wait for any more than that."

Leijaliuk smiled. "Wonderful, thank you, Sacred Den Master. You've no idea how much this will help us."

Belissar thought back to his days before the tower, especially the times he was living on his own. He remembered stumbling across a patch of berry bushes on a particularly tight year. He imagined someone suddenly giving him some more.

". . . I think I might, though."

With that, the bear folk got to work picking the food and flax. With the near-automatic harvesting of the resource nodes, they were done almost immediately. Most of them gathered under the direction of Leijaliuk, who took stock of the haul, while Juosiutik commandeered a few others to help her with the more medicinal plants. Soon, Leijaliuk had split the harvest into three piles, one large and two small. She then walked back over to him.

"Here you are, Sacred Den Master. Please let us know if this is sufficient."

Belissar turned and looked at the piles, with several sweetvetch roots and a pile of berries, along with several flax flowers. He rubbed his chin. He received more honey each day than he could consume by far. If that weren't enough, he had an entire orchard of apple trees. He had plenty to eat even before considering that the tower magic meant he didn't even *need* to. As for the flax flowers . . . well, Belissar had more of those than he ever wanted to deal with.

So, he wondered what exactly he would do with this stuff. It made sense to get some payment for letting the bear folk gather it, but he still had to do something with it all at the end of the day. He could try to give it to the bees, he guessed, but he wasn't sure what they would do with uprooted flowers or berries. He thought he remembered seeing bees land on a dropped fruit at one point, but it was unusual enough that he struggled to recall exactly.

It used to be highly rare for Belissar to have more than he knew what to do with, so he didn't have any great ideas. If he was in the village, he could have tried to trade it at least . . .

Belissar suddenly realized that he was being dumb and knew right away what he should do.

". . . Actually, that's a bit much for me. I already have a bunch of flax and food. So, um, would it be possible to trade this for something else? I could use some pots, or some finished cloth."

Leijaliuk thought for a second before replying. "That should be possible. Very well, is it alright if I bring some items tomorrow then?"

Belissar nodded. "Yeah, that works."

After that, Juosiutik also finished her gathering and separated her haul into piles as well. This time, Belissar accepted the pile, figuring he could use the medicinal stuff once Juosiutik taught him a bit more about potions. Juosiutik and Leijaliuk then arranged for the bear folk to carry the piles for the God of Bees to her shrine, placing it all in the chest. The two bear women knelt in front of the statue, with all the gatherers kneeling behind them. Juosiutik and Leijaliuk whispered in words too quiet for Belissar to hear.

The shrine of bees began to glow. Belissar suddenly stumbled back.

"Wha . . . ?"

A moment later, the bear people rose to their feet. Leijaliuk and Juosiutik walked over to him. "Sacred Den Master, is something the matter?"

Belissar took a moment to acknowledge them, then shook his head. "Ah, no, it's . . . fine. Yes, it's fine."

Leijaliuk and Juosiutik glanced at one another before turning back to him. "If you say so. Thank you again for your generosity, Sacred Den Master."

Juosiutik nodded her head repeatedly. "Yes, thank you! Um, would you mind if we delay the lessons for now? I'd like to get all this home and organized."

Belissar nodded with a distant look in his eyes. "Ah, yeah, that's fine."

With that, the bear people gathered up their shares and departed the tower, leaving Belissar alone. Alone to look again at the message that had distracted him.

Gained 84 DP.

He had gotten eighty-four DP, more even than Metsaitti's hunters, just from that offering? Something that took less than an hour of time? And they were even going to share the bounty with him; he would receive an abundance of food, flax, and herbs without lifting a finger. He could then trade the fruits of the bear people's gathering back to them for more stuff.

Suddenly, all the mana he'd spent on those resource nodes didn't seem so expensive after all. Belissar even wondered if he should move the orchard entrance closer to the main exit so the bear people could gather apples and wood too.

Belissar cracked a small smile. He had been . . . apprehensive, to say the least, about the bear people when they first arrived. But at this point, well, they didn't seem so bad. He was even starting to like having them around.

CHAPTER SIXTEEN

BEES TOGETHER STRONG

Chief, we found something. Partiokinik figured we should ask you to check it out."

Chief Rohsuak raised an eyebrow at the scout's report. The clan had more hunters than just Metsaitti and the group he took into the sacred den. However, most of the hunters were currently guarding the camp, keeping an eye on the Underway entrance, or else scouting out their new home. Metsaitti had taken only the youngest bunch, those with the greatest potential for growth . . . and whose absence would hinder the clan least. It seemed that now the remaining scouts had found something.

The chief slowly rose to her feet and nodded. "Lead the way."

And so, she made her way through the forest, along a small trail the hunters had cut. It was slow going; the hunters had cut as little as they could to minimize signs of their presence, so she constantly had to push branches out of her way. She could feel scratches accumulating here and there.

And yet . . . she was all smiles. Few remained who had witnessed it, but Chief Rohsuak had not always been one for calm leadership from behind. It was rare that she had the opportunity to leave her duties and brave the unknown, though a dull ache in her knees reminded her of why she generally restrained herself. Still, for all the little aches and pains she couldn't help but beam as she came out into a small clearing where crumbling stone ruins stood. She could still feel the thrum of mana lurking within the humble walls. She dropped her smile and turned to the hunters.

"You were wise to call me. This place is magic. Please, do not approach or touch anything."

The hunters nodded and spread out to keep watch. Chief Rohsuak slowly made her way toward the ruins, stretching her senses to keep track of the mana. Her

caution mostly seemed unnecessary as she made it to the ruins' walls without incident. The mana, while apparent, was quite faint, and she couldn't detect any particular pattern to its flow.

She heaved a sigh, closing her eyes for a moment. Memories came to her
unbidden. In the days of her youth, her clan had possessed great wisdom. There
had been masters of the mystic arts who were far more attuned to the flows of
mana than she, and keepers of lore who might connect what she saw to ancient
tales. She was neither. Despite what the clan might say, she was only truly good at
fighting and surviving.

And because of that, she was all they had left.

In the end, Chief Rohsuak couldn't glean any insights into the ruins. She had
seen similar ruins and similar markings to those that had nearly faded, but she
had no means by which to decipher them. All she could say was that ruins similar
to these covered quite the area, and the fact that most of them still held some
mana was a testament to skill in the mystic arts. Whatever people had built them
had once lived across the entirety of her clan's journey and had been able to weave
extremely enduring enchantments. But in most of the ruins, including these,
those enchantments had faded long past use or recognition. Those that hadn't . . .
tended to be dangerous.

She walked back to the hunters. They looked at her expectantly, but she shook
her head.

"Nothing of note, though we should still be cautious about the mana. Keep
an eye on this place, but do not approach it. Let's let sleeping bears lie."

The next day Belissar made some trades with the bear people, giving up his portion
of the harvest for some leather and pottery. Juosiutik apologetically asked to delay
the potion-making lessons, as she wanted to see how her recipes would work with
the dungeon ingredients before teaching them to him. Belissar agreed to that, since
it would let him focus on the beehouses.

And so, the week went on. Belissar continued working on the flower meadow
beehouse. He was making steady progress on the frame when he realized he had
a problem.

How exactly was he going to make the roof? It was a bit of an oversight.
Putting aside the question of getting the beams up to the top, he would also need
to manipulate the beams to slot them into the grooves he'd carved, since he didn't
have nails or anything similar. He might be able to build some sort of staircase
that he could use to drag a beam up, but then lifting that beam by himself for the
slotting would be . . . difficult.

He was frowning and rubbing his chin when Niobee started to dance in front
of him. "King okay?"

Belissar grunted. "Yeah, I'm just trying to figure out how to lift this stuff up there."

Niobee paused before dancing. "Bees help?"

Belissar smiled and reached out to brush her head. "Thanks for the offer, but this might be a bit heavy for you."

Niobee shook a bit at his touch . . . and then suddenly flew off. Belissar tilted his head at that. "Was it something I said? Or should I not have touched her head while she was flying?"

It turned out it was neither of those things. Belissar heard the buzzing before he saw it. The entire soldier bee army was now flying toward him, with Niobee at the lead.

"King! Bees help! If all help, can lift?"

Belissar stared with eyes wide open. "Oh. Um, maybe?"

Belissar walked over to one of the intended roof beams. He crouched down and lifted one side of it off the ground. "Okay, can you girls come and see if you can lift it?"

The soldier bee army saluted as one and then swarmed over him. Countless soldier bees hovered next to the beam, hooking their hind legs under the bottom. Once assembled, they all began beating their wings as one. Belissar kept a hold on the beam to keep it from falling . . . but he needn't have worried. The beam began to lift out of his hands.

"Nice, let me get the other side."

He lifted the other end off the ground so the bees could get a grip on the entire beam and level it out. Soon, they lifted it into the air . . . without his help at all. Belissar stared at the sight for a moment.

"That . . . is amazing."

He shook his head and then walked over to the frame, where two vertical beams stood upright. "Okay, can you girls bring it over here? We need to bring it to the top of these two."

The bees did as he asked. It took a bit of finagling to get the beam into the grooves, but the small size of the bees made them even more capable of minute adjustments than a person would be, and so they got it in.

Belissar then realized he would still need to get up there to add the stabilizing wax. He knew he could ask the bees for help with that too, but as far as he knew he would need worker bees rather than soldiers for that task. The soldier bees were pausing their training to help, but that wasn't too worrying since they could already handle purifications without issue. Asking the worker bees to pause their tasks, on the other hand, would cut down on honey production for the hives, so Belissar wanted to avoid that if possible.

As such, he was about to start building a staircase or a ladder when he suddenly had an idea. He had gotten the beams up there with the help of his bees, perhaps like a dungeon master might. So . . . perhaps there were other ways his dungeon master abilities might help here? In fact, he realized there was a very easy way they could do so.

He switched to tower sight and located one of his trees, selecting it. He moved the transparent image right next to the beehouse in progress and confirmed, then watched as light began to cover the tree. A moment later, the tree was now standing in front of him . . . right next to the newly installed beams.

He grabbed onto the branches, clambered up the trunk, and within moments found himself next to the beams, close enough to work his magic. He smiled to himself.

Being a dungeon master wasn't half bad, at times.

*

> *All hostiles defeated.*
> *Purification successful.*

Belissar smiled. Another day, another victory without sacrifice. Between the sprayers and the bee army's growing skill, minor+ purifications were handled with ease. The purifications were now swapping between single birds or double wolves at random, but the bees had perfected their strategies for both.

And, of course, a week of successful purifications meant a week of rewards.

> *Minor+ Purification completed!*
> *Please select a reward:*
> *- +75 DP*
> *- +15 Max Mana*
> *- Small Pond (Rarity: Common. Type: Water.)*

Belissar's smile widened at that. Today bore unexpected fruit. For the first time of all the options he had seen, something water-related was being offered. Belissar selected the option.

At five mana, it was a bit more expensive than the usual feature, but he could add one to any of his rooms. Besides, the mana expenditure was not a problem considering the tower's current state:

> *Mana: 86/405*

His mana had taken a significant dip due to all the new plant nodes. He had made several of the new plants plus two flax nodes for the bears, then one of each new plant node for both the flower meadow and the apiary queens to gather from. But with daily minor+ purifications offering fifteen mana each, he had been able to recover a bit. He did spend two of the rewards on particularly enticing boosts for his bees, but he was still in a good spot with an additional sixty total mana.

Belissar added a pond to each of his rooms, one by the flower meadow beehouse, one by the orchard grove, and one by the apiary farmhouse. The flower meadow and orchard ponds were set up near the hives for fighting fires.

The apiary pond, on the other hand, was set up for easy access from the farmhouse. Belissar now had access to water, and he had just acquired watertight pottery from the bear people. That meant he could now practice that basic potion Juosiutik had taught him.

And more than that . . . Belissar could attempt to resume his mead-making. And with all the ingredients available in the tower, he had countless potential recipes he could try.

He grinned as wide as he could.

CHAPTER SEVENTEEN

BEE-WILDERING PROGRESS!

After the victory celebrations, Belissar went to check out the nearest pond. It was . . . well, a pond. It was only about as long as he was tall and looked like it would come up to his ankles, maybe even as deep as his knees at the most. There were no particular plants or features. The crystal-clear water let him see the empty rock at the bottom.

It was a bit of water and that was it. But, at the end of the day, that was all Belissar needed it to be. He knelt down and cupped a bit into his hand, then took a sip. His first drink of water since becoming a dungeon master. It was cool and refreshing.

He then returned to the apiary farmhouse for the night. He sat back in one of the chairs, for he had something he wanted to think about before he went to bed.

DP: 1714

When reviewing the tower's status, he'd noticed his DP had grown *substantially*. He knew that he was receiving way more DP than before thanks to both the bear people's gathering group and their hunting group, but only now did he realize just how much he had received. He reopened the DP store for the first time since it had appeared.

DP Shop
- Room Feature Choice (Cost: 1000 DP)
- Monster Choice (Cost: 3000 DP)
- Room Choice (Cost: 3000 DP)
- Perk Choice (Cost: 10000 DP)
- Additional Room Slot (Cost: 5000 DP)
- Boost Maximum Mana (Cost: 5000 DP)

His eyes widened as he compared the numbers. When he had first seen the shop, his DP income had been all of one per day. Even the cheapest option would have taken him *years* to afford. So, he had basically written off the entire thing as too expensive to ever afford and largely forgotten about it.

Now? Now he could *already* afford a new room feature choice, and he was well on his way to being able to afford the others. So, it was time to consider *if* he wanted to buy a room feature now or save for one of the other options later. He asked himself what room features he needed, if any, but he couldn't think of anything specific. As luck would have it, he had already gotten a water source just today, which was the main room feature he'd been wanting. Other room features could be useful, like more plants for the bees, more traps for better defense, or maybe something to help the bear people and get even more DP. Yet he couldn't think of a specific thing that he *needed* right now, and since the choices seemed random, he had no idea if the feature in question would even be something he wanted.

So, he considered the other choices. Second on the shop's list was another monster choice, which was always a good thing. The sprayers had been incredible, dealing with shades while minimizing the risk to his bees. He had already seen plenty of monster options that would be useful. He could get digger bees if they ever showed up again. Carpenter or mason bees might help him with his current construction projects. Monster bee captains would make the army even stronger than it was. Plus, who knew what other options were out there?

The choice that appealed to him the most right now was a new room type, listed in the shop for three thousand DP. He still had a fourth room slot he hadn't used, and he had a bunch of plants unlocked that he didn't have a suitable place to grow. If dirt tunnels appeared again, for example, he could probably grow all those cave plants he had. Not to mention that Juosiutik had a bunch more she could share in that case as well. And even if dirt tunnels or other underground options weren't available, new room types might unlock more plant options from basic resource plants, so it wouldn't be a loss either way.

The fourth option was a new perk choice. At ten thousand DP, perks were the most expensive item in the shop, and thus far the effect of perks seemed subtler compared to new monsters or features. But they made his tower and his bees stronger and didn't require him to spend any more mana to do so.

He wasn't completely sold on a new room type yet, so he considered the final three options as well. For five thousand DP, he could expand his room limit and get more rooms to work with. He could make an orchard just for the bear people, maybe even an apiary if he was willing to let them interact directly with the bee colonies. He still hesitated on that, but the bear people had respected his bees thus far, so maybe it wouldn't be a terrible idea. Plus, a second farmhouse might provide a good place for lessons with Juosiutik.

For the same price, five thousand DP, he could boost his maximum mana. This option was the least appealing to Belissar, since he could expand his mana just from the daily purifications. As such, a new room type did seem like the best option he could pick.

Still, he was in good shape to wait and see what might appear. He had already received new features from the minor+ purifications and new plants from the bear people. He also figured that new types of bees might show up from all those new plants, so he might also get some new monster types as well.

Well, he would have to wait a bit longer before he could afford a new room type anyway, and who knew what might appear before then? In any case, Belissar had a plan for his growing DP, so he said goodnight to Niobee and then went to sleep.

It turned out Belissar's thoughts would be correct. Belissar awoke and was making his rounds through the apiary beehouses when he came to one of the new ones. The queen was waiting out at the front and began to dance rapidly as he approached. Next to her stood a worker bee. A worker bee with red and black stripes.

Belissar grinned. He had a feeling he knew what was going on.

"Good morning. You want to show me something?"

The queen danced her salute and then the worker bee flew up toward Belissar.

Burning Monster Bee Worker

Vitality:	*Minimal*
Strength:	*Minimal*
Speed:	*Average*
Magic:	*Minimal+*
Defense:	*Minimal*
Resistance:	*Minimal+*
Special:	*Minor*
Notable Skills:	*Burning Poison Sting, Heat Resistance, Sacrificial Strike, Brood Offspring*

A monster bee worker raised on honey infused with Fire mana.
Both its body and its venom run hot. Stings will burn and may cause fever.
Can produce fire and heat-resistant wax, a necessity for its
Fire mana-infused honey.

Belissar nodded. As he'd expected, one of the queens had raised a new bee type from the flame radishes.

"Good work. If you can, try to raise some more of these, we could use them."

The queen froze, standing completely still for a moment before she burst out into as rapid a salute dance as she could. Belissar chuckled.

"Well, there's no rush, so don't overdo it, okay?"

She saluted once more before rushing into her beehouse, the burning worker following after her. Belissar shook his head. He was a tad worried she might get carried away now that he had asked something directly, but it *was* true that he could use those bees. Flame-resistant wax would be a godsend given that all of the building materials currently available in the tower were flammable. These burning worker bees could very much resolve that concern *and* reinforce the firebreaks he was planning. If there were enough of the burning worker bees, then brush fires would no longer represent an existential threat to the flower meadow.

And that was only from the first of the new plants he had received. Belissar couldn't help but whistle a tune as he continued on with his morning.

With the help of the soldier bees, construction on the new beehouse accelerated dramatically. The soldiers working together could lift a beam faster than Belissar could. In addition, after lifting one beam, the soldiers would rotate out for another group, allowing the work to continue while the first group rested. Within a day, they had already finished the framework.

Belissar was now sawing planks for the floors, walls, and roof. The bees did attempt to help with that task, but the small handle on the saw made it hard for the bees to get sufficient leverage. Belissar had some ideas on that, but he didn't have the resources or skills to make a metal saw. Perhaps he should ask the bear people about it. They had to have gotten their metal tools and weapons from somewhere, after all.

But for now, Belissar didn't mind. He wanted to do this *for* the bees, so it would defy the point if the bees took care of every part of the task. The bees also could lift the planks without too much trouble, so they began laying the floor even as Belissar created the planks.

As the purification cooldown approached, Belissar halted the work and reviewed their progress. It wouldn't do for the soldier bees to go into a fight tired, after all. His eyes widened a bit as he saw the frame with part of the floor taking shape. At this rate, they'd be done much sooner than he'd anticipated. Belissar grinned.

Everything seemed to be going very well.

DOUBLE, BUBBLE, BEAR AND TROUBLE

Back in the bear people's camp, Juosiutik sat just outside her tent and watched her pot as it bubbled. Others of the clan passed her by, but most knew better than to interrupt her mid-brew. She focused inward, stretching out with what little mana she had herself to monitor the potion as it bubbled and swirled. She frowned.

A true potion-maker would be able to follow the flow of mana throughout the entire process, and even predict how it would develop. They would have been able to make micro-adjustments at the very start so that the whole thing would coalesce at the end, even if the middle seemed chaotic and volatile. Juosiutik, on the other hand, did not have the mana reserves to keep such a close and detailed eye. She barely had enough to infuse the potion and kick off the process. Nor did she have the knowledge of what changes she needed to make, what sort of chaotic flow was counterintuitively desirable, and what sort of apparently smooth flow would actually ruin the entire mix. It was one reason why so many of her experiments went up in flames.

But there was nothing for it. Only a handful of records had been left behind when the last potion-maker passed, so there was no choice but to figure it out through trial and error—a process made much more difficult by the clan's lack of resources. She had neither the mana-infused foodstuffs that would have boosted the growth of her own reserves nor the extra potion ingredients for her to make more than the occasional attempt.

That was beginning to change, however. The God of Bees had given her slight blessings, boosting Juosiutik's mana reserves just a bit. In addition, Juosiutik now had a consistent source of high-quality ingredients. She could afford to waste a few on failed experiments. And she also had a powerful source of mana that proved capable of infusing *any* combination of ingredients she had tried.

Her thoughts turned to the sacred den and its master for a moment. He was small and strangely furless. She thought that might have been just part of his species, whatever it was, but he had a small patch on the top of his head, so it clearly wasn't impossible for him to grow any. She was originally going to investigate his condition but Chief Rohsuak had told her no, so she would let it lie. Maybe he was sensitive about it?

It would make sense. The sacred den master was incredibly timid. He reminded her more of Noigakkuq, the runt of the clan who mostly kept to herself, than of a leader like Chief Rohsuak. That wasn't all bad, though. Juosiutik didn't mind Noigakkuq's company when the other girl was willing to speak with her. She and the sacred den master were both far less likely to ignore Juosiutik's warnings and tip over a brew in progress. There was a reason Tyhgak wasn't allowed near her pot anymore.

Still, Juosiutik couldn't make heads or tails of the sacred den master. The man commanded an entire army that could wipe out most of the clan. He possessed riches beyond imagining, and even Juosiutik's limited senses could tell his personal mana reserves were nothing to scoff at either. So, why then was he so timid? If *she* had that much power at her disposal . . . well, she probably would be marching back toward—

In any case, it was strange that someone with that much power would not be waving it about, much less be frightened of those far weaker than he.

Juosiutik was taken out of her thoughts as she felt the bubbling mana begin to settle down. She leaned over the pot to stir it with a ladle. The mana remained settled even with her disruption, letting her know the mixture was now stable. She allowed herself a small smile.

Yet another successful brew. At this point, she was beginning to understand some of the properties of the mana honey. The magical, ridiculous properties that defied her understanding of potion ingredients. Mana honey was greedy. It wanted to absorb more mana and harmonize it with its own, taking on its properties. It shared its own mana in the process, creating a current of mana-exchanging characteristics between different ingredients. It was an excellent binding agent that could tie clashing ingredients together, using itself as the medium. And the mana it already possessed would kick-start any such process, taking the burden off of Juosiutik.

In some ways, it wasn't fair. It wasn't fair that *honey* was a better potion-maker than she was. But that was fine, because she had the mana honey now, and felt confident enough in her understanding of it to try something.

She emptied the pot and stored its contents. She had to wait for the pot to cool down before she could wash it thoroughly, then she went back into her tent and began rummaging through her bags until she found the ingredients she was looking for. She filled the pot with water once again. This time, though, she built a small fire underneath it rather than using flame radish. This was a difficult and complicated brew, so she couldn't afford to use flame radish for heating as the volatile ingredient and its additional fire mana could throw off the entire mix-ture. Just one of many reasons she hadn't been able to attempt this yet.

Another major reason was her limited supply of ingredients. Sleepy chamo-mile and quickblossom were supposedly abundant in their old home, but Juosiutik had never seen them. All she had left of them were a couple of dried flowers and a handful of seeds. For the quickblossom, she didn't even have enough for the sacred den to absorb, so she would have to try and grow some of the seeds once she was sure her clan wasn't going to move again. So, she could not afford to waste what little she had left on failed attempts.

And that was a problem, because this brew was not only complicated. It didn't even make *sense*. Sleepy chamomile and quickblossom had opposite effects, such that mixing them together canceled the other out and left the drinker with nothing but a stomachache. And yet . . . the previous potion-maker had been able to blend them together. Somehow, they had been able to manage the clash and the chaos such a mixture would create and bring a stable product out of it all. A miracle drink that was unparalleled in its ability to relieve fatigue, restoring and relaxing the body while simultaneously energizing it. Juosiutik, for the life of her, couldn't figure out how it would ever be possible. And without access to new ingredients, the small reserves she had would not be enough for her meager skills to work it out.

But no longer. The sacred den could now provide her with as much sleepy cham-omile as she needed. From what little she recalled of the recipe, the mix required far more sleepy chamomile than quickblossom, so that went a long way toward making an attempt possible. Still, that alone would not justify using up the last few dried quickblossom flowers. But she had received something else that would.

Mana honey. That mystical, unfair binding agent. Juosiutik had tested it recently with as many ingredients as she could spare, and as far as she could tell, it would work even with ingredients that were supposed to clash. So, Juosiutik might not be able to get the opposite ingredients to work together, but now, she might not have to. Mana honey might be able to do that for her. She was confident enough in it that it was worth an attempt.

She checked her ingredients and her tools, then double- and triple-checked them. She took her spear and jabbed it into the ground, topping it with a small wolf-mole skull. The agreed-upon sign within the clan that she was *not* to be disturbed.

She took a deep breath as the water began to heat up. Her heart began to pound in her chest as she held the pouch containing the quickblossom, confirming the contents hadn't gone bad.

"Okay . . . here goes . . ."

She placed the pouch of quickblossom down for now and then dumped a whole armful of sleepy chamomile into the pot. She sent a small jolt of her mana into the water to begin the process, and then began stirring the mix. She danced around the pot, stirring in random patterns. A circle here, then a circle the other way, then a figure eight, then back and forth. The goal was to prevent the sleepy chamomile from settling while its mana activated.

She then tossed in a sweetvetch and some cloudberries, ingredients that had also come from her homeland. Juosiutik vaguely remembered such things being added to the mix, though she wasn't sure why. She did feel the mana react slightly.

She then took another deep breath. The sleepy chamomile mana was now leaking into the water. If she didn't act now, it would settle and turn into a basic sleepy chamomile tea. It was now or never.

Narrowing her eyes, Juosiutik picked up her pouch and a piece of mana honeycomb she had broken off the tray. She took a dried quickblossom flower from the pouch and rubbed it on the honeycomb, coating it in the honey. Then she dropped both into the mix.

The mix began to bubble and boil over as the ingredients reacted. Juosiutik stirred furiously, spreading the quickblossom mana throughout the pot. She could feel the mana roiling, and she could see wisps of steam and small sparks flying out from the pot. It was tempting to send her mana into the mix, to try to soothe over the growing storm.

But she resisted. She had no idea what this mix was supposed to look like at this stage, so intervening haphazardly would be a mistake. Instead, she felt for the mana of the honeycomb and focused on that. She sent what little of her own mana she had through her ladle to the piece of honeycomb and tried to carry it on into the mix as she stirred. Her entire plan here was to trust in the properties of the mana honey, so that was what she focused her interventions on. Juosiutik hoped against hope, and even prayed to the gods, that the mana honey would do what she thought it would.

Juosiutik stirred the mixture for what seemed like an eternity. Her heart pounded harder and harder as the mix grew ever more chaotic. She started frowning as a particularly large spark nearly singed her hand. Her face began to fall. If this kept up, she would soon need to abandon the mixture and run. The possibility of it spontaneously combusting was now too high to ignore.

But right as she was about to call it, something changed. The mana shifted, and then the mana flows began to rapidly disperse. The sparks and the bubbling died down almost immediately. Juosiutik's eyes widened and she leaned over the pot. She gulped.

"Did it . . . fail?"

Had the mixture collapsed and dispersed all of its mana? She had to force herself to move and take a scoop with her ladle. She trembled as she reached out into the liquid . . .

And then she froze. The liquid was still filled to the brim with mana. She began to stir the pot and her eyes went wider. The whole pot was still full of mana. Settled mana that did not react further to her disruptions.

The mix was stable.

She took another scoop and lifted it with a trembling hand. She blew on it until it was just barely cool enough not to burn her and took a sip. Her trembling grew and her eyes filled with tears. She spoke in barely a whisper.

". . . I did it . . . Mom, I did it . . ."

She stood completely still for a moment as her mind processed what she had just achieved. Then she thrust her hands up into the sky.

"I DID IT!"

Juosiutik filled two water pouches with the potion and then took off running as fast as she could. Her heart soared as she smashed through branches, ignoring them as she sprinted toward the sacred den. She burst past a surprised Metsaitti and his hunters, ignoring their calls to her as she rushed into the sacred den.

She didn't stop until she came to the shrine of bees. She then skidded and fell to her hands and knees, giggling as she did.

"I did it. Thanks to you, I did it."

She began to tear up again and wiped her eyes.

"It's all thanks to you, both you and your sacred den master. Thanks to you, I revived my mom's recipe. I . . . I . . . maybe I can become a potion-maker like her after all."

She slowly rose to her feet and brushed the dirt off her. Then she took one of the pouches and placed it into the shrine's chest. She fell to her knees.

"Thank you. I can't thank you enough. Without your blessing and the sacred den's honey, I couldn't have done this. So, please, if it pleases you, please be the first to accept this."

Even as Juosiutik spoke, the chest and the shrine of bees began to glow, far brighter than before. It grew so bright Juosiutik had to shield her eyes.

When it died down, Juosiutik gasped. In the center of her vision hung a string of words, floating in the air.

The God of Bees offers you her full blessing.
If you wish to accept, please select one of the following blessings:
- Blessing of the Alchemist
- Blessing of the Mystic
- Blessing of the Healer
- Blessing of the Honey Herbalist

Juosiutik's mouth fell wide open.

CHAPTER EIGHTEEN

BLESSING BEES-NESS

Belissar had just dismissed the soldier bees to prepare for the daily purification when Juosiutik suddenly burst into the tower. Belissar raised an eyebrow.

"Huh, wonder what she's doing here? It's kind of late, isn't it?"

Then, she began to repeatedly thank the God of Bees and put something in the shrine of bees' chest. Well, Belissar certainly didn't disapprove of that, but he still wondered why she was doing it now, and why she seemed . . . frantic? Excited? He wasn't sure.

At least until a moment later, that was.

A challenger has been fully blessed.
Gained 20 DP.

A challenger has selected a blessing unique to your patron.
Gained additional 10 DP.

Belissar gasped and focused back on Juosiutik. She was kneeling before the shrine of bees, which was glowing, and had tears streaming down her face. She was repeatedly saying something, though as usual Belissar couldn't hear her speak at the shrine.

Belissar crossed his arms. On the one hand, he *really* wanted to ask her what had happened. On the other hand . . . she didn't seem in the best of shapes, so she might not want to talk? Belissar groaned a bit before deciding he would at least approach her. If she didn't want to talk, she didn't want to talk, but if she *was* willing he would very much like to know how she received a full blessing. This was the very first progress that had been made on that particular mission, so any information on how he could assist would be extremely helpful. He started to make his way over, with Niobee and the soldiers following along.

Juosiutik was just starting to gather herself and rise to her feet as Belissar approached.

"Um, hi. Sorry to bother you."

She quickly spun around. Her eyes widened slightly. "Sacred Den Master . . ."

Belissar was about to respond when she suddenly jumped forward and wrapped her arms around him.

"Thank you! Thank you so much! It's all thanks to you!"

Belissar, of course, began to panic as he was wrapped in furry arms by a bear woman quite a bit taller than himself.

"Huh? Um, what?"

Niobee flew in front of Juosiutik's face while the soldier bees began to surround her and extend their stingers. Juosiutik gasped and let go of him, then backed away with her hands raised.

"Sorry, I didn't mean any offense."

Belissar shook his head. "No, it's . . . fine. Um, I'm fine, everyone, please don't hurt her."

Niobee turned sideways to keep an eye on Juosiutik as she danced. "King sure? Not attacked?"

Belissar shook his head. "No, not attacked. It's a human . . . err, human is what I call myself, but what about you?"

Juosiutik nodded. "Human, huh? For us, we call ourselves the karnuq."

"Right, it's a human and karnuq sign of affection, I think? Hugs are a sign of affection for you, right? Actually, why *did* you hug me?"

Juosiutik flushed and looked away. "Ah, yes. I got a bit . . . excited." Then her face brightened and she held up a water pouch. "Because of this! Check this out, Sacred Den Master!"

Belissar tilted his head. "Um, what is it?"

Juosiutik beamed. "It's my mother's old recipe! It's a potion that simultaneously relaxes, restores, and energizes your body! You can use it to restore fatigue, to stave off exhaustion, to help the body fight off illness, all sorts of things!"

She looked at the pouch. Her eyes began to tear up slightly. "My mother . . . passed before she could teach me. The recipe was too hard for me to figure out, and I barely had any of the ingredients left. But with the mana honey you gave me and the sleepy chamomile you're growing, I was able to recreate it. It's all thanks to you and the God of Bees."

She extended her arms and held out the pouch to him. "Please, accept this. I wanted to give you and your patron god the first batch."

Belissar felt his chest grow tight. Something from her late mother, huh? He slowly reached out and took the pouch. He took a deep breath as he considered what to say.

". . . Thank you. I'll treasure it."

Juosiutik smiled, nodded, and then wiped her eyes. Belissar waited for a bit before beginning to speak again. "By the way, I saw you got a full blessing from the God of Bees?"

Juosiutik beamed once again. "Yes! I offered some to the God of Bees and then she gave me her blessing! I'm a honey herbalist now!"

Belissar tilted his head. "Honey herbalist?"

Juosiutik nodded. "If I'm not mistaken, it's one of the God of Bees' unique blessings. Chief Rohsuak told us that could happen but that we should only expect the regular ones, so I was surprised! I didn't even expect to get blessed today! But look, watch this!"

She held out her hand. Mana condensed and grew visible, forming into a familiar hexagonal pattern made of golden light. Honey began to drip from the pattern into Juosiutik's hand.

"I can make honey now, too! And I'm getting all sorts of ideas on what I can do with it! This is going to be amazing! I can finally become a real potion-maker!"

Belissar was still trying to follow the rapid-fire conversation, but he eventually caught up and nodded with a smile. "Ah, congratulations."

Juosiutik beamed once more. "Thanks!"

Eventually, Juosiutik said her goodbye and left the dungeon, walking at a normal pace for once. Belissar stood watching the tower entrance and rubbing his chin. Niobee flew in front of him.

"King okay?"

Belissar nodded. "Well, I think I sort of get the blessing thing? Maybe the bear people . . . or karnuq . . . have to accomplish something? Or was it because she used mana honey . . . or ingredients from the tower? Or . . . was it because she was really grateful? Well . . . I guess I don't get it after all, but I have an idea of how to help, at least. I think if we help them make and achieve things, maybe that will help with the blessing mission?"

Niobee swayed in the air for a bit before beginning a slow dance. "King should be careful. Stay safe."

Belissar smiled at her. "Thanks, I will. But . . . I don't think we have to worry about them. At least not Juosiutik, anyhow."

"Okay . . . if King says so."

With that, Belissar and the bees returned to preparing for the next purification. Belissar considered how he could do more to help the bear people, or rather, the karnuq. Perhaps he had already done so by giving them access to food, flax, and herbs, but maybe there was something more he could do? Right now, there were a handful of things in his tower that the karnuq didn't have access to. The apple trees and wood tree resource nodes of the orchard, the mana flower and flame radish nodes, and then, of course, the beehives themselves and the honeycomb they produced. Belissar still wasn't comfortable exposing his bees' homes to the karnuq, and he wasn't about to make a beehive the bees couldn't use, so honeycomb would still have to go through him, but the others bore thinking about. He, of course, could make mana flower or flame radish nodes right on the spot. As for the orchard . . . at the moment, he would have to escort them there because of the remnants. Unless he could do something about that . . . ?

He waited for a moment but sadly, no new messages from the tower appeared. It did not seem he would be able to control remnants outright, at least for now. He had seen a rest zone feature that would block them, which wouldn't make sense to choose if he could just stop them at will, he supposed.

So yes, he would have to escort the karnuq through the flower meadow if he wanted to give them access to the orchard. Although . . . he *did* have an extra room slot open. Couldn't he make another orchard and place the door to it right by the entrance? Remnants didn't appear by the shrine of bees or a small area around it, so it would be safe, right? Though, that would only get the karnuq *to* the orchard. If they then spread out to gather apples, would remnants start appearing in the orchard? Belissar might need to guard them anyway in that case.

He put that idea aside for now and considered the other options. Flame radishes were a bit expensive and something the karnuq both already had access to and didn't necessarily need anymore, so they probably weren't worth it unless the karnuq specifically requested it. On the other hand, mana flowers were something they very much wanted and had no opportunity to receive.

That is, *if* Belissar was willing to devote a patch of the bees' most favorite flower to the karnuq's use. He didn't want to make something like that that the bees wouldn't have full access to, but he *did* have a mission to help the challengers get blessings from the God of Bees herself. Belissar groaned a bit before deciding to compromise. He made four new patches of mana flowers, one in the karnuq's gathering zone, one by the flower meadow hives, one in the orchard bee grove, and one in the apiary. That way, he could be sure his bees had mana flowers to spare before he offered any to the karnuq.

It was a notable hit to his remaining mana, but that was what the mana was for, in any case.

Belissar decided to be satisfied with that for now, as the purification cooldown had just about ended.

CHAPTER NINETEEN

HAPP-BEE CELEBRATIONS

Juosiutik returned to the camp to find Chief Rohsuak waiting for her, for her mad dash had not gone unnoticed. The chief had her arms crossed and an eyebrow raised, flanked by hunters she was about to send out to ensure the girl's safety. Juosiutik looked away sheepishly.

"Well, I trust you had a good reason for running off like that?"

Juosiutik flushed but couldn't help breaking out into a smile. "Let me show you!"

Chief Rohsuak shook her head and dismissed the hunters. Juosiutik then led the chief over to her tent. Chief Rohsuak noticed the pot and walked over to it. Her eyes widened as she detected a familiar scent.

"Is this . . . ?"

Juosiutik nodded. "It is. I did it."

Chief Rohsuak turned to her and gave the girl a warm smile. She pulled Juosiutik into a hug. "Congratulations."

Juosiutik's eyes moistened again but she shook her head and returned the embrace, then broke out and stepped back. "Thanks, but that's not all. I . . . rushed out, because I wanted to offer the remade potion to the God of Bees and the sacred den master who helped me figure it out, and, well . . ."

Juosiutik held out her hand and formed the honeycomb pattern once again. "The God of Bees approved."

Chief Rohsuak blinked a bit before breaking into a wide grin. "It seems further congratulations are in order, champion."

Juosiutik's face lit up.

That night, the karnuq held a grand celebration. For the first time since their sojourns began, one of their own had been blessed by the gods, worthy of becoming a champion capable of great deeds. Tyhgak was upset someone had beaten him to the punch. Juosiutik gloating to him did not help.

And in the midst of it all, one young karnuq woman hung at the edge of the celebrations. She was small for a karnuq, about the same height as the sacred den master. She slouched as she sat on a log on the outskirts of the camp, sitting alone as she sipped from her mug.

"Sacred dens and champions, huh?" she said aloud to herself.

Her eyes fell upon Juosiutik lifting a mug up into the air and cheering. The rest of the clan was cheering and laughing as well. Her eyes narrowed and she slowly turned her head in the direction of the sacred den. She began to clench her mug tightly . . .

Belissar triggered another minor+ purification that night, another pair of wolf-shades. The bees once again handled it without issue, and Belissar gained another fifteen mana. During the celebration, he took a sip of the potion Juosiutik gave him. He smiled.

The sweetness of honey blended nicely with the tang of the berries, and the whole mixture filled him with the pleasant warmth of mana. He felt his muscles relax and the tension leave his shoulders, even as a surge of energy raced through his chest. It was evening after a long day of work and yet he felt as if he had just awoken after a good night's rest.

He felt so good that when he laid down that night to sleep, sleep refused to come to him. He stared at the ceiling for about half an hour before shrugging and getting up. With his tower sight he could see in the dark as well as the day, so he took his newfound energy and began sawing more planks for beehouse construction. He worked late into the night before finally feeling fatigued enough to rest.

The next morning he awoke later than usual. He looked over at the potion pouch and nodded. He would use it carefully from now on.

Once he got up, he made his way over to the tower entrance, intending to greet the karnuq gatherers. He arrived shortly after they did . . . and as he expected, he found Juosiutik standing completely still, her eyes fixed on the new mana flower patch next to her other herbs.

Juosiutik's head slowly creaked up to look at him. "Sacred Den Master, is this . . . ?"

Belissar smiled. "The God of Bees has approved of you, so I figured I'd lend a hand too. Feel free to take from this patch. Just leave any others in the tower for the bees, okay?"

Juosiutik nodded as rapidly as she could with a massive smile on her face. "Yes! Of course! Thank you so much, Sacred Den Master!"

Belissar chuckled and then spoke with Leijaliuk to exchange his portion of yesterday's harvest for some goods. Today the karnuq had brought some more dried wood, which they'd agreed upon as the default payment unless Belissar had any special requests. Dried wood meant more supplies for current and future bee-hive construction, and it would keep much better than extraneous food, so Belissar figured that was the best thing to stockpile at present.

Belissar then returned to the beehouse and looked up at the soldier bee army following him.

"Shall we get to work, then?"

He chuckled as he was greeted with hundreds of salutes, and then they all got to work. The beehouse was taking shape very quickly, even faster than before. Planks for the walls, roofs, and floors were much thinner and lighter than the beams for the frameworks, so the bees could lift them with ease, and there were hundreds of bees to do the job. They were limited only by the speed at which Belissar could saw appropriate planks . . . and thanks to last night's little potion situation, they started the day with a stockpile already done.

In fact, they worked so quickly that the work was *done* by the end of the day. Belissar just stood, staring in silence for a while at the completed building before him.

A long wooden cabin now stretched across the exit of the flower meadow. Its right end had an archway through the structure, forming an entrance hallway for the door to the orchard, with the shrine of bees and the memorial just to the right of that. The archway was separated from the rest of the building's interior save for small holes that the bees could fly out from. Its left side stretched out toward the flower meadow hives, and held the living spaces for the hives. The front was a solid wooden wall with several small windows just under the roof for the bees to come and go through. The only ground-level entrance was on the far left wall, which Belissar closed off with a flap made of cloth.

Inside, the structure was mostly open, though there were smaller beams forming built-in frames that the bees could use to support their honeycomb. These frames were topped by a lighter roof with regular gaps, forming areas where soldiers could gather before flying out the windows on the front, as well as providing some cover for the frames from anything coming through those windows. Belissar had initially planned to further separate the interior with walls and additional cloth flaps . . . but to his surprise, the queens indicated that wasn't necessary.

And as Belissar put up the last cloth flap, the shrine of bees began to glow . . . followed by the entire beehouse. Soon the whole thing lit up with golden light, and Belissar was forced to shield his eyes. Words appeared before his eyes.

New feature detected.
New feature unlocked.
Bee Barracks now available!

Belissar's eyes widened. He now felt the thrum of mana flowing through the wooden walls of the structure. He gently walked up and placed a hand on the nearest wall.

Bee Barracks

Mana Upkeep: 10 (5 with Blessing of Bees)
Current Occupants: None

Slight boost to monster bee growth rate, medium boost to combat monster bee growth rate, slight boost to coordination for bees housed within.
Houses multiple colonies.

Belissar stepped back in a daze, and then began to grin. It seemed the tower and the God of Bees liked his work. But, of course, even they were not the ultimate judges.

He turned to find the soldier bee army waiting behind him. Their queens had come out of their hives and now flew ahead of their army. Belissar smiled at them.

"Well, what do you think?"

A slight gust blew into Belissar's face as the bees danced hundreds of "Amazing!" "Incredible!" aerial motions all at once. He chuckled and then stepped to the side.

"In that case, enjoy!"

The bees all saluted as one and then burst into motion. The soldiers flew back toward their hives as the queens gathered in a circle and began to dance to one another. Soon, swarms of workers were flying into the barracks, the queens directing them to specific frames which they immediately began filling with honeycomb. Belissar watched in awe as the mana of the barracks began to stir, speeding up the construction. In fact . . . if his eyes weren't deceiving him, the wax structures were growing faster than the bees themselves could build them. He guessed that was why this thing cost mana to upkeep. And it made sense. The beehives could make honeycomb without any bees at all, so it only followed they could make empty wax too.

Above all, the bees were flying more rapidly and dancing more excitedly than Belissar had seen in a while. That alone made him beyond proud of what they had built here. He turned to Niobee.

"I'm going to skip the purification for the night and let them get settled. Can you let them know if they ask about it?"

"Okay!"

Niobee flew off to join the other bees. Meanwhile, Belissar quietly excused himself and made his way back to the apiary farmhouse, humming a tune as he walked.

GRAND PLANS FULFILLED

The Firstborn hovered in the air as she again looked upon the towering fortress spread out before her. Legions upon legions of her and her fellow queens' offspring flew in and out of the grand gates, a couple of soldiers holding open the great weaves to ease their passage.

The King . . . was truly incredible. And generous beyond all imagining. They now had walls that even a soldier could not pierce. They had entrances taller than any foe which they could use to launch their assaults. They had areas to gather and organize their forces before they ever left the hive.

The fortress was even *magical,* like the palaces of the apiary were said to be. Mana flowed through the walls, touching every bee that entered and assisting their efforts to rebuild their hives. And as the queens moved their young brood in, the Firstborn felt the mana flow into them as well, helping to nourish them and stimulate their growth. If her predictions were correct . . . they could now maintain a larger army than before without even expanding their foraging efforts.

But even that was not what the Firstborn was focused upon at the moment. The thing that held her gaze were the grand pillars upon which to build their combs. The same pillars that the Conduit had once told her about when she was a young queen. The same pillars the King had built for the fallen First Dynasty, upon which they had built their civilization. In fact, the Conduit even claimed these pillars were far larger and sturdier than those ancient ones.

The Firstborn began to tremble. They had done it. They had returned to the time before the First Invasion. They had fully avenged the fall of the First Dynasty. The King now trusted them enough to turn his attention to grand constructions and leave the bloody work of war to them.

The Firstborn allowed herself one more moment to bask in the glory of the fortress before she returned to work. There was much to do, and her hive needed her to direct their efforts. Their cooperation with the King had revealed the potential of the soldiers for more than simple combat. Even now, workers were chewing off entire sections of honeycomb in her old hive, which a single soldier could carry all at once. The soldiers carried these portions of her old hive to the pillars that were designated for her, where workers forming new wax would integrate them into the new constructions. The King had declared that there would be no invasion today in order to give them a chance to move, and the flower meadow queens intended to fulfill his will. Therefore, the whole soldier bee army was deployed to support the effort. And with hundreds of soldiers, each of which could carry many cells, the work was proceeding beyond expectations. Tasks they thought would take days could now be accomplished in mere hours.

And then, the queens of the flower meadow would take full advantage of their new home. The extra mana and space and the ease of cooperation would accelerate their efforts, while the new flowers grown by the King would sustain their expansion.

The Firstborn and her fellow queens had succeeded. They had built an army that had proven victorious where the First Dynasty had fallen. They had grown enough that the King had begun to trust them enough to turn his attention back to his initial plans.

And that would only be the beginning. This she promised.

The Second of the Sixth stood still in her hive, staring at the glistening, slightly glowing blue and green honey in front of her. She . . . was unsure of herself.

She had been extremely wary when the First of the Fifth offered her access to a brand-new flower . . . and her suspicion had only grown as scout reports and nectar samples came in. The flower was like one of the healing herbs but contained noticeably more mana, like the mana flowers. It produced nectar on par with processed healing herb honey which, was then elevated even further by her workers. As well, its productivity far outstripped that of a regular healing herb flower. There were no downsides to this flower that the Second of the Sixth's workers had noticed. It was not difficult to gather from, limited in quantity, or lower in quality. It was, by all metrics, an excellent flower and a great boon to her hive.

This was beyond suspicious. The Second of the Sixth just *knew* the First of the Fifth must have some sort of ulterior motive with this. The schemer who had maneuvered herself into uncontested control of the apiary and all of its resources would not have simply given up a treasure of this caliber. No, she must have some sort of plan, some sort of catch. And yet, for the life of her, the Second of the Sixth could not figure out what it was. She could not see how the First of the Fifth would benefit from this.

And that was why she was suspicious. The First of the Fifth was crafty and powerful; that much all the apiary queens had to acknowledge. There was absolutely every possibility that she saw something the rest of them did not, which meant that the lack of an apparent motive was the most dangerous situation of all. It was why all of them had been wary yesterday, when the King doubled the number of mana flowers in the apiary and the First of the Fifth again did something that none of them had anticipated. She gathered the apiary queens up and assigned each and every one of them a mana flower. Every hive now had exclusive access to its own mana flower, with the rest to be shared communally.

The apiary queens had wanted to refuse, as they could not determine what the First of the Fifth's game was. However, the Second of the Sixth had to admit that the First of the Fifth was truly *good* at what she did. Whatever her angle ultimately was, she'd made them an offer none of them could refuse. The queens begrudgingly agreed to her terms. All of them stewed in worry as their hives began to grow, wondering when the First of the Fifth's final designs would be revealed.

So the Second of the Sixth could not help but worry. She thought long and hard on how best to leverage the new flower the First of the Fifth had dared to "grant" to her. Its nectar was rich and powerful . . . but it was ultimately just a single flower. No matter how productive, it would be difficult to support any sort of mass endeavor with it. At first, she'd wanted to offer its honey to the King, but filling an entire tray off the nectar of one flower would take a long, long time. She thought about raising new workers on it . . . but that, too, would have only resulted in a handful of new workers. Not enough to make any sort of dramatic difference for her hive. Not enough to surpass anything that the First of the Fifth had already accomplished.

No, none of that felt like a sufficient use of this treasured resource she had acquired. Her instincts whispered to her of something else she could do. The nutrition, quality, and mana concentration of the new honey was just right for a use that even the First of the Fifth had not attempted.

The Second of the Sixth had recently gathered the necessary quantity to make the attempt. She could try it right now. And if she succeeded . . . not just her honey or her workers but her entire *hive* would be transformed. They would become something different, something altogether new in the King's realm. She would achieve something even the First of the Fifth had not.

And that was why she hesitated. Surely the First of the Fifth would have noticed the potential in this flower? Surely the First of the Fifth must have realized the implications? The Second of the Sixth hated to admit it, but the First of the Fifth did produce the finest honey of all the queens. It would be foolish of her to believe she understood something regarding this nectar which the First of the Fifth did not.

So, why then would the First of the Fifth permit this to happen? Why would she allow the Second of the Sixth to achieve something she herself had not? Was there something the Second of the Sixth was missing about this? A reason the First of the Fifth had not embarked upon this path? Was this the result the First of the Fifth was hoping for? Was the Second of the Sixth falling for her trap? Would she seal her fate if she took the next step?

She did not know. She couldn't know. She thought and she thought and she thought some more. She discussed it with her scouts. She discussed it, if in necessarily vague terms, with the other apiary queens. But in the end, none of them could determine the First of the Fifth's purpose in this. None of them could see any angles or schemes.

So, the Second of the Sixth came to her decision. She gave the order to her workers and they began to surround a cell larger than any they had ever built before, filling it to the brim with the new honey. And then, she herself climbed in, curling up to fit her large body in. The workers immediately began to cover the cell over as the Second of the Sixth circulated her mana, resonating it with the honey all around her.

She would take the plunge and do what she thought best. To forgo this opportunity was to forgo her best chance at becoming something more than just another apiary queen. It was to forgo her hive's best opportunity at greatness. And if this was what the First of the Fifth wanted, if there was some scheme in the works that would seal the Second of the Sixth's fate, she would just have to admit she had been beaten. It would be no different than it had been before, and no different than if she rejected the opportunity entirely.

She continued to circulate her mana and began to drink the honey as the wax shut out the light . . .

CHAPTER TWENTY

BEE-VIEWING THE NUMBERS

A young karnuq woman, the one smaller than the rest, waited in her tent, her things packed into a bag. She had waited until the sun set and night fell, when most of the rest of the clan had already gone to sleep. There was only a waning moon out tonight, just enough light to avoid complete darkness, but dark enough to restrict even a karnuq hunter's sight.

Well, she probably needn't have bothered. Most of the clan wouldn't care where she went or what she did. She gritted her teeth at that thought. She figured most of them wouldn't even care if she disappeared entirely.

But for just this night, that was convenient for her. She was able to slip past the night watch without any fuss and make her way to her destination, a small clearing near their camp, where the tunnel to the Underway opened up. She peered around until she found the night lookout, yawning as he leaned on a tree.

The chief would have taken his hide for negligence in this duty. For the girl, however, it was perfect. She waited for him to drift off fully, then took a deep breath and left the cover of the forest, creeping across the clearing as fast as she was willing to risk. Her heart pounded louder and louder the further she got . . . but eventually she hit the dirt and was soon making her way below ground.

She allowed herself to smile. She'd made it.

And now all she had to do was traverse the Underway. Alone. Where shades or creatures just as terrible prowled, ones that could threaten even a fully grown karnuq hunter. Not to mention a runt who hadn't even been taught as much as how to thrust a spear.

But she had made her decision. And so, with one final check of her belongings, she set off into the deep . . .

The next morning, Belissar made his way around the apiary, gathering honeycomb and checking in with the queens. As he continued on his way, he found one queen waiting for him outside. And he didn't need to ask why, for his jaw dropped as soon as he saw her.

Her color had changed from yellow to greenish blue. He focused on her and words appeared before his eyes.

Medicinal Monster Bee Queen

Vitality:	*Minimal*
Strength:	*Minimal*
Speed:	*Average*
Magic:	*Minor*
Defense:	*Minimal*
Resistance:	*Minimal*
Special:	*Above Average*
Notable Skills:	*Herbal Shot, Poison Sting, Brood Mother, Command Offspring*

A monster bee queen raised or evolved on Medicinal Mana Honey.
Lays medicinal variant offspring by default.

She watched him as he read through the description. He then turned to her with wide eyes.

"Wow, that's amazing. So, you can raise all medicinal bees now?"

She paused and then slowly danced the affirmative. Belissar smiled. "That's great, congratulations."

She froze, and then broke out into a happy dance. Belissar grinned and chuckled. This was a significant development, to be sure. So far, only a handful of worker or soldier bees of the specialized types seemed to appear in the different colonies. But now, there at least one hive would be mostly comprised of medicinal bees. Belissar figured he'd be getting a lot more medicinal honey, which could be crucial if the bee army took significant casualties later.

Additionally, if more queens could specialize like that, it'd open a lot of options. An army of pure maddening soldier bees? A hive of the new burning bees who could easily make fireproof wax constructs? Plus, who knew what might result from the new flowers they had received from the karnuq?

All in all, a great way to start the day!

After the karnuq finished their gathering, Belissar noticed Juosiutik still hanging around. He hadn't planned on speaking with her today, not seeing a particular need to, but since she wasn't leaving he figured he should ask. He walked over to the entrance.

"Hi, did you need something?"

Juosiutik turned to him and nodded. "Ah, there you are, Sacred Den Master! I wanted to ask if you wanted to resume potion lessons?"

Belissar rubbed his chin a bit before replying. "Sure. It's actually a good time."

With the bee barracks completed, all he had left to do was to replace the new apiary beehives with his own beehouses, and then figure something out for the two queens in the orchard. He wasn't entirely sure what he was going to do for them yet, so he was planning to tackle the apiary first. But since he already knew how to build those beehouses, and they were much smaller to begin with, he wouldn't need as much time or focus to finish the job. So, if he wanted to continue on the potion-making, now would be a good time.

Juosiutik smiled. "Great! I do need to figure out some ideal recipes considering the ingredients you made for us, and I also need to figure out how my blessing works. But since you also can do the magic honey thing, I could try to do so with you? You could see the process of working out a potion recipe and your blessing will probably work for it too."

Belissar nodded. "Ah, that makes sense, I think? Um, hang on just a second."

It had slipped Belissar's mind a bit to make a safe potion area for these lessons, so he went ahead and did so now. With his tower sight, he cleared an area of flowers near the entrance, turning it back into bare dirt. Just in case, he also moved the pond he had made from the end of the flower meadow to the entrance. Belissar then turned back to Juosiutik.

"Okay, this should be a safe place for the potions . . . um, are you okay?"

He found Juosiutik staring at him with wide eyes. She suddenly gulped and shook her head. "Fine, fine, Sacred Den Master, sir. Um, should I set up here, then?"

Belissar nodded. Juosiutik then slowly walked to the center of the newly cleared dirt area and opened up her bag. She laid down a large cloth and began removing some ingredients and tools, glancing at Belissar and at the pond every now and again.

"Right, um, would you like to begin?"

Belissar spent the morning helping Juosiutik experiment with some recipes, listening intently as she explained about flows of mana and such. It was still a bit esoteric to him, and Juosiutik herself was still figuring out those exact recipes, but she explained this was just how her experimentation went. They agreed to keep that up on a regular basis. After the lesson, Belissar started sawing some wood for beehouse construction until time came around for another minor+ purification. Another bird shade appeared this time but again, the bees handled it without issue. Belissar added another fifteen mana.

Mana: 76/435

The night, after celebrating the victory, Belissar paused as he reviewed his mana. He had passed the four hundred mark. On a hunch, he thought about expanding again.

Attempt expansion purification?
Estimated purification strength: Small.

His hunch was correct; he had gathered enough mana to attempt to expand once again. He crossed his arms and began to hum. The question was, should he?

On the one hand, the last expansion had been remarkably beneficial: a brand-new room for his bees to live in, a new soldier bee type that could kill shades without risk to itself, and a new floor's worth of rooms to fill in. He had started to see glowing mana-flower like versions of the healing herbs and poison flowers, so apparently cross-pollination was also working. And beyond that, the ability to conduct daily minor+ purifications had increased the rewards he was receiving each day, accelerating his tower's growth. So, who knew what another expansion would bring him?

Additionally, his defenses had also improved. The soldier bee army was stronger and better at handling shades than ever before. The sprayers brought an entirely new dimension to the army, the flame radishes allowed for much more efficient use of the pit traps, and the bees themselves had fully adjusted to fighting aerial opponents that flew faster than them. The barracks was completed, and while it did not yet have all the defenses Belissar planned for it, it did provide a final opportunity to ambush any shades that managed to break away from the army.

On the other hand, was it worth the risk to attempt it right now? The last expansion purification had nearly gone badly and there was no guarantee the next shade would be anything they had prepared for. In fact, at this point, Belissar was anticipating it would be something *other* than what they had prepared for. How could he be certain that any of their improvements would suffice against something they couldn't predict?

Additionally, the flower meadow queens had just moved into the barracks, and there were only two queens in the orchard. It might be worth letting the former get settled and the latter expand a bit more before trying anything big. Plus, there were new flowers that the bees were still sampling. For all he knew, they might have another new bee type ready if he just waited.

He also was getting a lot more DP from the karnuq now. In fact . . .

DP: 2014

At this rate, he was just a bit over a week away from being able to afford a new room or monster choice. Something that might provide a notable advantage against whatever shade the Hunger threw at them next. Even if it didn't, it would still provide another way his tower could grow without taking the risk of an expansion purification.

So, what should he do?

This time, though, Belissar answered that very quickly. When in doubt, ask the bees. He turned and found Niobee resting on the farmhouse table in front of him.

"Hey, Niobee?"

She perked up and rose to her feet. "Yes, King?"

Belissar opened his mouth, then paused for a second as he thought about how to word his question before continuing.

"How are the flower meadow queens doing? How are they settling into their new home?"

Niobee began dancing rapidly. "Great! Queens love! We're planning to expand, King's big hive perfect!"

Belissar smiled, and then rubbed his chin. "Planning to expand?"

"Yes! New queens, bigger hives!"

Belissar nodded. "Got it, thanks Niobee."

"You're welcome!"

Belissar nodded again, this time to himself. That settled it. If the flower meadow queens had plans of their own, Belissar didn't want to disrupt them. He knew if he asked them about another big purification, they'd likely drop whatever they were doing to prepare. So, he would wait for now. He'd let the flower meadow queens finish their plans, and in the meantime, he would get a new option from the DP store and give the bees a chance to work with the new flowers. And then, once the flower meadow queens were settled and he had set up whatever the new option turned out to be, he'd think about tackling another expansion.

And so, Belissar made his choice, and then headed off to bed.

CHAPTER TWENTY-ONE

BEE SUPPORTIVE?

Belissar made his way over to the entrance after finishing his morning routine and helped Juosiutik experiment with her potions. She was having him generate mana honey, both for the sake of the recipe but also to help him learn to mix his mana into the potions.

Then, after the lessons concluded, Belissar began work on another beehouse for the apiary. With dry, construction-ready wood from the karnuq, it didn't take him long to finish.

Upgrade Apiary Beehive to Belissar's Beehouse?
Cost: 25 DP
DP: 2093

Metsaitti and his hunter group were still fighting remnants, but Belissar had already gotten some DP from the gathering group. He *did* want to conserve his DP for the store purchase, but twenty-five DP was fairly affordable. It was less than he was getting each day, in any case, and the bees were worth it.

The queen of the beehive in question was already at the entrance of her hive, watching as he put the final touches on the beehouse. Belissar glanced over at her.

"Ready?"

She danced her salute and Belissar confirmed the purchase. The beehouse and beehive both began to glow until the beehouse disappeared and the beehive molded into shape. The queen began a happy gratitude dance.

Then the apiary lit up as all the beehouses he had formerly built began to glow and reshape themselves, replacing the rough-cut wet wood with more precisely sawed and dry planks. Belissar grinned at that.

One down, five more to go, and then the two orchard queens, and he'd have housed every queen in the tower. Then he just had to wait for the challengers to get blessed. Juosiutik had already accomplished that, and he figured the other non-combatant karnuq were working on their offerings as well. He wondered though if there was anything he could do to help the fighting group.

He . . . wasn't sure. Would helping them fight help them get blessed? The God of Bees wanted something they did themselves for the blessing . . . so it might actually hurt if he helped them with the fight.

Belissar eventually shrugged. He didn't know what he didn't know. But some of the karnuq did seem to know a thing or two about towers. He figured he'd ask Metsaitti on the way out if there was anything he could do.

And so, Belissar returned to working on the beehouses, waiting for Metsaitti's group to finish up for the day.

Belissar waited by the entrance as Metsaitti's group made their way back. They seemed surprised to see him, but Metsaitti approached and lowered his head.

"Hello, Sacred Den Master. May we help you?"

Belissar shook his head.

"I'm, um, here to ask you the same thing. Is there anything I can do to help with the blessings?"

The young hunters' eyes widened and they glanced around at each other. Metsaitti paused for a moment before offering a small smile.

"Directly, no. A challenger must be judged on their own merits. Assistance is not forbidden but will delay their progress."

Belissar frowned at that, but Metsaitti continued.

"Indirectly, the greater the feats and achievements, the greater the reward. If we had your permission to explore deeper and face greater challenges, that would help. Additionally, if you could come up with challenges of your own, where we can earn some rewards from your tower, that would also assist."

Belissar crossed his arms. "I see. What sort of challenges and rewards?"

Metsaitti shrugged. "That is up to you. Every sacred den is different in that regard. Some require feats of strength or endurance, or use mazes and traps to test agility and speed. Others use puzzles to test wits, or prefer mystical tests. In some dens, challengers face their defenders directly."

Belissar immediately narrowed his eyes. "No hurting the bees."

Metsaitti raised his hands and shook his head. "It is only an example, and not all fights result in death. The point is that there is no one way to do it. I have observed that most sacred dens have challenges inspired by their patron god."

Belissar nodded. "I see. And the rewards?"

Metsaitti rubbed his chin. "Those, again, are as varied as the sacred dens and the challenges, but mostly consist of mana-infused objects. If I could make a suggestion, the mana flowers and mana honeycomb you possess wouldn't be out of place in any other sacred den's challenges."

Belissar hummed for a second. "I see. I'll, um, think about it."

Metsaitti smiled. "Thank you for considering us, Sacred Den Master. If you do decide to propose a challenge, we would be honored to face it."

Metsaitti turned around as the other hunters also inclined their heads, thanking Belissar. Belissar . . . still wasn't used to being thanked like that, so didn't say anything. The group prayed at the shrine of bees and then departed the tower shortly afterward.

Belissar rubbed his chin and hummed. So, challenges, huh? Mana flowers were a bit out of the bag at this point, given he had made a patch for the karnuq to gather from for free. But mana honeycomb, on the other hand?

Belissar began to nod. He did have more of that than he could ever use himself, and he'd only be receiving more as he gave the queens beehives and bee-houses. He could even make extra beehives, seeing as they could produce honey without occupants, and the queens could always raise more children to fill them later on.

Belissar didn't want the karnuq just taking the labor of his bees for free. But . . . if they had to face some sort of challenge to acquire the honeycomb? If they had to do at least something to earn it? That might be a different story, then.

Though, that meant Belissar needed to think of such a challenge. Mazes? Puzzles? Feats of strength? Belissar didn't have much idea of what any of that would look like.

He glanced up at the shrine of bees. Metsaitti *had* said something about being inspired by the patron god. So . . . something bee-related? What would be a good bee-related challenge?

Belissar ended up having a lot to think about that day.

Juosiutik was finishing up a brew back at the karnuq camp, and just cleaning up her tools when someone approached. Juosiutik started to scowl but her face softened when she saw who it was.

"Oh, it's you, Noigakkuq. How may I help you?"

A small karnuq woman, Noigakkuq, walked up to Juosiutik and started helping her clean her tools. She was one of the few people Juosiutik trusted to help her, or even approach her, while she was making potions. Noigakkuq worked silently for a bit before she replied.

"Do you have anything to help someone stay up?"

Juosiutik blinked. "Um, I do but . . . what exactly do you need it for, Noigakkuq?"

Noigakkuq shrugged. "To stay up."

Juosiutik frowned. "You aren't doing anything dangerous, are you?"

Noigakkuq turned and looked her right in the eyes. "Everything is dangerous for me, remember?"

Juosiutik eyed for a bit before sighing. She went into her tent and found her mother's potion, pouring a small portion into a water pouch. She then walked back outside and handed it to Noigakkuq.

"Here."

Noigakkuq took it and nodded. "Thanks."

The two worked in silence until Juosiutik was all packed up for the night. Juosiutik furrowed her brow as Noigakkuq turned to leave.

"Noigakkuq . . . just, be careful, alright?"

Noigakkuq did not respond as she walked off.

When the sun had set and night had fully arrived, Noigakkuq once again snuck out of the camp. The night was dark and the sentry watching the tunnel to the Underway was dozing off once more, so she was able to reach her destination without issue.

She took a deep breath and began. She took a sip of the potion Juosiutik had given her, then reached into her pouch to pull out a knife and a faintly glowing crystal. She channeled what little mana she possessed into it, causing it to glow much brighter and light up the dirt walls. Then she descended into the deep.

Last night, she had looked around but couldn't find anything. Try as she might to resist it, the fatigue had gotten to her. The shadows had blurred together, and she couldn't pick out any scents from the smell of dirt and roots all around her. Willpower could only do so much to make up for her body's weakness. And if there was anything her body possessed in abundance, it was weakness. The rest of the clan had made sure she was fully aware of that.

So, against her wishes, she had to approach Juosiutik and, fortunately, the other girl had delivered. Noigakkuq felt her body relax and her fatigue fade away. A surge of energy rushed through her and her senses sharpened. The blurred shadows now turned into rocks and roots. The blend of smells now separated out. She could smell a cave carrot here, a tree root over there. She could feel the humidity rise as she made her way down toward the underground river her clan had followed here.

And above all, she could smell the mana. Mana had a smell, at least as far as she was concerned. She was aware that mana didn't really interact with the senses like physical objects did . . . but the chief had told her that everyone interacted with mana differently. Some could see it, some could feel it, and she apparently could smell it. So, she'd learned to ignore the others who laughed at her "delusions" and followed her nose.

They learned to stop laughing so much when she found a cave full of glowing crystals. And that was why she, the runt of her generation, had not been abandoned on their dangerous journeys, despite being considered incapable of fighting. She had been just useful enough to be worth protecting.

But that had changed. There was a sacred den now full of all sorts of magical treasures . . . none of which required her nose to find. Oh, she had asked to be part of the group exploring its halls, but she had been denied. It was too dangerous, they had said. They claimed to need her elsewhere, they said, though she knew few of them believed that.

So now, she would take matters into her own hands. Before the clan could decide they had no further use for her. No reason to keep protecting and babying her, as they put it.

Noigakkuq sniffed the air, and then set off into the deep . . .

CHAPTER TWENTY-TWO

SNEAKY BEE-LIVERY

All hostiles defeated.
Purification successful.

Minor+ Purification completed!
Please select a reward:
- +75 DP
- +15 Max Mana
- Monster Bee Sprayer Resistance Boost (Minimal+)

The bees finished up the day's purification with ease. Belissar then considered the rewards. Normally he'd just default to more mana unless there was an especially enticing perk or feature, but at this point he already had enough mana for the next expansion purification. More mana *was* always helpful, and would help him get a head start on the expansion after the next one, but it also felt a bit . . . unnecessary.

So, he took a moment to consider the other options. Seventy-five DP would help him reach his DP shop goal sooner, but it was less than what the karnuq were giving him at this point, so was it really worth a full purification reward? On the other hand, a boost for his bees was always welcome. He wasn't entirely sure what the resistance boost did, so that was worth checking . . .

Resistance: Governs the entity's ability to resist magic, negative statuses,
and non-physical effects.

That was helpful. So, resistance was like defense, but for magic? Well, that decided it then.

Monster Bee Sprayer Resistance Boost (Minimal+) selected.
Monster Bee Sprayers receive a slight boost to Resistance!

So far, the most dangerous attacks for his bees were the magical ones. Well, he wasn't entirely sure about that, but he assumed that the bird-shade's lightning and the wolf-shade's mist were both some sort of magical attack. It was absolutely worth a reward choice to shore up his bees' defenses against such dangers.

And more generally, Belissar figured he'd focus on perks and features while he waited, unless he specifically needed more mana. It was a good opportunity to boost the strength of his bees in preparation for the fight to come.

With that settled, Belissar celebrated the bees' victory and then made his way back to the apiary farmhouse. Before doing anything else, he took one of the jars he had received from the karnuq and took it out to the pond, filling it partially. He then made his way back into the farmhouse and walked over to the big jars holding the extra honeycomb trays he had accumulated from the apiary bees' daily production. He poured the honey from one of the trays into the jar, then swirled it about to mix it up with the water.

Yes, it was time to get started on mead-making again. For now, he was keeping it basic with just mana honey and water. Since the honey was notably different from what he was used to, he wanted to get a baseline before he iterated on any of his previous recipes.

Once that was done, he thought a bit on possible challenges for the karnuq before heading off to bed.

Belissar awoke just before the break of dawn. He had not awoken naturally, but rather from a pressure upon his mind. It was the tower's mana flowing into him, waking him up. He quickly determined the cause: someone had entered the dungeon in the wee hours of the morning. His tower sight turned to the entrance . . .

A small karnuq crept into the tower. They were covered in dirt and mud and Belissar couldn't make out their features very well, but he could tell this wasn't a karnuq he knew. This karnuq was smaller than any he had ever seen so far, barely taller than him . . . possibly even the same height or less.

He narrowed his eyes. He had no idea what they were doing here at this time of day, and without any of their fellows. That set him on edge. Still, the karnuq hadn't done anything to harm him, the bees, or the tower thus far, so he only kept watch for now.

The karnuq held some sort of glowing crystal, which lit up their immediate surroundings. They crept around until they found the shrine of bees. Belissar frowned as the karnuq stepped over to the Shrine . . . and then opened the wax chest. They reached into a pouch tied to their waist and pulled something out, placing it inside. They stared up at the shrine of bees and said something that Belissar couldn't hear. The shrine of bees and the chest glowed lightly in response.

Challenger blessed.
Gained 10 DP.
Tribute received. Your patron grants you this portion:
- Ground Mana Flower x1

Belissar's eyes widened. He was no longer suspicious of the karnuq's intentions. Well, that wasn't necessarily true, as it was still incredibly suspicious that they were creeping around alone at night, but he at least no longer had to guess what they were doing in his tower. The God of Bees seemed to approve—and, to be honest, if they were bringing him *new mana flowers*, then he didn't particularly care what they were up to.

In the glowing light, Belissar could see the karnuq look down at their hands. They started to giggle, their laughter growing until they were full-on cackling. They spoke and this time, Belissar's tower senses worked. He heard a high-pitched, feminine voice. So, a girl, most likely? Perhaps a very young one, from the small size?

"We have a deal, then. Wait for me, sacred den and your god. Promise me your power, and there's more where that came from."

Belissar watched as the karnuq left, still giggling as she crept away. He then shrugged and got up. If she was secretly bringing him ground mana flowers . . . then he could only wish her luck!

The day was about to begin, and since he was fully rested thanks to the tower magic, Belissar decided to start his day early. He had spent a while thinking of different challenges he could make and, after sleeping on it, he thought he had an idea.

He took a tray of mana honeycomb and walked off toward the flower meadow. He soon arrived at his destination, off to the center of one of the side walls away from either entrance or the bee barracks. There, he placed the honeycomb down out in the open.

Then he then surrounded the honeycomb with pit traps.

Well, it was a simple idea, but bees flew to get their honey, right? So, if he surrounded some honey with pit traps, it would be hard for normal people to get it unless they could fly like bees, right?

. . . The idea had sounded better last night, before Belissar had actually implemented it. But he shrugged and left it there. He guessed he'd at least see if it worked as a "challenge" for the karnuq, and if not, he'd adjust it later.

He then paused and rubbed his chin. The challenge did give him an idea, though. His bee magic so far let him make honey like a bee and make wax like a bee. Presumably, it would let him do bee-ish things in general.

So . . . wouldn't it be possible to fly like a bee using his magic?

Belissar stirred up his mana and sent it out of his body, thinking about bee wings and buzzing about in the air. A honeycomb pattern of light began to form around his back . . . but it began to slow down before finishing even a single hexagon. Belissar grunted and groaned as the mana grew harder and harder to move.

Then, suddenly, he gasped and lurched forward. The mana suddenly stopped flowing out of his body completely. The light shuddered and then dispersed in a bright flash of light. He fell to the ground, his face covered in sweat and his head pounding.

"Ugh, okay, guess wings are too hard for now."

It seemed he wouldn't be joining the bees in the skies anytime soon. A moment later, Niobee came rushing over to him with medicinal bees in tow. And since the sun was only beginning to rise, Belissar decided to rest a moment before resuming his day . . .

Belissar spent the next day learning potions with Juosiutik, building another beehouse, and watching the next purification. He got a minimum+ Vitality boost for his soldier bees this time.

He went to bed but woke up before the sun rose again. He apparently could just . . . decide how long to sleep and the tower mana would wake him up. That was incredibly convenient. He then gathered together some healing herb mana honey and mad mana honey and turned his attention toward the tower entrance.

He thought about it and realized he could help the sneaky karnuq. She was giving him a treasure considered priceless by both the karnuq and his bees, so it would absolutely be appropriate to give her some mana honey in exchange, or so he thought. He wasn't sure what she was doing or where she was getting the flowers, but he figured healing herb honey would always be valuable for its medicinal properties. The mad mana honey, on the other hand, could help if she was doing something dangerous. She'd said something about power, and the mad mana honey was just about the strongest weapon he had that he could share, in any case.

So, he made his way to the flower meadow and then waited. And waited. And waited . . .

Eventually the sun rose and Belissar frowned. He guessed she wasn't coming tonight, then? Belissar shrugged and took the honeycomb back. The flowers were supposed to be rare, after all, so maybe it would take her a bit to find another. He would just have to wait until the next time she came by, then . . .

THE NEW-BEES

The Firstborn crawled through her section of the fortress. The flower meadow queens had finished moving their hives a while ago and were now fully settled in. Everywhere the Firstborn looked, worker bees from many hives crawled, hovered, and buzzed about with their countless tasks. Foragers brought in new nectar, medicinal bees tended the brood, and she even saw a group of scouts dancing with the Fourth of the Seventh's workers, passing on their knowledge of the Beyond.

And, of course, workers beat their wings across trays full of honey of different types. The slightly golden glow of mana honey, the bluish-green tone of healing herb honey, the purple of the mad honey, and a few more. There was a small section devoted to the red honey from the flame radishes, though since that honey seemed to generate its own heat, they could only keep a small amount of it. Otherwise it could grow dangerously hot, threaten to melt its wax containers, or worse.

Honeys from the newest flowers were currently mixed together. The flower meadow queens were aware that not every flower type could raise a unique type of bee. They were also aware that the apiary queens would certainly experiment with and categorize each of the new flowers to determine which ones could. So, they decided to wait, and focus on maximum honey production instead. They were the hive of hives; honey was the apiary's specialty, battle was theirs.

Besides, right now, they needed all the extra nutrition they could get.

The Firstborn greeted the Second Queen of the First Spawner's Second Dynasty as they both crawled over the top of their trays before she moved down to her destination. In the center of one of the trays was a particularly large cell, currently covered in wax, as well as countless smaller ones. The wax cover on the biggest one was just starting to split. The Firstborn watched as two mandibles pierced through and the medicinal workers got to work. They helped pull apart the wax cover so the cell's occupant could crawl out.

The Firstborn's First Daughter, a princess ready for her mating flight, was now fully grown. The workers poured over her as soon as she crawled out of the cell, helping to clean her off as she beat and dried her wings. Once she was clean, the Firstborn approached her. The princess turned to face her and then began a salute, indicating she was ready to go.

But the Firstborn had other ideas. She gently brushed the young queen's antennas with her own before stepping back and beginning her dance.

"Go, wait for drones. Then, return here."

Her daughter looked up to her before beginning a slow and unsteady dance.

"Return?"

The Firstborn confirmed and then danced for the new princess to follow her. The two climbed up to the top of the frame. The princess began looking around every which way as the full barracks now spread out before her. She flinched and backed away as a worker with a different mana signature flew past, but the Firstborn touched antennas once more.

"We build a hive of hives, as King demonstrated. Many queens work together, many hives work as one. You also return and join hive of hives. Have space, will help you set up. No need to do it alone."

The new princess still swayed about, recoiling a bit every time another hive's workers flew past her, but she still saluted.

"As queen mother commands. Will return."

The Firstborn brushed her daughter's antennas once more and then stepped away. Two of her workers then landed nearby and stood on either side of the young princess. The young one turned to face her mother again, who simply danced a confirmation. The young princess thanked her mother and then began to fly, with the two workers escorting her. She was followed by the princesses from the other queens. A moment later, the drones began to hatch as well.

After half an hour, the Firstborn's daughter returned, now a queen ready to build a hive.

"Queen mother, have returned."

The Firstborn came out to greet her and danced for her to follow. She led the new queen into her frames, where a new nursery had been prepared. A couple of medicinal workers were crawling over it, checking the wax cells for hygiene.

"Can start laying brood here. My workers will tend, bring honey, so don't worry and lay as many as you can."

The Firstborn's daughter stood completely still before slowly, ever so slowly starting to dance.

"Is that . . . alright? Share wax, honey, and workers?"

The Firstborn immediately danced her confirmation.

"We hive of hives, remember? All help each other. I help now, you help later, okay?"

Her daughter still swayed a bit but managed to dance her salute.

"As queen mother commands."

The young queen stepped forward toward one of the cells, finding it full of honey already. She went ahead and laid one of her eggs. The medicinal workers then crawled over and began to check the egg with their mana. The young queen watched them for a bit before shaking herself and starting to lay more. The Firstborn walked over, brushed her antennas one more time.

"Will find you later, okay?"

After her daughter confirmed, the Firstborn set off to resume her own work.

Later that day, the Firstborn came back to her daughter's tray. A good number of the cells now held eggs. Her daughter was currently resting and replenishing her mana with the honey provided to her. She got up when she saw her mother and started to salute, but the Firstborn began dancing first.

"Come with me, something you must see."

The Firstborn led her daughter up to the top of the hive. There, they found all the other flower meadow queens, each leading her own daughter as well. The Firstborn's daughter glanced around at them until a loud buzzing drew her attention.

Soldier bees flew through the upper entrances and landed before each of the young queens.

"Get on."

At the Firstborn's command, her daughter crawled on the back of the larger soldier. The Firstborn then took off with her soldier following along. All the queens thus made their way across the flower meadow toward the room's entrance. Her daughter stared at the sight before her.

"What . . . is this?"

"The army."

The young queens all froze as they saw the massive numbers of soldier bees flying through the air. And then, they began to shiver.

"Queen mother . . . there's something . . ."

The Firstborn confirmed.

"Yes, the invader approaches. Watch closely."

Her daughter backed up a bit on the soldier carrying her but looked toward the direction the Firstborn indicated.

There, at the entrance of the room, two wolf-shades appeared. The young princess recoiled and began to beat her wings, instinctually wanting to flee. But the Firstborn remained still and had commanded her to watch, so she remained.

The Firstborn's daughter ceased all movement as she watched the soldier bee army set upon the shades and eliminate them in minutes, without the loss of a single bee. The Firstborn flew in front of her.

"This is hive of hives, this is our duty."

Her daughter danced her acknowledgement in a bit of a daze.

After that, the flower meadow queens gathered and introduced one other to their daughters. And so, a new generation was inducted into the hive of hives.

The Fourth of the Seventh, her lead worker, and the First of the Fifth's First Daughter stood at the entrance of their joint hive. In front of them were thirty-two workers arranged into eight squads of four. The lead worker began her dance.

"One squad in each direction. Preliminary scouting, only check flowers if in abundance or if possess mana. One scout memorize terrain, other three watch for danger. Turn back when sun begins to fall. Understand?"

The worker bees all danced their salutes. The lead worker saluted as well and then turned to face the queens. The First of the Fifth's daughter turned to the Fourth of the Seventh, so the Fourth of the Seventh started to dance.

"Go! See the Beyond!"

And with that, the workers began to beat their wings and flew away from the hive. As they left, the Fourth of the Seventh turned to both her lead worker and the First of the Fifth's First Daughter.

"Thank you both! Couldn't have done without you!"

The First of the Fifth's First Daughter immediately started a rapid dance.

"Of course! Will always help Fourth of Seventh, with anything!"

The lead worker paused for a moment. She . . . could not bring herself to state she would help with *anything*, knowing what her queen truly wanted. And that killed her, given an *unrelated queen* was offering to do just that. Her loyalty and her instincts warred with one another as she tried to determine what she would dance.

"As queen commands."

She settled on that, for it was true. If the queen commanded her, she would follow through, whatever it was. Previously, her instincts might have prevented her from following a command that might doom the hive . . . but with the First of the Fifth's First Daughter's cooperation, their hive would now always have a queen present, so there was far more leeway. So now, she could follow her queen with no reservations.

Besides, in the end, she trusted her queen. She knew the queen would not harm the hive. And her trust was proven as the Fourth of the Seventh danced happily.

"Thanks! We work now?"

The worker and the other queen saluted, and then all three returned to their hive.

As for the scout group, after leaving the hive they beelined straight for the flower meadow, and then flew straight toward the tower's entrance. Soon, they passed into the unknown.

They paused for but a moment as they saw the world beyond the King's domain for the very first time. The sun beat down, flowers spread out before them, and trees rose in the distance.

But this was an area the flower meadow hives had already scouted, so the workers quickly set to their task. As they had arranged, each squad of scouts flew off in different, evenly spaced directions, using both the sun and their ability to sense the tiny-lightnings all around them to stay on course. They flew out above the ground, racing forward until they reached the limits of the flower meadow's scout reports, just past the ruins in one direction and the karnuq hunters' camp in the other.

And once there, they slowed down. A more thorough search began, with one bee making note of the terrain while the others kept an eye out for anything unexpected.

And so, the bees resumed scouting the Beyond . . .

CHAPTER TWENTY-THREE

APPRO-BEE-ATING THE HONEY

Two more days came and went. From the purifications, Belissar received a minimum+ strength boost for his soldiers, as well as hidden wax cells. He didn't particularly have use for them yet but figured he would take them just in case.

Additionally, there were some developments among his bees. The flower meadow queens had successfully reproduced, introducing a new generation of queens to the bee barracks. The young queens would need time before they could contribute any soldiers, but Belissar was already noticing more and more workers in the flower meadow, so it seemed to be going well.

Additionally, some of the apiary queens had been waiting for him when he visited this morning. He found some new honey types when he gathered the trays for the day.

Sleepy Mana Honeycomb Tray

A tray of honeycomb containing Sleepy Mana Honey. Made by monster bees with the nectar of flowers with sedative properties, this honey has relaxing and, in high dosages, sedative effects.

Gelatinous Mana Honeycomb Tray

A tray of honeycomb containing Gelatinous Mana Honey. Made by monster bees with the nectar of flowers with gelatinous properties, this honey is thicker and retains a semi-solid state unless disturbed.

Antidote Mana Honeycomb Tray

A tray of honeycomb containing Antidote Mana Honey. Made by monster bees with the nectar of flowers with restorative properties, this honey can counteract the effects of numerous toxins, including weak mana-based ones.

The bees had successfully made a new honey type from each of the three new herbs Juosiutik had given him, which he had somewhat anticipated. However, there was an additional type that he did not expect to find.

Antifreeze Mana Honeycomb Tray

A tray of honeycomb containing Antifreeze Mana Honey. Made by monster bees with the nectar of flowers from cold climates, this honey maintains its temperature well, and helps the bees that ingest it to do so also.

Apparently, the cloudberries and sweetvetch plants contained some special properties of their own. Which was quite the happy surprise for Belissar. He offered the first trays of each new type to the shrine of bees, then figured he would bring some to Juosiutik in the future. And, if the past was anything to go on, there would soon be some new bee types based on these honeys. He was excited to see them.

It did make him wonder about something, however. He had already seen burning worker bees . . . but had not received a tray with any sort of burning honey. He took a look inside the hives with his tower sight until he found one with burning workers and saw a small patch of red honey. If he had to guess, it seemed like the bees were only making a small amount of honey from the flame radishes, just enough to raise some workers on it, but definitely not enough to fill an entire tray. Belissar then remembered the description of the burning worker bees. Particularly, the part about how their fireproof wax was necessary to store their honey. The hive in question was not, in fact, made of fireproof wax. So, it was likely the case the bees were being careful with the honey in question.

He shrugged. He guessed he'd have to wait for the burning workers to build some fireproof comb first, but that was fine. In any case, his bees were growing well, he was about halfway done making beehouses for the rest of the apiary queens, and the new flowers were coming into play. The one thing that wasn't going as well was the small karnuq's secret deliveries. Belissar had woken up early each day to try and meet her, but she hadn't appeared yet.

He was currently standing by the shrine of bees in the dark hours of the early morning. At this point, he was wondering whether it was worth waking up each day to wait for her. Still, it didn't seem to be negatively impacting him physically. He didn't really feel any more tired than normal. Tower magic sure was convenient.

And, tonight, his diligence was rewarded. The gates of the tower slowly opened and in came the karnuq, covered in dirt and carrying her glowing stone. She froze as she saw Belissar standing by the Shrine.

". . . Sacred Den Master."

Belissar raised his hand and waved. "Ah, yeah, that's me. Hi there."

The karnuq did not respond. They both stood there in silence for a bit until the karnuq gulped. "Um, can I help you?"

Belissar flushed a bit. "Oh, sorry. No, um, you're already helping me. So, I figured I'd help you."

The karnuq narrowed her eyes and took a step back. "Help . . . me? What do you mean?"

Belissar held out two trays of honey. "Here. The top one is healing herb mana honey, which will help if you get wounded. The bottom is mad mana honey. It's, um, a bit poisonous. It causes intoxication . . . and supposedly paralysis if you eat too much?"

The karnuq frowned and did not move, leaving Belissar holding out the trays. He was about to apologize and take them back when she finally spoke.

". . . Why are you giving this to me?"

Belissar tilted his head. "Um, because you gave Ground mana flowers to me?"

The karnuq's eyes widened. "So . . . it's because I did something for you? You're giving this to me because of what I did? And you, uh, don't mind what I'm doing here?"

"Um, yes? Or, I mean, you're bringing flowers for the shrine, right? I definitely don't mind that."

The karnuq relaxed a bit, stepping forward to take hold of the trays and inclined her head. "Thank you, Sacred Den Master."

She took out her bag and found some empty pouches inside. She broke the trays into smaller pieces, stacked them up, and placed them inside the pouches before storing them all in her bag. She then turned to Belissar.

"If you don't mind . . . can I pray to your patron now?"

Belissar nodded. "Oh, yes. That was all I wanted to talk to you about, anyway."

The karnuq nodded before hunching down. "I see. Thanks, then . . . um, would you mind keeping my visit to yourself?"

Belissar tilted his head. "Um, sure? Unless . . . you aren't stealing these from Chief Rohsuak or something, right?"

The karnuq quickly shook her head. "No, of course not! I found these myself!"

Belissar shrugged. "Well then, sure. I don't see why not?"

The karnuq visibly relaxed and let out a sigh. "Thank you, Sacred Den Master."

With that, she turned to the shrine of bees and placed another flower in the chest, praying in words Belissar couldn't hear.

Challenger blessed.
Gained 10 DP.
Tribute received. Your patron grants you this portion:
- Ground Mana Flower x1

The karnuq then sighed. "Not enough, yet, huh? In that case . . ."

She rose to her feet. She turned and faced Belissar again, this time standing straight and looking him in the eyes. He nearly took a step back from the intensity of her gaze.

"I'll be back again, once I find another."

Belissar took a second to respond, but then began to smile. "I look forward to it."

The karnuq's eyes widened. She stood there blinking for a bit before she smiled ever so slightly, nodded to him, and then took her leave.

Belissar, did, in fact, look forward to her return. Combined with the ones offered by the other karnuq earlier, he was now at four of the needed five Ground mana flower samples. One more, and he might have a new mana flower for his bees.

With the small karnuq gone, Belissar returned to the apiary to get a bit more sleep before the sun rose.

Metsaitti's group was exploring the flower meadow once again. Another shade appeared and this time Metsaitti said nothing, stepping back to let his hunters test their strength. The two spear wielders charged forward while the archers drew their bows. The archers released with perfect timing, such that the arrows landed just as the shade was about to move. The shade yelped, distracted as the other two karnuq lunged forward. One spear stabbed through its torso while the other struck its head, and then the shade vanished. Metsaitti nodded as he watched.

Three of the hunters turned to each other and grinned, but one of the archers had his eyes fixed forward.

"Hey, does anyone else see that?"

The other karnuq turned to look. The spearwoman gasped. "Is that . . . ?"

The other spear wielder, Tyhgak, smiled. "That's the mana honey, right?"

A large piece of honeycomb was just lying there on the grass, without a monster bee in sight. Metsaitti nodded but said little else. Tyhgak happily stepped forward before skidding to a halt.

"Wait just a minute . . ."

He began poking the ground ahead of him with his spear while slowly creeping forward. Suddenly, his spear poked right through the ground . . . which vanished to reveal a pit trap. Metsaitti allowed a slight smile. The boy was learning after all. As was the sacred den master.

Tyhgak and the other spearwoman nodded at each other and both began circling the pit trap in either direction. As soon as they reached the end of the pit trap, they found another trap on either side. And then another pair. The honeycomb was completely surrounded by pit traps, such that there was no way to reach it on foot. Metsaitti chuckled.

"It looks like we found our first challenge from the sacred den master."

Tyhgak frowned. "How are we supposed to get it, then?"

Metsaitti shrugged. "That's what you're supposed to figure out."

Tyhgak rubbed his chin, then suddenly smiled and turned to Metsaitti. "Can't you just jump over the pits?"

Metsaitti shrugged again. "I can, if you don't want any of the honey, that is."

Tyhgak frowned again. He opened his mouth, then closed it. He and the other karnuq grouped up and Tyhgak turned to the spearwoman.

"Can you make the jump?"

She just stared at him. "No, no I can't."

"What if we give you a boost?"

She sighed. "How am I supposed to get back afterward?"

Tyhgak frowned again. "Oh, right. Um, what if you take a rope with you?"

She rolled her eyes. "Did you bring any rope?"

"Um, no?"

She sighed again. "Did anyone?"

The archers shook their heads. Metsaitti couldn't help but chuckle as he listened in. He remembered his first sacred den challenge. These kids didn't know how easy they had it. This sacred den master was far less violent and cruel than some others he had known.

In the end though, the group concluded they didn't have the necessary tools. They hung their heads as they turned away from the honeycomb. Metsaitti raised an eyebrow.

"Giving up?"

The spearwoman sighed. "What other choice do we have?"

Metsaitti shrugged as the group hung their heads. Then he ran toward the pits and leapt across, just making it to the other side. He opened his bag, took out an empty pouch of sufficient size, then wrapped up and stored the honeycomb. He then leapt back over. The young hunters were staring at him. Tyhgak began to smile.

"Metsaitti . . ."

Metsaitti gave him a grin. "Oh, this is for me. You'll have to get your own."

The hunters all groaned. "Come on, that's not fair!"

Metsaitti dropped his grin. "And that's the lesson. You need to be prepared to encounter the unexpected. If you are not ready to take advantage of an opportunity, you will lose it. And if you are not ready to handle a threat . . ."

Metsaitti let them finish the sentence as he walked off. He nearly stopped as he licked a bit of the honey off his finger.

He decided he was all too pleased to teach the next generation this important lesson.

BEAR-Y SCARY TUNNELS

Noigakkuq once again arrived at the Underway. Three nights had passed since meeting the sacred den master, but she'd had no further luck in finding another Ground mana flower. The first two had been easy to find, located right around the immediate vicinity of the entrance to the surface. But she knew from experience that she was unlikely to find any more unless she ventured out further. This had been borne out last night when she combed the area and couldn't detect even the slightest whiff of concentrated Ground mana.

So, tonight, she intended to head deeper. She made her final preparations just inside the mouth of the tunnel. She took a bite of the healing herb mana honey and a swig of Juosiutik's potion, then took out her light crystal. She would need to be fully alert if she wanted to make it back in one piece . . . or at all.

Noigakkuq then walked through the dirt tunnel until she arrived at the underground river. Here, the dirt gave way to stone, the river carving its way down into the roots of the world. Mushrooms and cave plants grew along its banks, and she could catch a glimpse of the occasional fish in the river itself. Such were the means by which the karnuq had sustained themselves on their travels through the deep. And if there was enough food and water here to sustain the karnuq, there was enough to sustain other creatures as well. Noigakkuq would need to be extra cautious.

She put away her light crystal and waited for her eyes to adjust. A group of karnuq could afford to use such things, but since she was alone it would only make her a target. Fortunately, the river was not entirely devoid of light. Small flashes of bioluminescence sparkled in the dark as insects, fungi, plants, and fish made their presence known. Tiny sparks of mana spoke to minuscule battles being raged all through the dark as well. It was not enough to see much of anything, but with a karnuq's vision Noigakkuq could at least watch her step. She would then trust in her nose to find anything else she needed to know about.

And so, she crept ahead into the dark, sticking close to the wall to avoid falling into the river should she trip. Down, down the riverbed she went until, finally, the wall started to curve away from the river, opening up into a much, much wider area. The river she had been following extended into the dark, and she could hear the much larger one it fed into. The tunnel expanded to tower high into the air, the ceiling far higher than even several karnuq stacked on top of each other. Stalagmites, stalactites, and pillars wider than a karnuq was tall filled the area. Patches of moss created little floating lights while glowing mushrooms clung to the walls and pillars.

She had arrived in the Underway, the true Underway, a series of massive tunnels that crisscrossed underneath the surface of the world. They dove deep enough that the Hunger had not yet overtaken them all, allowing for a degree of travel underneath the corrupted surface.

Sometimes. Even down here, there were signs that the Hunger was seeping into the ground. More than once the karnuq had needed to change course because they found signs of corruption along their original route. More and more of the tunnels they knew had become inaccessible over the years, some very rapidly. And it was not unheard of to encounter shades in the deep. Noigakkuq would just have to hope that she wouldn't meet one tonight.

And so, she began to travel down the Underway, sticking close to the pillars and stalagmites. Few predators down here relied solely on sight, but it was still wise to stick to cover. She continuously sniffed the air, trying to work out the scents of different manas she could smell. Searching for the concentrated Ground mana . . . while hoping to detect anything she didn't want to find before it found her.

She stopped and slowly crouched against a pillar. She caught a cool and acrid scent that was tinged with hints of Dark mana. A scent she had been trained to keep an eye out for, as her skill in that regard had saved a hunter more than once. The scent of a cave panther. A dangerous foe even for a veteran hunter. A death sentence for Noigakkuq, should it set its sights on her while she was alone.

She sat completely still, not making a single sound or vibration. She had taken steps before this trip to eliminate her own scent as well, so, hopefully, the cave panther wouldn't be able to detect her. She stayed there for what felt like an eternity, breathing as softly as she could.

But then, finally, the scent started to recede. The cave panther was moving away. She remained still for a while longer, until she was absolutely sure she could detect no trace of the scent. Then, she slowly began to creep forward, hugging the wall of the tunnel. By all wisdom, she should have turned back now.

But Noigakkuq would not. By all wisdom, she shouldn't be here at all. She was small. She was weak. She couldn't fight. She couldn't survive on her own.

Until she started to sniff mana, she'd been nothing but a drain on the clan. She had heard the conversations between the adults when their supplies ran low.

She was sick and tired of it. And now, now she had the opportunity to gain some power of her own. To ensure that she could survive, that she could decide her own fate. That she would not be left at the mercy of those who thought of her as a burden.

And to do that, she would have to brave the dark, and all the dangers it held. She would have to defy wisdom and do what even a veteran hunter would not. So, she pressed on.

And then, finally, she caught a whiff of Ground mana, the combination of earthy and metallic scents that had already existed all around her but was now concentrated such that it no longer faded into the background of other scents. She nearly broke out into a run, but she caught herself. She forced herself to continue creeping, sniffing rapidly to search for any scents other than the Ground mana. But she found nothing, so she continued her slow advance.

She found a small tunnel in the wall she was following and cautiously made her way inside. The tunnel was only a bit taller than the average karnuq and began to turn from stone to dirt as she inched forward. Even smaller tunnels veered off to the sides, setting her on edge, but the scent continued down the main one, so on she went.

And then, finally, she found it. She was overwhelmed by the scent of Ground mana as she stepped into a small cave at the end of the tunnel. There, sitting in a patch of dirt, was a Ground mana flower. Its petals were as brown as its stem and glowed with a faint, brown light. The mana sat heavy on her, pushing her down toward the ground but surrounding her with warmth, making her want to roll into the dirt. She couldn't help but grin as she walked over to the flower and crouched down. She gently dug into the soil and then gathered the flower up, roots and all. She grinned and laughed a bit as she held the flower in her hands, before placing it into her bag.

Now, she could finally—

But before she could finish her thought, the ground exploded. Something heavy struck her back, and she heard loud snarling.

Noigakkuq fell to the ground, reaching for the knife at her side. She swung wildly, having no idea what she was even swinging at. But she managed to strike *something* as she heard a yelp, and then whatever it was backed off her. She quickly clambered away and scrambled to her feet, facing her assailant. She frowned and narrowed her eyes.

A wolf-mole shook its head, pawing at the scratch on its face Noigakkuq's wild swings had inflicted. It was a low, heavy creature with the massive claws of a mole and a long, snarling snout filled with teeth. And, worst of all, it smelt heavily of

Ground mana, its scent having been masked by the Ground mana flower she had found. That was why she hadn't any idea it was here.

And now, it was standing between her and the only exit. Noigakkuq had no illusions as to what would happen next. Her little knife could annoy the creature, but there was no chance she could kill it. Now that it was on guard, there was little chance she could get her weapon past its battering claws or snapping jaws. Her only hope was to escape, but the predator filled the tunnel's width. The wolf-mole watched her knife warily, but it made no move to retreat. It would not give her the chance to leave.

She was trapped. She gritted her teeth.

But then, she had a thought. She slowly reached into her bag with her free hand, keeping her eyes and her knife in the direction of the wolf-mole, and reached around until she found what she was looking for. She pulled out a small package wrapped in cloth and then tossed it at the wolf-mole. The wolf-mole scurried back to avoid the package, which landed on the ground. It then started to sniff . . .

The moment it did, it paused, and then crawled to the package, now sniffing it heavily. It pawed at it with a set of claws, scraping off some of the cloth. Noigakkuq smelled the air and smiled. Fortunately, she had grabbed the right one.

"Go ahead, monster. Eat your fill."

The wolf-mole did just that, gobbling up the piece of honeycomb she had broken off and packaged, scarfing down the mana-rich food with gusto. Unfortunately, that did not sate its hunger, and it turned to Noigakkuq once more. It growled and slowly crawled forward. Noigakkuq backed up until she hit the wall.

And then the wolf-mole paused again. It suddenly began to whine and paw at its nose. Its eyes twitched every which way, and then it shuddered. Then, it plopped down on the ground and made no further movements, though its eyes continued glancing around.

Noigakkuq took a deep breath. It was now or never.

Then she ran straight at the monster. It made no move to attack her. She leapt over it, onto its back, and still it did not respond. It couldn't.

And so, she slid off its back and then ran down the tunnel as fast as she could.

A BEAR-Y SATISFYING DAY

The moment Noigakkuq stepped out into the Underway proper, she was assaulted by a heavy, acrid scent. Her breath caught in her throat as two glowing eyes lit up the pitch-black tunnel, and then a dark shape pounced right toward her. She didn't even have time to scream.

Then, just before her end arrived, something shot past her face. She heard metal stab into flesh and the roar of a cave panther before someone grabbed her hand.

"Come on!"

She was pulled away into a run before she could process what was happening. They passed by a glowing mushroom, which gave her a glimpse of the figure pulling on her arm.

"Metsaitti?!" she asked incredulously, searching his face for an explanation.

He just shook his head. "Later!"

Noigakkuq swallowed her words and focused on running. Once she did, Metsaitti let go of her arm and fell back behind her, holding his spear at the ready as they retreated up the Underway. Ultimately, though, the two made it back to the smaller river tunnel without issue. They kept on in silence until they were back above ground. Noigakkuq bent over, resting her hands on her knees while she panted for breath. When she had finally recovered enough to speak . . .

"Why . . . are you here?"

Metsaitti raised an eyebrow as he gave her a knowing smile. "That's what I should ask you. As for myself . . . I've been tailing you since the first night."

Noigakkuq's jaw dropped and Metsaitti chuckled. "You're good at sneaking, Noigakkuq, but did you really think we'd leave the entrance to the Underway *that* unguarded?"

Noigakkuq frowned. Metsaitti sighed, then walked over and patted her on the shoulder. "I know the others can be dumb at times. But your contributions have not gone unnoticed. I'd hate to lose you."

Noigakkuq furrowed her brow. "Then why let me go? And why not let me come with you to the sacred den?"

Metsaitti sighed again. "I already told you, didn't I? We needed you by the camp until we scouted the area."

Noigakkuq crossed her arms. "That's just an excuse, isn't it?"

Metsaitti frowned. "It was not. To be honest . . . if I had the choice, I would have stopped you. Your ability to sniff mana is crucial to keeping the camp safe while we don't fully know the area. But the chief insisted we give you this chance, since you were not willing to wait."

Noigakkuq froze. ". . . The chief did?"

Metsaitti gave a small grin. "She did. I guess the Blazing Berserker knows a thing or two about sneaking out into danger." He then chuckled and shook his head. "I didn't expect you to go that deep, however. So, answer me this, did you find what you were looking for?"

Noigakkuq was silent, but slowly nodded as Metsaitti stared at her. Once she did, he nodded back. "Good. I hope that's enough, then, but if you must go that deep again, you need to take hunters with you, understand?"

Noigakkuq frowned but did not object. Metsaitti sighed and then turned toward the camp. "In that case, let's get some sleep. You can come with us to the sacred den tomorrow to offer up whatever it is you found."

Noigakkuq stood still, staring at Metsaitti. Metsaitti noticed she wasn't following and turned to her. "Is something the matter?"

"You're . . . letting me keep it?"

Metsaitti nodded. "Whatever it is, you found it. As far as I'm concerned, it's yours. Now, if you don't mind, I'd like to get some sleep."

With that, he left. Noigakkuq stared at the place where he had stood for a moment longer before clutching her bag tightly and following after him. She knew that Chief Rohsuak respected her, even if the others didn't, but she was the chief. She couldn't spend much time on any one karnuq, nor favor one over the others. But to find out she was valued to the extent that Metsaitti would come after her . . .

She shook her head. In any case, she had what she needed, though this was apparently the last one she would acquire with her own power. She could only hope it would be enough.

The next morning, as Metsaitti's hunters and the gathering team were preparing to head to the sacred den, Noigakkuq joined them. Tyhgak's eyes widened when he saw her, and then he averted his gaze.

"Um, why is she here?"

Noigakkuq narrowed her eyes at him. "And what is that supposed to mean?"

Tyhgak gulped. "Um, n-nothing, it's just . . ."

The spearwoman sighed and elbowed him in the gut. "Tyhgak, shut up."

Tyhgak decided to listen but kept stealing glances at Noigakkuq, who did her best to ignore everyone around her. She walked over to Juosiutik instead. Juosiutik tilted her head.

"Noigakkuq? I thought you normally stayed with the camp. Are you going to come help with the gathering?"

Noigakkuq shook her head. "You'll see."

Juosiutik raised an eyebrow at that but said no more. The group then made their way to the sacred den. Most of the karnuq began their daily gathering, but Noigakkuq separated from them and made her way to the shrine of bees. Ignoring the gazes of Juosiutik and Metsaitti's hunters on her back, she took the Ground mana flower from her bag and placed it inside the chest, without letting anyone else see.

"Please . . . I've done as you asked," Juosiuitik murmured, looking up at the shrine of bees. "Please give me your power . . ."

As she spoke the words, the shrine of bees began to glow far brighter than Noigakkuq had ever seen before. She could vaguely hear the other karnuq gasping behind her, but she wasn't paying attention to them. As the light died down, her eyes went wide.

The God of Bees offers her full blessing. If you wish to accept,
please select one of the following blessings:
- Blessing of the Forager
- Blessing of the Scout
- Blessing of the Geomancer
- Blessing of the Bee-ssassin

She stood there completely still, just staring at the words for a moment. Then she began to grin. Then she began to laugh. Soon she was full-on cackling. She turned around to face the rest of her people. All the karnuq were staring at her with eyes opened wide. Tyhgak was glancing around every which way.

"What . . . is this? What's going on? What happened to her?"

Metsaitti just gave a small smile and nodded at her. Juosiutik, on the other hand, came up to her happily.

"Congratulations, Noigakkuq! Or should I say, champion?"

Noigakkuq grinned back. "Yes, yes you should."

Tyhgak jumped at that. "Wait . . . seriously? Noigakkuq got a . . . seriously?!"

Noigakkuq turned and narrowed her eyes, though the grin was still on her face. "Better step it up, all of you. You're falling behind *me* now."

Tyhgak's jaw dropped at that. But the surprises weren't over yet. All the kar-nuq turned as they heard the sounds of buzzing soldier bees and saw the sacred den master approach with his army. He walked up to Noigakkuq, holding two trays of honeycomb in his hands.

"Looks like you got a blessing. Um, congratulations?"

She flashed her grin at him. "Thank you, Sacred Den Master. Is that . . . ?"

The sacred den master nodded and handed the trays over to her. "Thanks again. And it looks like I have enough to make those flowers now. They're, um, a bit expensive, so I can't make one for you here, but I can share some with you, if that works?"

Noigakkuq blinked and then grinned again. "Yes, that will be fine."

The sacred den master nodded and then turned to Juosiutik. "I'll wait until the gathering's done, then?"

"O-Okay."

Tyhgak then exclaimed, "Just what is going on?!"

Noigakkuq was all smiles as the gathering team walked back to the camp. Everyone kept staring at her whenever they thought she wasn't looking, but for once, she didn't mind. In fact, she basked in the attention. After all, the second champion in the clan was not one of the hunters, nor one of the craftsmen. It was she, the little runt who was good for nothing but her nose. Not only that, but now everyone was wondering what sort of relationship she had with the sacred den master . . . and what exactly he was planning to give her later. In a single morning, she had gone from the most expendable member of the clan to one of the greatest.

And, best of all, she now had the power to ensure that would remain the case. She grinned as she stirred up her mana, just enjoying the feeling of it flowing through her body. Now, no one would ever look down on her. Now, they'd regret begrudging her presence.

When the camp came into view, she saw Chief Rohsuak waiting there, motioning to her. She separated from the group and walked over to the chief with a grin. Chief Rohsuak smiled warmly at her.

"I take it we have a new champion?"

Noigakkuq's grin grew. "We do."

Chief Rohsuak reached out and patted her shoulder. "Congratulations, and well done. We'll have to arrange a celebration tonight, then."

Noigakkuq couldn't help but giggle. She couldn't wait to rub it in everyone's faces . . .

But then she felt the chief's grip on her shoulder tighten.

"However, you are aware how dangerous and reckless your actions were, correct? Going into the Underway alone, much less when you have not been trained as a warrior. And are you aware of what sort of consequences it would have had for yourself and the clan had you failed? I've told you before the important role you play, have I not?"

Noigakkuq's smile faded. "R-Right . . . I'm sorry."

The chief was still smiling, but for some reason Noigakkuq did not feel reassured.

"There's no need to apologize. It was our failure not to train you. But now that you are one of our champions, that is a task of the utmost importance. I will personally ensure you will be fully prepared before the next time you leave the camp."

It was strange. Personal training by Chief Rohsuak, presumably in the art of combat, was exactly what Noigakkuq had wanted for most of her life. And yet, now that it was finally happening, she could not help but feel a chill go down her spine.

FOR THE LOVE OF BEES

The karnuq were making a bit of commotion around the small one after she prayed at the shrine of bees and Belissar gave her more honey, but he ignored them. He was busy reviewing all the latest messages.

A challenger has been fully blessed.
Gained 20 DP.

A challenger has selected a blessing unique to your patron.
Gained additional 10 DP.

Tribute received. Your patron grants you this portion:
- Ground Mana Flower x1
Ground Mana Flower absorbed.

Sufficient samples gathered. Ground Mana Flower now available.
*Current applications: Flower Meadow, Apiary, *Orchard.*

(=Resource Node only)*

Belissar couldn't help but grin, and even laugh a bit. Another challenger had been fully blessed, granting him a nice haul of DP as well as progress on that particular mission. But all that paled in comparison to the treasure said challenger had brought him in the process. Mana flowers were his bees' favorite, and now he had a new type. Better yet, the message specifically mentioned Ground mana, the same type featured in the digger bee descriptions. Maybe, with this, he wouldn't have to pick that option in the future, for his bees might come up with a similar bee type all on their own.

Belissar immediately went to add a few . . .

Available Resource Plants for Flower Meadow:
-Ground Mana Flower (10 per node, 20 due to unsuitable environment.)

He went completely still, just staring in silence at the message for a while. Then he checked the apiary and the orchard . . . and found the same numbers for them as well.

Twenty mana. The price a monster bee queen spawner had been before he had the Blessing of Bees. Scratching out some math in the dirt revealed that one ground mana flower node could pay for four of the regular mana flower nodes.

That was . . . a tad bit expensive. A ground mana flower node would represent the single most expensive thing in his dungeon.

But, after only a brief moment of hesitation, Belissar concluded it was worth the cost. He added one ground mana flower node to each of his three rooms.

Mana: 16/435

And in one fell swoop, he was nearly out of available mana. He had been right to tell the karnuq he couldn't make a ground mana flower node for her personal use just yet. And, even if he could have afforded it, he needed any available mana for other purposes as well. He would soon be able to afford a new room choice from the DP shop, so he'd need the mana for a new room if all went well, plus whatever features and spawners he'd want to fill it with.

But enough of that. The important thing was that his bees now had a brand-new flower. Belissar set his tower sight on the new ground mana flower nodes and grinned, waiting to see how they would react . . .

The First of the Fifth was currently pacing around in a circle. This was fine. She had the news of the mighty fortress the King had built for the flower meadow queens with . . . joy. Yes. Joy. Nothing else.

Because, of course, the King loved all bees. So, it only made sense for him to ensure all bees had a home. To collaborate with the queens like he hadn't done for any of the apiary queens . . . and to spend weeks lovingly working on the designs and the construction . . . and to collaborate with the hives so they could work by his side throughout that time . . . then transforming the whole thing into a magical construction on par with, or perhaps even greater than, the magical palace she had received.

Yes, this was fine. The King loved all bees, so she would too. Therefore, she would celebrate the boon the others had received. Yes. This was just a sign of the King's favor for all bees, and therefore his favor for her as well. See, afterward, he went and upgraded the apiary hives, too! Her palace's walls were now made of dry and precisely cut wood, far less vulnerable to rot and decay! She was still part of the bees the King loved!

And she was becoming like him too! Like the King, she had also lavished great gifts upon the bees. She had given every queen their own mana flower to support their growth! The flame radish flowers with nectar so hot it nearly burned? She let another queen gather that and gain favor with the King for the new workers raised on it! The brand-new healing herb flower that resulted from the cross-pollinating gathering she tasked her workers with? She had given that to the Second of the Sixth, who had subsequently did something never before seen, and changed *herself* with it!

Yes, this was fine. Well, the last one definitely was. The Second of the Sixth transforming herself was certainly impressive . . . but in hindsight, the First of the Fifth would never have done so herself. The Second of the Sixth could now raise medicinal workers and produce healing herb honey from the nectar of *any* flower, no longer requiring specialized nectars to produce specialized products. But there was a downside to that. It meant that *any* honey the Second of the Sixth produced became medicinal, regardless of what flower the nectar came from. So, in other words, she was now incapable of producing any other type. That would have been an altogether unacceptable situation for the First of the Fifth, as it would have shut down all her attempts to experiment with, categorize, and improve various honey types.

Still, the First of the Fifth could now see the benefits of her new approach. She would never have taken the path the Second of the Sixth had, but it was good that someone had. Had she kept the mana-infused healing herb for herself, all that would have resulted was a slightly improved healing herb honey. But now, instead, the First of the Fifth would not have to worry about mass-producing healing herb honey the next time a major battle came around. The Second of the Sixth could do so with far greater ease than any other queen, leaving the First of the Fifth free to focus on experimenting with new types and making high quality mana honey for the King's table instead.

And most of all, the King was greatly pleased with the Second of the Sixth's transformation. Thus, the First of the Fifth donated a similar flower that appeared in the poison flower patch to yet another queen, not even sampling its nectar for herself.

This was all fine. The First of the Fifth continued to repeat that to herself as she paced around endlessly.

That is, until she felt the stirrings of mana shifting through the entire realm. It was a subtle thing, further away from her senses than normal. As if it were traveling beneath the ground instead of through the air. The First of the Fifth perked up and crawled outside. What she found . . . was not nearly as subtle as she had first thought. A patch of the ground near the prime gathering area was glowing brightly.

Which meant she was about to receive new flowers. But even the First of the Fifth was not prepared for what appeared when the glow faded. A third patch of mana flowers now appeared . . . but this flower was entirely different from the other two. Instead of the blue and clear glow of the regular flowers, these ones were pure brown from stem to petal, blending in with the dirt beneath them. Their stems and leaves hung low while their roots spread wide, clinging tight to the ground. And whereas the other mana flowers left their mana to drift through the air in aimless puffs of mist, these ones directed their mana down. She saw the sparkle of mana traveling through their roots into the soil around them, solidifying and strengthening it.

This . . . this was something altogether different. Not the base mana flowers, which held mana but not much else, doing little with what they accumulated. Nor the specialized but mundane flowers that produced interesting but ultimately normal compounds. No, this was more akin to the flame radish flowers, gathering and transforming mana into a new form that could act upon the world all by itself . . . but to a far greater degree than even those.

The First of the Fifth was halfway to organizing foragers and guards to stake her claim on the new flower when she paused. And then she began to tremble. The King . . . loved . . . *all* bees. Which meant he made this for . . .

She slowly, ever so slowly, forced herself to begin dancing.

". . . Forget previous order. Go to apiary queens, tell to gather by new flower."

The workers seemed confused but moved to carry out her command. The First of the Fifth then turned to the new flower patch and stared at it, trembling the entire time.

Yes . . . this was . . . fine . . .

The Second of the Sixth couldn't help but buzz her wings loudly as she flew over to the gathering area . . . and saw the brand-new flowers. There it was. The First of the Fifth's plot had finally been revealed. This new patch of flowers was more unique and powerful than any the Second of the Sixth had ever seen . . . and it was just the latest of a whole slew of new flower types, on top of the number of mana flowers doubling. There were so many new flowers, in fact, that no one hive was large enough to monopolize them all. Not even the First of the Fifth's.

So, what had that crafty queen done? She had parceled out the existing flowers one by one, pretending she was being charitable so that each hive would be pacified with the leftovers she had long finished with. And now, once the greatest prize of all had appeared, she was going to swoop in and snatch it all for herself.

And all the other apiary queens, having accepted the previous favors, would be entirely unable to complain. Including the Second of the Sixth. It was beyond frustrating . . . but she had been played. She could only buzz as the First of the Fifth slowly flew over to the new patch and pointed to one of the strange brown flowers.

"This one, mine."

The Second of the Sixth buzzed her wings again. Yes, she knew! They all knew that! Was the First of the Fifth not satisfied in merely staking her claim?! Did she want to go through and claim every last flower, one by one, just to rub it in?! Did she . . .

The First of the Fifth then, even more slowly, flew to the next flower. She trembled as she danced.

"This one, First of Sixth's."

The Second of the Sixth froze, as did all the other apiary queens. Her eyes . . . must have deceived her.

"This one, First of Seventh's."

The Second of the Sixth slowly descended to the ground and landed on a blade of grass, remaining completely still as the First of the Fifth continued. Her eyes were apparently working? Unless she had somehow forgotten what the dances meant entirely. Maybe her evolution had unintended side effects. But the First of the Fifth continued, and her dances kept saying the same thing, no matter how unbelievable it seemed. One by one, she called out each queen, assigning them a flower.

"This one, Second of the Sixth's."

Including her. Just what was going on?

BEAR THIS IN MIND

Tyhgak was strangely silent as he walked with Metsaitti and the others into the sacred den for yet another hunting trip. The others were giving him looks but he didn't notice, lost in his thoughts as he was. He'd had much to think about lately.

When Tyhgak first saw the sacred den . . . he couldn't say he was impressed. The older generations had told him all sorts of stories about sacred dens. Some were labyrinths of death meant to push their challengers to the limit. Others were the bastions of mighty armies, led by imperious warlords who demanded submission.

This one opened with a field of flowers. Sure, a pit trap could be dangerous, but it was a far cry from the magical bombs and invisible blades he had heard stories of. And the bees? Sure, there were a lot of them and they were big for bees, but they were just bees. They didn't come close to the monsters Metsaitti and Chief Rohsuak had taken down. Most of the hunters had taken down something worse during their journeys through the Underway.

And the sacred den master? He was a sickly young runt, barely older than Tyhgak. He was even smaller than Noigakkuq, and most of the fur had fallen off of his body, if it had even grown in the first place! Now Tyhgak knew that the strength of a person did not indicate their value, but he also wasn't going to feel threatened by someone like that. And if even Tyhgak could take him on, then the sacred den master wouldn't last five seconds against Metsaitti, much less the chief, the Blazing Berserker herself. So, he didn't understand why the chief and Metsaitti were bending over backwards to be all submissive to him. He had heard of the daring raids the two had led on the tigerfolk and the lizardmen, and had assumed that it was his time to follow in their footsteps. And this sacred den . . . well it seemed like land for the taking!

. . . Okay, Tyhgak wouldn't go that far. Sacred dens were connected to the gods, and attacking one was a huge taboo. But still, Tyhgak thought they should at least be negotiating more confidently when they held the clear advantage. Like with the mana flowers! Those things were super valuable! He had learned that well enough when Juosiutik and the Chief had torn him a new one after he knocked over a pot with one inside it! He figured they'd be pretty happy if he brought one back! But no, he had to stay away because of a couple of bees. They had plenty of flowers all over, so what was the harm of taking one?

At least, that was what he once thought. Then he saw the bees in actual combat.

Tyhgak was brought back to the present as he felt a chill settle on his fur, and had to fight back a shiver despite standing under the sun in a bright field. A shade appeared before him, a tiny one, barely coming up his ankles, and yet still his body wished to recoil away from it. He felt the same even as the shade fell to his and his comrades' spears.

He still remembered his first trip to the sacred den, and his first time fighting a shade. His body had been trembling, and he'd struggled to keep a hold on his spear. His thrusts were hesitant and poorly aimed, barely scraping into the shades. If Metsaitti hadn't been there, the shade would have been free to pounce right on him. But Tyhgak couldn't have helped it. The Hunger was more than just another monster. It was, well, a *hunger*. When he looked at a shade, when he felt the Hunger nearby, he knew, deep down inside, that he was prey. He was paralyzed by the feeling that the Hunger would not merely rip apart his flesh, but that it would consume him on a deeper level. It would take all that was inside of him, all that made him who he was, and devour it, to be replaced by more of the Hunger itself. He looked into even the tiniest shade and saw the death, destruction, and corruption of all that he was.

And then, later, he had watched the bees he thought little of rip those shades apart, plunging directly into bodies made of pure Hunger without any hesitation. And he watched the sacred den master escort them through the fields. He walked with no hesitation, no fear of the shades appearing around them. He casually pointed out the shades to his bees as they appeared. He acted and spoke with the confidence of one who knew he was not at risk, fully trusting that his bees, his soldiers, would eliminate the shades at his command.

Tyhgak understood, then. The sacred den master was far more powerful than he appeared, and underneath his timid and frightened demeanor lurked courage and confidence. The kind of courage and confidence that could only have come from facing true danger and emerging victorious. The kind of courage and confidence Tyhgak hoped, but couldn't be sure, he had himself. He turned pale when he thought of what might have happened if they had raided the sacred den like he'd once thought of doing, or if the sacred den master had been more inclined to violence. Chief Rohsuak and Metsaitti could probably have survived . . . but the rest of them wouldn't have.

But, fortunately for everyone involved, the sacred den master was not that sort of person. He was a gentle soul, one who did not lord his power over others, and who treated people weaker than him with respect. At first, Tyhgak thought that was just because he seemed frightened of everyone, but he had recently changed his mind.

And that was because the clan now had two champions, and neither of them had been warriors. It was a surprise that Juosiutik had beaten them to the punch without fighting a single shade, but it wasn't that shocking in the end. Juosiutik had a drive and a fire that matched the heart of any warrior and let nothing stand in the way of her potion-making . . . something that Tyhgak had personally found himself on the receiving end of. If anyone could earn a god's blessing without fighting, it was her. Still, though, she apparently had the cooperation of the sacred den master, who seemed to take her instruction without complaint despite the obvious difference in their power. And she had, from those interactions, received treasures from him that Tyhgak and the others had so far been unable to earn with their might.

But the real kicker was just yesterday. When they found out that *Noigakkuq* had been cooperating with the sacred den master in secret . . . and was the second karnuq to be blessed as a result. Everyone in the clan knew that Noigakkuq was to be protected. It was something that Noigakkuq herself was unhappy about, but what could they do? A cave panther wouldn't care about her wishes and would absolutely take advantage of her smaller size and weaker arms. She was physically the least likely to survive danger.

Others in the clan even spoke of her as a burden. Tyhgak knew she was not, even before she'd revealed her ability to sniff mana, but he also knew she couldn't be exposed to danger. He, ah, may have even promised to protect her . . . though he, um, hadn't managed to actually convey that to her.

But then, Noigakkuq had suddenly gone and become a champion. She had gone and done something unbelievably dangerous, and the sacred den master had *rewarded* her for it. And she seemed happier than Tyhgak had ever seen her. That made him think about a lot of things. He may have valued Noigakkuq more than the others, but he had still thought of her as weak. The sacred den master apparently did not . . . and then she had gone and proven what she was capable of. And now she had the blessing of a god and wouldn't need anyone else's protection any longer.

Tyhgak's silent pondering continued even as they finished their hunt and started to return to the camp. When he arrived, he decided upon something. He made his way to the chief . . .

Chief Rohsuak lifted an eyebrow. "A hunt in the Underway?"

Tyhgak nodded his head. Chief Rohsuak crossed her arms. "What brought this on?"

Tyhgak couldn't help but fidget under her gaze. "It's, um, for the sacred den master."

Chief Rohsuak frowned. "The sacred den master? Tyhgak, be honest with me. Are you envious of Noigakkuq's deeds? Are you growing impatient that you have not been blessed?"

Tyhgak lifted his hands and quickly shook his head. "Ah, it's not that."

Chief Rohsuak's eyes narrowed on him, making him gulp. "Then what is it?"

Tyhgak trembled a bit but took a deep breath. "It's . . . an apology."

Chief Rohsuak tilted her head. "An apology?"

Tyhgak nodded. "I, um, was pretty rude to the sacred den master, talking about taking his flowers from his bees and stuff. But . . . he's a good man who didn't deserve that. He's strong, he's treated us well, and he even helped Noigakkuq . . . when we wouldn't. So, um, I wanted to apologize, and maybe do something for him."

Chief Rohsuak stared at him for a moment before her face softened. "I see."

She hummed and rubbed her chin. "Noigakkuq found a cave panther and a wolf-mole den too close to the entrance for comfort. I had intended to organize an expedition to scout the Underway and identify the dangers in our surroundings. If Metsaitti approves, I will consider including you in the group."

Tyhgak started to smile, but Chief Rohsuak frowned and glared at him once again. "Be aware, though, that even if you are allowed to join, getting something for your own purposes, including to give to the sacred den master, will come third to the expedition and your own survival."

Tyhgak nodded, still smiling. "Yes! I promise!"

Chief Rohsuak sighed, but slowly nodded. "I will speak with Metsaitti, then. Be aware that I will defer to his decision on if you are ready, and I will not listen to any complaints on it. Understood?"

Tyhgak nodded again. That was fair, since he still couldn't compare to Metsaitti as a hunter, but they *had* been hunting in the sacred den for a while now. He could only hope he had proved himself in that time.

CHAPTER TWENTY-FOUR

THE BEE-SIRED OUTCOME

Belissar fell into a rhythm for the next few days. He made potions with Juosiutik, received wood from the karnuq gatherers, watched his bees swarm over the new mana flowers, and continued monitoring the purifications. No new names were added to the memorial, several new perks and features were added to the tower's status, and all was well.

He had received a Monster Bee Sprayer Speed Boost, a Monster Bee Soldier Mana Boost, and a Worker Bee Vitality Boost, all minimum+. He didn't get any new features, but he didn't need any right this moment, so that was fine.

He also had started work on the orchard beehouse. At first, he tried to create a beehive up in the trees to see if he could, but the transparent image remained red, so he guessed he couldn't stick it among the branches. He could have just built one on the ground, or even built a new bee barracks, since the two queens shared a joint hive, but that would somewhat defeat the purpose of the grove he'd made for them.

So, he was currently working on something else. He knew he could move trees, so now tried to move individual branches. He found he could, albeit slightly, so he did his best to flatten them out and join them together. Then, he started building a flat platform out of sawed logs up in the branches, hoping that if he made something flat and stable, he'd be able to put a beehive feature up there.

He requested some assistance from the flower meadow soldier bees once again, since there was little chance he could lift these planks up into the grove's canopy on his own. The entire army wanted to assist him but he refused. The flower meadow queens were still helping their children get set up, and he was planning an expansion purification soon and did not want the army to neglect their training. Belissar ordered most of the army to continue training, taking only a small group, the minimum number of soldier bees that could lift the planks. It was slow going since they had to rest after each plank, but Belissar didn't mind. He absolutely preferred to take his time on this than to leave the army unprepared for the coming fight.

But now, it was time for something new. Because, now that the karnuq had finished their gathering and hunting for the day, his DP had finally crossed the threshold.

DP: 3110

He could finally afford a new room. He opened up the DP shop and selected a new room choice.

Extra room choice purchased.
One room choice now available.

Please select a room:
- Swamp (Rarity: Common. Type: Nature, Water, Field.)
- Farm (Rarity: Common. Type: Resource, Settlement.)
- Dirt Tunnels (Rarity: Common. Type: Ground, Labyrinth.)

Belissar smiled, and only hesitated for a brief moment. Swamps didn't sound particularly appealing, but that was only if he considered them as a human. As a dungeon master, on the other hand? Wet mud and surprisingly deep water to drag down a shade and prevent it from moving quickly? Novel and aquatic plants that could offer new flowers for his bees? That could offer significant potential for his tower's defenses. The next option, a farm, needed little explanation. More food would be great for the karnuq, who had already provided him with grain plants to grow in it, and new crops could mean new flowers for the bees.

But his choice was already made.

Dirt Tunnels are now available.

It just made sense. He had subterranean plant types from the karnuq, and they even had some more they hadn't offered since he had nowhere to put them. He had Ground mana flowers, which would hopefully result in new bee types that could make use of the new area and the new flowers, and which would hopefully be cheaper in an underground room. And, while the bees could certainly handle flying shades at this point, an underground area would make it all the more difficult for those types of opponents . . . provided his bees could actually operate in such a place. Farms, while helpful to the karnuq, just couldn't provide much for his bees that he didn't already have with flower meadows and orchards. A swamp could, but it was an option he didn't have anything prepared for. It was not appealing enough to delay taking dirt tunnels any longer.

Plus, he had learned his lesson with the digger bees. Dirt tunnels may have shown up every time so far, but if he didn't take them now there was no guarantee they'd continue to appear.

And then, his smile dropped. Because now that he had a new room came the hard part: deciding where to actually put it. For the sake of the defense, it would make the most sense to put it closest to the entrance, forcing the shades to pass through it before they could reach the bee barracks or any other hives. And if it were still just him and his bees, that's probably what he would have done. However, he now had to consider the karnuq . . . and all those resource nodes he had created for them at the front of the flower meadow. They'd all be much harder to reach if Belissar put an entire additional room between the bear folk's camp and the entrance. The karnuq still hadn't made a trip to the orchard, after all.

So then, put it somewhere behind the flower meadow? Putting in between the flower meadow and the orchard . . . was not a good idea. The orchard bees made regular trips to the flower meadow and were even sending scouts outside of the tower—which reminded Belissar, he probably should check out the newly purified area at some point. Maybe he could ask the karnuq for help with that? Or he could just wait for his bees' scouts, since they were already searching . . .

Belissar shook his head. He was getting distracted. The point was that adding a room's worth of distance to the orchard bees' trips would disrupt their current efforts. The same would apply to putting it behind the orchard, as the orchard bees also regularly travelled to the apiary.

So, maybe he should put it after the apiary, or even off to the side of one room? But if he did that, then the room wouldn't contribute to defense at all. If it were behind the apiary, then any shade that reached it would have already passed through all the bees and their hives, at which point Belissar would already have lost. A room that was off to the side might just be ignored entirely.

Belissar groaned. If only there was a way to keep it out of the way of both his bees and the karnuq while also having it in the way of any shades . . .

Belissar paused and his eyes widened. Maybe there was a way to do just that? He switched over to his tower sight, not viewing a single room but sending his sight higher until he could see all three rooms, like when he tried to place a new one. And then, just to see if he could, he thought about moving the orchard. The orchard turned transparent and he could move it around. He tried moving it in front of the flower meadow . . . and it moved just fine, with the flower meadow moving back to take its former position. He didn't confirm anything, and let the orchard move back to its original spot.

It *was*, in fact, possible to move the rooms after he had placed them. In other words . . . it would be possible to place the dirt tunnels conveniently off to the side

during normal times, but then move them in front of the entrance before purifications. Or, at least before the bigger purifications, since it might be disruptive to
rearrange the tower twice every day.

With that knowledge, Belissar prepared to place a new room of dirt tunnels,
relieved in the knowledge that the decision wouldn't be permanent. Since he didn't
want to move the orchard up a floor, he decided to place the tunnels off to the
side of the apiary. When he went to place the dirt tunnels' entrance, however, he
found a surprise.

In addition to the usual entrances on the side of the walls, he found he could
place an entrance directly on the apiary's floor, in which case the dirt tunnels
appeared stacked underneath the apiary. But still counted being as on floor two,
somehow? Deciding not to question it, Belissar experimented more with the door
instead, wondering if he could make a tunnel *to* the dirt tunnels that would then
pop up elsewhere in the apiary? He found that he could as a second entrance
appeared. He could make several entrances and exits, even.

Well, that was interesting, but Belissar wasn't entirely sure how to use it, so
he just made one entrance near the door to the first floor and left it at that. Now,
he had to adjust the room itself. He found a twisting maze of different tunnels,
which splitting off into dead ends and circular turns, or connected back to other
paths. Some even sloped up or down instead of turning side to side, making multiple floors within the room itself. Belissar could now adjust those tunnels as he
saw fit.

But, well, Belissar hadn't exactly designed an underground maze before, and
so he left it as it came and confirmed the placement of the room. He felt the
mana of the tower surge as a brand-new room came into being. He returned to
his normal sight, then turned to Niobee with a smile.

"Shall we go check it out?"

"Okay!"

CHAPTER TWENTY-FIVE

BEE-FICIENT ARRANGEMENT

Belissar stood just inside the entrance to the new room. Sunlight trickled in from the entrance, illuminating a tunnel made of dirt about ten feet across. A new shrine of bees stood in a small alcove off to the side, perhaps a tad shorter than the others, designed to fit within the cramped space. Besides that, there was dirt on the ground, dirt on the walls, and dirt on the roof . . . and nothing else in the few feet he could see. Beyond the initial slope down from the apiary was pitch-black darkness.

Belissar turned to Niobee. "Um, can you see inside?"

"Can!"

Belissar blinked at that. "You can? You can see in the dark?"

Niobee paused before beginning a slower dance. "Not with eyes. But can feel!"

"Ah."

Belissar began to nod. At this point, he had figured out that Niobee had a pretty deep connection to the tower, so it only made sense she could also use the tower sight to see beyond what her own eyes could. He, too, could use his tower sight to view the dirt tunnels as if in the light of the sun . . . but that somewhat defeated the purpose of coming here in person. Although . . . from what he *could* see, there was nothing but dirt.

As the name and description stated. Now that he was here, he, ah, wasn't entirely sure what else he had expected. He ended up shrugging.

"Well, since we can't see much ourselves anyway, might as well get to work."

"Okay!"

He chuckled a bit at Niobee zooming around him before considering what to do next. Obviously, the dirt tunnels were due for both traps and resource plants, but there was just a slight problem with that . . .

Mana: 11/435

He had allocated quite a lot of his mana to all the new flowers the karnuq had brought him, ending with the Ground mana flowers that were oh-so expensive. He also had not been expanding his mana reserves with the daily purifications while he waited for the expansion purification. So . . . his available mana was quite low. He wouldn't even be able to afford another Ground mana flower node if they were as expensive here as they were in the other rooms, though he was very much hoping they wouldn't be. On top of that, there were the cave carrots, the cave potatoes, and the burrowing stonecrop, plus whatever else the karnuq might be willing to share now if the dirt tunnels were suitable to grow them all. And, of course, he would need traps if he wanted to use the room for defense. Eleven mana . . . was probably not enough for all of that.

Belissar decided to at least check the numbers, though.

<u>Available Resource Plants for Dirt Tunnels:</u>

- Basic Medicinal Mushrooms (Mana Upkeep: 3 per node.)

- Basic Poisonous Mushrooms (Mana Upkeep: 3 per node.)

- Cave Carrot (Mana Upkeep: 3 per node.)

- Cave Potato (Mana Upkeep: 3 per node.)

- Burrowing Stonecrop (Mana Upkeep: 3 per node.)

- Mana Flower (Mana Upkeep: 5 per node.)

- Ground Mana Flower (Mana Upkeep: 10 per node,
5 due to suitable environment.)

Belissar blinked at the list, which was longer than he'd expected. So, basic medicinal and poisonous mushrooms? Maybe those were supposed to be the underground equivalents of the healing herbs and poisonous flowers. Well, that was nice, though as far as he was aware mushrooms didn't really make flowers, so maybe not. Though, he *did* recall seeing bees land on some he saw in the forest, so maybe there was something they could gather from it?

He was at least happy to have confirmation that all those plants the karnuq had given him would, in fact, grow in the dirt tunnels. And, most of all, that Ground mana flowers were not only not as expensive, but *significantly* cheaper in the dirt tunnels. The same upkeep as a normal mana flower, even. If only he could move the Ground mana flowers from the other rooms to here . . .

Belissar suddenly realized that he could. He walked out of the dirt tunnels' entrance and over to the flower patches of the apiary, where countless bees were flying to and from the new Ground mana flowers. They all stopped as they saw him approach.

"Um, sorry, could you give me a second? I'm going to move these slightly, but they should come right back, okay?"

The bees all saluted and backed away from the Ground mana flower patch. Belissar then reclaimed it, watching as glowing light covered over the flowers and then melted back into the ground, leaving an empty patch of dirt as if nothing had ever existed.

Belissar then swapped to his tower sight and thought about adding a new dirt tunnel entrance, opening up a hole right where the Ground mana flower patch had been. He placed a new Ground mana flower node right by that entrance, illuminated by the sun and visible from above, then returned to his normal sight. He looked around at the bees and nodded.

"Thanks for waiting. You can go back to gathering now."

The bees saluted and then dove into the new hole in the ground. Fortunately, there was enough sunlight for them to work with, so they resumed gathering from the new Ground mana flowers just the same as before. Belissar nodded with a smile as he checked his mana.

Mana: 26/435

Success. He had reclaimed a few points of his mana while still leaving the apiary bees with access to the new flower. He briefly considered whether he could do the same for the flower meadow and orchard patches as well . . . but they were a bit too far away from the dirt tunnels, as the bees would need to fly at least the full length of the orchard to reach it. But that was fine, as he probably had enough mana to work with now.

He added a dirt tunnel entrance to both the orchard and flower meadow. He found he couldn't actually place them directly in the sunlight streaming from above, so he placed them to the sides of each entrance, where they would be shaded from the light but still visible enough for the bees to see them. He even added the two types of mushrooms for good measure, just to see if there was anything the bees could do with them.

Mana: 11/435

When he was done, his mana was right back where he'd started. It seemed all those resource nodes cost exactly the same amount he had saved by moving the Ground mana flowers, so that was convenient. And that gave him a decent amount of mana left for traps, seeing as both the pit traps and the sticky honey traps only cost one mana . . . or would they? Belissar frowned as he recalled that the sticky honey traps were as cheap as they were because the bees were refilling them with their own honey. But these traps would be located deep inside the tunnels, where the bees would have trouble reaching. He would have to check how much the sticky honey traps would cost if the bees couldn't reach them.

In the end, Belissar shrugged and added two sticky honey traps and a single pit trap by the main entrance to the dirt tunnels. He put one sticky honey trap in the roof of the tunnels, and the other in the pit trap itself. He figured he'd wait to add anything deeper in until his bees had a way to actually reach it.

Mana: 8/435

He'd get a bit of his mana back once the bees started filling the sticky honey traps themselves, but even so, his mana was almost depleted. He'd done all he wanted to for the dirt tunnels at the moment, though that could change if the Ground mana flowers resulted in a subterranean bee of some sort. Or if he wanted to make nodes in the dirt tunnels for the karnuq to gather from, not to mention if they gave him new subterranean plants now that he had a place to grow them. Still, at this point it was worth considering whether he should go back to expanding his mana from the daily purifications. The only question was . . . should he attempt the expansion purification now, or wait for new types of bees and flowers?

On the one hand, everything he had been waiting for was now finished. The bee barracks' main structure had been completed and the flower meadow queens had finished moving inside. The new queens had been born and now had enough workers to contribute to their hives, though they were not yet large enough to begin laying soldiers. The dirt tunnels were ready and could be placed in front of the flower meadow as an additional obstacle to any flying shades. The sprayers were fully integrated into the army, new bee types were growing, and some basic anti-fire measures had been taken. And the benefits of a successful expansion had already proven quite dramatic. He had just filled his final room slot, so now seemed like an excellent time to acquire new floors and slots.

On the other hand, there was still value in waiting before attempting the expansion purification. With extra time, the new flower meadow queens would start producing soldiers and dramatically expand the size of the army. The bee barracks' main structure was complete, but Belissar could still add defenses to the exterior, such as a palisade for the perimeter. He also had only the orchard grove beehouse to design and build before he could complete another mission from the God of Bees. The new bee types would spread if he waited, and who knew how helpful burning soldiers or sprayers might be? And, again, if the Ground mana flowers resulted in a bee type that could operate underground, he could consider using the entirety of the dirt tunnels as a battleground instead of just the entrance.

So, what was the right choice? Expand now and gain even more rooms, monsters, and resources, but at the possible cost of losing bees? Or take the slow path, letting the bees explore the fullest extent of the new resources before exposing them to any more danger, but delaying his tower's growth as a result?

But, just then, Belissar noticed something that would delay this decision. Something that made his heart stop and his blood run cold. Despite a lack of any purification notices, he felt the Hunger creeping along the tower's mana once more.

CHAPTER TWENTY-SIX

INCURSION

Belissar immediately focused on the entrance of the tower . . . and found nothing. He frowned and then began to zip around the tower with his tower sight, but he still couldn't find anything out of place. The karnuq weren't present in his tower at the time, so he didn't think there'd be any remnants, but still he searched. Not finding anything, he began to zoom out his tower sight, hoping to catch sight of anything out of the ordinary, but as far as he could tell all was normal in his tower.

And yet, he could still feel the Hunger. His heart began to pound. "Where is it?"

Niobee zipped in front of him. "Bees looking!"

Belissar nodded. "Thanks, let me know if they find anything."

He could see his bees stir and start to spread out through the tower. Without any further options to check the tower himself, Belissar tried to focus on the feeling in the tower's mana. He couldn't find a shade anywhere in the tower, but it was *definitely* touching the tower's mana, so it had to be somewhere . . .

Belissar froze, and then his eyes opened wide. He realized . . . that the tower's mana was not limited to its own walls. And that attacks by shades were not unknown in his former, tower-less life.

He immediately began to look outside the tower, jumping through the eyes of the scout workers still out there. Most of them were on their way back, but a few were further out. They felt his presence and followed his will, turning around and spreading out. However, there were only a handful of scouts, what one joint hive could spare on exploration, and there was a lot of ground to cover.

A bad feeling crept into Belissar's chest. Because as far as he knew, there were only two things in the area a shade might go for. His tower . . . and the karnuq camp. His mind was filled with the image of a big wolf-shade tearing through tents. Of Metsaitti and Chief Rohsuak and the hunters trying to face one. Of Juosiutik and the gatherers trying to flee.

His blood ran cold. "Move to the karnuq, check the area around them!"

The bees closest to the camp flew as fast as they could, flying above the scene. Fortunately, the camp itself was not under attack—yet. Belissar exhaled the breath he was holding, but then looked closer. There was a lot of movement around the camp, and he could see armed hunters gathering at the edge of the camp furthest from his tower.

"There, head that way!"

The bees did as asked . . . and then he saw it. It was shaped like a massive boar, but with six tusks, six eyes, and eight legs, and taller than even a karnuq. It knocked over the trees as it walked, not slowed down in the slightest by the obstacles in its path. A trail of death lay in its wake, grass, flowers, shrubs, and fallen trees rotting and dying in the oily black mist of the Hunger.

Belissar didn't even spare another thought before he was running toward the entrance of his tower.

"Niobee, gather the army! We need to move!"

"Yes!"

The army heard Belissar's intent before Niobee even left his side and began to fly into the air as one. They spared not a moment in rushing forward, arranging into their squads and formations mid-flight as they rushed toward the tower entrance.

As for Belissar . . . he continued running, even as the bee army flew him by and rushed ahead. Images and memories kept passing through his head of burnt villages and dead flower fields and of standing by the bedsides of bodies lying still.

He could only hope they would make it in time.

Chief Rohsuak frowned as she stood in the forest. Metsaitti directed the hunters as they spread out. She had known that this was a distinct possibility. It had been a risk to set up their camp where they had. The area the young tower had purified was a bit too small for comfort. Yet, she had hoped that same youth would mean an incursion by the Hunger would be far off, and so she had been more worried about the threat posed by the sacred den master than about the dangers he warded off. Apparently, she had been wrong on both counts.

But she couldn't have known that when they first arrived, so there was nothing for it now. The hunters would have to stop the incursion here, in the forest. If they could not, the survivors would have to flee to the sacred den and beg for the master's protection. Rohsuak was relatively optimistic he would be receptive, but it would also mean her people becoming entirely dependent upon him. She was not yet certain if that was a wise step to take.

Her people would have to do what they needed to, however. Immediate survival trumped long-term caution. She put aside her thoughts as Metsaitti walked up to her.

"How's it looking?"

Metsaitti frowned. "Will you be able to assist?"

Chief Rohsuak shook her head. "I have the power to attack, but not to control the fires that would result. Burning down the forest would not count as a victory. If you can immobilize it, I could concentrate my attack, but if I miss I will not have a second attempt."

Metsaitti's frown deepened. "I . . . am not certain we will be able to do that. Not without losses."

Chief Rohsuak narrowed her gaze as she glared out into the trees beyond. "We will do what we have to."

Metsaitti slowly nodded and returned to the hunters. The karnuq stood scattered about, armed with spears and bows mostly carved from the bones of their prey. Only a handful still held the masterfully forged weapons of their forebearers. Chief Rohsuak's shoulders sagged as she let out a sigh. They were a far cry from the war parties she had followed in her youth.

They felt it before they heard it, the ground rumbling with each step the enemy took. They heard trees crack and fall and saw the rustling in the canopy. Many of the younger hunters began to fidget and gulp.

"Steady."

Metsaitti raised his spear, his voice stopping the hunters from shuffling back. As long as he stood, they would stay and fight. Chief Rohsuak could only hope he would not fall.

And then, the shade burst from the trees, towering over even the karnuq hunters. It paused as it looked around. Then it let out a roar and began to dig into the ground.

"Loose!"

At Metsaitti's shout, the karnuq archers let their arrows fly. Their aim was true and the arrows sank deep into the monster.

It hardly seemed to notice. The shade began to charge, shaking the very world around them. Metsaitti took but one look at its building momentum before he made his call.

"Dodge!"

The karnuq hunters, prepared to stand their ground, paused at his cry. That moment of hesitation nearly cost them their lives as they finally threw themselves out of the path of the monster. They hit the dirt, unable to launch any counterthrusts as the shade dug into the dirt, leaving huge furrows in the ground as it slid to a stop and prepared to charge once again.

Chief Rohsuak frowned as the monster began a second charge surprisingly quickly. Despite its bulk, it would not remain still long enough for her to target her spell. What was worse, shades were inherently drawn to mana. It would notice once she began to gather hers . . . and she was not confident she could finish her attack before it could charge her down. How ironic that the Blazing Berserker would now find herself helpless in a fight, forced to conserve her strength until it was *safe* to unleash it.

Metsaitti, at least, still had the strength to fight. He stirred up his mana, drawing the shade's attention away from a group of archers as he strengthened his body and his spear. The shade immediately turned to him and narrowed its eyes. A moment later, it began another charge with a roar.

Metsaitti stood in place, digging his own feet into the dirt. He stood completely still, his eyes fixed upon the monster bearing down on top of him. Then, at the very last second, he pushed off and leapt to the side, moving faster than any normal karnuq could and barely evading the tusks of the beast. He planted his feet and thrust his spear into the monster's side as soon as he landed.

The shade roared as it continued to charge ahead. Metsaitti's eyes widened as his spear, still stuck in the boar-shade's side, was suddenly yanked forward. He held on and was pulled off his feet as the monster charged forward. But he was forced to let go as he nearly crashed into a tree, tumbling across the ground as the shade skid to another halt. It turned to face him once more, eyes blaring red as it adjusted its stance. Metsaitti looked up and grimaced.

Chief Rohsuak grimaced even more. Metsaitti's spear was one of the better weapons they had left—most of the others would have snapped from such force. The other karnuq hunters were currently keeping their distance, launching arrows when they could but otherwise staying away. Only Metsaitti had the mana and the abilities to consistently dodge the shade at close range.

This fight was not going well.

CHAPTER TWENTY-SEVEN

THE CAVAL-BEE IS HERE!

Metsaitti tensed as the boar charged toward him. Again, he leapt to the side at the last moment and then grabbed onto his spear as the shade passed. He tried to pull it out, but was instead pulled along by the boar, unable to get enough leverage before an approaching tree forced him to let go once more.

Meanwhile, Chief Rohsuak shouted at the other hunters, taking command and ordering them to stop attacking. Metsaitti was fast and experienced enough to consistently dodge the shade's charges, but without his weapon it would be hard for him to keep its attention if someone else was harming it.

Still, Metsaitti could not exactly fight unarmed forever. Chief Rohsuak, there-fore, began to stir up her mana. Should she miss, she would no longer be capable of contributing to the fight . . . and may cause another big problem on top of it, but at this point she had little choice. Someone needed to give Metsaitti a chance to get his weapon back, and no one else was capable of the task.

Chief Rohsuak herself was not certain she'd be able to escape the boar's atten-tion afterward, but protecting the clan was her duty as chief. She'd just have to trust that Metsaitti would take advantage of the distraction and give her a chance to escape.

But then they heard it. A slight buzzing noise that grew louder with every second. One of the hunters pointed up in the sky.

"Look!"

Chief Rohsuak took a second to glance up and her eyes widened. A massive yellow-and-black cloud was rushing toward them. One that she very much recognized.

The bee army approached.

"The sacred den master . . . has come to help us?"

The bees soared overhead and then dove down toward the boar just as it was charging at Metsaitti once more. A squad of soldier bees slammed into its side, their stingers piercing deep. The boar roared in pain and turned to face the new threat, but that group of soldiers had already flown away. A few moments later, another squad stung the shade from the other side. It snarled and spun around to swing its tusks in the other direction but hit only air.

The karnuq scattered at first, but stopped and started to cheer as the bees attacked their foe. Nearby, Metsaitti waited as he watched the bees dive from above. Then, when a squad dove in from the opposite side, he sprinted forward. He grabbed hold of his spear right as the bees stung the shade's other side and then pulled as the shade spun away toward the bees. Finally, using the shade's movement against itself, he was able to recover his spear. The rest of the hunters turned to Chief Rohsuak as they watched the bees fly circles around the shade.

"Come on, let's help!" one shouted.

But Chief Rohsuak held out her hand and shook her head. "Only intervene if you are confident that you won't hit any of our friends. For now, regroup and stay vigilant. That monster could very well charge this way in a rage, we are not out of this yet."

The karnuq gripped their weapons and refocused on the fight.

Belissar rushed through the forest, ignoring the branches scraping at his arms and legs. Through his tower sight, he watched as the soldier bee army flew past the karnuq's camp and ahead to the actual battlefield. Metsaitti and Chief Rohsuak were there, both unharmed for now, though Metsaitti was facing the shade alone . . . and unarmed.

"Take it down but be careful. We don't know what it can do!"

Belissar's words traveled through his mana, and he saw the queen in charge of the army dance her salute. The soldier bee army organized into their formations and a moment later the squads began their attack runs. Fortunately, the shade did not appear any faster than the wolf-shades and couldn't fly like the bird-shades, so the soldier bees were able to attack it without incident.

But Belissar didn't dare hope that would remain the case, given how every shade thus far had surprised him. So, he kept running until he, too, arrived at the edge of the battlefield. He paused for a moment as he saw the true size of the boar with his own eyes, but then shook his head and shouted.

"Chief Rohsuak!"

Chief Rohsuak glanced toward him and made a bright smile. "Sacred Den Master, thank you for coming to our assistance."

Belissar nodded and then got right into it. "Can you tell me what that shade can do? Any special or magical attacks?"

Just then he saw the boar take a deep breath, causing Belissar's own breath to catch in his throat. A shade inhaling was generally a bad sign, but fortunately the bees were ready. They scattered as they'd trained to do as the boar roared and charged in the direction of the closest bees. Belissar felt the ground shake under the massive shade's hooves. His bees, however, were not intimidated, and simply flew out of the way as the shade barreled into the trees.

"We cannot tell!" Chief Rohsuak yelled over the buzzing of the bees. "It has used nothing but its body to attack so far. Brute strength appears to be—PALOIKU! MOVE!"—she cut off and shouted at a pair of hunters. They barely leapt out of the way as the shade smashed through a tree behind them—"its main focus!"

Belissar turned back to watch the battle. On the one hand, the shade was far less agile than the wolf-shades and lacked their whiplike tail, so his bees were having an even easier time dodging it than normal. On the other hand, this was the largest shade they had ever dealt with. His gigantic soldier bees almost looked like regular bees in comparison. If he focused in close, he could see their stingers barely piercing its hide.

He frowned. If the shade couldn't effectively attack back, then his bees could handle it. Still, it seemed like their attacks weren't doing a lot either. And with the shade's sheer bulk, the army could keep it surrounded but they couldn't keep it from moving if it wanted to.

"If there are no special attacks, I think we can take it down eventually, but it looks like it's going to take a while. Did you have a plan to deal with it?"

Chief Rohsuak held up a finger and lit a flame on it even as she kept an eye on the boar's movements. "I have enough mana for one big fire attack, but only one. And with the forest surrounding us, I can't afford to miss. If you can get it to stop or at least slow down without your bees in the way, then I should be able to finish it off."

Belissar nodded and then relayed as much to the queen in charge, telling her to focus on slowing the shade down. She saluted and began to dance, sending her commands to the rest of the army.

Three squads approached the shade, one from the front and two from behind. The squad in front consisted of sprayers, who unleashed their toxins right into the shade's face while the other two squads took advantage of the distraction to sting its hind legs. The shade roared and smashed forward through several trees to try to get to the bees, but the sprayers had never lowered into its range in the first place.

The bees repeated this tactic over and over until the shade wised up and began kicking with its back legs before it charged. The bees managed to dodge the relatively short and thin legs, however, and changed their approach. They began to randomize their assault, sometimes diving from the sides, sometimes from behind, and sometimes even from the front. But with every attack, they made sure the boar charged away from Belissar, moving deeper into the forest.

The shade left a trail of destruction in the forest, but it displayed no means of attacking aerial foes. Belissar held his breath every time the shade paused or took a breath, but ultimately it did nothing but kick and charge. Still, the monster's bulk was a defense in and of itself and for a long time, Belissar thought the bees' attacks weren't actually doing anything more than irritating it.

But eventually, the shade began to slow down. Its charges were less frequent and ended earlier, and it was breathing heavily and even beginning to sway a bit. Its eyes were swollen shut from all the poison that had been sprayed on them. Belissar turned to Chief Rohsuak.

"It's starting to slow down now."

Chief Rohsuak narrowed her eyes. "Let's approach, but let's stay vigilant. A cornered beast is the most dangerous. Metsaitti, you're with me. The rest of you, stay here."

With that, Chief Rohsuak, Metsaitti, and Belissar followed the trail of destruction until they caught up with the boar. The hunters dutifully remained back. It was just finishing another charge, crashing into a tree. This time, rather than flattening it, it merely left a massive dent that caused the tree to bend and creak.

Chief Rohsuak stirred up her mana and Belissar felt the surrounding air heat up. "That'll do. Can you have your bees clear the area around and above the shade?"

Belissar wasted no time telling the bees to get clear. Barely a moment later, they took some distance, specifically moving so that no bee was hovering directly above the monster. Chief Rohsuak held her arms out with her palms facing together. A ball of fire formed between them, growing brighter and hotter until Belissar couldn't look at it directly. Then, Chief Rohsuak thrust her hands forward and the ball shot straight toward the boar.

The shade was still catching its breath and so didn't notice the attack approaching until it was too late. It was only just beginning to move when the ball crashed into its side.

And then a pillar of fire shot into the air, engulfing the shade. They heard it roar and squeal but the venom of countless bee stings had taken its toll. The shade rolled a bit on the ground and then fell still.

SETTING A BEAR-ING

A hostile has been defeated in your purification zone.
Gained 20 DP.

Belissar let out the breath he had been holding as the message crossed his vision. A moment later, the shade's body dispersed into mist, taking most of the flames with it. He could feel the chill of the Hunger fade as his tower's mana flooded the area. Dead grass and flowers left in the shade's wake began to regrow. He, Chief Rohsuak, and Metsaitti had to stamp out a few small fires, but in the end the situation had been dealt with. And with not a bee harmed in the process.

"Looks like we got it. Did, um . . ." Belissar hesitated but swallowed and cleared his voice. "Was anyone hurt? I might be able to help, if so."

Chief Rohsuak smiled and shook her head. "No. Thanks to you, we got through unscathed. Which reminds me . . ."

She glanced at Metsaitti and he nodded. Then they both turned to Belissar and bowed their heads, slamming their right fists into the left side of their chests in unison as Chief Rohsuak spoke.

"Thank you, Sacred Den Master, for your assistance. You saved many lives today and we will not forget it."

Belissar fidgeted a bit but calmed himself and nodded. "You're welcome. I'm just glad no one was hurt."

Having confirmed that all was well with the karnuq, Belissar turned to the soldier bee army. Niobee and the commanding queen were hovering in front of him, waiting for his next command. Belissar smiled at them.

"Great work, everyone. Let's go home and celebrate."

The air buzzed as all the bees saluted as one. Belissar couldn't help but grin. An invasion by the Hunger. A disaster that had destroyed entire villages in the past. Once one of the greatest fears in his life, a calamity he would have been help-less against before.

Now, thanks to his bees, it had been dealt with. And neither a bee nor a kar-nuq had been hurt in the process. He could not help but be proud of how far his bees had come. And, perhaps, how far he too had come from the helpless peasant he had once been.

Belissar made his way home with his head held high and a spring in his step.

Chief Rohsuak stood for a moment and watched as the sacred den master left with his army. She rubbed her chin and hummed for a moment before turning to Metsaitti.

"What do you think?"

Metsaitti smiled and inclined his head. "I will follow your lead. You've always been a better leader than I."

Chief Rohsuak rolled her eyes and knocked the top of his head. "I wouldn't waste my breath if I wanted to hear flattery."

Metsaitti chuckled before turning serious. "Well, he just risked his life for ours on his own initiative. Mine especially, given the situation. I owe him my life . . . and I'm guessing possibly yours?"

Chief Rohsuak slowly nodded and hummed for a moment more. She then crossed her hands behind her back and straightened her spine, ignoring the pain in her back.

"When you return, assemble the family heads. We have much to discuss."

After the karnuq hunters had been accounted for and returned to their camp, Chief Rohsuak stood before a large gathering. Each family in the clan had sent a representative. Juosiutik and Noigakkuq were there, as well as a number of other young karnuq who represented the oldest, or in too many cases the last, living member of their families. Chief Rohsuak held back a sigh as she saw how many young faces were present.

The rest of the clan huddled around the outer edges of the gathering, intent on eavesdropping as much as possible. But that was fine for tonight. Chief Rohsuak wasn't trying to be secretive. Officially gathering the family heads was just a way to keep the meeting from getting too chaotic.

After all, she had quite the proposal to make. As evidenced by the current situation, in which all the karnuq were staring at her in silence after she had finished.

One of the older men furrowed his brow.

"Chief . . . this is . . . are you certain? You're asking us to surrender our free-dom, our way of life."

Chief Rohsuak nodded. "I am."

One of the younger hunters crossed his arms. "Wouldn't it be better to stick to ourselves? What if we need to leave again? We've made it this far on our own."

Chief Rohsuak heaved a sigh . . . and allowed herself to slump over. She felt an itch in her throat, and she allowed herself to cough and hack until Juosiutik brought her a drink. She thanked the girl as she drank.

All the karnuq were staring at her, many with their eyes open wide. It was, after all, one of the first signs of her age she had truly permitted them to see. She cleared her throat once more before beginning to speak.

"Our people have teetered on the edge of a knife for a while now. We've made it through, yes. But our good fortune will not last forever. We are one mistake, one instance of bad luck away from ruin. And even if our good luck does continue . . . we cannot keep on like this forever. As you can see, my time is dwindling, much more quickly than you think. Metsaitti is not getting any younger either, and we have no champions as of yet who can match him. What will happen ten years down the line, or twenty? What if Metsaitti is wounded and a shade like the one we faced tonight appears?"

She turned and looked the young hunter in the eyes. "Could you stand against something like that alone?"

The younger karnuq held her gaze for a couple of seconds before glancing away. Chief Rohsuak coughed once more, then took a deep breath and straightened her spine, rising to her full height. Even now, she stood above most of her people when she wasn't hunching over.

"We have survived, but we have made no progress. We have only lost more and more on our journey. But now . . . now we have a chance to change that, and to grow."

She turned to Leijaliuk. "For the first time since our journey began, we know where tomorrow's meals will come from."

Leijaliuk nodded. Chief Rohsuak pointed to Juosiutik and Noigakkuq. "We have raised our first new champions since we lost our home, with more on the way."

And then she turned to Metsaitti, who nodded as everyone turned to face him. "And, as of tonight, we have protection from an army whose might exceeds our own."

She turned and looked each member of the meeting in the eye, one by one. "For the first time, our people can grow in strength, prosperity, and numbers. But that is only true as long as we remain here. If, for some reason, we are forced to leave, we will lose access to that protection. We will lose access to the first consistent source of food we have had since we began our sojourn. And our two champions will lose access to the sacred den of the patron who has granted them unique blessings, while no further members of our clan will have an opportunity to receive any blessings at all."

She then smiled at them. "What I propose is that we do what we need to make our current good fortune permanent and ensure that we will continue to grow far into the future, even after all of us here are gone."

The karnuq slowly began to nod, though one of the eldest frowned. "But . . . didn't you say it's dangerous to trust a sacred den master? Don't you remember what happened to our fathers and mothers?"

Chief Rohsuak looked him right in the eye. "I did. And I do. And that was why we held back. That is why we still live in tents, ready to leave at a moment's notice. That is why we live on the outskirts, where we are still exposed to the Underway and the Hunger."

She let her expression soften. "But I no longer think that. We gave this sacred den master a chance to show us his true colors and he has. From the time we arrived here, he has not hesitated to share with us the bounty of his sacred den, or the blessings of his patron. And in exchange he has only demanded one thing: that we not harm his bees. Tonight, he risked those same bees in order to protect us, even though we hadn't even asked for his help, and he demanded nothing of us in return. This sacred den master has earned my trust."

She turned to Metsaitti, who saluted. "Mine as well. I owe him my life for tonight."

A wave of murmuring passed through the karnuq . . . which only grew as Noigakkuq stepped forward, tossing a dagger in her hand.

"I'm in favor of it."

Juosiutik stepped forward as well. "As am I. I would not have reclaimed my mother's legacy without his help."

Leijaliuk joined them. "I do not wish to return to rationing like I once did . . . and I imagine none of the rest of you want me to either. We *need* this sacred den, and I am in favor of anything that helps us keep it."

Chief Rohsuak waited for the murmurs to quiet down.

"Then, it is time to make a choice about the future of our people. All in favor?"

She stood tall as she waited for the responses.

THE WILL OF THE GODS

Ruckanos diverted course the moment he was out of sight of his lord father's tower. Well, he knew his lord father had eyes and ears everywhere in his domain, so it wasn't like he'd remain unaware. But Ruckanos had a plan, one that was fully in line with both his mission and his punishment, so he believed he could get away with this much.

And so, they touched down in the charred ruins of the village where this all started. His guards frowned as he disembarked. The captain followed and walked up to him.

"Commander, may I ask your intentions? Our orders were quite clear."

Ruckanos scowled as the captain dropped the "Lord" title from his name. But he had no time to lose, so instead he turned and walked over to one of the other wyverns, the one carrying the oldest member of their group.

"Augur, time to earn your trade. Do anything you can to try and trace where my tower went."

The augur furrowed his brow. "Commander, I must warn you that tracing a tower after its birth is impossible."

Ruckanos narrowed his eyes at the man. "We are about to embark upon a suicide mission. If we want even the slightest chance of survival, we need a direction at the very least. If there was any time to innovate on your trade, it is now, old man. You should be motivated most of all, as I imagine the journey will be hardest on you."

The augur sighed, moving to disembark. "I will do what I can, but do not expect a miracle."

Ruckanos scowled. "Know that we will all perish if you cannot produce one."

The augur and Ruckanos walked to the field behind a charred apiary, the place where they had seen the tower's birth, while the captain ordered the remaining guards to rest for a bit. The augur knelt down, feeling around the grass.

"I believe it was around here, or at least this is as close as we can tell given the passage of time. I will attempt a divination, but that is about all I can do."

Ruckanos heaved a sigh. "Stop blabbering and get to it."

The augur heaved his own sigh and then reached into his robes. He began to carve a circle full of ancient symbols into the dirt and the grass. He then pulled out a bottle full of bright red liquid and placed it in the center before turning to Ruckanos.

"Commander, do you have anything you can offer to the gods? Perhaps they will look more favorably upon us if so."

Ruckanos heaved a dramatic sigh this time. "What do you think, augur? Do you think my lord father showered me in riches before sending me off to die? No, I have nothing in my possession that can be spared. I am offering my very life, as well as all of yours, in the service of the gods. The least they can do is show me where to go."

The augur frowned but turned back to the circle and closed his eyes. He began to speak in a soft whisper and the magic circle glowed with blue light as he filled it with his mana.

Suddenly he gasped, and his eyes shot open. The blue light began to turn into a golden yellow and then the bottle disappeared. The augur trembled.

"C-Commander . . . it's a miracle."

Ruckanos glared at him. "Out with it. What has happened?"

The augur continued to shake as he looked up into the sky. "T-The gods have spoken. Somehow, they spoke without words, so I know not which one but . . . I have a heading. The journey . . . will be incredibly long, but I know where to go. The gods have smiled upon our mission."

Ruckanos paused for a moment before his face broke out into a grin. So, the gods themselves approved of his mission, huh? That tiny spark of hope in his chest now exploded into a roaring inferno. He now had the location of his lost tower, one that he knew for a fact would be young, weak, and ruled by some dying peasant. Maybe the gods had already struck the fool down for his transgressions, and the tower would be waiting for its rightful ruler. Either way, his chances of surviving . . . and more . . . had improved dramatically.

And what were terrible odds in the face of the will of the gods? If they themselves were supporting his quest, then what did he have to fear? Or maybe . . . maybe he had been chosen for even *more* than the usual tower lord. Maybe this would all be better for him in the end, to reclaim his tower in a location far beyond the reach of his lord father, the Conclave, or even the High Council. He rose to his feet and walked back to the captain.

"Captain, we leave immediately. And now, we know where we're going."

A queen bee inspected her hive once more. Her antennas drooped as she took stock of their current honey stores.

They weren't going to make it.

When a rival hive of humans had arrived and burnt down the Hive-Builder's own colony, she and all of her rivals had been forced to flee. They had lost their homes, their broods, and, worst of all in the current situation, their winter stores. They all were forced into a mad scramble to build new hives and gather enough nectar to survive the coming chill.

And that was when this queen had made a fatal mistake. She once had a special worker, different from all others. The worker had somehow accumulated enough mana to become something more. Her dances were more complex and precise, while her stings were more powerful and deadly to their enemies . . . and her body held together even when stinging foes many times her size. She also lived for many years, far beyond any of her sisters, and any honey she made was of the highest quality, imbued with bits of mana that elevated it beyond the rest. Drinking that honey had caused the queen to accumulate some mana of her own, opening her eyes and mind in ways she still couldn't fully understand.

The queen had come to rely upon that worker above all others. And so, when the inferno came and the queen found said worker was missing afterward, she panicked. She had committed the majority of her workforce to search for that one worker . . . and found nothing. So, while the rival queens had managed to rebuild their hives to some semblance of function, she had expended her hive's dwindling resources on a fruitless chase.

Her hive, built on an exposed tree branch, wasn't even fully enclosed, and the days were already growing colder. Her honey stockpiles were barely enough to last for another week, much less the frozen months that were coming. If she had found her missing worker, she could imbue the honey with mana to increase its nutrition, allowing them to stretch it out. But she had not, and now the situation was dire. She had no idea what to do. She had no idea how they were going to survive.

And it was all her fault.

It was then that she heard a noise. The noise of humans. Since she had not scouted for good locations, she had been forced to set up her hive just beyond the ruins of their old home. Now, she saw humans walking there once more. Humans she recognized.

The very ones who had taken the Hive-Builder and her worker from her.

No, she realized, it was not her fault alone that her hive was doomed to death. Indeed, the greatest share of the blame lay with the humans who had taken the Hive-Builder, her worker, and her hive. The very humans who now stood before her again.

Her wings buzzed and her hive stopped their work as they looked toward her. She began her dance, preparing to fly once more. The queen stirred what little mana she had and sent it through her remaining workers, overriding their instincts and calling them to heed her command. She planned to take her entire hive on this flight . . . this last mission.

Perhaps this was for the best. If her hive had any chance of survival, she would have had to let this opportunity slip away. But if they were doomed anyway, if they could not possibly survive the winter no matter what they did, then at the very least they would take down the monsters responsible for their plight. She could avenge her hive, her worker, and the Hive-Builder.

But then, golden light filled every inch of her vision. Suddenly, she found herself in a hive beyond all hives, with golden walls of honey and wax stretching out further than her eyes could see in any direction, with fields of every color of flower imaginable coating the ground. Worker bees crawled and flew all around her. Bees of sorts she had never seen passed her by . . . and queens worked alongside the workers.

And at the center of it all was a bee. A bee she had never seen and had not known . . . and yet instantly recognized, for she had always known her. She stood before the Queen of All Bees herself. She moved to dance a salute, but the Queen of All Bees moved first. The queen froze as she watched the Queen of All Bees dance. When it was over, how else could she respond but to salute?

When her perception returned to her own hive, she found her workers crowding around her, waiting for her to instruct them. And indeed, she did, though not at all as she originally intended. As she'd first planned, the entire hive rose into the air. But unlike as she had planned, they hovered over her hive, chewing the half-built wax into smaller pieces. They picked up whatever honey and brood they could and then flew off as one.

They kept low to the ground, just barely above the blades of grass and the flowers of the field. They constrained the beating of their wings to the slowest speed that could keep them aloft, minimizing their buzzing. And then . . . they ignored the humans, instead making their way toward the giant, winged reptiles that were tied down nearby, hovering over to the largest of the beasts.

The hive landed on one of the large bags tied to the reptile's side and crawled inside. They crawled their way to the very bottom of the package, where a grand stock of provisions rested. There, they curled up into a ball and began building a small amount of wax, just enough to give them shelter.

No sooner had they finished when the queen felt the beast stir and lift into the air. She could only wonder where the Queen of All Bees was sending her.

And when she would be permitted to have her revenge.

CHAPTER TWENTY-EIGHT

WILL YOU BEE MINE?

Belissar sat in the apiary farmhouse after celebrating the bee army's latest victory. He rubbed his chin as he let the silence of the night waft over him. Niobee watched him from the table but made no noise, not wanting to interrupt his thoughts. Eventually he nodded and then gave a light sigh.

This incident had decided things for him. He was going to conduct another expansion purification sooner rather than later. The boar-shade had been really easy for his bees to take down without losses . . . but that was because it had been outside of the tower. What if this boar had appeared in a purification? Sure, the boar couldn't actually hit any of the bees, but its sheer bulk and resilience meant the bees couldn't stop it from moving around, and it had lasted a long time before being noticeably affected by their venom. If the shade had been assaulting the tower, it could have made a break for the flower meadow exit and likely would have reached it before the bee army brought it down. It, therefore, could have done major damage to the bee barracks, the orchard, or the apiary before perishing. It might even have been able to reach the core, if it made a straight run there. The glowing sphere at the final room of the tower had turned Belissar into a tower lord when he first touched it and he could channel most of his tower abilities through it . . . and it could apparently be corrupted if a shade reached it like the first one had. Given that even that partial corruption resulted in bits of the Hunger climbing the walls of the core room, Belissar didn't want to find out what would happen if core corruption ever hit one hundred percent.

Well, it probably wouldn't have gone as badly as that—the boar seemed to charge whatever attacked it, so they likely would have been able to lure it into a pit trap, but that wasn't what concerned Belissar. It was clear at this point that the Hunger continuously changed its approach . . . and was not limited to the contained purifications Belissar could conduct at his leisure. The Hunger was at war with his tower and would do everything in its power to slip past his defenses, both during and outside of the purifications. Belissar had, perhaps, gotten a bit too comfortable thanks to the recent string of successful purifications. It was good for him to remember that the Hunger was not a passive threat.

As such, while it didn't mean that he should rush, it would be wise of him not to delay his tower's growth. More expansion meant more options. New bees, new rooms, new features, and new flowers could all provide tools to deal with whatever the next shade turned out to be. And more territory purified meant more ground a shade would need to cover before it could reach the karnuq or the tower, should one attack from the outside once again.

Belissar still wanted to do everything he could to put the odds in his bees' favor and avoid casualties. But ultimately, he knew he could trust them to get the expansion purification done. And so, he would.

Now resolved, Belissar headed off to bed. Tomorrow would be a busy day.

The next day, Belissar and Niobee gathered the queens at the orchard's shrine of bees, as close to a midpoint of the tower as he could arrange. He took a deep breath as the queens hovered around him, waiting for his words.

"I am planning to conduct another expansion purification."

The queens paused, then burst into salute dances. The flower meadow queens affirmed they were ready to fight. The apiary queens promised donations of honey, particularly the medicinal queen. The orchard queens danced about, saying they would help however they could. Belissar smiled a little before continuing.

"Thank you all. We won't do it just yet, though. After the karnuq finish their gathering for today, I'm going to move the dirt tunnels to the front of the tower. They'll restrict and slow down any shades, especially flying ones, and maybe we'll even catch one in the traps. But, um, since this is a new thing, I want to give you all the chance to adjust. So, we'll try moving the rooms today and let the army practice fighting at the entrance to the new room, then conduct the purification once they're ready?"

The flower meadow queens started a dance indicating they were ready now . . . but the biggest one, the Second First of the First, paused. The others quieted down once they noticed, waiting for her to dance. Slowly, she began to salute, and then the others followed.

Belissar then turned to the apiary queens and bowed his head. "I'm sorry, but that does mean the new underground plants will be moving further away for the next day or two. Is that going to hurt your hives?"

The apiary queens saluted immediately.

"All flowers King's flowers! If want move can move!"

Belissar held back a frown. He felt bad about making the bees' foraging harder and their enthusiastic response only made him feel worse, but this was necessary.

So, instead, he forced himself to smile at them, resolving to do whatever he could to avoid such situations going forward.

"Thank you, I'll move them back as soon as I can. Everyone, let me know if there are any issues, or if you have any ideas that could help with the upcoming purification."

It was at that moment the karnuq arrived, and Belissar tilted his head. Chief Rohsuak had come with the group . . . a large group different from the normal gatherers and hunters. He turned to Niobee.

"Um, looks like the karnuq want to talk. So . . . guess we'll go talk to them. Afterwards, can you show the army where the entrance to the dirt tunnels is?"

"Okay!"

"Thanks, Niobee. Okay then, let's get to work."

The bees made their most rapid salute dance yet.

Belissar, Niobee, and the soldier bee army made their way over to the entrance. The karnuq, unusually, had not begun either gathering or hunting. Belissar guessed they were waiting for them, which was borne out when they saw him and walked to meet him.

"Hello, Sacred Den Master."

Belissar waved to the chief. "Hello, Chief Rohsuak. Um, did you want to talk?"

Chief Rohsuak nodded, her face unusually serious. "I do. We have a great request of you."

Belissar gulped at her tone. ". . . Um, what sort of request?"

Chief Rohsuak turned back to face the other karnuq and looked each in the eye. One by one, they saluted to her. She then turned to face him once more. Belissar nearly stepped back at the intense gazes of so many large bear people, but he tried to think about the bees flying above him, which gave him the courage to stand his ground. And then . . .

Chief Rohsuak and all the karnuq bowed their heads toward him.

"Sacred Den Master, if it pleases you, we wish to swear ourselves to your service."

Accept offer of allegiance?

Belissar stared blankly, then blinked repeatedly.

". . . Um, what?"

Fortunately, Chief Rohsuak seemed to have anticipated his confusion, as she took him aside to explain in more detail.

"From what I understand, sacred den masters are able to accept outsiders as their defenders and servants. We would like to become yours, if you would accept us."

Belissar furrowed his brow as he tried to follow along. "I . . . see. And, um, what exactly would that look like?"

Chief Rohsuak extended an open palm toward him. "Whatever you would like it to."

Belissar tilted his head. "Huh?"

Fortunately, Chief Rohsuak immediately elaborated. "From what I have seen, every sacred den master's relationship with their sworn defenders is different, so the exact details would be yours to decide. But, at the most basic level, we are hoping for food, shelter, and protection from external threats. In exchange, we will become your people. We will fight your battles, work your lands, defend your sacred den, and follow your commands."

Belissar rubbed his chin, but then suddenly his eyes widened. "You're . . . offering to become my tower guard?"

Now it was Chief Rohsuak's turn to rub her chin. "I am not familiar with the term, but if that is what your people call those who serve sacred dens, then yes, most likely."

Now that gave Belissar pause. He still wanted nothing to do with the tower lords or the way they did things. However, it was also true that he didn't know how they treated their own tower guards, and besides, Chief Rohsuak said their treatment would be up to him, so there wasn't an issue in doing things how he wanted. The question was: *Did* he want tower guards? And did he want the karnuq to fulfill that role? The tower itself had sent him a message when the karnuq made their request, so apparently there was more to it than just verbal promises.

But well, if he set aside his memories of the tower lords . . . this was a good thing, right? If the karnuq wanted to help defend the tower, he could certainly use their help during the next purification. Maybe they could also help him with building beehouses or processing flax or tasks like that.

But was this too good to be true? Chief Rohsuak said he'd have to provide them with food and shelter and protection. What exactly did that mean? What exactly would they want from him if accepted? Would they try to swindle him, maybe ask for all that stuff and then make excuses when it came time to fight?

Belissar looked over at Chief Rohsuak, and then beyond her. He saw Metsaitti, Juosiutik, and Noigakkuq among the karnuq who had come along. All of his concerns and anxieties boiled down to one question:

Did he trust the karnuq?

Belissar's eyes widened. He took a deep breath and opened his mouth. "Let's discuss what exactly this will look like for us."

Chief Rohsuak paused for a moment, then broke out into a smile. "Yes, of course."

To Belissar's own surprise, the answer to his question was yes. The karnuq had treated him well so far, better than any human ever had, save for his own parents and the old beekeeper. They had listened to his requests, delivered on their promises, and hadn't done anything to his detriment. And, most of all, they had respected his bees.

He was already providing them with food and protection, come to think of it. And he also did not want to see them harmed, as he had recently learned. So, he felt that they were worth taking a chance on, despite his fears.

And so, Belissar and the karnuq began discussing a new relationship with one another . . .

CHAPTER TWENTY-NINE

BEE-COME A DEFEND-BEAR

I see, so you're planning to expand tomorrow?" Chief Rohsuak confirmed.

Belissar nodded. "Yes, so it'll probably be best to wait and see what space I have available then."

Chief Rohsuak rubbed her chin. "I'll have the clan move just outside the sacred den in that case. Will you require assistance with the expansion?"

Belissar's eyes widened. "Ah . . . actually, yes. It's basically a fight against a big shade, like the boar we fought. And, um, that can spit clouds of death mist or something. Or that can fly and summon lightning."

Chief Rohsuak crossed her arms. "I see. If you wish, I can bring our hunters to help?"

Belissar paused for a moment, as he hadn't considered that. But if they wanted to become his tower's defenders, then wouldn't that make sense? "If you're sure . . . the help would be appreciated. I believe my bees can handle it, but we've been surprised before."

Chief Rohsuak narrowed her gaze. "Yes, we, too, have suffered from the unpredictability of the Hunger. Very well, you will have our support."

Belissar smiled. "Thank you, that's appreciated."

In more ways than one, in fact. Not only would the karnuq give him a good backup plan if a shade managed to overwhelm or escape his bees, but the fact that they were willing to help him fight also reassured Belissar that he wasn't making a mistake with this. They really did intend to make good on their promises and become his tower guard.

With that, he and Chief Rohsuak hammered out some other details. Belissar was already providing them with food and supplies, so, to his surprise, there was very little he needed to do that he wasn't already. Ideally, he would prepare a place for them to stay within the tower, but that would have to wait, as Belissar wasn't sure what rooms he'd want to place after the next expansion. Additionally, there was the issue of remnant spawning, which Chief Rohsuak was a bit surprised to find Belissar had little control over. He had seen a rest zone feature, however, so they both hoped they'd find a way to avoid spawning mini-shades everywhere the karnuq went.

So, to Belissar's continued surprise, most of the discussion was on what the karnuq would do for him. Chief Rohsuak basically told him that the tribute they offered him when they gathered stuff from his tower would now apply to everything they did, seeing as they were his people now.

"Um, are you sure about that?"

Chief Rohsuak nodded. "You are offering your protection and we are becoming your people. It is only natural. And, Sacred Den Master, may I offer some advice?"

"Um, sure?"

She looked him in the eyes, causing him to flinch a bit. "It is not wrong for you to seek your own benefit, you know? You have been extremely generous, and we trust you to be fair."

She sighed as Belissar frowned. She then placed her finger on her chin and glanced up at the bees hovering above. "How about this? Think of us as part of your bees. You take care of them and they obey you and offer you the fruits of their labor, correct? It is something similar for us."

Belissar paused. For a brief moment, he imagined Chief Rohsuak flying around on a pair of wings, attempting a "King best king!" dance.

He couldn't help but burst out laughing. Chief Rohsuak blinked and tilted her head. "Sacred Den Master?"

"Heh, it's . . . nothing, haha." He took a deep breath and then smiled at her. "Well, you're no bees, but I think I understand what you're trying to say. I build you a home like I did for them and you help me like they do?"

Chief Rohsuak returned his smile. "Exactly."

Eventually, they had hammered out as much detail as they could. Chief Rohsuak took the karnuq back to their camp, intending to move the rest of the clan over to the tower. Belissar busied himself by accompanying the soldier bee army to the apiary. They gathered by the main entrance to the dirt tunnels, the one built into the walls of the apiary, and then practiced fighting an enemy emerging from the tunnels. They tested making short dives into the cave, having sprayers attack from outside, and forming different encirclements to stop an enemy from leaving.

As the day wore on, Chief Rohsuak returned to the tower once more, followed by the entire karnuq clan. Belissar and the soldier bees made their way over. The karnuq all gathered before him, every man, woman, and child. Chief Rohsuak stepped toward him.

"We are ready, Sacred Den Master."

Belissar nodded at her. "Me too."

She then smiled. "Just one thing. May I ask for your name, or do you prefer Sacred Den Master?"

Belissar flushed as he realized that he had never given any of the karnuq his name. "Oh. Um, I'm Belissar. Err, nice to meet you?"

Chief Rohsuak chuckled softly. "Nice to meet you too, Sacred Den Master Belissar."

Fortunately for Belissar, the conversation finished and Chief Rohsuak returned to the karnuq. She then led them in striking their chests with their fists and lowering their heads.

"I, Chief Rohsuak the Blazing Berserker, in the witness of the God of Bees, swear myself to the service of Sacred Den Master Belissar. To be his shield and spear, to be his hands and feet, and to ensure that his sacred den stands. Let the gods bear witness and hold me to my oath."

The other karnuq all followed suit with their own names. Belissar gulped but tried to repeat their motions. He felt he should at least say something in return.

Accept offer of allegiance?

"Um, I, Belissar, master of this dungeon . . . in the witness of the God of Bees, accept. I . . . promise to do my best to house and protect you all. Um, let the gods bear witness and hold me to my oath?"

He turned to face the shrine of bees. His eyes widened, along with those of the karnuq, as the shrine of bees began to glow brightly. He, along with each and every karnuq, was surrounded by a golden glow, which then flashed once and disappeared.

You have gained 132 sworn defenders.

Sworn Defender: An outsider who has sworn to defend a dungeon. Bound not to harm the core or the dungeon master, and to defend it from existential threats. Immediately gains a minor blessing from the dungeon's patron and may interact with dungeon mana. Remnants will not spawn around a sworn defender unless they specifically intend to be challenged. Sworn defenders do not cost mana to upkeep, but mana may improve the bond with a given individual.

Both Belissar and the karnuq were left blinking as the glow receded. The karnuq all began to stare at their hands, and Belissar could now feel them stir up their mana. In fact . . . he could now feel them like he did his bees, though the connection was noticeably weaker.

There was a lot to take in, for both parties. But Chief Rohsuak kept her wits about her and bowed her head toward Belissar once more with a smile.

"Thank you, Sacred Den Master Belissar, for accepting us."

"Oh, um, you're welcome? It feels like I should be thanking you for promising to protect the tower."

Chief Rohsuak's smile grew. "If all goes well, perhaps we shall both thank each other?"

Belissar slowly smiled at that. "That sounds nice."

But the biggest surprise was yet to come. Niobee flew down in front of Belissar and began to dance. "King! Outsiders now King's workers?"

Belissar smiled at her. "Something like that."

She turned to face Chief Rohsuak and began to dance. "Good! Work hard for King!"

Chief Rohsuak paused only for a moment before nodding. "Yes, of course."

The rest of the karnuq were not so calm.

". . . Did that bee just talk?"

"Um, I didn't hear anything, but I somehow did? What?"

"Maybe we can hear her dancing? Is that the blessing of the God of Bees?"

"L-Look, the other bees are dancing, too!"

The bees, for their part, were also conversing.

"Outsiders . . . can dance now? Part of King's hive?"

"Part of hive of hives? But . . . they're not bees?"

"Not bee . . . but like King? So, okay?"

Niobee flew up before the soldier bees and began her own dance.

"Not bees, but belong to King now, so okay! As long as work hard for King, can join hive of hives!"

With that, all the soldier bees saluted as one. "Yes, Conduit!"

With that, the soldier bees began greeting dances to the karnuq. The karnuq were left with wide eyes as they said hello to the soldier bees. Belissar crossed his arms and nodded at the sight with a smile.

Well, there was a lot going on, but he was happy that the bear folk could talk to the bees now. And very happy to see them doing so without issue. That was a crucial step if the karnuq were truly going to make their home in his tower. He was also pleased to hear the bees were okay with this and had accepted the new defenders. He . . . probably should have spoken with them before accepting the karnuq's oath. He should probably speak with the queens regularly, in fact.

And in particular, he should probably talk to Niobee and the queens about the karnuq before they started putting them to work, from the sound of things . . .

CHAPTER THIRTY

PURIFICATION CAN BEE DIRTY

The next morning, Belissar and the soldier bee army gathered by the tower entrance. Chief Rohsuak soon arrived with Metsaitti and a group of karnuq hunters and moved to greet Belissar.

"Hello, Sacred Den Master."

Belissar nodded at them. "Hello, thank you for coming."

Chief Rohsuak inclined her head. "Of course. Would you mind sharing your plan with us?"

Belissar nodded and motioned to the bee army overhead. "The bees have been training for this, so they should be able to handle it. If you don't mind, could you come with me to the other side of the room? It would help if you could guard the exit on that side, in case something goes wrong."

Chief Rohsuak saluted in the karnuq fashion and turned to Metsaitti, who commanded the hunters to move out. Belissar turned to the queen leading the army today.

"We'll start soon, good luck and try to stay safe, okay?"

The bees all danced their own salute as one, and then Belissar moved to join the karnuq hunters as they walked to the other side of the flower meadow. The bear folk were glancing around and gripping their weapons, but the Hunger didn't stir. Chief Rohsuak smiled slightly.

"So, it's true. We really won't be challenged just for our presence in the sacred den."

Belissar nodded. "Looks that way. That's really convenient, you should be able to move in once we're done here."

Chief Rohsuak's smile grew. "So it seems."

With no remnants appearing, the group made their way to the flower meadow exit without any issue. The karnuq eyed the bee barracks curiously but Metsaitti barked orders at them.

"We have a shade incoming, prepare for battle!"

They saluted and began to take up positions in front of the barracks, right by the hallway through the structure that led to the flower meadow's exit. Chief Rohsuak turned to Belissar.

"That's the place you'd like us to guard, correct?"

Belissar nodded. "Yes, thank you."

Chief Rohsuak nodded and watched the hunters arrange themselves. A few moments later, she turned back to Belissar with a serious expression.

"We are ready whenever you are, Sacred Den Master."

Belissar nodded and then shifted to his tower sight. He had already moved the dirt tunnels in front of the flower meadow, all that was left was to remove the second entrance by the Ground mana flowers, so that the only exit was out at the end of the maze.

Once Belissar confirmed the changes, the tower's mana rumbled. The gate in the flower meadow shifted into a cave that opened into the dirt tunnels. Meanwhile, the orchard moved up to the second floor, and the exit of the flower meadow now displayed the staircase heading there.

The soldier bee army buzzed their wings and held their positions.

Belissar sent them a message. "Everyone ready?"

The queen in command saluted. Belissar took a deep breath.

Attempt expansion purification?
Estimated purification strength: Small.

"Okay, here we go."

Expansion purification attempt commencing.

The karnuq jumped and glanced every which way as the tower's mana began to surge. Soon the tower's entrance gate slammed open and the Hunger began to coalesce once more. The karnuq shivered as the chill of the Hunger passed through the tower's mana. The bees stood at the ready.

Belissar paid them no mind, focusing his tower sight on the entrance as the Hunger formed. It appeared down on the ground, so it probably wasn't a flying shade . . . but then it split into two before the shade began to take shape. Or, in this case, shades.

Two sets of paws dug into the subterranean dirt. Short, rounded feline heads emerged with two pairs of glowing red eyes each, one set forward in the normal position, a second set on the sides of the shade's heads. Their bodies were mostly feline, similar to the mountain lions Belissar knew but a bit smaller and far lither, with long, thick tails stretching out behind them. The similarity ended there as a pair of bug-like wings extended on their backs.

Expansion purification begun. Remaining hostiles: 2

"It's started!"

The karnuq refocused at Belissar's shout, while in the dirt tunnels the shades let out a roar and began to run. Belissar's eyes widened as they crossed the entrance room in an instant.

Fast!

The shades' feet launched their light forms across the rooms, their wings beating to push them forward even faster. They didn't fly but they moved so far with each step they were practically gliding. Their long tails extended outward, keeping them stable even as they soared.

They launched right over the first pit trap without even touching it. Belissar wasn't sure if they had dodged it . . . or if they hadn't noticed it at all.

They did slow down somewhat as they approached the first turn, but their wings spread out and their tails whipped around, allowing them to reorient themselves with minimal speed loss. They flipped around and began to run along the walls for a bit before straightening out, one taking up a position behind the other as they flew down the tunnels. The sticky honey trap Belissar had placed on the tunnel roof activated, but the shades were long gone before the honey even left the nozzles.

It seemed this time the Hunger didn't plan to fight the bees at all.

"Be careful! There are two ground shades moving super-fast! They're probably planning to run right past you!"

The commanding queen saluted and began to give out orders to the army. The bees tightened their formation around the entrance, forming a near-solid wall of chitin around it. Belissar was incredibly grateful for the dirt tunnels, as the twisting labyrinth gave the bees a chance to adapt. Still, he was worried. With the bees so tightly packed, a single attack like the wolf-shade's mist or the bird-shade's lightning would cause massive damage. But with the sheer speed the shades were currently displaying, he didn't think there was a good alternative. He would just have to hope these shades didn't have an attack like that.

The shades rushed through the tunnels, though several times they hit dead ends and had to backtrack. Belissar noticed that they never checked the same tunnel twice . . . probably because of the trail of blackened dirt they left whenever they touched the ground. That was unfortunate, but the dirt tunnels still bought some time, far more than they would have had otherwise. Still, the shades' sheer speed meant they were approaching the exit far faster than

Belissar might have hoped. He called out as they rounded the last corner before the exit.

"Here they come!"

A group of sprayers took up positions right in front of the entrance, abdomens already pointed down the final hallway. The shades rounded the corner and slowed slightly. They growled at the sight of the bees in front of them and then spread their wings, gathering black mist around them before flapping their wings back as quickly as they could. A burst of more black mist blasted behind them, pushing them forward and sending them hurtling down the hall.

The sprayers, though, were already launching their attack. The queen in command, heeding Belissar's warnings and Niobee's further description of the shades, had ordered them to spray their toxins before the shades came into range. The venom spray was flying through the air before the shades even made it through.

The venom caught the first shade right in the eyes. It howled and twisted, trying to paw at its face. As a result, it tripped and tumbled to the ground, falling right into the final pit trap of the dirt tunnels. It fell with a crash and then was covered by the honey trap at the bottom.

Unfortunately, with its wings spread wide, the shade had taken the entirety of the toxic spray, blocking any from reaching the second shade. The unaffected shade pushed forward, leaping over the pit. It beat its wings and caused a gust of wind to pour out of the entrance, pushing aside the sprayers as the shade burst into the flower meadow.

At which point it was set upon by the soldiers.

A solid dome of soldier bees collapsed onto the shade from all sides. It beat its wings again and pushed some of the ones in front off course with another gust of wind, but the bees on its side and top managed to land and thrust their stingers into its body. The shade howled and took off running, but the soldier bees clung on tight, having expected it to try and escape. They continued to sting it over and over.

The shade tried to whip its tail and beat its wings, but its features were designed for speed, not damage. The tail was too thick to whip all the way around, and the bees evaded it with ease. The wings were too light to do any meaningful harm to the tough soldiers, and they simply ignored the ineffectual blows. The shade tried to stir up its black wind, but the soldiers clung on regardless.

With no other course, the shade took off running as fast as it could, hoping the bees would fall off. But as it did, a second encirclement of bees took up positions and launched their attack. With its attention focused on the bees already on its back, the shade failed to react in time. A third group of bees landed on its face and shoulders to begin their own attacks.

The shade howled and collapsed to the ground about halfway through the flower meadow, just within range of the karnuq. The hunters gripped their spears tight as they saw the shade approach . . . but the ball of bees and black mist didn't move any closer.

Hostile purified. Remaining hostiles: 1

Belissar released the breath he was holding and then turned his attention to the other shade. Smoke billowed out of the entrance to the dirt tunnels. The apiary soldier bees had already dropped flame radishes on the other shade. He only had to wait a moment more.

All hostiles defeated.
Purification successful.

CHAPTER THIRTY-ONE

THE MASTER'S SPECIAL-BEE

The tower's mana surged and passed in a wave out into the world beyond, reclaiming even more territory from the Hunger. The karnuq glanced around in a daze. Even Chief Rohsuak had a curious look on her face as she turned to Belissar.

"Is it over, Sacred Den Master?"

Belissar nodded. "Yes, sorry you all came this way without doing anything, but fortunately the bees handled it."

Chief Rohsuak slowly shook her head. "It's a good thing we didn't have to fight. You will not hear complaints from me about a lack of danger."

Some of the others gave pointed stares toward Chief Rohsuak's back, but she didn't respond, so Belissar decided not to mention them.

"Yes, that makes sense. I normally hold a celebration for the bees now, would you all like to join?"

Chief Rohsuak smiled. "We would be honored, Sacred Den Master."

With that, Belissar asked some of the karnuq to come with him. Their eyes widened upon entering the orchard, and again when they reached the apiary. They were stunned into silence when Belissar started gathering the vast trays of mana honeycomb he had stockpiled. He placed the trays in the karnuq's hands and had them haul the honey back down to the flower meadow, with the apiary hives assisting. Soon, all the bees and the karnuq gathered by the flower meadow's shrine of bees. Belissar turned to the bees.

"Great work, everyone! We won again, thanks to you, and we didn't lose a single bee!"

The karnuq watched in silence as the entire soldier bee army broke out into celebratory dances in the air, and then began to swarm the honeycomb trays. Belissar broke off a few pieces and handed them to the karnuq as well. Chief Rohsuak and Metsaitti couldn't help but grin massively as he did.

The other karnuq hunters soon understood why.

Since Belissar had conducted the purification in the morning, it was barely mid-day by the time the celebrations finished. Most of the bees returned to their work, while Metsaitti led the karnuq hunters back to report their victory to the rest of the clan. Meanwhile, Belissar requested that Chief Rohsuak and the bee queens remain.

Because now it was time to discuss the rewards.

Expansion successful.
Reward: Floor limit increased to 3. Receive one perk choice,
and two random reward choices.

Belissar had told Chief Rohsuak that they'd discuss the karnuq moving inside the tower after the purification rewards, so it made sense to consult with her on those rewards. And once Belissar had decided to do that, there was no way he wouldn't also consult the bees on the choices. They had helped him make his last round of choices too, after all.

"Okay, so, first things first, we have a new floor. That means we can add two more rooms. Additionally, we have a perk choice and two random choices. Let me check them now."

Please select a perk:
- Enhanced Toxins (Rarity: Common.)
- Boosted Beehouses (Rarity: Uncommon.)
- Bee Specialist (Rarity: Common.)

Belissar rubbed his chin as he read the choices to Chief Rohsuak and the bees. The perk choices were all ones he had seen before. That . . . should have been a good thing, right? It meant he could now pick up something he had missed before. Yet, for some reason, he couldn't help but feel disappointed. But he had two more choices to read, so he continued on.

Please select a reward:
- Uncommon Room Choice (At least one uncommon or better option.)
- Uncommon Room Feature Choice (At least one uncommon or better option.)
- +1 Room Slot

Please select a reward:
- Rare Monster Choice (At least one rare or better option.)

- Uncommon Room Feature Choice (At least one uncommon or better option.)
- +100 max mana

Belissar stared at the choices for a bit. A rare choice! The first he'd seen in a while! He couldn't recall perfectly, since he had been a bit confused at the time, but the monster bee queens themselves were a rare choice, right?

"Sacred Den Master?"

Belissar flushed a bit as he remembered that everyone was waiting on him to actually read the choices aloud. He also had to explain a bit about what each type of choice might provide.

"So, um, what do you all think?"

Niobee was, of course, first to respond. "Whatever King chooses!"

The rest of the bee queens soon followed, though they had some additional suggestions. More bees, more flowers, and more beehouses were the general trends. Belissar then turned to Chief Rohsuak, who was chuckling at the display. She then noticed his gaze and rubbed her chin with a hum.

"I will admit I'm a bit out of my depth here. It is fascinating to learn how the sacred dens function, but I cannot claim to have ever built one. More resources, new rooms, and stronger defenders all have their own appeal and I cannot tell you which should be your priority. As for my people: food, water, and shelter are our immediate concerns. You are already capable of providing those, however, so I would prefer you do what serves your sacred den best. From my perspective, you have led it well thus far. You should continue forward with your vision for it."

Belissar couldn't help but frown a bit, as he had hoped Chief Rohsuak would have had a stronger opinion. If he thought about it, though, she had been a relatively normal person just before this. She was like he'd been when he was first put in charge of a tower . . . and taking it far more calmly than he had. So, perhaps he *was* more experienced when it came to tower affairs at this point. Not that he felt like it.

But ultimately, he was the one who had to make the decision, so he got down and thought about it. At the moment, he didn't feel like his tower had any urgent needs in particular. The bees had a bunch of new flowers, the karnuq apparently wouldn't trigger remnants now that they were sworn to him, and the soldier bee army had dealt with a new shade type easily. The bees' requests were fairly general, and overall, they seemed happy with their current situation. The karnuq might have more needs in the future, but for now just having a safe place to stay and food to eat was plenty.

As far as the shades went, the dirt tunnels had proved they were worth their weight in mead. They slowed the shades down and gave the bees time to prepare, and they allowed Belissar to observe the shades before the actual fighting began so he could warn the bees about their speed. The purification might not have gone as well without that extra forewarning. It seemed there was significant value in having some rooms ahead of the bee army.

So, what would help his tower most? Which new options could help him face the next new trick of the Hunger, like the dirt tunnels had? What would best prepare them for the future?

Belissar slowly began to speak as he continued rubbing his chin.

"I think . . . we should take the extra room slot. That will give us an extra room for each floor, as well as three rooms on the new floor. We could make a floor for the karnuq with three whole rooms. Then, we could add a new dirt tunnel room for the apiary bees to gather from while leaving one by the entrance so we don't have to keep moving the current one? And taking the extra room slot now should give us plenty of space for new rooms, since new room choices are cheaper than new room slots in the DP store."

Chief Rohsuak's eyes widened slightly and then she bowed her head.

"We are honored you would offer so much to us, Sacred Den Master."

Belissar rubbed the back of his head and decided not to mention that he just didn't want his bees to have to share their rooms or flowers. The apiary queens also thanked him and began a long dance detailing just how much they liked the new flowers. Belissar grinned at that.

Room limit increased! Room limit is now three per floor.

He then rubbed his chin as he considered the next decision. "Any opinions on the perks? Ah, let me read the descriptions for you."

Chief Rohsuak and the bees listened attentively as Belissar explained what each perk was supposed to do.

And then, for the first time ever as far as Belissar was aware, the bees disagreed. The flower meadow queens favored enhanced toxins, while the apiary queens preferred boosted beehouses. Which made sense. The flower meadow queens were responsible for the soldier bee army, and so would naturally want anything that would strengthen their attacks. The apiary queens devoted themselves entirely to honey production, which boosted beehouses would assist them with. Belissar could see the argument for either, which was why this choice was so difficult. He turned to Chief Rohsuak, hoping she might have some advice. She took on a thoughtful look before speaking.

"Any of the choices would seem to help you. As a warrior, however, I must note that poison seems to be your sacred den's most potent weapon. There is both danger and opportunity in specializing in a single field, but maximizing your strengths is generally not a bad call. You'll find the further you commit down a single path, the more options it will grant you to overcome its own weaknesses.

And, of course, we will now offer our assistance should you face a foe your choices are ill-suited to deal with. In my opinion, enhanced toxins will grant your sacred den the most power, if that is your concern and should open additional doors down the line if you wish to continue down that path. On the other hand, Bee Specialist is an apt description for your current sacred den and fits your patron, so reinforcing that will not disappoint. As far as the beehouses go . . ."

She gave him a grin and licked her lips. "I, personally, would not mind more honey."

Belissar hummed and maybe groaned a bit. Part of him wanted to move on to the next choice and see if that would help . . . except that Bee Specialist itself might affect the next choice, so if he ended up choosing that it would best to have it before the next choice, right?

Belissar looked toward the shrine of bees and then nodded. When in doubt, he would choose bees.

Bee Specialist selected.

Bee Specialist would help all of his bees with the boost to their stats. And, as Chief Rohsuak had pointed out, it fit the God of Bees and his vision for the tower. He hadn't thought about it before, but when she mentioned a vision he tried to imagine what his tower might look like in the future, what he might want it to look like.

He saw a tower full of and surrounded by happy bees.

Bee Specialist would work with the Blessing of Bees to guide future choices in the direction of that vision, so that was what he chose. Though, he'd see what he could do to still improve the beehouses and maybe find some more poisonous flowers, to address his bees' requests.

And now came time for the final choice. Belissar couldn't help but be a bit excited . . .

CHAPTER THIRTY-TWO

EXPLORING RARI-BEES

Belissar very briefly thought about the last choice to ensure he wasn't missing something or acting foolish, but in the end his choice was made. Extra mana? He could get that from daily purifications. An uncommon room feature choice? Room features were the cheapest option in the DP store and could even show up as minor+ purification rewards. He would have considered it if his tower had a specific need or lack that an appropriate room feature might have addressed, but at the moment he was satisfied with his current features.

So, with no specific reason to pick anything else, he chose the monster option. He couldn't wait to see what a rare option might entail.

Please select a monster:*
- Monster Bee Blader (Rarity: Uncommon. Type: Bee, Blade.)
- Monster Bee Communer (Rarity: Rare. Type: Bee, Mind.)
- Bloodsucking Bee Queen (Rarity: Epic. Type: Bee, Blood.)

*(*One or more choices upgraded due to Blessing of Bees.)*

Belissar couldn't help but grin. Not just a rare option, but an epic one too! Though . . . was rare better than epic or the other way around? He wasn't entirely sure, but epic sounded like it should be better? In any case, he should have two good options, plus an uncommon to boot! Belissar could barely wait as he opened up the descriptions for each.

Monster Bee Blader

Vitality: *Minor*
Strength: *Small*

Speed: *Average*

Magic: *Minimal*

Defense: *Minor*

Resistance: *Minimal*

Special: *Minimal*

Notable Skills: *Poison Slash, Death Blow, Brood Offspring*

Evolves From: *Monster Bee Soldier*

A monster bee soldier evolution. This bee trades its stinger for an edged blade and grows claws on its front two legs, as well as having greater size and strength. This allows it to attack more directly via cutting and slashing. It can coat its abdomen blade in venom, though its venom is no more powerful than a normal soldier's.

Belissar whistled as the tower showed him the usual image of the monster. While the monster bee workers were the size of regular bees and the monster bee soldiers a bit larger than his hand, the monster bee bladers were the size of a small dog. And while the soldiers were basically just larger bees, the bladers were more monstrous in shape as well as size. Their front legs had curled blades like those of a praying mantis, while their stingers were flat, wide, and sharp on either end. The flower meadow queens hovered closer and closer to him as he read out the description of the bee.

An impressive option that could do some serious damage without relying on poison at all. And that was just the uncommon choice.

<u>Monster Bee Communer</u>

Vitality: *Minimal*

Strength: *Minimal*

Speed: *Average*

Magic: *Small*

Defense: *Minimal*

Resistance: *Minor*

Special: *Average*

Notable Skills: *Poison Sting, Death Blow, Brood Offspring, Brood Link*

Evolves From: *Monster Bee Worker*

A monster bee queen can command her offspring, but must also remain safe within the hive, meaning this ability often goes unused save for the direst of circumstances. The monster bee communer is the solution to this.

*The monster bee communer expands the link between a monster bee
queen and her offspring. It not only increases the range of a monster bee
queen's command but also allows her brood to exchange information
with her from a distance, allowing the entire hive to benefit from their
queen's abilities. The communer itself has very little in the way of defense
and so must be protected.*

All the bees fell still as Belissar finished the description. The Second First of the First slowly began to dance.

"Lets queens . . . command from inside hive? Strengthens link between hive?"

Belissar slowly nodded. "I think so?"

One of the queens from the orchard then hovered closer to him. "King . . . new bee . . . lets queens see what workers see? Even when far away?"

Belissar slowly nodded once more. "If I understand this correctly . . ."

The orchard queen trembled and then suddenly exploded into a high-speed dance. "That one! Want that one!"

Belissar blinked as workers from that queen's hive, who had stuck around the queen meeting for some reason, pulled their queen back. Well, that was at least one unambiguous opinion. Belissar chuckled a little as he checked the epic-rarity option.

Bloodsucking Bee Queen

Vitality:	*Minor*
Strength:	*Minimal*
Speed:	*Average*
Magic:	*Minor*
Defense:	*Minimal*
Resistance:	*Minimal*
Special:	*Minor*
Notable Skills:	*Drain Bite, Poison Sting, Brood Mother, Command Offspring*

*A sweat bee evolved by mana to seek other fluids. Drains sustenance
and mana from the blood of living creatures and has anticoagulant venom
along with enlarged stingers to encourage the flow of blood. This one
is a queen, and capable of building a hive of monster blood bees.*

Belissar just stared in silence for a bit, before gulping. Well, that was certainly an option. Bees that . . . drank blood? Now that image put the *monster* in monster bee. Belissar gulped again and rubbed his chin.

Well, they certainly sounded powerful. Bees that could not only make small stings, but open small cuts that would continue bleeding far longer than normal.

And not only that, but this one was a queen, and could therefore build an entirely new set of hives. And what if the other options he already unlocked applied? Would he have bloodsucking bee soldiers? If he tried to scale up the bloodsucking bee stinger to soldier bee size, it would almost match a monster bee blader's stinger as a cutting weapon. Bloodsucking bee sprayers? What would they spray—blood, maybe? But they were supposed to drink blood, so probably something else?

However, there was a significant problem. Where exactly was Belissar going to get the blood to feed such monsters? At the current moment, the only sources of blood in his tower were himself and the karnuq. He didn't have enough blood to feed even one hive by himself, and he didn't think the karnuq would appreciate being turned into a food source. Maybe he could get some sort of animal option? But the Blessing of Bees and his new Bee Specialist perk would make that unlikely, right? He hadn't seen any monster options that weren't bees as of yet, and Bee Specialist would only make it less likely.

So, if he chose Bloodsucking Bee Queens . . . he'd probably have to wait until he had a sustainable source of blood before spawning any. He turned to Chief Rohsuak.

"Um . . . do the karnuq raise any animals?"

Chief Rohsuak's face was scrunched up. "In the past, yes, but none survived our journey here."

"I . . . see . . ."

Belissar took a deep breath. On the one hand, this option was epic. Who knew when he'd see it again, or if he ever would? It was powerful and could potentially open up an entire world of possibilities for his tower. But it wasn't something he could support yet . . . and something he wasn't sure he'd ever be able to. He had yet to see a non-bee animal offered to him, and there weren't many bee-related animals save for those that preyed upon bees—and Belissar knew he was never picking any of those. And while he may have preferred bees to people, he wasn't about to feed the karnuq to them.

So . . . he decided to let it go. He believed in his current bees, and they had a clear opinion this time.

Monster Bee Communer now available!
Monster Bee Workers may now evolve into Monster Bee Communers.

The bee queens all paused as a wave of mana passed over them. And then, the orchard queen who had expressed her opinion earlier exploded into another rapid dance. "YES! Amazing, incredible! Thank you, King! King is best king!"

A moment later, the other bee queens joined her in thanking him, and proclaiming him the best. Belissar grinned and chuckled.

"Heh, you're welcome, glad you like it."

It pained him to watch the epic option fade, but the rare Monster Bee Communer seemed like a good choice as well. And, most of all, it was the one his bees preferred and one that made them extremely happy. That was enough to reassure Belissar that he wasn't making a mistake. It was his bees that did the fighting and defeated the shades, so an option they wanted was probably the most beneficial in any case. Better to pick something that would make his current hives stronger than to roll the dice on a brand-new one.

"That should be it. I'm going to talk with Chief Rohsuak about getting the karnuq set up. You girls can stay if you want, or you can get back to your hives, whichever you prefer."

The orchard queen gave one final dance of gratitude before zipping out of the room. The flower meadow queens exchanged dances with one another, and then all but one of them returned to the bee barracks, the last one indicating that she would stay to listen and report back to the barracks. The largest apiary queen then started a dance exchange of her own. When it finished, all the apiary queens save for her left, while she moved to hover by Belissar. He nodded at the two bees who stayed and then turned to Chief Rohsuak.

"Okay, should we discuss where you're going to set up?"

Chief Rohsuak smiled at him. "It would be my honor, Sacred Den Master."

THE CONDUIT'S WORR-BEES

Belissar and Chief Rohsuak discussed a bit and decided to allocate the second floor to the karnuq. Belissar would add a flower meadow, an orchard, and a dirt tunnel room there for the karnuq to use. There was, however, a slight problem.

Mana: 11/435

It turned out Belissar didn't have enough mana to actually add that many rooms right now, much less any additional room features. So, he and Chief Rohsuak agreed to wait a day or two for him to expand his mana reserves before the karnuq would move in.

With that, Chief Rohsuak left to rejoin the karnuq and Belissar dismissed the two remaining queens back to their hives. He decided to spend the remainder of the day resting after all the recent battles and conversations.

But, unbeknownst to Belissar, the queens did not immediately disperse and return to their hives. Niobee took the Firstborn and the First of the Fifth aside. The Firstborn gave a salute dance and then began to dance unsteadily.

"Yes, Conduit? Need us?"

Niobee danced unusually slowly for her. ". . . Yes. Worried."

The Firstborn and the First of the Fifth glanced at each before the First of the Fifth began to dance.

"That's concerning. What worried about?"

Niobee turned to glance toward the entrance of the tower. "Before King was king, King was part of hive of humans. Human hive treated badly. Hurt King, stole King's food. Niobee would sting but King wasn't part of hive, so only Niobee fought. Wasn't enough."

The Firstborn and the First of the Fifth both began to buzz loudly and extend their stingers at that. Niobee had to brush their antennas to calm them down. The First of the Fifth began a slow, but unyielding dance.

"So . . . Conduit believes karnuq are threat to King?"

The Firstborn saluted. "Want me to gather army?"

Niobee danced the negative before continuing unsteadily. "No. Karnuq different. Swore to join King's hive. Think will be okay, but still worried. Can queens keep watch, make sure not tricking King?"

Both the Firstborn and the First of the Fifth saluted immediately. The Firstborn waved her abdomen about, stinger still extended. "Will protect King from every threat."

The First of the Fifth was still buzzing her wings. "Anyone hurt King . . . will die."

Niobee thanked the two queens and then left to rejoin the King. The Firstborn and the First of the Fifth slowly made their way back to their hives, for they had much to think about.

When she returned to the bee barracks, the Firstborn called for a meeting of the queens and relayed the information granted to her by the Conduit. The other flower meadow queens were silent. The Firstborn could sympathize. The tales of the King before he became king were always fantastical and hard to believe. Especially this one.

How could the King have ever found himself at such a disadvantage? How could others like him fail to see his wisdom and grace? And how powerful were they that they could harm the King and get away with it?

It was a solemn reminder to the flower meadow queens. Their army was mighty and could bring down invaders without the loss of a single bee. They had avenged the First Dynasty and allowed the King to turn his mind away from war. They had defeated two new types of invaders without being caught off guard. But they were not the most powerful force out there, not by a long shot, and they still had a long way to go if they wanted to protect the hive of hives. It would not do for them to grow complacent from their recent victories.

Fortunately, the King had granted them great tools to do just that. Every queen felt the tower's mana pass through them. It strengthened all the bees, making the soldiers hit harder, letting the workers fly faster, and granting the queens greater mana and endurance. And, beyond that, it spoke to the queens. It told them of a new type of bee, the one the King had told them about. A bee that would let a queen see through the eyes of her workers and send them commands from the safety of her own hive.

For the flower meadow queens, it was perfect. The need for a queen to command the army for maximum responsiveness and adaptability? They could now do so without exposing themselves to danger. The drop in worker efficiency they noted whenever the queen was away? The queen no longer needed to leave to take command, and so she could continue to manage her workers at the same time. The delays when a queen commanded soldiers that weren't of her own brood? Now each queen could command their own offspring simultaneously. It was a solution to all of the problems they had encountered since taking personal command of the army.

Additionally, this new type of bee would help with the issue raised by the Conduit. The queens could assign workers to follow the newcomers and then watch them with their own eyes. Their responses to any threats would not be delayed by the need to wait for a scouting report to arrive.

So, the flower meadow queens soon began to discuss what all of this would mean for them. Every queen would begin raising communers immediately, while worker bees would be spread out across the entire room in order to keep eyes on every corner . . . and so keep them aware of everything occurring in the flower meadow.

They would never cease in their efforts. They would take this opportunity to continue to grow the might of the army. And they would keep the hive of hives and the King safe from any and all threats.

The First of the Fifth paced about in her hive as she considered the implications of what the Conduit had told her. To hear that the King had been wounded and humiliated? *Unthinkable.* Had it been anyone other than the Conduit who told her, she would have had them stung for a most egregious and despicable lie.

But it was the Conduit, and that meant that it was true. Her wings buzzed again as the mere thought of it made her mind go blank with rage. Should any of the King's old human hive appear again, she swore she would make them suffer.

But they were not here. So instead, she would not fail the Conduit's request. She would ensure that these karnuq would *never* have the chance to do anything like the King's old hive.

The question on her mind right now was . . . how?

She had the worker force to spread across the apiary, or even beyond, and she could request her daughter's help with the orchard. The flower meadow queens would handle their own domain and, for once, the First of the Fifth did not doubt that they would complete this task with all due diligence. The issue was that to do so would ultimately compromise her honey production. Workers spread out across the apiary would disrupt the allocation of her foragers to the best flowers, the patches the King had grown himself. They could still gather from the mundane flowers spread across the room, but the honey quality and quantity would suffer as a result.

The First of the Fifth was willing to do even this if it came down to it. She would *not* permit the King to suffer such injury and humiliation ever again, no matter what she had to do to prevent it. But she was the First of the Fifth. She aimed to be the King's ideal queen. She produced the most and the best honey. She would love all bees as he did. She never compromised and never settled for less than the best and would spare no effort to achieve her aims.

So, she considered how she could complete her given task without compromising her honey production. If there was any method by which she could avoid the inefficiency inherent in giving her workers this secondary goal.

And, as she could have expected, the King had provided.

At first, the First of the Fifth had been somewhat dismissive of the new option. These communer bees cost more mana and honey than a regular worker to raise, and yet held no advantage over any other worker in either work or battle. Certainly, she could see the value in extending her eyes and dances beyond the range of her own sight . . . but it was not necessary for her hive. Her hive was amazingly efficient already. She had perfect knowledge of its every operation and full confidence that her workers would carry out her will. Relying on communers to manage her own hive was a crutch that an ideal queen would not require.

But as she thought more about it, she began to see the value. Her gravest mistake came from being unaware of events going on outside of her hive. If, for example, she had assigned a communer to her daughter's hive, she could have received real-time updates on her daughter's status. In fact, she intended to send one to her daughter now for that very purpose.

And then, she had an idea. Why should she limit that to her own daughter? What if, instead, she sent a communer to every single hive in the apiary? That way, she could keep track of every hive there, and so offer assistance whenever and wherever it was required? Would that not be the ideal way to show her love for all bees? Would that not bring her closer to the King and the Conduit, both of whom could keep track of the bees without seeing them directly?

And, this would provide a solution for her current quandary. Because if she did this, then she could collaborate with the other apiary queens on this task. She knew the flower meadow queens and even her daughter cooperated with other queens besides their own kin, and that such cooperation had apparently borne fruit, but still she hesitated. The First of the Fifth now loved all bees, but she still refused to compromise the quality of her work. She did not wish to share her tasks with any queen who could not achieve the level of performance she expected of her own hive. How much more so when it could be the King's own safety at risk?

But what if the other queens took her eyes with them? What if all the queens of the apiary spread their eyes and ears throughout the room to receive immediate reports on any threats, which they could then immediately pass on to the First of the Fifth? That . . . would be sufficiently effective, would it not? And it would only require a fraction of the workers from each hive to achieve, resulting in a drop in productivity that was ultimately manageable.

The First of the Fifth finally stopped pacing, and then began to issue commands to her workers. It was time to call the apiary queens to gather once more.

UN-BEE-LIEVABLE HAPPINESS

The Fourth of the Seventh zipped through the hive, bouncing off of all of the walls. Her workers had given up on calming her down at this point, even the lead worker.

Largely because the First of the Fifth's First Daughter had also joined her.

"Amazing! Incredible! Can watch workers even when in hive! King is best king!"

"Amazing! Incredible! Can talk to Fourth of Seventh even if she leaves! King is best king!"

The lead worker, however, froze solid as the First of the Fifth's First Daughter slowed down just enough for her to comprehend the frantic dance going on. She began to tremble.

There . . . would be a way to contact their queen? *Wherever* she went?

And, to the worker's further surprise, the tower's mana began to speak to her as well. It turned out the new bee type the King had spoken of was not a queen, or some modified soldier. It was a *worker* evolution, and concerned her directly, thus making her eligible to receive the new information herself.

Her trembling grew as she considered the implications of the new information she had received. Plans began to coalesce in her mind.

However, the hive's surprises were not yet over . . .

Belissar strolled leisurely out of the flower meadow. However, he stopped as soon as he got to the orchard, turning to glance at the grove where the two orchard queens lived. He began to rub his chin.

The bigger orchard queen's sheer excitement at the communer bees reminded him of something. If he recalled correctly, the orchard queens were the ones sending out scouts beyond the tower. It had been their workers that managed to locate the shade attacking the karnuq and enabled him to respond before tragedy struck.

He had been neglecting the world beyond his tower, but he realized that couldn't continue. Even if the karnuq moved inside the tower, threats could still come from beyond. The Hunger itself would probe the exterior, and then there was the risk of visitors who were not as friendly as the karnuq. And on the more positive angle, there were opportunities he was neglecting as well. It was outside the tower that his bees found the first mana flowers, not to mention all the plants the karnuq had brought with them. And each time Belissar did an expansion purification, the amount of ground reclaimed from the Hunger grew, which meant both new opportunities and new exposure to danger.

It would not do for him to remain unaware of what was occurring in his own tower's range.

He nodded and stepped toward the grove, waving at the bees above. Shortly thereafter, the two orchard queens came down to greet him . . . and continuously thanked him for the communer bees. He couldn't help but chuckle as they kept up their dance, not pausing for even a moment.

"You're welcome, I'm glad you like it. And, I was thinking . . . would it be possible to step up the scouting? Now that you have the communers, maybe set up a mini-hive where the scouts could stay so they don't have to keep flying back and forth all the time?"

He knew the orchard queen called the Fourth of the Seventh had moved a couple of times at this point, so he figured she would have experience in setting up and managing multiple hives at once. And with the communers, the queens could stay in contact with their workers at a distance, so he figured it should be possible.

The Fourth of the Seventh immediately stopped dancing. She hovered in the air, barely moving save for the beating of her wings. Belissar began to frown. Maybe he had been mistaken . . .

And then she burst out into yet another rapid dance. She was moving so fast and frantically he could barely keep up.

"YES! WILL DO! WILL DO RIGHT AWAY! KING IS BEST KING!"

Belissar blinked at the sudden dance, but chuckled and shook his head.

"Take your time and let me know if you need anything for this."

"OK! WILL!"

That settled it for the Fourth of the Seventh's lead worker. The King himself had commanded them; her queen's dreams were now their hive's primary mission. All efforts would need to be taken to ensure it came about.

And so, she flew to catch her dancing queen.

"Queen, need to talk."

"OK!"

The Fourth of the Seventh continued bouncing off the walls. The lead worker waited until she approached and then landed on her queen's back, clinging on with all her might. She slowly tapped out a dance with the leg she didn't need to use to hold on.

"Queen, really need to listen. Please stop for second."

"Oh, okay!"

The Fourth of the Seventh finally landed on the ground, letting her worker climb off. She was staying mostly still, though she was fidgeting a lot as if she couldn't contain herself. The lead worker quickly started her dance while she had her queen's attention.

"King commanded, we set up new hive in Beyond, expand scouting patrols."

"YES! Amazing, incredible!"

The worker quickly stepped forward and brushed her queen's antennas to prevent her from resuming her flying dance.

"Yes, amazing, incredible, we know. Need to prepare now, okay?"

The Fourth of the Seventh still danced about but listened to her worker and remained on the ground. "Yes! Okay! Let's prepare! What we need?"

The worker aimed a dance at her queen. "Need queen to raise more workers. Need lots more for this."

"Okay!"

Then the worker aimed a dance at herself. "Worker wants to evolve. Become one of new bees so can talk to queen anywhere. Is okay?"

The Fourth of the Seventh walked up to her and began to brush her with her antennas. "Okay! Good! Worker always helps a lot, worker evolving should be amazing!"

The worker nearly broke out into a happy dance at the praise but she contained herself. "Queen is best . . . ahem, thanks, queen. But worker won't be able to help while evolving. So, queen NEEDS to stay in hive. Needs to raise brood, manage hive until worker wakes up. Stay with First of Fifth's First Daughter and help her with work. NOT leave until worker is done evolving. Okay?"

To the worker's surprise, her queen immediately agreed. "Okay! Will make sure hive is ready! Worker can go evolve!"

The worker . . . wasn't sure about this. But then she felt another set of antennas brush hers. She turned and found the First of the Fifth's First Daughter. "Don't worry, will help! Will make sure everything ready. Can gain King's favor and help Fourth of Seventh at same time. Will not fail."

The worker slowly saluted to both her queens, and then made her way to the brood chambers, where the most mana-packed honey was stored. The entire way, she gave some final commands to her fellow workers. She still wasn't sure how the hive would do without her, but her queen had promised to watch things and the First of the Fifth's First Daughter would be there to help.

So, with only a moment of hesitation, she chose an empty cell and curled up inside of it. The brood tenders filled the cell with mana-rich honey, and then began to wax it shut.

It felt strange to spend brood honey on herself, and to leave the hive to its own devices. But she believed in her fellow workers, and they all knew this was the right choice.

The Fourth of the Seventh was excited for the communers because it would let her see through her worker's eyes. It would let her explore without exploring. But her workers . . . her workers had a different plan. Because, if they could speak to their queen wherever she was, then it wouldn't matter if the queen left the hive, right? And beyond that . . . communers could not only pass information and communications between the workers and the queen . . . they could also reach out to the nearby bees themselves.

That meant that if the lead worker became a communer, she would be able to see, hear, and command the workers of the hive like a queen could. That meant that she could fulfill most of the queen's tasks without any loss of efficiency.

And if she could do that while also being able to speak to her queen at any time?

In that case, her queen would be free to go anywhere she wanted to without any interruption in the hive's function. So long as she made sure to lay enough brood . . . and the worker had ideas on that as well.

Her last thought as she settled into sleep was that finally, she could make her queen's dreams come true.

As the worker went off, the First of the Fifth's First Daughter was left with the happily dancing Fourth of the Seventh. She could barely contain her own happiness as well. With these new communers, she could take care of the joint hive while also contacting the Fourth of the Seventh at any time. And then the King himself had personally given them a mission! Her mother would be beyond pleased to hear about this!

And, she had her own idea about how to make it happen. She just . . . had to gather the courage to state it. She stopped walking and grew still, her antennas twitching. The Fourth of the Seventh noticed and flew down in front of her.

"First of Fifth's First Daughter okay?"

The First of the Fifth's First Daughter looked at her savior and partner queen. She twitched at the attention and nearly fled. But the Fourth of the Seventh, the Fourth of the Seventh's worker, and the King himself were counting on her. So, she gathered her courage and began to dance. Slowly, unsteadily, and with frequent pauses, she forced herself through each of the steps.

"Fourth of Seventh, been thinking. Orchard is big, two hives not enough to gather from. And now . . . King wants us to scout, set up new hives. So . . . was wondering . . . just because King commanded . . . and because definitely need . . . would you . . . d-drones and queens?"

She tripped over herself at the end but managed to finish the dance. She was barely able to force herself to stay and wait for the Fourth of the Seventh's response. But her mother had raised her to be an exceptional queen, and so she did not give into her fears.

The Fourth of the Seventh watched her for a torturous moment before beginning to dance. The First of the Fifth's First Daughter nearly tore her gaze away but forced herself to remain still.

"Drones? Queens . . . Oh! First of Fifth's First Daughter wants to raise new queens?"

". . . Yes."

"Okay!"

The First of the Fifth's First Daughter froze as her mind attempted to comprehend the immediate reply.

When it finally did, it was her turn to begin a frantic happy dance.

CHAPTER THIRTY-THREE

BEE-ORGANIZING THE ROOMS

The next day, Belissar got to work. He moved the original dirt tunnels back up to the second floor so that the apiary hives could resume foraging the subterranean plants and mushrooms, then spent the rest of the day working on the orchard tree-hive. He and the squad of soldier bees helping him managed to build a relatively flat platform across the tree branches, with a frame of thicker beams reaching down to the ground to provide additional support and a basic ladder for Belissar.

Then came the moment of truth. Belissar held his breath as he selected a beehouse feature and tried to move it on top of the platform . . .

The transparent beehouse did not turn red. Belissar grinned as he clenched his hand into a fist.

"Yes! Looks like it works."

"King is best king!"

Niobee led the soldier bees and the curious workers from the orchard hives in a celebratory dance. Belissar would be ready to begin construction on the actual beehouse now, though he held off. It was just about time for the daily purification, so the beehouse would have to wait until tomorrow. Belissar made his way to the flower meadow where the soldier bee army was already gathering. After confirming they were ready, he opened up the purification menu.

Please select a purification strength:
- Minor (Cooldown: 14 hours)
- Minor+ (Cooldown: 22 hours)

Belissar tilted his head at that. "No new ones?"

Niobee flew in front of him. "King, something wrong?"

Belissar shook his head. "Last time we did an expansion, we got access to tougher daily purifications. It looks like this time we didn't, though I think those cooldowns are a bit shorter now. I wonder why?"

Niobee wavered in the air. "Sorry, don't know."

Belissar chuckled and shook his head. "Don't worry about it. It's a Tower of the Gods, after all. Let's just focus on what we do know and go with the normal purification, then. Is the army ready?"

The queen in command for the day saluted him and confirmed. Belissar nodded and selected the minor+ purification.

"Okay, here we go."

In the end, the minor+ purification was no different from any other they had faced, and the bees handled it flawlessly. Belissar was able to safely add another fifteen mana to his pool as he led the victory celebrations.

The next day, Belissar started by checking his mana.

Mana: 26/450

It wasn't much, but it was a start, and it was enough to handle the basic rooms. Belissar reviewed his tower once more. The first floor currently held the flower meadow and orchard, along with an empty space for a new room. The second floor contained the apiary and the dirt tunnels, along with yet another empty slot. Finally, he had an empty third floor, which at the moment only contained his core room and a staircase room to the second floor.

It was time to change that. He walked over to the closest apiary hive, the one with the largest queen. He turned to Niobee.

"Niobee, this queen is kind of the leader of the apiary, right?"

Niobee danced her confirmation. "Yes, First of Fifth lives closest to King, makes most and best honey! Other apiary queens listen to!"

Belissar thanked her and then walked over to the hive. The First of the Fifth had already crawled out and happily greeted him. Belissar smiled as he greeted her back, then asked her his question.

"Hey, so, I'm thinking of moving the apiary up to the third floor now. I want to put the karnuq on the second floor so they won't be right by the entrance, but also not right by my core room. Is that alright? Are there any downsides to moving your hives further from the first floor and the entrance?"

The First of the Fifth paused, going completely still. Then she began to tremble. Eventually, she erupted into dance.

"YES! IS FINE! WANT TO BE BY CORE AND BY KING!"

Belissar blinked, then shook his head and chuckled. At this point, he should probably expect such reactions from his bees. Close to him, huh? That wasn't how he had been thinking of it, but if that was what the bees wanted, then that was what they would get. He'd have to make sure to visit each hive regularly as his tower began to spread out.

In this case, though, he had just wanted to make sure he wasn't interrupting the bees' foraging with this move. But, well, clearly the First of the Fifth wouldn't mind even if it did. He thought of trying to calm her down and ask more specifically, but then shrugged. The point of this was to make sure he wouldn't inconvenience his bees, but this queen clearly wanted him to go through with the move even if it would.

So, he proceeded with his plan. He moved the apiary and its connected dirt tunnels up to the third floor, and then added a bunch of new rooms to the tower. To the now-empty second floor, he added a new flower meadow, a new orchard, and a new room of dirt tunnels. The new flower meadow was both the entrance and exit for the entire second floor, with doorways leading down to the first floor and up to the third floor placed right next to each other. This would allow his bees to bypass the second floor without disturbing the karnuq, and via the shortest possible trip. The new dirt tunnels and orchard, on the other hand, were connected to the second-floor flower meadow on the far side from the staircases, sectioned off from the rest of the tower for the karnuq's convenience.

Mana: 6/450

Belissar rubbed his chin. Building the three new rooms had drained most of his available mana, so he wouldn't be able to do much with them just yet. He enabled the free flower types he had available for the flower meadow just for variety, but otherwise left the rooms alone. At the bare minimum, he would need to add a few ponds at five mana a piece so the karnuq would have sources of water, which he didn't have enough mana to complete today.

He could move features between rooms, he found, and in fact he planned to move all the resource nodes he made for the karnuq up to their new home once they moved in. However, that wouldn't work for the ponds because he wanted one in every room in case of fires, so cannibalizing from the existing rooms wasn't an option. Besides, it would only take a day to get enough mana for the ponds and the karnuq were right outside the tower where he could help them in case of an emergency, so Belissar figured it would be fine to wait. He turned to Niobee.

"Okay, the second floor is built, though there's not much in those rooms yet. That's going to be where the karnuq live. The bees can still visit and use the flowers there, and even move there if they're comfortable living around the karnuq, but they should be aware that the karnuq will be free to gather whatever resources are on that floor. Can you let them know?"

"Okay!"

Niobee landed by the First of the Fifth and began to dance with her, so Belissar left them to it. Now that the new rooms were built and his mana was spent, it was time for the other task of the day. The one he was most looking forward to.

Now that the orchard grove had a platform that could hold a beehouse, it was time to ensure the last of his queens had a home built by him. And to complete one of the missions from the God of Bees in the process. He walked down to the orchard with a spring in his step.

Meanwhile, the Conduit gathered the First of the Fifth and the Firstborn once again. She passed along the King's decrees on the second floor . . . and then the queens and the Conduit began to discuss. The First of the Fifth was still somewhat in a daze from her earlier discussion with the King, who wanted *her* to live closer to his core and stand between him and the outsiders, but she managed to understand the Conduit's dance enough to respond.

"So, King doesn't want bees to claim second floor?"

The Conduit took a moment before starting a slow and unsteady dance. "Not . . . exactly. Think King is worried about bees. Karnuq will take good flowers on second floor, so bees there might have less. Might also want to take honey from hives on second floor."

The First of the Fifth buzzed her wings at the thought of anyone other than the King taking her honey. Fortunately, she would not be subjected to such a travesty with her now-guaranteed proximity to the King, but it still bore considering. Previously, she might have been tempted to raise another queen so that the new territory could be claimed by her children. And while she was no longer as concerned about territorial claims, it was only natural to want to see any unclaimed resources put to good use in service of the King and his bees. But now? Would she be willing to see a child of hers subjected to the treatment the Conduit warned of? To surrender flowers . . . or even honey . . . to these newcomers of uncertain trustworthiness?

No, no she would not.

The Firstborn replied while she was deep in thought. "Then . . . could just send some workers? Gather from flowers if can, but not make hive. Can gather a bit without getting in the way, and can keep an eye on newcomers?"

The Conduit's dance grew a bit steadier as she replied. "Good idea. Queens cooperate, both send less workers?"

The First of the Fifth danced her confirmation. In this case, the gathered nectar would be secondary and not at all guaranteed, so it made sense to share the burden between the queens, especially those who did not need to worry about sustaining their hives like herself. And keeping an eye on these newcomers was a task of great importance.

And so, the queens agreed to adopt a wait-and-see approach to the second floor. They would take measure of the karnuq before any queen would make her home among them.

CHAPTER THIRTY-FOUR

COMMUNITY BEE-VELOPMENT

Belissar grabbed his usual construction squad from the soldier bee army and headed over to the orchard grove. He tasked them with ferrying the wood he needed for the beehouse up to the platform before climbing up himself. His ladder wasn't the most solid construction, and he had a slip or two, but he managed to pull himself up safely. After only a brief moment to gather his breath and feel relatively solid wood beneath his feet, he got to work.

The two orchard queens had already crawled out of their hives, curious as to his presence up in the canopy of the grove. He smiled at them. "What are you two called?"

The larger of the two answered immediately with a rapid dance. "Fourth of Seventh!"

The smaller was more hesitant, trembling as she stumbled over herself. "F-First of Fifth's First Daughter, h-honored to speak with King."

Belissar tried to give a reassuring smile to them. "Fourth of the Seventh and First of the Fifth's First Daughter, got it. I'm going to build a house for you two now, do you have any ideas on how it should look? Any features it should have?"

The First of the Fifth's First Daughter began trembling so hard she couldn't even dance anymore, and so didn't say anything. But, to Belissar's surprise, the Fourth of the Seventh began dancing immediately.

"King is best king! We share hive, so should be big! Going to raise more queens, so big for them too!"

The First of the Fifth's First Daughter spun around to stare at the Fourth of the Seventh. However, Belissar was already nodding his head. "Got it, hm, I don't think we have enough space up here for a full bee barracks, but I'll make the house as big as possible. Anything else?"

The Fourth of the Seventh paced in a circle for a moment before responding. "Nope! King's hives are best!"

Belissar grinned and turned to the other queen. "How about you? I want to make it the best it can be for you, so if you have any ideas please let me know."

The First of the Fifth's First Daughter resumed trembling but managed to get a dance out. "N-None, sorry. King's hives already best."

Belissar chuckled at that. "Okay then, I'll get started. Let me know if you think of anything."

"Okay, King is best king!"

"Y-Yes. King is best king!"

With that, Belissar got to work. He placed some beams outlining the future walls, planning to use up as much of the platform's area as he felt was safe. He made it wide, but short enough he'd have to hunch over to stand inside. Between magical monster bees being less vulnerable to disease and parasites, his tower sight that could see inside a beehouse without opening it, and this hive's inaccessible location, he realized there was no real reason to build a beehouse here with human access in mind. As such, he built it from the inside out, since the entrances wouldn't be human-sized or shaped.

He made rows upon rows of large, square frames for their convenience. As with the flower meadow bee barracks, he didn't put any interior walls or separations, since the two queens were building a joint hive already. The entrances would be circular holes, small for an adult human but still quite large compared to even a soldier bee. He covered these with cloth sheets weighed down by wood tied to their bottoms, something that could be pushed aside by bees while keeping out the elements. He made smaller entrances purely for workers as well, even carving a hole in the bottom so the bees could fly straight toward the flowers at the bottom of the grove.

It took most of the day, but with the help of the construction soldiers and a few soldiers of the Fourth of the Seventh's own, he managed to finish. He looked over it and grinned.

And then his eyes widened and he frowned. He just realized that, normally, he would place a beehive feature, assemble a beehouse next to it, and then merge the two together. And this time . . . he had forgotten to actually place the beehive feature. He gulped.

"Hope this works . . ."

He tried to do so now, bringing up the beehive feature and moving it over the beehouse . . .

Compatible feature detected. Upgrade to Beehive?

He let out a sigh of relief as instead of displaying a transparent beehive, his tower sight instead illuminated the completed beehouse. It appeared he could also build the beehouse first and then upgrade it into a feature. That was convenient to learn, especially now.

He went ahead and did so.

New feature detected. New feature unlocked.
Wooden Platform is now available!

New feature detected. New feature unlocked.
Bee Apartment is now available!

Beehive upgraded to Bee Apartment.

Belissar's eyes widened as the tower's mana began to flow into the new house. He knew this beehouse was a lot different from any other he had built, but he hadn't expected a new feature out of it, much less two. He quickly brought up the details on both.

<u>Wooden Platform</u>

Mana Upkeep: *1*

An elevated platform made of wood. May hold features within its weight limit. Weight limit may be improved if supported by other features.

<u>Bee Apartment</u>

Mana Upkeep: *10 (5 with Blessing of Bees)*
Current Occupants: *None*
Current Product: *Honeycomb*
Base Production Rate: *3 honeycomb per 24 hours*
A larger variant of Belissar's Beehouse. Improves maximum products stored to 3 per occupying queen, increases bee productivity, and increases bee happiness. This larger version may hold multiple queens and hives, each of which increases the honeycomb production and storage.

The description of the wooden platform was pretty straightforward, to the point that Belissar wondered why it was a separate feature. On the other hand, he had seen simple dirt trails offered as a feature before, and this was much more complicated than those, so he supposed it made sense. If nothing else, it would be extremely convenient if he wanted to build more elevated hives. He only wished he'd had it before needing to build one from scratch.

The bee apartment, on the other hand, was like his beehouse, but bigger. Which made sense, because that's exactly what it was. He was pleased to see it still had the same magic effects as the beehouses. It was a bit more expensive in terms of mana, but it could also hold more queens, so as long as they got along maybe it was even better than separate beehouses? He wasn't sure, he'd have to write out the math to know for certain, but he assumed the mana-to-bees ratio wouldn't be worse, at the very least.

He was worried for a second about the higher mana cost than he expected, not to mention having to account for the unexpected Wooden Platform feature, so he double-checked his mana.

Mana: 0/450

He exhaled his breath. He'd had exactly enough for the new features. But now he truly couldn't do anything else until the day's purification.

Ultimately, though, new features and tower mana were not the point of this. So, he turned to face the existing orchard hive built in the branches. He found the two queens and their entire hive hovering behind him. He gave them a smile.

"Well, what do you think?"

He chuckled as he was subjected to countless "Amazing!" "Incredible!" dances all at once. He had to admit that at this point he had expected and even looked forward to that reaction.

"I'm glad you like it. Enjoy!"

Belissar began climbing down the ladder as the two hives swarmed over the bee apartment, inspecting every angle of it inside and out before the two queens began moving their joint hive inside.

And once he safely reached the ground, the words he had waited for passed across his vision.

Mission: House All Bees completed!
Reward: Uncommon Monster Choice

His grin only grew. Not only had he built something he was proud of and made a home for each and every one of his bees, but now the God of Bees herself acknowledged his efforts. And what better reward could there be for building bee-houses than more bees?

Belissar took a deep breath . . . and then he dismissed the message for now. From now on, he wanted to consult with his bees before making any major choices. Possibly with Chief Rohsuak as well, although from their last conversation it seemed like it would be fine to make monster choices without her. The bees, however, would be directly impacted and might have strong opinions on what would help them most. And at this point, it was nearly time for the daily purification, after which the queens would gather anyway for the victory celebration. So, Belissar decided to wait until then to check what the choices would be.

It only took an intense amount of his willpower to do so. For once, Belissar couldn't wait for the purification to arrive.

CHAPTER THIRTY-FIVE

BEE DIFFERENT?

Belissar might have been incredibly distracted during the purification. Fortunately, the bees handled it entirely on their own, so there were no issues. Belissar fidgeted about during the victory celebration, not helped in the slightest by the energizing effects of the sweet mana honey. And then, finally, when the celebrations calmed down, he turned to Niobee.

"Niobee, can you gather the queens? We have another choice to make."

"Okay!"

It took but a moment for the queens to rush to his side. Belissar could no longer contain his grin. "We have a new monster choice to make, and I'd like you all to check the options with me."

The queens burst out into celebratory dances at that. Belissar's grin grew as wide as it could go as he finally opened up the choice he had waited on.

*Please select a monster:**
- Monster Bee Burster (Rarity: Uncommon. Type: Bee.)
- Monster Carpenter Bee (Rarity: Common. Type: Bee, Nature.)
- Monster Bumblebee Queen (Rarity: Rare. Type: Bee.)

*(*One or more choices upgraded due to Blessing of Bees.)*

Belissar immediately proceeded to read out the descriptions for the queens.

Monster Bee Burster

Vitality: *Minimal*
Strength: *Minimal*
Speed: *Average*

Magic:	*Minor*
Defense:	*Minimal*
Resistance:	*Minimal*
Special:	*Below Average*
Notable Skills:	*Death Burst,*
	Brood Offspring
Evolves From:	*Monster Bee Soldier,*
	Monster Bee Sprayer

This monster bee sprayer variant's venom has grown so caustic and volatile that it cannot be safely contained. The monster bee burster holds its venom ingredients in separate glands, only to be mixed at the moment of attack. Once it does so, it soon explodes, subjecting its surroundings to a powerful blast that showers the area in toxins.

Belissar immediately frowned. A monster bee that was designed to die, that couldn't do much of anything without sacrificing itself. It did seem quite powerful . . . but Belissar still didn't like the idea. Maybe he could resign himself to losing bees that were born to die—it might even be a good idea, as he could subsequently use those bees for situations where death was certain anyway—but he'd still rather avoid bee death than embrace it. He'd take the option if he felt the tower needed it, but he was definitely checking the other options first.

The queens, likewise, remained silent. He was grateful for that, as he probably would have felt compelled to choose this option if the bees themselves wanted it.

The second option was a repeat: the monster carpenter bees he had seen earlier on. He hadn't consulted his bees at the time, however, so he still read out the details for them.

Monster Carpenter Bee

Vitality:	*Minimal+*
Strength:	*Minimal+*
Speed:	*Average*
Magic:	*Minimal*
Defense:	*Minimal*
Resistance:	*Minimal*
Special:	*Minimal*
Notable Skills:	*Poison Sting, Wood Cut*
Spawner Upkeep:	*1*

*A carpenter bee that has accumulated enough Nature mana to become
something more. Sharp mandibles meant for boring into wood
allow for painful, if small, bites.*

They made even more sense now than they did the first time. Belissar now had the orchard, which was full of trees and could grow wood tree resource nodes. Carpenter bees would have plenty of space to grow and plenty of work they could help with. Belissar may have just finished building beehouses for all his current queens, but he figured there'd be more to come. The soldiers had helped immensely just by lifting the wood and moving it around, so Belissar could only imagine how quickly the task would go if he had bees that could help him cut and process the wood as well. Not to mention, the karnuq would be building homes of their own before long. Carpenter bees could very much help with that.

Still, carpenter bees wouldn't help much when it came to the purifications. Likewise, they weren't a brood offspring, and so they wouldn't interact much with the existing hives. They would be an addition to the tower that would only be involved with woodworking. The only use for that in the immediate future would be to help the karnuq . . . who were fully capable of woodworking on their own. In fact, the karnuq themselves could now help Belissar with tasks like woodworking, should he need additional assistance. So, was it worth committing a monster choice to that?

Belissar supposed that would depend on the third and final option.

Monster Bumblebee Queen

Vitality:	*Minimal+*
Strength:	*Minimal+*
Speed:	*Below Average*
Magic:	*Minimal*
Defense:	*Minimal+*
Resistance:	*Minimal*
Special:	*Above Average*
Notable Skills:	*Poison Sting, Brood Mother*

*A bumblebee queen that has accumulated enough mana to become
something more. Similar to her mundane cousins, but more aggressive,
and with slightly magical venom. This one is a queen, and capable of building
a hive of monster bumblebees. Compared to monster bees, monster bumblebees
are tougher, stronger, and have the potential to grow significantly larger.
Yet they are slower, not as numerous, don't produce as much honey,
and don't coordinate as closely with one another.*

Belissar hummed and rubbed his chin. It was the third queen choice he had seen, and this one was an entirely different species. So, still not related to the monster bee queens . . . but it had the Brood Mother skill. Would they be able to raise other bee types like soldiers or sprayers, then? Sadly, the tower did not tell him one way or another.

At first glance, the monster bumblebee queens didn't seem all that different from monster bees, especially compared to the how different the bloodsucking bees would be. But one line in particular stood out to Belissar: the potential to grow significantly larger. He had already seen how helpful soldier bees could be just on account of their size. Could monster bumblebees grow larger than that? And how much larger? Would they grow as big as the small remnant shades? The minor purification wolf-shades? As large as a human? As big as the giant boar-shade? At the moment, Belissar had no idea. But if it were on the larger end . . . then Belissar could definitely see a place for such a hive. A bee with bulk could be a very helpful addition indeed.

However, all that was guesses and hopes. It could be the case that "large" was just in comparison to normal bees, and not very large at all in the grand scheme of things. There was also the chance that the monster bumblebee queens were considered different from the others even with the Brood Mother skill, and that none of the previous monster choices would apply to them. Belissar might end up having to commit more monster choices before they would become useful. And, as a separate species, they'd definitely be starting from scratch. They'd have to raise new hives and would need to share the flowers used by the existing bees. There was a risk that it wouldn't be worth the effort.

Belissar looked around at each of his queens. "So, what do you think?"

This time, the queens stood still, hovering in the air. It seemed that they did not have as strong an opinion as last time, if the lack of immediate dancing was any indicator. Niobee flew over to the Second First of the First and they brushed antennas. She did the same with the First of the Fifth and the Fourth of the Seventh before flying back over to Belissar.

"Bees say whatever King chooses. Don't know about new bees, but trust King."

Belissar frowned at first, but then he nodded. At the end of the day, he was the dungeon master. It was his responsibility to make a choice, and to make the best choice for the tower as a whole. He consulted with the bees to see if they had any needs or wants, to see if they would catch something that he missed. If they didn't have a strong opinion or didn't see any issues he missed, then it was ultimately up to him to decide on his own.

It also made sense, in this case. The only brood offspring option this time was the monster bee burster, and Belissar guessed the bees could tell he was not enthusiastic about that one. They, at least, were not as excited as they had been about the communers, or even the monster bee bladers. The other two options were different species from the usual monster bees and so represented potential competition. If the bees had an opinion on those, it probably wouldn't be a favorable one.

So, what, then, should Belissar choose? The monster bee bursters that would guarantee he'd watch bees die? Or the monster carpenter bees or monster bumblebee queens, both of which were of uncertain benefit and would compete with his current queens for resources? This choice might just be the hardest monster choice he had faced yet.

Belissar ended up glancing toward the shrine of bees, wondering what she would think . . .

But then, his eyes widened as he realized one simple fact. His patron was the God of *Bees*. Without qualifiers. Not of honeybees, not of monster bees, but of bees, as a whole. As a beekeeper, honeybees were the only ones he considered most of the time, but he had acknowledged just yesterday while designing the orchard's bee apartment that not all of his concerns as a beekeeper were relevant now.

So . . . could he build a tower worthy of the God of Bees if he only stuck to a single type? The answer was clear. As such, Belissar made his choice.

Monster Bumblebee Queens are now available.

His tower would, therefore, be a tower for all bees. His current queens might be reluctant to welcome new competition, but Belissar would make sure there were enough flowers that they could all forage to their hearts' content. He hoped that these new bumblebees would grow into something that would make surrendering some flowers worthwhile even to the other bees. As queens of a species stated to grow large, he had great hopes in their potential.

Belissar turned back to look at his queens. "I'm going to go with monster bumblebee queens. But I promise to make sure there's enough flowers for everyone. So, treat them nicely, okay?"

One by one, the queens saluted him. Belissar just hoped it would go well.

CHAPTER THIRTY-SIX

BUILD A BEAR HA-BEE-TAT

Belissar wanted to add some monster bumblebee queens right away but, unfortunately, his available mana was still exceedingly low. He had only fifteen mana to his name after the day's purification reward . . . and he intended to use all of that to add ponds to the three second-floor rooms. Then, there were still the two empty room slots, one each on the first and third floor, for him to fill. And then, he would likely need to add new resource nodes both to make sure the karnuq were well-supplied and to fulfill his promise to feed all the bees to their hearts' content even with the arrival of a new species of queen. With all that in mind, it would likely be some time before Belissar could confidently add a monster bumblebee queen spawner.

He heaved a light sigh before turning in for the night. Well, the solution to all of those issues was the same. Stay patient, conduct purifications, and expand his mana. So, there was nothing for it but to wait for tomorrow.

The next morning, Belissar placed three new pond features in the new second floor rooms. It pained him to watch his mana drop back to zero, especially when he knew that fifteen was more than enough for a monster bumblebee queen spawner. But he held to his course for now and made his way to the tower's entrance, Niobee and the soldier bee army escorting him as usual. He stepped outside to find the karnuq preparing to gather resources. They paused what they were doing and then saluted to him in their fashion. Leijaliuk, who had been organizing the gatherers as she normally did, walked up to him.

"Hello, Sacred Den Master, did you need us for something?"

Belissar nodded. "Is Chief Rohsuak around?"

Leijaliuk turned and motioned to another karnuq who ran into the camp. "Yes, I'll send for her. She should meet you shortly."

Belissar thanked her and then stood off to the side. A moment later, Chief Rohsuak walked up to the tower. "Hello, Sacred Den Master Belissar. How may I help you?"

Belissar greeted her. "Hello, Chief Rohsuak. I've finished the basics of the place for you all. Could you come, or send someone, to check it out?"

Her eyes widened slightly before she smiled. "We are honored, Sacred Den Master. Yes, I will come with you. I'd like to bring Metsaitti as well, if that's fine?"

Belissar agreed and soon, Metsaitti joined them. The trio and the bees watching them then made their way back into the tower and up to the second floor. The new flower field stretched out before them, the sea of colorful flowers broken up only by the occasional tree providing shade. At the end of the room, a gate through the wall of trees at the edges of the room led to the second orchard, where rows of apple trees stood in lines, and a hole in the ground opened up to a large cavern that split off into the network of the dirt tunnels. The entrances to the other two rooms each had a pond of crystal-clear water. Behind Belissar and the two karnuq, at the start of the room, were the two staircases leading to the first and third floors, with the shrine of bees nestled between them.

Metsaitti glanced around every which way. "This is all for us, Sacred Den Master?"

Belissar smiled. "Yes. Well, um, I do still want the bees to go where they want, so be nice to them if they come here. But yes, these three rooms are for you. Do you have any suggestions? I can change things up while we're here."

Metsaitti tilted his head. "That depends. What are you able to change?"

Belissar picked up one of the trees and moved it closer. "I can move the trees around, add more, or remove them, though there's a maximum number for this room. I can change the types of flowers that grow here, though some cost mana to add so I can't afford them right now. I can also move the ground up and down a bit, like this. And I can move any existing features around, like the pond over there. Oh, I can also move or add more entrances to the other two rooms."

Belissar demonstrated each of these as he spoke. Metsaitti's eyes widened just slightly, while Chief Rohsuak simply chuckled a bit. Then she turned to Belissar with a serious expression.

"Sacred Den Master Belissar, I notice that the entrances to the lower and the upper floors are both here, which would make it simple for an invader to bypass our floor entirely. Do you not intend for us to guard the way further in?"

Belissar shook his head. "Um, it's a bit different, but no, not here. We normally fight the shades in the first flower meadow, since that's where the bee army lives. So, um, if a shade gets here . . . we're probably already in trouble, so it'd be better to stay out of the way."

Chief Rohsuak and Metsaitti glanced at one another. Metsaitti crossed his arms and hummed. "So, would you have us join the initial defense instead?"

Belissar nodded. Metsaitti then frowned. "I can't say I know much about sacred dens, but wouldn't letting the Hunger deeper inside be a problem? Maybe we should have some backup defenses, even if we plan to stop it before it can get here?"

Belissar's face turned dark. "Yes, but . . . it's . . . happened before."

He took a deep breath and shook his head to clear the memories of that day. "If a shade reaches the core, it will vanish and the core will become partially corrupted. It . . . seems kind of bad, to be honest, but we can also extract and purify that corruption later. I think as long as we don't let it build up too much, it shouldn't threaten the tower as a whole. So, if we can't stop it before here, it's probably better to let it hit the core than to risk our lives."

His face turned dark again. "And if the bee army fails, we probably won't have much choice but to get out of the way and try to survive."

Belissar flinched as he felt a hand touch his shoulder. He looked up to find Chief Rohsuak patting him. Niobee and the soldiers hovered a bit closer but did not intervene.

"We will do our utmost to ensure it does not come to that, Sacred Den Master."

Metsaitti saluted as well. Belissar took a deep breath and tried to focus away from the dark thoughts.

". . . Thank you. Um, should we talk more about the rooms?"

Chief Rohsuak gave him a smile as she stepped back. Chief Rohsuak and Metsaitti then made their recommendations and requests. Belissar created a small incline starting from the entrance to the room, with a bunch of the trees clustered at the top to give shade to anyone watching the staircases. The two karnuq mapped out where they'd start building a settlement, and Belissar moved the pond to the center of that area. Chief Rohsuak rubbed her chin as she looked at the water.

"It's a bit small for all of us . . . but you said this is some sort of built-in feature of the sacred den? Can I assume the water will be replenished regularly?"

Belissar hummed for a moment. "I'm . . . not sure, but I think so? I, um, don't even know where the water came from, but it cost mana so I'd guess there'll be some magic involved?"

Chief Rohsuak slowly nodded. "We'll have to test it then, but if you needed mana to make it then it should work that way."

The group then toured the other two rooms. The karnuq had little to say on the orchard, save that Belissar promised them wood tree nodes so they wouldn't have to cut down the apple trees. They had a bit more to say on the dirt tunnels, given their long sojourns through the underway, and Belissar complied with their requests. He cut down on the winding and twisting labyrinth the dirt tunnels would spawn as, instead widening the tunnels as large as they would go and creating some bigger caverns at regular intervals. He added several more entrances between the dirt tunnels and the flower meadow, and even the dirt tunnels and the orchard. Apparently, the tower would let him do that now that he had three rooms per floor.

When it was all said and done, the group arrived back at the flower meadow. Chief Rohsuak looked over the land and smiled.

"It's wonderful, Sacred Den Master Belissar. If you would allow us, I'd like to begin moving in right away."

Belissar blinked at that. "Oh, okay. Um, I can move the existing resource nodes you gather from to here, but it will be a day or two before I can add anything more, if that's okay?"

Chief Rohsuak smiled. "You have already been beyond generous and accommodating. What you have already given us is plenty for now."

Belissar stood there for a moment. "Oh, um, thanks?"

Chief Rohsuak shook her head with a light chuckle. "It is we who should thank you. Thank you for everything, Sacred Den Master Belissar. I swear we shall repay your generosity."

Metsaitti joined her and the two both saluted him. Belissar fidgeted a bit, unsure of how to respond to that. Fortunately for him, he didn't have to, as the two karnuq took their leave to organize the move. Niobee flew in front of him once they had separated.

"King okay?"

Belissar stretched out his hand for Niobee to land on, slowly beginning to smile. "Yes, it's just . . . I'm not used to people, um, thanking me for things. They used to just take whatever they wanted. It still feels weird but . . . I guess it's not bad. Much better than before, if I'm honest . . ."

Niobee began to dance quickly, tickling Belissar's arm. "King is best king, everyone should thank! If take King's things again, Niobee will sting!"

Belissar blinked at that, and then smiled and chuckled. "Thanks, Niobee, that's reassuring to hear."

Come to think of it, his bees praised and thanked him for everything he did. So, maybe it wasn't all that strange that the karnuq would thank him too. Maybe . . . getting thanked for providing stuff wasn't strange at all.

CHAPTER THIRTY-SEVEN

BUMBLING ABOUT

Soon, Chief Rohsuak and Metsaitti returned to their camp and arranged the move. The karnuq were used to packing up quickly, and so the entire clan was heading into the tower before long. The karnuq who hadn't been inside before glanced every which way . . . or else nervously watched the bee army hovering over their heads. Soon, though, they arrived at their new home in the second-floor flower meadow and set up their tents once more. Belissar then moved the resource nodes intended for the karnuq to the places Chief Rohsuak had specified previously.

He had intended to let them set up in peace, but later in the day he recalled there was one more thing he should discuss with them. He quickly found Chief Rohsuak.

"A purification?" she repeated, once he explained the situation.

Belissar nodded. "Smaller than the one you saw, though. We do them every day around this time. So, um, you should be careful around now."

Chief Rohsuak immediately turned to Metsaitti, who nodded and began shouting for the hunters to gather. She turned to face Belissar and saluted.

"We're ready to do our part, Sacred Den Master Belissar."

He immediately began waving his hands. "Ah, it's okay. These ones are pretty small. The bees can handle it no problem."

Chief Rohsuak shook her head. "Still, would you permit us to join you? It's our duty to help . . . and if nothing else, I'd like our hunters to see what they may need to face one day."

Slowly, Belissar lowered his hands, thinking for a moment before starting to nod. "I . . . guess that makes sense? Okay, we'll wait for you to get started, then."

And so, the karnuq hunters gathered and followed Belissar to the first-floor flower meadow. The soldier bee army had already assembled into their formations. Metsaitti took the hunters and moved closer to the entrance, where they'd be able to get a good look at the fight. Chief Rohsuak remained with Belissar near the bee barracks.

"Okay, here we go."

The bees saluted and then Belissar triggered the purification. This time, a small bird-shade appeared. The bees immediately adjusted their formation and the shade was set upon the moment it coalesced. It screeched as soldier bees landed on its back and clung on, stinging it repeatedly. Only moments later, it crashed to the ground. The karnuq hunters blinked as they stared at the scene.

And so, the karnuq joined the daily purifications.

The next day, Belissar . . . wasn't sure what to do. Having completed beehouses for every bee in his tower, he was left without an urgent task. He did use his replenished mana to add some new resource nodes for the karnuq, mainly some cave carrots and potatoes in the dirt tunnels section and a couple of wood tree nodes in the orchard, but that only took a minute. He considered helping the karnuq with their camp, but they were all noticeably larger and stronger than him, so he wasn't sure how much help he'd actually be. He could have asked the bees for help again, but since this wasn't something he needed to do or something related to them, he didn't want to take them away from their own work.

So, instead, he spent the day practicing his magic, trying to form wax into larger shapes. He also prepared some more honey for mead. It wouldn't be too much longer before his first batch was ready!

And so, time passed. After four days, the karnuq were mostly settled. But Belissar wasn't paying attention to them at the present moment. Because, after four days of purifications and mana increases, it was finally time.

First, Belissar added a new flower meadow to the third floor, connected to the apiary. In the new flower meadow, he added another resource plant node of every flower he had available. Mana flowers, healing herbs, poisonous flowers, textile flowers, flame radish, sleepy chamomile, gelatinous heather, snakebane, and more. Next to them, he added an entrance to the third floor's dirt tunnels that opened into a wide cavern with nodes for the subterranean flowers. He held off on the mushrooms until he could see if the bees could truly use them, but otherwise made cave carrots, cave potatoes, and, of course, Ground mana flowers.

It had been a lot more than he had expected, and so a lot more days of purifications had been needed to afford it all. While Belissar waited, he built some beehouses as well, ready to upgrade into beehive features once there were bees to occupy them.

And now, he was finally ready to add those bees.

Mana: 16/555

His maximum mana had crossed the five-hundred mark, and he could even start a new expansion purification if he wanted. He didn't, however, seeing as he hadn't even filled up all the new room slots yet, and the bees were still evolving their new communers. But now, finally, he had added all the new flower nodes to ensure that his current bees wouldn't need to give up a single one of their current resources, a new room to ensure sufficient space for the new bees, and enough mana to actually afford the spawner.

And so, finally, Belissar was ready to add a monster bumblebee queen spawner. He turned to Niobee with a grin. "Ready for new bees?"

Niobee danced around rapidly. "Ready!"

He selected the option. Whereas the monster bee queen and monster bee soldier spawners had taken the form of beehives hanging from a tree, this spawner took the shape of a hole in the ground. In its center was a pile of haphazardly placed bumblebee-sized wax pots. Belissar placed the spawner next to the collection of resource nodes and confirmed. He stared at the spot in the ground that began to glow as the tower's mana streamed toward it. When the light faded, there was the spawner. And then the tower's mana began to flow toward it once more. Belissar began to grin as one of the little wax pots began to glow.

A moment later, a little ball of black-and-yellow fuzz climbed out of the pot. Belissar's first monster bumblebee queen. She was a bit bigger than the bumblebees Belissar remembered, about the size of his finger. She shook herself and then extended wings that seemed entirely too small for her fuzzy body. But she beat them anyway, and soon took off into the air. She turned toward him and made her way over, hovering in the air in front of him.

"Hello," Belissar said. "Welcome to the tower."

The monster bumblebee queen responded by flying in a wide circle around Belissar. Her motions didn't come across as exact words like the monster bees' dances, but Belissar could still decipher her intent. She was happy, and ready to work.

Belissar smiled and stepped to the side, pointing to all the various flowers he had made and the beehouses.

"Go ahead, use anything you want in this room to make your hive."

The monster bumblebee queen turned to look at all the flowers. A moment later, she began zipping around Belissar in wide circles, completing several repetitions as fast as she could. Belissar grinned.

"I'm glad you like it, enjoy."

After one final circle, she zipped toward the mana flowers and began to drink nectar and gather pollen. After she was satisfied, she left the flowers and flew . . . away from the beehouses. She began to land on the ground and look around. Belissar frowned and rubbed his chin.

"Does she not like them? Does she need something else?"

Niobee flew over to the bumblebee queen and the two began to brush antennas. After a bit, Niobee flew back over.

"King! New queen says looking for hole, place to hide underground!"

Belissar's eyes widened a bit. "Ah."

He began to nod as he recalled bumblebees he had seen before. He remembered finding a nest in the ground at one point. If that was the case . . . then his normal elevated beehouses wouldn't be particularly desirable for the monster bumblebee queens.

New mission received: Create a home for bumblebees.

And now the God of Bees had confirmed it as well, so Belissar got to work thinking about what to do. His first thought was to try and dig something for her, but then he realized he should check if the tower's powers could help.

The flower meadow . . . didn't seem to have anything that would work. He could move the dirt up and down but couldn't make holes in it or anything. However, he did have the dirt tunnels now, and he already had an entrance leading underground, just one that was far too large for any bee. So, instead, he added a new cavern to the tunnels, one that was about the size of a beehouse's interior, as close to the top of the dirt tunnel room as he could place it. He then tried to make a small, monster bumblebee-sized entrance between it and the flower meadow.

He managed to succeed. The bumblebee queen paused as the ground began to stir and glow next to her, opening up into a hole in the ground. She crawled over to it and peered inside, then climbed down. Belissar watched with his tower sight as she crawled down into the cavern, checking out the space.

A moment later, she crawled out, and began to fly around in a circle again.

Mission: Create a home for bumblebees completed!
Reward: One common room feature choice.

Belissar smiled at the queen zipping around him.

"I'm glad you like it."

As the queen completed her flight and crawled back into the hole, Belissar opened up the room feature choice, because he had an inkling of where this was going . . .

Select Room Feature:
- Basic Resource Plants (Rarity: Common. Type: Nature, Resource.)
- Bee Nest (Rarity: Common. Type: Bee, Monster Nest.)
- Thorned Roses (Rarity: Common. Type: Nature, Trap.)

And, as he expected, the God of Bees had intervened. Belissar obediently selected the option both he and the God of Bees wanted.

Bee Nest

Type: *Bee, Monster Nest*

Mana Upkeep: *2 per nest (1 with Blessing of Bees)*

A hive for bee types that prefer more rugged and freeform colonies, as well as solitary bees. Boosts the growth of any bees living inside of it.

Belissar had exactly one mana remaining, so he applied the new feature to the cavern. Mana infused the floor, walls, and ceiling of the cavern, and little grooves and divots appeared for cells to go into. Small wax pots like the one in the monster bumblebee queen spawner began to grow on their own.

Belissar grinned as the bumblebee queen paused, and then began running around her new home.

BEE-MUSING COMMUNING

She slowly awakened. Everything was pitch-black. She began to squirm, wondering where she was, what had happened.

But then, suddenly, there was light. Or rather, mana. It flitted across her vision and flooded into her body. There were patterns, dances within the mana.

"Larva in section two is hungry, need honey."

"Honey production good! New palace full of mana, barely need to add any to nectar! King is best king!"

"New flowers have mana but make sleepy, make worker fly slower. Inefficient. Don't recommend."

Her vision spun and she felt dizzy. A hundred different dances impressed themselves on her mind all at once. She . . . needed to feed the brood! Or . . . was she checking the honey? Or giving a scout report . . . or was she receiving it? Or was she trapped, curled up somewhere dark? Her head began to pound and she squirmed about in her confines.

That is, until she saw a dance that stood out above the rest.

"King made new room! Want to go see!"

Suddenly she burst into motion.

"No! Queen promised to stay until done evolving!"

In an instant, the Fourth of the Seventh's worker burst out her cell all in one go. She paused as her mind finally caught up, her focus on her queen causing the rest of the mana and the dances it carried to fade to the background.

That's right, she was a worker of the Fourth of the Seventh. The worker who helped the others work whenever their queen was distracted. The worker who had subsequently decided to evolve to better fulfill her role. The worker who . . . was probably done evolving now?

But she put all of that aside . . . because she knew that dance! The scouts must have reported the King had done something new again! Which meant she had to find her queen, now!

Strangely, though, she somehow knew exactly where her queen was. She could see as her queen suddenly paused, and somehow turned in her direction.

"Worker? Worker is awake! Going to go see!"

The worker paused. Her queen . . . had noticed she was awake? And was immediately coming to see her, despite the new scout report?

Before she knew it, she had stopped moving and broke out into a happy dance. When her queen rounded the corner of the honeycomb tray, the worker immediately flew over to her. Her queen began to brush her with her antennas.

"Queen!"

"Worker!"

It took a while before the worker could think coherently again.

"Worker, you're evolved!"

The worker finally calmed down enough to perceive her queen's dances. That . . . was right? She was evolved, right?

Suddenly, she was no longer looking through her body. Rather, she was now looking *at* her body, from up above. Was this her queen's vision? She saw a little worker, no bigger than any other. However, her antennas were far fuzzier than normal, with countless branches extending out from them and swaying as if in a breeze. Also, her eyes were glowing as mana swirled around her body.

That's right. She had evolved. She was no longer a worker. She was now . . . a communer. Her body was filled to the brim with mana, far more than she had ever had before. Her antennas directed and swirled that mana around, extending it out to connect with the mana of her queen and her sisters. That mana danced along with them, carrying information about them back to her.

It was a lot. But she kept her focus on her queen, a bright star of mana shining through the light of the rest, and which all the rest focused their attention on. Even the second star, the First of the Fifth's First Daughter, turned toward the first . . .

She paused. Wait. She could also . . . feel the mana of the other queen? One that was part of her hive but also not? And now that she turned her attention to the mana of the other queen, she could also feel the mana of the other workers in the hive, though it was faint and required her active attention to notice. The ones who weren't her siblings, but acted like they were.

She briefly wondered if that was normal before turning her attention back to her queen.

"Queen . . . stayed? Managed hive?"

The Fourth of the Seventh danced happily. "Yes! King built new hive, so had to move!"

The communer froze. Wait, what? The King . . . had built them a new hive? She briefly looked around and started to tremble. She was not in the hive she had built. She was in a mighty palace with massive pillars of wood supporting the comb, with huge currents of mana surging through them and into the cells, enriching the honey and feeding the young. With her new sight, focusing on the mana caused the entire hive to light up like the sun. She stumbled back and quickly refocused on her queen, letting the ambient mana fade into the background.

And the surprises didn't stop there.

"First of Fifth's First Daughter and I going to raise queens, too! Been saving honey for!"

That was also big news. They . . . were going to have new queens? Were they going to send them out or keep them in the hive? Did they have the workers to support that?

"And then outsiders moved into King's land! Conduit, Firstborn, and First of Fifth asked if we could help scout!"

At this point, the communer's thoughts became jumbled. Something from the Beyond . . . moved inside the King's realm? The Conduit and the two foremost queens asked them to do something about it?

"And now heard King made new room! Even made new kind of queen! Want to see and greet!"

The communer collapsed to the ground, her antennas twitching. The glow in her eyes flickered and then shut off, immediately cutting off the dances swirling in her head.

Just how long had she been evolving?!

The First of the Fifth flew through the sky. She was, as usual, loathe to leave her hive behind, but this time she had to. The King had raised a new bee of his own, the first since he raised the soldiers that guarded the apiary. And this new one was apparently a queen, no less, the first since the last of the apiary queens was born. It was imperative that she meet this new queen and take her measure . . . and, of course, figure out how to support her.

This was all the more important as the King had placed the nascent queen in a new room connected to the apiary itself, placed as close to the First of the Fifth as possible without infringing on the existing hives. It was a clear sign that she should help take care of this newcomer.

She flew through the new room, a second flower meadow. She paused briefly at the sheer abundance of flowers before shaking herself back to focus. The King himself had promised that all bees would have enough nectar to eat to their hearts' contents, so it was only natural he had provided extreme riches to the new queen. It was even a sign of his love for the rest of the bees, as this would ensure they wouldn't need to reduce their foraging for the newcomers!

Or so she repeated to herself as she flew to the closest palace. She landed outside.

No one came to greet her. That was . . . a somewhat inefficient use of time, for both of them. The First of the Fifth buzzed her wings, but she would show patience and grace. So, she waited.

And waited. And waited . . .

Eventually, when she was buzzing loudly, she gave up and told one of her workers to check inside. The worker peeked her head in and immediately came to report.

The palace was empty.

The First of the Fifth paused for a moment before drooping a bit. So, she had waited for someone who wasn't even there. That was an unfortunate waste of time, but at least it meant she had not been specifically ignored. So, she made her way to the next palace, where, surely, she would find the newcomer.

A minute later and the worker she sent to check confirmed that this palace, too, was empty.

At this point the First of the Fifth abandoned courtesy and ordered her workers to immediately check the other two. They came back confused, reporting that those palaces were empty too. The First of the Fifth couldn't help but float around aimlessly.

All of the King's palaces were empty? Then, where was the newcomer?!

It was then that one of her workers got her attention. She turned to face the ground and nearly dropped out of the air.

Instead of the King's personally crafted palaces, the newcomer was crawling out of a hole in the ground. She was large for a newly born queen, maybe a fifth the size that First of the Fifth was now. She was covered in far more hair than normal, giving her a round and fuzzy appearance. She beat her wings and slowly rose into the air, moving far more ponderously than the First of the Fifth's sleek and efficient workers.

The First of the Fifth's instincts vaguely hinted at the identity of this newcomer. A different type of bee, one that was larger and less elegant, that had small, chaotic hives instead of the efficient order of her own. But, fortunately, one that was not at odds with her own, besides the general competition for resources that the King had sworn to prevent.

The newcomer suddenly paused, and then began flying over to her. She then simply floated in the air, not bothering with a dance or anything. It appeared it was up to the First of the Fifth to initiate. But that was fine. She was, after all, the older and more experienced queen. It was only natural for her to have to lead a newborn.

"Hello. I'm First of Fifth. Welcome to King's hive of hives."

The newcomer stood still, not replying with a dance of her own. The First of the Fifth hung there, waiting to see what she would do. And just when the First of the Fifth began to wonder if she was being ignored again, the newcomer moved.

But she did not dance. Instead, she simply began flying in a circle around the First of the Fifth. The First of the Fifth began cleaning her antennas to calm herself.

Taking care of new bees . . . might be more difficult than she thought.

CHAPTER THIRTY-EIGHT

DIRT-BEE DEVELOPMENTS

With the bumblebee spawner established and the bumblebee queen settling into her new home, Belissar turned his attention back to the karnuq. In fact, he could hear Chief Rohsuak calling for him.

"Sacred Den Master Belissar, if you have a moment, would you mind stopping by?"

Belissar tilted his head at that. He hadn't known someone could call for his attention like that. He heard the chief's voice through his tower senses even though he hadn't been focusing on her at the time. His bees hadn't done that before . . . although, in hindsight, it might have just been that the bees didn't normally call him directly. The few times they'd specifically sought his attention they had gone through Niobee instead, who herself was almost always by his side.

He shrugged and made his way over to the second floor, where a group of soldier bees had already come up from the first floor to meet and escort him. He trusted the karnuq enough at this point that it was probably unnecessary, but he'd also admit that having the bees around boosted his confidence in general, so he let them come along regardless.

Chief Rohsuak was waiting for him there as well. "Hello, Sacred Den Master Belissar. Thank you for coming."

He nodded back. "Hello, how is everything?"

Chief Rohsuak gave him a smile. "Wonderful. It's been a long time since we've had a home, and the one you've made for us is very pleasant."

Belissar started to smile a little. "Glad to hear that. Um, did you need something?"

Chief Rohsuak motioned around. "Now that our camp is settled, I'd like to send some hunters to the Underway. They'll both hunt around for game and resources, and scout the area for potential dangers. Would you permit us to do so?"

Belissar tilted his head. "Um, sure? I'm, uh, not sure why you're asking me, though."

Chief Rohsuak shook her head. "Sacred Den Master Belissar, we are now under your protection and sworn to defend your home. Sending out our hunters reduces your defenses, possibly permanently, should any of them be injured or killed, and any actions we take outside could be perceived as being done in your name. It is only natural that you have a say in our activities now, especially outside of our camp."

Belissar furrowed his brow. "Oh. That . . . makes sense."

Chief Rohsuak smiled. "So, with that in mind . . . do you have any need for our hunters in the near future? And do you have any thoughts on how we should act when outside of your dungeon, especially if we make contact with another intelligent people?"

Belissar's eyes widened. "Oh, there are others nearby?"

Chief Rohsuak placed a finger on her chin. "That depends on how you define *nearby*. They are not so close that contact is inevitable, but not so far that contact is impossible. And that's only considering the route we traveled to arrive here. We do not yet know what lies beyond your sacred den. I'll say it's not something you need to decide right away, but it is something you should consider, preferably before it happens."

Belissar hummed for a bit. ". . . Okay, I'll think about. Um, will it be okay if you just act how you did before for now?"

Chief Rohsuak's smile grew strained and she glanced away. "Um, about that . . ."

Belissar did not like that reaction. "Yes?"

Chief Rohsuak continued avoiding his gaze. "We, um, may not have the best of reputations with all of the peoples we've encountered. We often did what we had to in order to survive. So, we engaged in raiding and thieving on occasion."

Belissar blinked a few times before frowning. He . . . wasn't sure how to respond to that. "Um . . ."

Chief Rohsuak sighed and shook her head. "I'll speak to the hunters firmly before they go. Now that we have a home and a source of food, we will not need to be as . . . aggressive in any negotiations. Should I tell the hunters to avoid contact, and provocation, until they report back on anything they find?"

Belissar felt more than a bit uneasy at this point, but wasn't sure what else to say. "Um, yes. That sounds good, I think?"

With that, they discussed a few more things, such as the hunters resuming their remnant hunts, before parting. Once the chief was out of his sight, Belissar frowned. So, the karnuq were not as nice to everyone as they were to him. It was a bit hard for him to imagine that, given his interactions with them. But they were quite strong and intimidating. If they had come across him in his old village instead of in a tower with a bee army, would they have been as nice? Or . . . would it have ended as the tower lords claimed, with the karnuq killing and rampaging like savage beasts?

Belissar eventually sighed and shook his head. He didn't know, and the karnuq *had* been nice to him, so he supposed it didn't matter now. He just hoped that their past wouldn't end up causing any trouble.

He made his way back to the third floor and the apiary, intending to clear his head a bit. As he did, though, the First of the Fifth flew over to him, along with several of the other apiary queens. He smiled at them.

"Hello everyone, do you need something?"

The First of the Fifth danced happily before him.

"Oh, something to show me?"

Belissar grinned as the First of the Fifth turned to the others and then brought one of her workers forward. The worker's size and body appeared the same, but her eyes were large and her antennas wide and fluffy, more like a moth's than a bee's. Belissar could also feel mana swirling around her body, and her eyes and antennas occasionally glowed.

"This is one of the communers, right?" he asked, investigating the bee. "I hope they help out!"

The First of the Fifth saluted and then danced to the other queens. One by one they came before him and presented workers of their own. These were ones Belissar hadn't seen before but had been anticipating.

Sedating Monster Bee Worker

Vitality:	*Minimal*
Strength:	*Minimal*
Speed:	*Average*
Magic:	*Minimal*
Defense:	*Minimal*
Resistance:	*Minimal*
Special:	*Minor*
Notable Skills:	*Sedating Poison Sting, Sacrificial Strike, Brood Offspring*

A monster bee worker raised on Sedative Honey. It now produces the sedative compounds in the honey in its own venom glands. Its stings, in addition to containing the normal bee toxin effects, may cause fatigue, sluggishness, or in particularly high doses, unconsciousness.

Of the new flowers he had received from the karnuq, it seemed only the sleepy chamomile had produced a new bee type so far. But this one could be highly useful. The intoxicating effects of mad honey had already helped greatly against the shades, honey and venom that could knock a shade out could instantly end a fight. He had high hopes for that one.

Next was one of the queens herself, who had noticeably turned purple.

Maddening Monster Bee Queen

Vitality:	*Minimal*
Strength:	*Minimal*
Speed:	*Average*
Magic:	*Minor*
Defense:	*Minimal*
Resistance:	*Minimal*
Special:	*Above Average*
Notable Skills:	*Mad Poison Sting, Brood Mother, Command Offspring*

A monster bee queen raised or evolved on Mad Mana Honey.
Lays maddening variant offspring by default.

After a queen evolved into a medicinal queen, Belissar figured it was only a matter of time before a maddening queen would follow suit. Extra mad honey would ensure he could equip any future sticky honey traps with the deleterious honey type. And extra maddening bees could improve the strength of the soldier bee army . . . though this queen lived in the apiary, so maybe not, unless she was willing to either move or share soldiers and honey with the flower meadow queens.

But ultimately, it was the last of the new worker bees that really excited Belissar. The one he had been waiting for the most. She was a bit squatter, with shorter legs and longer antennas. She had large, thick mandibles that looked more suited to crushing than cutting, and her color was now a dull shade of brown rather than bright yellow.

Digging Monster Bee Worker

Vitality:	*Minimal+*
Strength:	*Minimal+*
Speed:	*Below Average+*
Magic:	*Minimal*
Defense:	*Minimal+*
Resistance:	*Minimal*
Special:	*Minimal*

Notable Skills: *Dig, Poison Sting, Sacrificial Strike,*
Brood Offspring
A monster bee worker raised on honey imbued with Ground mana.
Trades a bit of its speed for resilience and is optimized for
building subterranean hives and burrowing.

And, there she was. A bee born from the honey of the Ground mana flowers. Something like the digger bees he had given up his chance to choose, only born from the normal monster bee queens. A bee that could operate in the dirt tunnels . . . or in the Underway the karnuq said they came from. Exactly what his tower needed.

Belissar broke out into a wide grin. "Great work, everyone, this is definitely going to help."

The queens and new workers burst out into happy dances. Belissar chuckled and then rubbed his chin. Now that he had a bee that could go underground, couldn't he send his bees to scout the Underway as well? Well, that would take a bit, since one worker wouldn't be able to scout the tunnels alone . . .

And then his eyes widened as he had an idea. Why, exactly, would the bee have to go alone, when there was a group already going? Belissar turned to the queen who brought the digging worker.

"Can I borrow your worker? There's a job I could use her for."

The queen froze, and then started to tremble. It took a while, but eventually she burst out into a salute dance so rapid Belissar could barely make out what she was saying. The worker quivered as Belissar smiled and held out his hand to her.

"Great, let's go, then."

CHAPTER THIRTY-NINE

A VISIONAR-BEE PLAN

Belissar made his way to the second floor once again. There he found Metsaitti leading a group of hunters, including the group that used to hunt remnants in his tower, as they prepared for their expedition. Metsaitti noticed him and approached.

"Hello, Sacred Den Master. May I help you?"

Belissar nodded and held out his hand, holding the digging monster bee. "Could you take this bee with you on your trip? She's specialized for working underground, so she'll let me see the area. Oh! You could also talk to me through her . . . though you might be able to just talk to me directly now too, come to think of it. I guess we should test that when you leave."

Metsaitti nodded and held out his hand. "Of course, Sacred Den Master. I'll take care of her."

The digging bee looked to Belissar and he nodded. Instead of crawling onto Metsaitti's hand, she instead took off and landed on the bear man's shoulder. Belissar and Metsaitti then arranged to test if Belissar could see and talk to the karnuq like with his bees once they were outside of the rooms, and then Belissar left them to their preparations.

He rubbed his chin, because this all had given him an idea. He'd thought he would have to wait for digging bees to begin scouting underground until he had remembered the karnuq were already planning to do just that. So, he figured he should consider some other plans and whether there were alternative ways to achieve them.

He turned to Niobee. "Hey Niobee, could you speak with the queen from earlier, the one who evolved into a maddening monster bee? I'd like to know if she's happy living in the apiary and making honey there, or if she had anything else she might want to do."

"Okay, will ask!"

Belissar watched as Niobee flew off, then followed after her at a leisurely pace. In truth, a maddening monster bee queen would be most useful in the flower meadow, joining the soldier bee army. She could raise maddening soldiers and sprayers based on the unspecialized but highly productive mana flowers, greatly boosting their numbers among the soldier bee army. Even her workers had maddening stings, so even though they weren't soldiers, they could still help out in a pinch. If the queen wanted to move, having her join the flower meadow queens would be beneficial for the tower's defense.

But Belissar didn't want to make her move if she didn't want to, which was why he was trying to have Niobee ask her more subtly. He knew if he asked, she would immediately and enthusiastically reply yes regardless of what she actually felt.

Besides, the flower meadow queens no longer acted like normal bees. Normal bees could barely stand having two queens in the same hive. A situation like that would generally end in violence. Yet the flower meadow bees had grouped up together in the bee barracks, forming one massive hive with over a dozen queens. The apiary queens, on the other hand, kept to themselves as normal bees did. So, forcing one of the apiary queens to join the bee barracks if she were not already prepared to do so could cause some discomfort to both sides, maybe even conflict.

There was a benefit to keeping her in the apiary as well: mad honey was useful for the sticky honey traps, so there was also a need to produce it in large quantities.

Niobee met Belissar about halfway toward the hive in question, zipping about in the air. "King! Queen says loves hive King built for her! Loves making honey! No other wishes! Says King is best king!"

Belissar smiled and nodded. It seemed he had managed to be subtle enough to get a good answer. And now that he'd confirmed she wasn't thinking about moving, it was time to propose the other idea he had come up with.

"Niobee, do you think the bees would be willing to share honey with one another? Specifically, would an apiary queen be willing to share honey with the flower meadow queens?"

Niobee paused for a second before resuming her zipping about. "If King asks, will! Happy to help King!"

Belissar nodded at that. "Got it. Let's speak with her, then."

"Okay!"

At first, Belissar thought he'd have to wait until the flower meadow's poisonous flowers cross-pollinated with mana flowers, and then for the flower meadow hives to gather up enough of the hybrid nectar, for one of their queens to evolve. But now, he realized that wasn't the only option. The apiary queens produced a vast surplus of honey—they were giving him sixteen trays' worth a day, with still plenty for their hives. So, Belissar wondered, why wait for the flower meadow queens to produce their own honey before evolving? Now that there was a maddening queen and a medicinal queen who could both produce their respective honey types in bulk, couldn't he have them just share the specialized honey types with the flower meadow queens? The flower meadow queens could then use the honey to evolve their workers and soldiers in much greater quantities. A flower meadow queen might even be able to evolve herself. Meanwhile, the apiary queens could continue to devote themselves purely to honey production and pass on the benefit of any specialized honeys they developed.

Belissar wondered whether it was fair to take honey from the apiary queens just because they produced a lot, but then he remembered they were each giving him a tray of honey every day. Besides, he was a beekeeper. Taking some honey for his own purposes was part of the deal. Worst came to worst, he could just give his trays to the flower meadow queens himself. In fact, he should probably start doing that anyway. The mad honey trays were definitely starting to accumulate.

Belissar arrived at the hive and the maddening queen crawled out and saluted him. He greeted her and then got right into it.

"I have a favor to ask. Would you be willing to share some of your honey with the flower meadow queens? It would really help out if they could raise some more maddening soldiers with your help. Please give honey to them instead of me if you don't have enough."

The maddening queen paused before saluting once more. Belissar smiled at her. "Thank you, it will help a lot. Let me know if there's anything you need, or if you need more flowers or something."

The maddening queen quickly declined, but Belissar shook his head. "I know I'm asking a lot of you, so please, allow me to give you something. Hard work should be rewarded."

The maddening queen paused and fell still. She glanced at Niobee, who flew over and brushed her antennas against the queen's. Then, slowly, the queen began to dance.

". . . Mana flowers? Next to hive?"

Belissar smiled and nodded. "Sure, as soon as I can."

The maddening queen paused once more, and then burst out into a maximum-speed dance. It was so fast the dances were getting jumbled, but Belissar definitely caught the "KING BEST KING!" parts and chuckled.

"No, thank *you* for helping out."

Belissar thought a bit as they left the queen to her work. He then nodded and made his way over to the medicinal queen, repeating his request and offer. She had much the same response as the maddening queen.

Belissar smiled as he walked away. A vision for the future was starting to come together in his mind. A tower full of happy bees . . . happy bees that worked together. Apiary queens that gave their all producing all sorts of diverse and magical honeys, which they offered to the flower meadow army that kept them all safe. Such a setup would even solve a growing concern of Belissar's, which was that the dirt tunnels and the orchard both had plants and flowers that he could not plant in either the flower meadow or the apiary. Up until now, he had been trying to ensure that both the apiary and flower meadow queens had access to every flower type he had available . . . but that didn't seem to be practical going forward. As of now, the first floor's dirt tunnels lacked subterranean plants, and the third floor lacked an orchard altogether. He couldn't resolve that situation because right now as his mana was sitting at a grand total of zero. His future mana was accounted for as well: he now had two mana flower nodes he had promised to the donating apiary queens, the karnuq could probably use a few more resources, and the new bumblebee queens would need nests once they spawned.

If he continued to try and insist that every hive have every flower available, the situation would only get worse. What would happen as he acquired new rooms that might have unique flower types? What if those rooms were incredibly mana-expensive? Or what if he just didn't have the room limit to have every room type on every floor?

But if the queens began to share honey with one another, that would solve the problem. Queens in different rooms could specialize in their local flowers, or even evolve themselves like the maddening and medicinal queens had, and then just exchange their products with one another. Then, Belissar would only have to give one set of queens access to a given flower type for its honey to be available across his tower. He could specialize the first-floor rooms for defense without worrying if the flower meadow queens could raise the bee types necessary to defend them. He could expand new floors with new apiaries without needing to completely rebuild every room and resource plant node like he had for the bumblebees.

He nodded to himself. He was no longer a mere beekeeper, but a dungeon master. His abode was no longer a mere apiary, but a Tower of the Gods. And his bees were no longer regular bees, but magical monster bees who could speak with him directly. It was time for them all to elevate to something more. The bees had already been doing so on their own, and if Belissar was to be their king, it was time he helped out with that.

THE KING'S REQUEST

This was fine.

The First of the Fifth was currently pacing about in her hive. Her first communers had just emerged from their cells. Her mind lit up with the dances of countless bees as the communers focused their attention on their queen and connected her to her workers' mana as a result. It was nearly overwhelming, but the First of the Fifth had not created a hive of peak efficiency by lacking will. She managed to organize the incoming information within her mind and get her bearings . . . and, as a result, caught a glimpse of the King walking through the apiary. She had the worker in question escort the King, just in case he should have need of her, and so saw the conversations that resulted.

The King had made a personal request to one of the other apiary queens. The other apiary queen that had evolved. The apiary queen that had evolved specifically through access to a hybridized poisonous flower. A poisonous flower that had grown because the First of the Fifth's workers had cross-pollinated mana flowers with poisonous flowers. Poisonous flowers the queen had gotten access to because the First of the Fifth had then given up her own rights to a new flower type that her own workers had been responsible for, in the name of loving all bees.

This . . . was fine. Another bee had gotten to experience the personal favor of the King as a result of her efforts. This was good. Truly, she had demonstrated her love for all bees, and had become like her King. Which was why she was not even bothered by the idea of sending the apiary's hard work over to the Firstborn! Nor by the idea of the King handing over a full patch of mana flowers to an apiary queen after she had gone and shared access to her own with those same queens!

This . . . was . . . fine . . .

She was halted in her thoughts by a loud buzzing noise, as well as a thousand urgent dances impressing themselves on her mind. It appeared that thanks to her communers, the dances of her mind had been conveyed to her workers. Who were apparently agitated and preparing to marshal for war as a result.

Okay, maybe this wasn't fine.

She took a moment to calm herself and then danced that all was well to her workers, and that they should continue with their work. She would not permit her own inner turmoil to impact her hive's honey production. As her workers slowly stopped beating their wings and resumed their duties, she tried to take stock of the situation, to come at it from a different angle, that of efficiency.

And from that point of view, the King's actions made complete sense. The flower meadow queens' lower honey production meant they couldn't spare as much effort on cross-pollination or on producing specialized honeys. Yet, at the same time, the mad honey and bee types that resulted from the poisonous flowers would certainly aid the King's army more than it would boost honey production. So, if she set aside her natural hesitation to share honey between hives, it absolutely made sense to have an apiary queen produce specialized honey for the flower meadow queens. It took advantage of their differing roles to achieve maximum effect for the King's domain as a whole.

It also made sense why the King had requested that specific queen, instead of herself. Sure, her hive produced the most honey and the most excellent honey and had the most workers and the most efficient organization, but in this one minor use case there was good reason to request another. The maddening queen could produce mad honey from any source, including the highly productive mana flowers, with no additional effort. In contrast, to produce mad honey in bulk would have taken the First of the Fifth's hive significantly more effort, as they would have had to produce it solely from the nectar of the mana-less poisonous flowers. Cross-pollination would assist with that in the long term, but as of now there was only one of each hybridized flower, so it was not a factor in the short term. The maddening queen, even if her honey production and quality were lower and her hive less efficient, could produce mad honey in bulk with no drop in efficiency. The First of the Fifth could not, even though her production and quality would certainly remain the best even with the drop.

Yes, it made sense. The question was . . . what should the First of the Fifth do as a result?

But then, the First of the Fifth paused as an urgent report came into her mind. She had assigned one of her workers to escort the King after the karnuq moved in. That worker now indicated . . . that the King was moving directly toward her hive. The First of the Fifth dropped all thoughts to prepare for his arrival . . .

As Belissar was walking back to the apiary farmhouse, Niobee suddenly flew in front of him. She hesitated slightly, causing Belissar to raise an eyebrow.

"Niobee? Is something the matter?"

Niobee still hesitated before beginning a slow dance. "King, have . . . request."

Belissar blinked before breaking out into a wide smile. Niobee never asked him for anything, despite all that she had done for him. He owed her everything, including his very life, so he would jump at any chance to help her out.

"Of course. Niobee . . . you're my best friend and you've done more for me than I can ever repay. You can ask me for anything."

Niobee started to object before pausing and continuing with her original dance. "Okay . . . can King talk to First of Fifth?"

Belissar nodded. "Sure. Anything specifically I should tell her?"

Niobee was still moving slowly but picked up a bit of speed. "First of Fifth's workers pollinated new flowers, helped other queens evolve."

Belissar rubbed his chin and nodded. "Ah, so it's thanks to her we got the new queens and flowers? I'll have to thank her then."

Niobee paused for a bit before bursting into a rapid dance again. "Thanks, King! King is best king!"

Belissar smiled and shook his head. "No, I should be thanking the bees for everything they do, that much is a given. And I was serious. You can ask me for anything, Niobee." He then rubbed his chin. "Say, Niobee, the First of the Fifth is sort of in charge of the apiary, right? She was also the first to make medicinal and mad honey, right?"

"Yes, is most powerful apiary queen. Best at making honey, tries to make new types."

Belissar nodded. "I've been thinking about the future and I have an idea. Tell me how it sounds and if you think the First of the Fifth could help with this . . ."

The First of the Fifth flew out to meet the King, greeting him as he deserved. He smiled at her with the warmth of the summer sun, before speaking words that rumbled her very core.

"I need to thank you for pollinating the plants. It was thanks to you that we got some new plants and new bees that will be very helpful for the tower. Thank you, excellent work."

The First of the Fifth had a bit of trouble remembering what happened in the next few minutes. Something like falling to the ground as her mind went blank, followed by some sort of dance so rapid the world around her blurred. The King . . . had seen her efforts. He *approved*. She had helped the bees and helped the King. Her path was not wrong after all.

But that was only the beginning of a conversation that would change everything. The First of the Fifth listened with rapt attention, and then immediately agreed with as much gusto as she could muster. She then spent the rest of the day doing a full-speed happy dance.

The King had grand plans. He was going to take new flowers and entire new rooms, and then categorize and specialize them. He would have queens, like the two that had recently evolved, devoted entirely to specialized honey types, which they would then share with the rest. He would thus maximize honey production across all flower types and hives and rooms, while still ensuring that all bees retained access to all flowers, even ones their workers never saw.

It was exactly what she did in her relentless quest for better honey. The King was taking her methods and applying them on a much grander scale, utilizing entire hives as she utilized single trays.

And he wanted *her* help. He asked her, as the one who had developed the new honey types and even new flowers, to take the lead. To determine which flowers were suitable for specialization, to ensure all queens had sufficient resources in the process, and to arrange for the exchanges of nectar and honey.

It was not a dream come true, because the situation *far* exceeded any dream the First of the Fifth had ever dared to imagine.

But finally, when she had calmed down, she paused. To bring the King's vision to pass would take more work from her than ever before. And, moreover, it would require her to organize the other queens as she did her own hive. She had no concerns about her ability to do so, since she had raised communers for exactly that purpose. The issue was . . . what of the other queens? She . . . would admit that she had not treated them appropriately in the past. She had thought of them as rivals and so attempted to overcome and contain them. They, therefore, trusted her about as much as any rival would. She knew that even her recent efforts had not convinced them otherwise. But if they would not trust her, then it would be hard to enact the King's plan.

So, the First of the Fifth gathered herself and did something that would have been unthinkable for her beforehand. She left her hive and flew to the King's abode. She did not dare step inside without permission, instead waiting by the window-sill. Fortunately, she did not have to wait long before the Conduit noticed her and came out to greet her.

"Hi, First of Fifth. Need something?"

The First of the Fifth hesitated only a moment before beginning to dance. "Need . . . help. King's plan . . . needs queens to work together. I . . . didn't work with other queens before, and other queens don't trust now. Will Conduit . . . help me? I know is a lot to ask, but need Conduit's help for King's plan."

Requesting help from another, one she formerly considered a rival, even. It was unthinkable. But the First of the Fifth realized that if the King wanted all bees to help one another . . . then she should be willing to request help when she needed it as well. To admit that she needed it . . . well, that was unthinkable too.

But if the other queens did not trust her, she could not efficiently fulfill the King's request of her. And that, of course, was the most unthinkable. So, she did what she had to.

She could only hope that the Conduit would be willing to—

"Okay! Will help!"

The First of the Fifth was silent for a bit as she tried to process what had just occurred.

PLOTS AND CONSPIRA-BEES

A worker from the First of the Fifth's hive crawled into a flame radish flower, drinking deeply of the nectar. Many of her sisters disliked foraging from the flame radish flowers, claiming the nectar was too spicy and burned their insides. Likewise, the pollen from said flowers increased the ambient temperature around itself, which her sisters said would cause them to overheat and force them to fly more slowly, reducing their gathering efficiency.

This worker had none of those problems, for she was a burning monster bee worker who had been raised on the nectar from these very flowers. The nectar of these flowers didn't burn her at all; indeed, she found nectar from most other flowers to be rather bland and chilly in comparison. The pollen's heat felt pleasant and warm to her, energizing her and helping her fly faster. As such, she was now the main forager for these particular flowers, a task she could handle on her own as her queen had decreed a limit on the amount of flame radish nectar gathered at any one time.

However, she did not fill herself up on the tasty and warm nectar as she wished, for she had another task. Since flame radish nectar could not be gathered in large enough quantities for her queen's normal honey production, she was ordered instead to focus on variety and visit multiple flowers on each trip. So, when she was half-full, she reluctantly crawled back out of the flower and took off into the air. She shivered a bit as she left the warm and comfortable flame radish patch.

She then flew off into the apiary, to a corner where a lone mana flower grew. This one wasn't from the magical patches, but rather one of the few spread out around the room, and far out of the way. As far as flowers went, the mana flower was her second favorite. While it was still a bit cool for her taste, the mana had a warmth of its own and she hungered for it. The mana flower could thus fill her in a way that even the flame radishes did not. And so, she landed and drank deeply.

As she did, a bit of pollen on her legs rubbed off into the flower. A slight glow illuminated the fallen pollen and then it vanished, melting into the flower. As the worker began to fly away, she did not notice the mana flower begin to take on a reddish glow. The glow concentrated into a little ball of light that lifted off from the flower and began to drift as if on the wind, even though the air of the apiary was calm.

It floated through the room, occasionally drooping, but never touching the ground. And despite the lack of a breeze, it continued to move, even turning and changing course. Until it floated above the flame radish patch. It then began to fall, drifting toward the patch as if being pulled on a line. It settled amid the flame radish flowers, its light growing brighter the closer it got. It then landed on the ground and melted into it.

A moment later, a new mana flower broke through the ground and rapidly grew. A mana flower with a red stem and leaves . . .

The Second of the Sixth was on top of the world. She had wondered whether evolving to a medicinal monster bee queen had been the First of the Fifth's plan for her. Her worries only grew when she realized that no matter what nectar her foragers gathered, her new offspring could only make medicinal honey now. That meant that while she could surpass the First of the Fifth in that one honey type, she could never match her in any other, including the honey served to the King. She had effectively removed herself as a rival for the King's favor.

And as the proportion of medicinal honey in her combs grew, more and more of her originally normal workers began to evolve to match their mother and siblings. Soon, her entire hive was made up of medicinal monster bees and no further possibility remained of going back. If she had made a mistake, it was a permanent one.

But it turned out she had not. Instead, the King had noticed her new advantage and personally come to her with a request. Only she could produce the quantities of medicinal honey needed to supply the queens of the flower meadow and their army, and Queen of All Bees knew they needed the help.

In exchange, he had promised her a personal mana flower patch of her own. He did not need to do so, for all hives in his realm were his own to command as he saw fit, but he did so anyway. Soon, she would have access to as many resources as the First of the Fifth did. Possibly more, given how the First of the Fifth had allocated her own patches to the apiary queens.

Lately though, the First of the Fifth confused the Second of the Sixth. Her actions no longer made any sense, and the Second of the Sixth couldn't make heads or stingers of them. Try as she might, she couldn't determine what, if any, benefit the First of the Fifth was gaining from offering up the flowers she had claimed to the rest of them. It had come to the point that the Second of the Sixth had to just stop thinking about it and take whatever benefit was offered.

Though, today, she thought she might just find out. A worker from the First of the Fifth had just arrived at her hive, informing her of a gathering of the apiary queens. She could not help but admit she was curious. Would today be the day the First of the Fifth's ultimate plan was revealed?

The Second of the Sixth made her way to the apiary's shrine of bees . . . and was surprised to find the Conduit waiting there along with the First of the Fifth. That was unexpected . . . and concerning. On the one leg, the Conduit wouldn't go along with pure selfishness on the part of the First of the Fifth, so whatever was about to occur couldn't be directly harmful to them. On the other leg, the Conduit's first priority above all else was the good of the King and of his realm. If the First of the Fifth had a plan that was technically beneficial to the whole, the Conduit might support it, even if it wasn't beneficial to the Second of the Sixth personally. She would have to remain wary—not that she could do anything, though. The Conduit was second only to the King, after all, so if she ordered them to do something they could only obey.

So, she watched with great trepidation as the First of the Fifth finally began to dance. Slowly. Painfully slowly. The Second of the Sixth resisted the urge to beat her wings. She should just get on with—

"Need . . . your help."

The Second of the Sixth froze solid. Um, what? The First of the Fifth? The arrogant top producer of honey in both quantity and quality, a fact that she made sure none of them ever forgot? *She* needed help? From them?

"King and Conduit both have requests. Too much for one hive. And . . . King believes in hive of hives. Hives working as one, not apart."

The apiary queens, the Second of the Sixth included, continued to watch in stunned silence. What exactly was the First of the Fifth up to?

"King noticed Second of Sixth and Third of Fifth evolved, make lots of medicinal and mad honey. Asked them to provide special honey to flower meadow so they can raise new soldiers. Also noticed queens evolved because of new flowers from my workers pollinating. Wants more flowers and more queens to evolve."

The Second of the Sixth twitched a bit as the attention focused on her for a second. The First of the Fifth . . . was acknowledging her achievement? Well, she was also partially claiming credit for it, which, while technically true, was a bit more in line with what the Second of the Sixth had expected.

"So, have new idea. I want access to all flowers, will test for special honey and pollinate new flowers."

The Second of the Sixth finally stirred into motion even as her wings began to buzz. Ah, there it was. The plan was finally coming together. She was about to grow indignant—

"Once flowers with special nectar identified, will be offered to a single queen. Queen should focus on evolving and then King will reward."

. . . and she was once again confused.

"We should all help give honey to flower meadow queens. Queens that contribute most, besides me, will be offered special flowers first."

The Second of the Sixth cleaned her antennas. Um, maybe the First of the Fifth was trying to spread out the burden of something requested by the King? But . . . that made no sense. If the King requested it, the First of the Fifth would want to handle it all herself and monopolize the King's favor, right?

"Conduit has also asked we watch newcomers to ensure loyalty. Would like foragers from each hive to help. Should raise communers, at least two. One so scouts can report to queens right away, another to stay at my hive and pass reports to me."

Yes, there it was! The First of the Fifth wanted to be the only one reporting so that it would seem like she was doing all the work!

"Will also teach communers staying with me organization and honey-making methods so queens can produce more efficiently. All King's hives should be excellent. If not enough honey to raise communers, let me know. Will give you honey to raise."

The Second of the Sixth was confused again. At this point, the First of the Fifth turned to the Conduit. All the other queens turned to her as well.

The Conduit danced her confirmation. "Is will of King! All bees work together for King and for hive of hives! Let Niobee know if any problems, okay?"

The Second of the Sixth gathered herself and tried to take stock of the situation. So, there was a request from the King. The First of the Fifth was requesting their cooperation, though in a way that put her on top of the hierarchy. Yet, the proposal was to their benefit. The First of the Fifth would be giving away her secrets, providing resources, and granting them all a chance to receive the personal attention and rewards of the King. It was . . . beneficial to both parties? Possibly even more beneficial to them. The First of the Fifth was giving away much in exchange for their acknowledgement of her nominal authority. Would that authority allow her to steer things in a way more beneficial to herself?

But ultimately, the Conduit had confirmed that this was the will of the King. So, there was no choice but to agree. Besides, no queen would reject an opportunity to receive personal orders and rewards from the King, as she had. And so, they all agreed.

The Second of the Sixth once again hoped she wasn't making a mistake. But somewhere, deep down inside her, a new thought was born. What if . . . she was wrong about the First of the Fifth?

Only time would tell if that were true.

CHAPTER FORTY

BETTER BEE VIGILANT

The karnuq hunting group had finished their preparations and left the tower. Belissar watched them a bit through the digging worker's eyes, but they didn't go very far today. They stopped at the entrance to the Underway and set up a small camp next to it. Once Metsaitti tested the link, Belissar found he could speak with the karnuq and could remain aware of their general location and status, though he had trouble seeing through them like he did with his bees. So, the digging bee would remain with them as Belissar's eyes, even though she wasn't necessary for basic communication. Through the link, Metsaitti explained that the expedition could potentially take multiple days, so it was important to have a base to return to. They might even make another one underground, depending on how far they ventured.

But since the karnuq wouldn't be heading into the Underway today, Belissar turned his attention back to the tower. It was just about time for the next purification.

And this time, something changed. Rather than a wolf-shade or a bird-shade, one of those fast cat-shades appeared. There was only one of them, but it was the same size as the ones from the expansion purification . . . and this time, there were no dirt tunnels in its way. Belissar wasn't moving the dirt tunnels for the daily purifications, and while he planned to add a new dirt tunnel room to the first floor, he hadn't actually done so yet.

So, this time, the bees only had the short amount of time it took the shade to form to rearrange themselves. A handful of sprayers launched their attack before the monster finished coalescing, while the soldiers rushed to tighten the encirclement.

The shade roared as toxins sprayed all over its back. It immediately pushed forward with its wind and began running. The soldiers hadn't finished getting in their positions, so it broke through their formation and began sprinting across the field. Belissar's eyes widened from his position by the bee barracks. He quickly turned to Chief Rohsuak.

"Get ready! A shade has made it past the army!"

Chief Rohsuak's face turned grim. Fortunately, not all of the hunters had left with the expedition, and those that remained had prepared to join the purification. Chief Rohsuak directed them into a tight formation in the hallway through the bee barracks that led to the next floor, with Belissar and the chief herself behind them. Belissar hoped against hope that the shade would prioritize moving deeper over attacking the exposed barracks.

But it turned out he needn't have worried. While the soldier bees' formation hadn't been completed, it hadn't been useless, either. A handful of soldier bees had latched onto the shade as it sprinted past them and were stinging it repeatedly. The shade began to slow down as it crossed the flower meadow.

The karnuq tensed and lifted their spears as they saw the shade approaching them. During the first few purifications, the bees had handled the shades so efficiently that most of the hunters hadn't gotten a good view. This time, they could see the shade's full form. Its big fangs and claws, the glowing red lights that replaced its too numerous eyes, the shifting and amorphous fog wafting off it that obscured the exact limits of its body. The wings that didn't fit on a feline animal. One of the karnuq gulped.

And the bees continued to cling on and sting the shade, ignoring all of that. It was bleeding drops of Hunger that quickly faded as it ran. It saw the karnuq in its way and growled, lifting its wings as it rushed forward. Belissar frowned.

"Careful, it's going to try and push us out of the way with wind."

Chief Rohsuak nodded, not taking her eyes off the shade for even a moment. "Brace yourselves! Don't let it push you a step back! Don't let it set a foot into our new home!"

The karnuq shouted and steadied themselves, bracing for impact. The queens of the bee barracks began to gather by the entrances with their workers, prepared to fly into action as well. The shade was just about to swing its wings forward . . .

And then it fell into the pit trap placed before the room's exit, just before the bee barracks. The bees' attacks had slowed it just enough that it didn't make it all the way across this time and instead fell in with a crash. The soldier bees clinging onto it let go and flew away before the sticky honey trap activated and drenched the shade in mad honey, and then the apiary soldiers dropped a flame radish sliver down on top of it without missing a beat.

The karnuq blinked and then glanced at one another, while Belissar took a large breath and let it out. "Whew, that was close. Thanks for the help."

Chief Rohsuak nodded. "Not at all. It's our duty and our home too, now." She gave him a wry smile as she glanced at the now-burning pit. "Besides, we didn't do all that much in the end."

Belissar chuckled and then frowned. If these fast shades could now appear in the minor+ purifications, then he should put some dirt tunnels in front of the flower meadow as soon as possible. Additionally, he was reminded of his initial plans. He had forgotten since the tower upgraded it to a feature, but the bee barracks wasn't complete, per his original intentions. The structure was only the start; he had also planned to fortify the exterior. The problem was that Belissar's attempts to make any sort of palisades hadn't gone well before, and he had prioritized finishing beehouses for the rest of the queens. But now . . . now it was apparent that the bee barracks could use some extra defense. He turned to Chief Rohsuak.

"Hey, do you know how to build fences or palisades or stuff like that? I'd like to fortify the bee barracks here, but the last time I tried it didn't go well."

Chief Rohsuak rubbed her chin and slowly nodded. "It's been a while, but we know the basics. Either way, more hands should help. We would be happy to assist if you need us, Sacred Den Master."

Belissar nodded. "Ah, yes. That'd be great."

And so, one quick promise to meet the next day and a victory celebration later, Belissar again had fifteen mana to work with. The dirt trails feature offered this time *was* a bit more useful now that the karnuq lived in the tower, but not enough to surpass Belissar's desperate need for more mana.

The very first thing he did was place a new dirt tunnel room on the first floor, between the flower meadow and the tower entrance. This purification and the previous expansion had made the benefits of having extra space between the entrance and the soldier bee army abundantly clear. Belissar did worry about putting an underground room in front of the entrance for the sake of the bees he had asked to scout the area around the tower, but his recent experience with the bumblebees provided a solution. He placed the dirt tunnels "underneath" the flower meadow, arranging it so that the exit from the dirt tunnels to outside of the tower was right underneath the bee barracks, with an entrance between them at the opposite side of the room. Then, he made a second entrance between the dirt tunnels and the flower meadow, a little soldier bee-sized tunnel in the ground next to the bee barracks that connected to the ceiling of the starting cavern of the dirt tunnels. He made sure that starting cavern was very tall to make the bee entrance harder to reach . . . at least for shades that couldn't fly.

This way, any invader larger than a bee would have to go all the way through the dirt tunnels and then through the entire flower meadow, while the bees themselves could head right to the tower's entrance from the bee barracks. Not only did that let the bees bypass the dark underground tunnels they'd have trouble flying through, but it also made their trip shorter than it had been before, since they now could bypass most of the flower meadow. And, if a shade did manage to find, reach, and fit through the bees' entrance . . . well, then it would be small enough that the bees could face it head-on in a place it couldn't avoid them. At least, Belissar hoped that would be the case . . .

In any case, with the new room to buy time, he knew the soldier bee army could handle fast shades, so that should be sufficient for now, and the karnuq would also help him fortify the bee barracks starting tomorrow. So, he turned his attention to other commitments. He made two more mana flower nodes next to the maddening queen and the medicinal queen's hives, as he had promised them.

And, just like that, he was nearly out of mana again. Fortunately, he had enough for another bee nest, since another bumblebee queen would spawn tomorrow. At this point, though, he felt so starved for mana that he wondered if he should consider removing some features. Most of the pit traps had largely been ignored, after all.

Still, Belissar had gotten what he wanted done today, so he put the matter aside and turned in for the night.

GENEROSI-BEE

The next day, Belissar made his way to the new flower meadow. The original bumblebee queen greeted him with rapid circles, making him smile. After he greeted her, Belissar headed over to the spawner. He arrived just as a new monster bumblebee queen was crawling out.

Monster Bumblebee Queen Spawner

Monsters:	*Monster Bumblebee Queen*
Cooldown:	*23/24 hours*
Current Monsters Spawned:	*2/4*

The bumblebee queen spawner was identical to the monster bee queen spawner, spawning one queen per day until it reached four. Belissar greeted the new queen and showed her the bee nest he had made for her last night. The queen responded by zipping in circles around him.

After that, he made his way over to the karnuq. Right at the entrance of the second floor, Chief Rohsuak had gathered a group of karnuq. She turned to Belissar and nodded.

"Welcome, Sacred Den Master Belissar. May I introduce you to Rakenliuk? He's our construction expert."

Belissar turned his gaze to the karnuq man who towered over him. Rakenliuk shook his head. "*Expert* is a strong word. We've rarely had to chance to build anything lasting. But I'll do my best, Sacred Den Master."

Belissar shook his head. "Ah, it's, um, fine. I don't really know what I'm doing either, so anything will help."

Soon after, Belissar led the karnuq back to the first floor and the flower meadow. He pointed around the bee barracks.

"So, I was thinking a ditch in front of this building with a palisade behind it? Um, unless you know of anything better to help guard this area?"

Rakenliuk slowly nodded. "Sounds like a plan to me."

Belissar then turned to find the soldier bees gathering around him. He smiled at them.

"We're going to improve the defenses of your home, and they're going to help. Want to help too?"

The soldier bees saluted, and a moment later the air filled with hundreds of beating wings as the entire soldier bee army ceased their training and returned to the bee barracks. Belissar turned back to find the karnuq staring at the scene with wide eyes.

"Um, the soldier bees helped me build stuff before. They can lift and move things."

Rakenliuk just wordlessly nodded his head.

The Firstborn watched through the eyes of her soldiers as the King approached alongside a group of the newcomers, her newly born communer now allowing her to see through her children. She longed to rush out to greet the King, but it was not her day to command the army. Her place remained in the barracks, managing the growth of her hive. As usual, her workers were small in number but tireless in their labor, and so they needed her support to ensure the army would remain fed. Ensuring the hive ran well and had sufficient honey was even more important than usual because her daughter had started to grow. The communer had also strengthened her connection to the young queen, and the Firstborn could now sense that she wished to grow to her next stage, which would allow her to begin laying soldier eggs of her own.

That was a wonderful thing, but it would take her daughter out of commission for a bit and would require a significant amount of honey to fuel her growth. And since all the flower meadow queens had raised daughters at the same time and subsequently began sharing resources, all of their daughters had grown at the same rate and were now at that same stage. Which meant half of all the queens in the bee barracks now needed extra honey and time away from their work. Not for the first time, the flower meadow queens' drive to build the largest army they could possibly sustain was coming back to haunt them.

The Firstborn and the other mother queens redoubled their efforts to ensure efficient honey production, trying to squeeze out as much extra honey as they could without overstraining their busy workers. They would normally cut down on soldiers to raise a few extra workers, but the recent purification had nearly gone badly, so they were also worried about the strength of the army. As usual, there was just too much they needed to do, and not enough honey for them to do it all.

Little did the Firstborn know, however, that everything was about to change.

Through her soldiers' eyes, she caught sight of another visitor. One that made her cease her work for a moment. The First of the Fifth had just flown into the flower meadow, leading a wave of soldier bees, the ones born from the soldier bee spawner in the apiary, as well as a cloud of workers.

All of them were carrying cells full of honey.

A moment later, the group landed at the entrance of the bee barracks. The Firstborn and the other flower meadow queens arrived. The Firstborn danced unsteadily.

"First of Fifth? Nice to see but confused, why here now? Not time for celebration? Need something?"

The First of the Fifth danced the negative. "King has idea. Wants hive of hives to work together. Flower meadow queens raise army, but not great at making honey. So, apiary queens help."

She then danced to her workers and the soldiers, who began to deliver the honey and sort it into three piles. "This one, regular honey from all apiary queens. This one medicinal honey from Second of Sixth, good for brood tenders. This one mad honey from Third of Fifth, good for soldiers."

The Firstborn danced in a daze. "You're . . . giving to us?"

The First of the Fifth's antennas twitched. "Yes. Was paying attention, right?"

The Firstborn stood still, and then began a dance of gratitude. "Thanks, helps a lot! Is perfect, even. How can repay?"

The First of the Fifth stood still for a moment herself before slowly dancing back. "Protect King and hive of hives. Will be bringing every day. Use to make strong army, okay?"

The Firstborn didn't even know what to dance. But eventually, she gathered herself and marched firmly through her steps, giving the First of the Fifth a salute dance.

"Thank you. Will not let down."

With that, the First of the Fifth took her leave. The Firstborn and the flower meadow queens gathered and distributed the honey throughout their hives. Empty cells were now filled to the brim. Whereas it normally took several days to gather enough honey for a single maddening soldier or sprayer, now each of the queens was laying a soldier egg in a cell full of the purple-tinted honey. The medicinal honey was even rarer, and the Firstborn used her batch to lay a new generation of workers that would ensure the health of her hive.

And then, with the normal mana honey, she prepared a large cell for her daughter. The young queen hesitated, but the Firstborn brushed her antennas.

"Go ahead. Have plenty of reserves now, will be okay."

Her daughter slowly saluted and then curled up into the cell that was much too large for her . . . for now. The Firstborn watched until her workers had completely covered up the cell before walking away. She aimlessly wandered the barracks for a moment.

The First of the Fifth had once again blazed a new trail. The Firstborn had made deals with her before, exchanging flowers for honey. The Fourth of the Seventh and the First of the Fifth's First Daughter had built a joint hive, working together for a common purpose, and the flower meadow queens had followed suit. The flower meadow queens had joined their armies and exchanged command of their soldiers with one another. But in all these cases, both parties benefited. They gave in expectation of receiving in turn.

Now, the First of the Fifth and the other apiary queens had given them vast quantities of honey . . . and asked for *nothing* in return. They worked for the hive of hives not as rival queens coming to an agreement, but as workers supporting their queens. They gave without expecting to receive, because there was work to be done and so they did it. They demonstrated how a queen in a hive of hives should truly behave.

The Firstborn was humbled yet again. She began to turn her mind to what her response should be. One could say the flower meadow queens were already acting selflessly, as they had taken on the defense of the hive of hives upon their shoulders, but the Firstborn was not satisfied with merely that. She considered how she, too, could contribute to the hive of hives. She would never catch up to the apiary queens in honey production, so sharing resources was not possible. So, was there something her hive could do that the apiary couldn't?

Her eyes turned toward the King as he worked with the karnuq and the soldier bee army that had naturally started to assist him. She watched as the karnuq dug deep trenches into the ground while the soldier bees carried large pieces of wood. She remembered the King's efforts to build the barracks, and how they had been able to assist him.

And she started to realize . . . soldier bees could do far more than simply sting, couldn't they? And if there was work to be done that a bee could do, then that is what that bee should do.

She soon came up with a proposal for the evening gathering of the barracks queens . . .

CHAPTER FORTY-ONE

UNEXPECTED BEE-NEFITS

Belissar turned his attention to the karnuq hunter group, which was just beginning their descent into the Underway from the tunnel entrance in the forest outside of the tower. The digging bee surprisingly couldn't see that far beyond the lights the karnuq carried with them, making Belissar wonder how she would operate underground without such assistance. His question was answered, though, when the bee flew off Metsaitti's shoulder and landed on the ground. The moment she touched the ground, a little pulse of mana shot out from her. Information on the surroundings came streaming back to her, and she could feel the vibrations of all the karnuq moving around her as well. It seemed the digging bees didn't intend to rely on sight in the first place. After the pulse returned to her, she flew back to Metsaitti's shoulder. She continued to land and send out pulses at regular intervals, building a steady map of the tunnel they were traversing.

But at that moment, something drew Belissar's attention away from the hunting group.

New plant detected. Fire Mana Flower is now available.

Belissar's vision blurred as he whipped his tower sight around and quickly found the culprit. A new flower had bloomed in the middle of the flame radish node in the apiary. It looked like a mana flower, but the stalk was colored shifting shades of yellow, orange, and red, and the petals at the top were bright red. The mana surrounding it was not a subtle, slowly pulsing glow like that of the mana flowers or Ground mana flowers, but rather a flickering light that illuminated the flame radish flowers around it. The air around it grew slightly hazy.

Belissar's eyes widened and then he grinned. He knew cross-pollination was working its magic, but this was the first time it had produced a flower so different the tower classified it as a separate plant. And what a flower it was. Belissar could practically feel the heat emanating from it . . . until he realized that with his tower senses he actually *could* feel it, if he wanted to.

It felt like it was burning him, so he decided to stick with vision alone.

In any case, it seemed like a flower that was practically on fire. And while he could sense that the regular mana flowers and Ground mana flowers both held equally as much mana as this one . . . there was still something impressive about it. The mana and Ground mana flowers, for all the power held within them, didn't truly appear that different from regular flowers beyond the occasional glow. The Fire mana flower, on the other hand, was very clearly magical, even to Belissar's barely trained eyes.

He grinned as he opened up the menu.

Available Resource Plants for Apiary:
-Fire Mana Flower (10 per node, 20 due to unsuitable environment.)

He pursed his lips as he immediately calmed down. Right, he had somewhat forgotten how expensive Ground mana flowers were when placed anywhere save the dirt tunnels. And well, he didn't exactly have some sort of fire tunnels at the moment. So, if he wanted to make a Fire mana flower node, he'd have to shell out a lot of mana.

And right now, he had a grand total of five available . . .

Belissar froze, and then smacked his forehead. He had completely forgotten that Ground mana flowers were far cheaper when placed in a dirt tunnel room . . . and he currently had two Ground mana flower nodes in the first floor's flower meadow and orchard that he could now move to the new first-floor dirt tunnels. He used his tower voice to let the flower meadow and orchard queens know he was about to move those patches, then he modified the dirt tunnels a bit, creating a cavern just below the flower meadow's resource nodes. He then moved both Ground mana flower nodes there, and created another small, soldier bee-sized tunnel up to the flower meadow so the bees could access the cavern directly. For the flower meadow bees it would be practically the same as before, and for the orchard bees it was a slightly longer trip but still quite short. And as for the results of his efforts?

Mana: 35/570

Dropping both Ground mana flower nodes' upkeep from twenty to five each freed up a lot of mana for him to work with. Enough that he could now afford a Fire mana flower node. So, the question now was, should he spend his mana on that?

He turned his sight back to the Fire mana flower . . . and frowned. A handful of worker bees were hovering around the flame radish patch, but they weren't moving any closer. Only the handful of burning monster bee workers that had grown so far were able to fly to the new flower, or even the flame radish flowers around it. If Belissar had to guess, the Fire mana flower was now raising the ambient temperature beyond what his worker bees could handle.

He let out a sigh. That settled it, then. If most of the bees couldn't actually gather nectar from the new flower, then there was no point in spending the mana on an entire patch of them. He'd have to wait for the queens to raise more burning workers . . . or maybe even for a burning queen to evolve.

Besides, he had just recently come up with the idea of specializing the bees, and the apiary queens had already begun delivering honey to the flower meadow. His original instinct to provide one of every type of possible flower node to every single room where bees lived was perhaps already outdated. So, he decided this time he'd wait for some sort of fire queen to evolve, and then make just one Fire mana flower node for her. And who knew? Maybe he'd manage to get a new room type that would make the Fire mana flowers much cheaper in the meantime.

Well, in any case, that meant he had another thirty-five mana to work with, or fifteen if he wanted to keep twenty in reserve for a Fire mana flower node. The question was . . . what to do with it?

Strangely, despite how mana-starved he had been lately, Belissar couldn't think of much. Well, he would need new bee nests for the next two bumblebee queens, but they wouldn't spawn until tomorrow and the day after. He could also make more resource nodes for the karnuq, if they needed any. Or he could add more pit traps and sticky honey traps, and maybe use them to reinforce the new palisade for the bee barracks?

Belissar decided he should see how his DP was doing, and how long it would take him to be able to get something new . . .

He froze. His eyes went as wide as they could go.

". . . How did this happen?"

Because displayed before his eyes was a number he had not expected to see.

DP: 3015

His jaw hung open. He . . . had enough DP to afford another choice from the DP shop? Already?!

When he finally snapped out of his daze, he realized something. He turned his gaze to the second floor. The karnuq were going about their day as usual. A group of four karnuq strolled through the orchard, picking apples off the trees. As they returned to their camp, they stopped by the shrine of bees, dropping off some apples and speaking a few words.

Gained 16 DP.

Small messages like that had been constantly passing through his vision ever since the karnuq moved in. He had eventually started to tune them out. They were notably smaller than the DP gained from the hunting group or the original gathering group, so Belissar hadn't considered them important. He had even thought that his DP income had dropped since the hunters had stopped fighting remnants.

Apparently, he'd been wrong. What he had not considered was that there were *many* more karnuq in his tower than before . . . and they never left. The gathering group and hunters used to come in groups of five or ten. Now there was a camp of over a hundred. Since the karnuq just stopped by the shrine of bees individually as they went about their days, the DP accumulation wasn't all at once like before. But if he added them all up . . . wouldn't it be a lot more?

Apparently, yes. Yes, it would. Belissar could afford a new room, a new monster, or a new room feature *right now.*

Belissar considered what he should pick. Well, he'd confer with Niobee, the queens, and Chief Rohsuak after today's purification, but he figured he should also think about it a bit on his own. As far as Belissar was concerned . . . a new room would probably be ideal, if only for the chance to get something fire-related for the new flower.

But on the other hand, he had currently filled up his available room slots for all three floors, so any more would require either removing an existing room or expanding again. And he wasn't certain he was ready for another expansion purification just yet. His tower's defenses hadn't changed all that much since the last time . . . save for the addition of the karnuq, which to be fair was a pretty notable addition. But the bees were still at largely the same strength as before, as the newest bee types hadn't started appearing in significant numbers. The communers would help the bee army organize their attacks, but they didn't add much in terms of direct fighting power, and the bumblebee queens were just starting to build their colonies. So, maybe a new bee type would be a better choice? If he got another option like the monster bee bladers, he could then conduct an expansion with more confidence, which would give him more choices to boot.

Or . . . he could go with new room features. They felt less impressive individually, but he could afford three of them, so there was a greater chance of getting something useful. On the one hand, it seemed like pit traps were less and less useful, as new shades had appeared that could avoid them. But on the other hand, pit traps had proven *very* useful, considering they were a mere common option that cost only a single point of mana to upkeep, and yet still became a death trap for anything that did fall inside. So, if a common trap did that much, what would an uncommon or rare trap be capable of? Additionally, room features included the basic resource nodes, which were perhaps the most important part of his dungeon. They were what allowed the bees to grow and the karnuq to move in. Maybe there would be more than just basic resource plants out there that could really help his tower grow with the bees it already had?

Belissar continued to ponder his options as he went about his day . . .

NEW DISCOVER-BEES

After making her delivery to the Firstborn, the First of the Fifth then gathered up another batch of honey and made her way to the third-floor flower meadow where the new queen lived. She found a handful of the large, fuzzy bees gathering nectar from the nearby flowers. While smaller than their queen, the workers were still quite large and round compared to her own, and moving more ponderously about. The First of the Fifth wondered how in the King's name the new hives would produce any quantity of honey given the speeds at which they were working and the number of workers active. The math didn't seem to add up to her.

But, well, that was why she was here.

The new queen was also foraging, along with a second queen that had emerged from the spawner just today. The First of the Fifth approached them.

"I'm First of Fifth. Welcome to King's hive of hives."

The two queens looked at her for a moment before the first began flying in a circle around her once again. The second slowly took off and began to follow her peer. The First of the Fifth resisted the urge to buzz.

Well, the King's mana informed her that this was a display of happiness, which she supposed would do. These bees seemed a bit . . . slower, in many ways. She wondered if she would have to teach them how to dance.

"Here, brought honey. Hive of hives helps each other. Please use to grow hives quickly."

The new queens stopped and watched as the First of the Fifth's workers dropped off cells full of golden honey just in front of that hole in the ground the first queen called home. The first queen suddenly began zipping around in the air, flying circles around the First of the Fifth as fast as she could.

". . . You're welcome."

The First of the Fifth turned to the new queen even as the first continued her loops.

"Where are you building hive? Have honey for you too."

The second queen froze, and then began to zip circles around her as well. The First of the Fifth's antennas began to twitch. While she appreciated the gratitude, she'd much prefer this second queen actually answer the question so she could drop off the honey and they could all get back to work . . .

It took longer than expected, but the First of the Fifth made her delivery and then returned home. Her communers alerted her to a bit of a situation with the foragers that required her attention, so she made her way over.

Soon, she saw it with her own eyes. A new flower. And not just any flower . . . a new *mana* flower. A treasure unlike any other.

But there was a problem. The temperature grew dramatically as she drew closer to the new flower, to the point that she had to stop before she could touch it. Her workers, smaller and more vulnerable to temperature than herself, couldn't even get that far. Only the burning workers raised on the honey of the flame radishes could manage to gather from this new flower, and she had only a handful of those.

One of them finished gathering and flew to her, saluting. The First of the Fifth asked her to bring the nectar closer so she could inspect it, and the worker did as she asked.

The First of the Fifth hovered for a bit with her antennas twitching. She then drooped a bit as she finished calculating. She would not be able to put the honey from this flower into production.

The nectar from the flame radishes alone already raised the temperature of its surroundings at an alarming rate. Anything more than a single cell or two spread out through the hive required the special fireproof wax that only the burning workers could make. Even then, anything more than a few of those cells put together still affected the rest of the hive. The First of the Fifth had been forced to limit production before the rising temperatures could start to impact the growth of the brood and the production of other honey types.

The nectar from the new mana flower had an even denser concentration of Fire mana than that of the flame radishes, with a corresponding increase to the heat it was putting out. Even if she had her burning workers work overtime to construct additional fireproof cells, she would not be able to fill even a fraction of a tray with this nectar without harming the rest of her hive. It seemed that a specialized hive would be necessary to make more than a few drops of honey from this flower.

Well, it was now the King's plan to do just that, but the First of the Fifth *had* hoped she could test the honey herself as well. But there was nothing for it.

She considered her options before quickly deciding. "Send word to Third of Sixth. I request her presence."

The Third of the Sixth was the only other queen to raise burning workers so far, so she was best positioned to specialize in the new honey type. Not only that, but the Third of the Sixth had been supremely motivated ever since the King had given her a magical palace of her own, since she had been born just a moment too late to claim one of the originals. Since then, she had made dramatic strides in catching up to the other queens, so the First of the Fifth had high hopes for her productivity.

She gave one final look at the new mana flower that was frustratingly just out of her reach, and then turned away to await the other queen's arrival.

The Fourth of the Seventh danced around her hive in no particular fashion. Her communer's mana was streaming into her own. When she focused on it, she was suddenly transported to a field full of flowers . . . and full of towering figures shaped like the King but with significantly more fur.

She could do it! She could see what her workers saw even while she was back at home! This was amazing!

She exclaimed as much to her communer, but her communer reminded her to pay attention. Not only would this be the first test of scouting with the support of a communer, but this was also a task assigned to them by the Conduit herself. Observing the karnuq was a low-risk scouting mission still within the King's realm . . . but it was still an important one, and it would require immaculate execution. The Fourth of the Seventh calmed herself a bit and focused her attention.

The karnuq were an impressive sight. The Fourth of the Seventh didn't think anything could be bigger than the King, and yet, they were. They were even a little intimidating, as something about their appearance touched something in her instincts. But they belonged to the King now, so she ignored that feeling and continued watching them.

The first two karnuq they found were just standing by the entrance of the second floor, leaning against a tree. Maybe sentries for their hive? The Fourth of the Seventh wasn't sure why else they wouldn't be working now, so probably.

Further in, she found karnuq workers gathering food for their hive. Unlike her own workers, they didn't extract the nectar directly, instead gathering entire plants. Like the King did with the flowers for the ropes! Maybe they were going to try and weave the stems like he did?

She focused closer on them. Through the communer, the scouts themselves followed her line of sight and flew closer to give her a better view. She flapped her wings a bit as she confirmed. Like the King, these karnuq were wearing woven stems, so it seemed her guess was probably correct.

And then, the Fourth of the Seventh froze. Her vision snapped onto one thing in particular and the scouts turned to face it.

There was a protrusion on the karnuq workers that the Fourth of the Seventh had thought held their stingers. But on closer look . . . the protrusions weren't a part of their bodies. Some were made out of what appeared to be dried skin, which had been the reason for the Fourth of the Seventh's mistake. But some were also made out of the woven stems, which was what clued her in now.

These protrusions had openings at the top. Whenever the karnuq workers picked up a plant, they placed it into that opening. The scouts flying closer could see the protrusions filled with many plants. The karnuq could thus continue to gather while carrying many plants . . . all the while their limbs remained completely free.

The Fourth of the Seventh thought back to this morning, when she had watched the First of the Fifth's hive carrying honey to the flower meadow. And then she thought of the ropes the King had made for the apiary soldiers that enabled them to carry his big fire sticks.

She turned to her communer. "Have idea. Can call soldiers?"

The communer saluted. "Already did."

A moment later, the Fourth of the Seventh's soldiers arrived, along with the soldiers the First of the Fifth had loaned to her. All the soldiers that had helped the King make his ropes.

The Fourth of the Seventh began to explain her idea and the soldiers gave her their full attention. Even the Fourth of the Seventh's communer watched intently as, once again, her queen came up with an idea she never would have thought of . . .

CHAPTER FORTY-TWO

BEE DECISIVE

The day went on. Belissar occupied himself by watching the karnuq expedition. They made their way down the Underway passage until it opened into a much larger tunnel, complete with stalactites, stalagmites, and pillars. A full-on river flowed down the center, with mushrooms and even mosses growing along its banks. The Underway proper.

The karnuq stuck in a group and advanced slowly down the hall. Metsaitti explained that they hadn't yet gone beyond the tunnel that had led the karnuq to his tower, so Metsaitti wanted to scout that way first and ensure the area was safe. He led the way. Noigakkuq was right behind him, sniffing the air, and the digging bee sent out mana pulses at regular intervals. Metsaitti was very pleased to have the two of them on the trip.

They didn't find anything of note before it was time for the daily purification, so Belissar turned his attention away. The purification was just a pair of wolf-shades this time around, running together through the first-floor dirt tunnels. Belissar waited to see if they would fall into the pit traps . . . before remembering that he completely forgot to add any traps to the new room. He very quickly scrambled to move the pit traps and sticky honey traps he'd left behind in the third floor's dirt tunnels down to the room they would actually see use in.

And then he ran into a problem. The transparent pit trap turned red as he moved it close to the shades.

Corruption detected. Please purify corruption before installing features in affected areas.

Belissar frowned. The wolf-shades left a trail of Hunger wherever they went that wouldn't vanish until it was purified, so it appeared Belissar would not be able to place any traps anywhere the shades had been. He groaned and then placed what traps he could at the last hallway before the flower meadow. Well, it was good to learn this now during a minor+ purification, rather than something more dangerous, but he still felt worried and a bit embarrassed to have forgotten something so obvious.

What followed was a surprisingly, frustratingly long time of waiting for the shades to stumble their way through the dirt tunnel maze before finally finding the exit. The soldier bee army stayed a bit further back from the opening, since the wolf-shades had their breath attack, and so the two wolf-shades rushed forward without a care in the world, unaware of the bees awaiting them.

The shades were quickly caught in the traps and then the bees struck. The rest of the purification was handled quickly; the hardest part had been waiting for the shades to arrive. Belissar sighed and then moved the rest of the traps to the front of the dirt tunnels before preparing for the victory celebration.

And then, it would finally be time to decide what to buy with his DP.

The First of the Fifth ordered her workers to begin transporting the usual victory feast, and then made her way over to the third-floor flower meadow. The bumblebees were just returning to their burrows as the day came to a close. The two queens turned and flew toward her. They didn't give any sort of greeting dance, just flew around her once and then hovered in front of her.

. . . She supposed that was supposed to be a greeting of some sort.

"King assembling queens to celebrate. Please follow."

She figured that the King would want his newest bees there, too, but somehow doubted these newcomers were aware, seeing as the first one hadn't shown up last night. The two bumblebee queens looked at her, and then started to fly around her rapidly.

"Yes, celebrating, but not here. Please stop and follow."

Belissar grinned as he watched his bees celebrate, now joined by the two bumblebee queens. Both the flower meadow and orchard queens had surrounded the two newcomers, curiously inspecting them while the bumblebee queens drank their fill of honey. He was very grateful to the First of the Fifth for remembering to bring them along. The tower was growing large enough that he was starting to forget things. It was a good thing he had asked the First of the Fifth to help organize the apiary queens after all.

In any case, soon the celebrations came to a close and the queens and Chief Rohsuak gathered around Belissar to see if he had anything to talk about. And tonight, he did.

"So, I wanted to ask you all . . . is there anything you want? Or anything you think the tower needs?"

The bees mostly remained still. There were a few calls for more flowers, but that was about it. Eventually, one exclaimed that "King's tower best tower!" at which point they all just started repeating that dance while the two bumblebees just rapidly circled around him. Belissar chuckled and turned to Chief Rohsuak. She smiled and shook her head.

"I am certain we will have plenty of requests for you once we are more settled, but for now you have given us plenty. Please, do as you will, Sacred Den Master, and do not concern yourself with us."

The bees danced their agreement with that statement. Belissar frowned slightly but nodded. "Okay then. I'll be making a choice now, or maybe several."

Well, it turned out he would be making the choice himself, with no guidance other than his wits and his gut. So, he went about with the option he had thought about earlier, and purchased a room feature choice from the DP store. He wanted to see what other kind of traps or resources might be available, since he had rare and uncommon monsters and rooms, but his room features were for the most part common. Besides, he could afford up to three room feature choices for the price of one monster or room, so there should be a good chance he got something helpful. Alternatively, if he stuck with just one room feature, he should be able to afford a monster or room just a bit later.

And with that, it was time to see what he got!

Extra room feature choice purchased.
One room feature choice now available.

Please select a room feature:
- Basic Resource Minerals (Rarity: Common. Type: Ground, Resource.)
- Beeswax Candles (Rarity: Common. Type: Bee, Fire, Decoration.)
- Grasping Vine (Rarity: Common. Type: Nature, Trap.)

Belissar frowned. All common options, apparently. Which . . . probably made sense? The tower said their rarity was common, so it would make sense that they were, well, commonplace. But still . . . most of Belissar's other choices had included at least one uncommon or rarer option, so it wasn't unreasonable to be disappointed that everything was common, right? Especially when Belissar had chosen room features specifically to get an uncommon or better one . . .

He sighed and shook his head. Complaining about it now wouldn't help, so he started to read out the descriptions to the bees and Chief Rohsuak.

Basic Resource Minerals

Type: Ground, Resource

Mana Upkeep: *Depends on resource selected.*

A spot where useful mineral resources may be found and mined.
Compatible minerals will depend on the room. Existing compatible
minerals may be converted to nodes.

Belissar couldn't help but nod as he read the description. That option was a good one, common though it may be. He even caught a glimpse of Chief Rohsuak's eyes light up as he read the description, though for now she held her tongue. All sorts of useful things could be found in the ground, after all. If they were lucky, either salt or iron would be extremely useful to the karnuq. And in the worst case . . . even just gatherable stone would allow them to build significantly more enduring structures, and equally more enduring defenses. This option shouldn't be a loss no matter what it gave.

On the other hand, though, it wouldn't help his bees much in any way he could think of . . . unless they needed salt? Did bees need salt? Belissar wasn't sure. In any case, he had two more options to read.

<u>Beeswax Candles</u>

Type: *Bee, Fire, Decoration*
Mana Upkeep: *1 (0 if wax is regularly provided.)*
A beeswax candle that provides light, and a bit of heat.
Effects may vary if special wax types are provided.

Well, that one was pretty straightforward. Belissar guessed that the candles would basically keep burning, like how the sticky honey traps could replenish themselves even if honey wasn't provided or how the beehives could produce honeycomb even without any bees, which could be convenient. Maybe he could use them to light up the dirt tunnels so his non-digging bees could operate there?

But he could easily make candles of his own, and he had digging bees for the dirt tunnels, so none of that was strictly necessary. He moved on to the final option.

<u>Grasping Vine</u>

Type: *Nature, Trap*
Mana Upkeep: *2*
A vine that constricts upon being touched. May trip or restrain a target.

Well, that was another trap, for sure. But, if Belissar was honest, he didn't see a point to this one for his tower. After all, he already had sticky honey traps to slow down an enemy and pit traps to trip them up. What could these vines do that those two traps couldn't? He couldn't think of much.

"What does everyone think of these?"

Belissar looked out across the queens, but they did not have any strong opinions this time. Chief Rohsuak just smiled at him. He stared at her until she chuckled.

"Well, if you must know my opinion . . . more resources are always appreciated."

Belissar sighed but nodded. Getting the bees to share their honest opinion was tricky enough, so he had hoped that Chief Rohsuak would be more forward with hers. "Well, that's what I was thinking too."

Basic Resource Minerals selected.

It wasn't really a contest. Basic resource minerals were the only option that could provide something his tower currently lacked. Neither candles nor vines were worth the thousand DP he had spent on this.

Which led Belissar to his next choice . . . should he buy more room features, or call it for the night?

CHAPTER FORTY-THREE

LUCK BEE A LADY

Belissar considered it for all of about five seconds before shrugging. He couldn't think of any particular reason why he *shouldn't* pick another room feature choice, and he still wanted to see an uncommon or rarer option, if at all possible. So, he went ahead and purchased yet another room feature choice.

Please select a room feature:
- Thorned Roses (Rarity: Common. Type: Nature, Trap.)
- Snare Trap (Rarity: Common. Type: Trap.)
- Mud Pit (Rarity: Common. Type: Ground, Water, Trap.)

Belissar's face fell as he read through the options. Once again, all commons. He was starting to wonder if he was exceptionally unlucky today . . . or if he had been exceptionally lucky until now. He really hoped it was the former and not the latter.

But well, he had a choice to make, so he read them out to the bees and karnuq assembled around him.

Thorned Roses

Type: *Nature, Trap*
Mana Upkeep: *2*
Roses whose stems and thorns have been reinforced with mana.
Surprisingly tough and painful to get through. May take the shape of bushes
or climbers if placed near compatible features.

This option didn't seem all that impressive. The thorns looked like they'd be painful enough if someone stepped into a bush of them, but would a shade just walk right into a thorny bush? Well, he guessed if all else failed, they were a type of flower, so maybe the bees would like them. It would depend on the other two choices . . .

Snare Trap

Type: *Trap*
Mana Upkeep: *1*

A rope loop tied to a tree under tension. If a target steps within the loop, will snap and pull their leg up into the air. It is recommended to add bait.

Well, it was a trap. A very simple trap that Belissar or the karnuq could probably build themselves if they had suitable trees around. A trap that, like the grasping vines earlier, was just another way to immobilize an enemy, something that the pit traps and sticky honey traps could already do.

Belissar was pretty certain he wasn't going to bother with this one, which left one more.

Mud Pit

Type: *Ground, Water, Trap*
Mana Upkeep: *3*

Turns a section of ground into mud. Target will sink into it.

As a trap, this one was perhaps the least impressive. A bunch of mud, huh? Well, Belissar did have to wade through the muck on occasion, so he knew it wasn't a pleasant experience, and the mud pit did look larger than a pit trap, so maybe it would be helpful for slowing shades down? And if he ever got plants that preferred wet, swampy ground, maybe the mud pits would work if he didn't have a full-on room? Maybe.

Belissar sighed lightly and turned to his bees and Chief Rohsuak.

The bees slowly danced. "Flowers?"

Chief Rohsuak simply shook her head, indicating she had no particular opinion here. Belissar sighed.

"Well, might as well."

Thorned Roses selected.

More flowers would never hurt, if nothing else.

Belissar then stared at the DP shop for a bit. He had little over a thousand DP left, enough for just one final room feature choice. Maybe it would be best to wait. A lot of the expansion purification choices guaranteed uncommon or better options, right? So, if he specifically wanted an uncommon room feature, he could just wait for the next expansion purification. Then he could save up his DP for another monster choice. If he only got common options for the monster choices, at least he'd end up with a new type of bee, right?

Or . . . he could buy another choice right now. Yes, the common options were, well, common. But he didn't recall having ever seen a choice of only commons before, much less two in a row! So, surely the next choice would include something else, right? Surely, he wouldn't get nine common choices in a row, right?

Belissar made his choice.

Please select a room feature:

Belissar held his breath.

- Lotus Flowers (Rarity: Common. Type: Nature, Water, Resource.)

He took a deep breath. There were still two more.

- Beeswax Candles (Rarity: Common. Type: Bee, Fire, Decoration.)

Really, a repeat option? Just what were the chances of that? Surely less than getting at least one uncommon option out of nine!

"Come on . . ."

Belissar held his breath as he checked the third and final choice.

- Arrow Trap (Rarity: Common. Type: Trap.)

Belissar groaned. How? How had he gotten not a single rarity other than common in three full choices?!

"King! What wrong?"

Belissar took a deep breath as he saw Niobee fly in front of him, clearly worried at his response. "It's . . . nothing. I was just hoping for . . . well, I don't know, but I guess slightly rarer options than we got."

Niobee hovered for a moment before dancing slowly. "Sorry . . ."

Belissar shook his head and reached out so that she could land on his hand, then brushed her fuzzy back. "It's fine, it's not your fault. Besides, everything we can get is helpful, right?"

Niobee began dancing again. "Yes! Everything King makes is great! King is best king!"

Belissar chuckled as the rest of the bees followed Niobee's dance. He couldn't help but feel better about the options as the bees celebrated, so perhaps he should just look on the bright side. Even if it wasn't what he wanted, he was getting three new options tonight for his tower. The majority of his tower was built on common features, after all, so perhaps a few more would be helpful as well.

He still wasn't going to look at the DP shop for a while, though.

In any case, it was time to choose . . . and this time, the choice was easy.

Lotus Flowers selected.

Lotus Flowers

Type: *Nature, Water, Resource*

Mana Upkeep: *3*

An aquatic flower plant cultivated for food.

It was a flower, and it was edible. That meant it would be helpful for both the bees and the karnuq, and that was enough for Belissar. He was a bit worried about the aquatic part but figured they might work in the ponds? Well, if not, at least he would have something to use if he ever got a water room of some sort.

With that, the celebration and meeting came to a close, and Belissar decided to turn in for the night. Disappointingly common choices aside, it had still been a day of great gains for his tower.

He, uh, just wasn't going to buy any new room feature choices from the DP shop for a while. Maybe the karnuq expedition would find some more mana flowers or something?

Belissar awoke the next day smacking his head with a groan, for he realized he had once again been dumb. If he'd wanted new stuff . . . then why hadn't he asked the karnuq if they had more plants? And minerals now, too! He would have to check with them on that today.

Besides that, it might be time for a new expansion soon. Belissar did have the three new room features, but he didn't really expect any of them to dramatically change his tower's defenses. Most of all, he didn't expect thorned roses or lotus flowers to result in new bee types, so there wasn't much left to wait for, unless he wanted to give the bumblebees more time to grow. But that could take a while.

He *definitely* wasn't motivated by his failure to get an uncommon or better room feature last night.

He also realized he had a lot on his mind . . . and a lot he was forgetting. He should try to write some of it down . . . if only he had something to write on and with.

"King okay? Thinking about something?"

Belissar shook his head and smiled at Niobee. "Nothing too troubling, just there's a lot going on in the tower now. I'm wondering how I can keep track of it all."

Niobee immediately started dancing. "Bees help!"

Belissar was about to thank her but politely decline her offer. His bees were amazing, but he didn't think they knew how to write. But then, he stopped, for a new thought came to mind.

The First of the Fifth had remembered the bumblebee queens when he had not. Maybe the bees couldn't write for him or make something for him to write on . . . but they could remember things that he forgot. So, why didn't he ask them to help him remember? There were a lot of bees, so if he asked a different bee to remember each thing, then wouldn't each bee only need to remember one thing in order for the tower as a whole to remember them all? And then, if he had each bee remind him of their one thing at a regular interval, then he could be sure he'd never forget any of it.

He turned to Niobee and grinned. "Thanks, Niobee, that's a good idea. I think the bees can help me remember things, could you gather some?"

"Okay!"

Belissar tried to think of all the different things he wanted to remember as Niobee flew out the window. Soon, bees began flying in one by one. Belissar told each bee one of the things on his mind and asked them to remind him at the post-victory celebration meeting that evening, then sent them on their way.

Once again, everything became easier when he worked with the bees.

CHAPTER FORTY-FOUR

BASIC GEOLO-BEE

The wounded soldier focused on the air ahead of her. She beat her wings, creating a chain of lightning that surged around her body. She began to focus this lightning and move it about, twisting into a pattern that resembled the steps of the dance for "sting."

The pattern locked into place and then flashed as she pushed her mana into it. Lightning took the shape of a stinger and shot out into the air before her. She stared at it for a moment before breaking out into a happy dance.

She . . . had done it! She had found a way to fight again!

Well, it would take a lot more work. That lightning hadn't even traveled as far as a sprayer's attack, and she still couldn't fly, so actually using it in battle would be difficult. But it was a step in the right direction, and an important one at that.

She stopped dancing as she felt a pair of antennas brush against her. She turned to see the other wounded soldiers gathered around her. Her antennas twitched before she began to dance the affirmative to the question she knew they had.

The process by which she'd received her lightning was dangerous. She knew the others wanted to try, and not a single one of them would shy away from danger on behalf of the hive, but that was why she wanted to be certain. She wasn't going to put her sisters at risk unless she knew that her path would lead them where they wanted to go. But now . . . now she could be confident that it did. In time, she would be able to rejoin the fight.

And that meant that now . . . it was time to help her sisters follow her path.

Belissar stared with wide eyes through his tower sight as he watched the wounded soldier's lightning fly through the air. Now that he was asking the bees to remind him of important things, he also asked them to let him know if there was anything he should keep track of that he hadn't mentioned. One of them had told him the wounded soldier was doing something with lightning, so he had decided to look in on how she was doing.

Just in time to see a stinger made of lightning surge through the air.

He withdrew his tower sight and looked down at his own hand. So far, he had used his magic to create honey and wax. But then . . . why not a stinger? It was perhaps easy for him to forget, since his bees would never, ever sting him now, but stingers were also a defining characteristic of bees.

He held his hand out and tried to move his mana in the pattern he had seen the wounded soldier use, imagining a stinger thrust out toward the air.

A moment later, the pattern finished and flashed. A stinger, made of yellow mana instead of lightning, formed and thrust forward. Belissar blinked for a second before starting to grin.

Leave it to the bees to be way better at this than him. And now, thanks to the wounded soldier, he had gained his first spell that could be used to fight. He would have to stay diligent about practicing his magic, for who knew what else might be possible?

In any case, the next bumblebee queen should be spawning soon, so Belissar made his way over to greet the newcomer, build her a nest, and check in on her siblings.

After taking care of the new queen, and perhaps taking a moment to enjoy the sight of three bumblebee queens flying circles around him, Belissar made his way over to the karnuq and found Chief Rohsuak and Juosiutik waiting for him.

"Hello, Sacred Den Master Belissar." Both of them greeted him.

"Hello, um, nice to see you again."

Juosiutik shook her head. "I should be the one saying that! I don't know how I could ever repay you for everything you've given us. The sheer amount of herbs and flowers I have now means we'll never run out!"

Belissar rubbed the back of his head. "Ah, um, you're welcome? Glad you like it."

He then turned to Chief Rohsuak. "Speaking of, I was coming to see if you have any other plants or minerals now. I'll, um, make some nodes of whatever you have for you if I can."

Chief Rohsuak smiled at him. "Yes, I had expected as much. Please take a look."

She motioned to a mat they had placed on the ground, covered in various plants, seeds, and ores. Belissar picked up one of the pieces of ore, which was tinted red.

Absorb iron ore? Current samples: 0/3

Belissar tilted his head. He figured iron would have been a pretty basic resource that might have come with basic resource minerals, so did he need to absorb it? He then realized he should probably check what was initially available for the basic resource minerals. Basic resource plants had come with healing herbs and poisonous flowers, after all, so he suspected the minerals feature would also have some starting options.

Available Resource Minerals for Flower Meadow:
- Basic Stone (Mana Upkeep: 1 per node)
- Copper Ore (Mana Upkeep: 3 per node)
- Tin Ore (Mana Upkeep: 3 per node)
- Salt (Mana Upkeep: 3 per node)

As he suspected, there were some starting options, but apparently iron wasn't one of them. That was curious, though with copper he guessed they might be able to make bronze instead? Was bronze somehow worse than iron? Belissar didn't know enough about smithing or metallurgy to say. He was definitely happy that salt was included, though. Belissar checked the options for the other rooms but in this case, they were all the same, though he found the nodes were one mana cheaper in the dirt tunnels than in any other room. So, it looked like absorbing iron was a good idea after all.

Iron ore absorbed.
Absorb iron ore? Current samples: 1.27/3

Each piece of iron ore gave a different quantity of samples, apparently, that roughly corresponded to their size. It still only took three chunks of ore, however.

Sufficient samples gathered.
Iron Ore is now available.
Current Applications: Flower Meadow, Apiary*, Orchard*, Dirt Tunnels*

(=Resource Node only)*

The next ore Belissar picked up was a metallic gray one that gleamed in the sunlight.

Absorb silver ore? Current samples: 0/3

Belissar's eyes widened as he stared down at the rock in his hand. This . . . was silver? He had heard of silver, but never actually owned anything made of it.

Well, Mrs. Imkomos *had* owned a silver amulet, a symbol of one of the gods, but Belissar had made sure it got buried with her. Other than that, his village had mostly functioned on the barter system—or at least it did when trading with Belissar—so the most valuable metal he had ever held himself were copper coins. Silver . . . was something unimaginable.

But then he paused, tilted his head, and shrugged. He knew silver was valuable, but he didn't actually know *why* it was valuable. The ore was certainly shinier than the iron ore, but that was as far as Belissar's knowledge went. Besides, the karnuq hadn't used coins to trade with him even before they had become his defenders, so it wasn't like unfathomably valuable silver coins would actually have any use right now.

But well, another option was another option, so he absorbed it too.

Sufficient samples gathered.
Silver Ore is now available.

Available Resource Minerals for Flower Meadow:
- Basic Stone (Mana Upkeep: 1 per node)
- Copper Ore (Mana Upkeep: 3 per node)
- Tin Ore (Mana Upkeep: 3 per node)
- Salt (Mana Upkeep: 3 per node)
- Iron Ore (Mana Upkeep: 3 per node)
- Silver Ore (Mana Upkeep: 5 per node)

Those were the only two minerals the karnuq had sufficient quantities of for him to absorb. Well, the karnuq *did* have salt as well, but that was apparently already included in basic resource minerals so Belissar didn't need to absorb it. Interestingly, silver ore was the only one more expensive than the rest. Maybe because it was valuable? Did valuable things for humans cost more mana for the tower? Or was there something different about silver specifically?

Belissar shrugged and moved on to the plants . . . or rather, mushrooms, mostly. Juosiutik grinned as she knelt down by them, then pointed to a bundle wrapped in cloth with a very serious expression.

"That's an Underway death cap. It's extremely toxic. Be careful not to touch it when you unwrap it."

Belissar gulped, and maybe trembled a bit as he reached for the bundle.

Absorb Subterranean Death Cap? Samples: 0/7

Fortunately, it turned out he didn't even need to unwrap the deadly fungi to absorb them. As a subterranean option, they were only available in the dirt tunnels, but that was fine. Belissar did not intend to spread these around, after all. He'd have to ask Niobee to test if they were dangerous to bees first.

Juosiutik then handed him the next one. It was a mushroom with a wide, flat cap.

"This is a glow cap. It glows in the dark. We think it has Light mana, but we're not sure. It can have a purification effect if you process it right."

Belissar couldn't help but let out a small sigh of relief. That was significantly less concerning than something with *death* in the name. Juosiutik then pointed to yet another bundle, this one long and thin.

"That's shadow vine. Again, be careful. Its sap has a blinding effect. Ah, and you shouldn't place it near the glow cap, because it dislikes light."

Belissar absorbed that one without unwrapping it as well. All three of the new plants and mushrooms were subterranean, so they would only grow in the dirt tunnels.

"I'll go ahead and make some of these. Thank you both."

Both Chief Rohsuak and Juosiutik shook their heads. Juosiutik gave him a smile.

"Like I said, I'm the one who should be thanking you, Sacred Den Master. The potions I'll be able to make with all of this and the honey are going to be amazing."

Chief Rohsuak nodded. "Juosiutik is right. And once you can create some of the ores, please let us know if you have any metalworking requests. We still have a smith, so we should be able to make some basic products right away."

Belissar's eyes widened a bit. "Ah, that'd be great, actually. Um, should we move to the dirt tunnels while I place these? I should, uh, probably let you know where the super-poisonous mushrooms are going to be."

Both karnuq's faces turned serious and Chief Rohsuak replied instantly, "Definitely."

DANGEROUS ACTIVI-BEES

The First of the Fifth glanced through the mana of her communer, allowing her to see through the eyes of her scouts. It was her turn to arrange the karnuq watch today, and she was glad that it was. The King was already making his way to them, exposing himself to harm once more. But the First of the Fifth would be on guard, and she would not allow *anything* to befall him.

Particularly not at the hands of these karnuq. She knew the King had welcomed them in, but she could not help but dislike them. They blended the King's noble form with the features of a creature her instincts knew as honey-stealers and hive destroyers! Sure, they hadn't stolen honey or destroyed a hive yet, so perhaps the resemblance was superficial, but that did not mean the First of the Fifth trusted them—least of all with the safety of the King.

Especially the one who talked to him now, the one carrying mushrooms and plants. The First of the Fifth heard she had attempted to pounce upon the King before, and that only the King's intervention had stayed the Conduit and the soldier bees' stingers. The word of the King was law, so it could not be helped, but the First of the Fifth swore she would not allow this one to threaten the King once again. She would watch her with extra vigilance.

The dangerous one grunted and growled in the manner that their people did . . . though as the King had accepted them, his mana now converted their noises into intelligible language. Their voices were coarse and rough and irritating, nothing like the soothing warmth of the King's. The First of the Fifth would have ignored them if they were not speaking to the King, but her vigil required her to analyze their words for any hint of deceit.

The dangerous one was speaking about some new mushrooms and plants. Apparently, that one was supposedly extremely toxic, that one possessed an unusual bioluminescence, and the last one caused blindness? Interesting, especially as the

King absorbed them all with the intention to spread them about. The First of the Fifth did not trust the dangerous one's assessments, so she would have to confirm the characteristics of these new resources herself. But if the dangerous one spoke with any truth, there could be an opportunity to develop new honey types . . . and new types of bees as well.

If that occurred . . . well, at least then the karnuq would have been good for something. It was the least they could do, as they had already invaded the King's home, eaten his food, and threatened his person.

The First of the Fifth had to calm herself before her hive started preparing for war again.

So, yes, new plant types would be a start. Not enough for the First of the Fifth to tolerate their presence, much less approve of it, but a start. *If* the dangerous one could be trusted. Which was a big *if.*

And then, she heard the dangerous one speak yet again. "Like I said, I'm the one who should be thanking you, Sacred Den Master. The potions I'll be able to make with all of this and the honey are going to be amazing."

The First of the Fifth's attention snapped to the dangerous one like a bolt of lightning. Her wings began to buzz and her stinger extended. The dangerous one . . . had acquired honey? How had she done so? Where had she gotten it? Had the hive of hives been robbed already?

This . . . this could not stand. If such a thing had occurred, if these honey-thieves had stolen what was rightfully the King's, then their intentions were absolutely clear. They would have deceived the King and repeated the insults and injuries of his former life after all the generosity and grace he had shown them. The First of the Fifth would not suffer them to live if so.

Still, the King did not react to that shocking declaration, which was the only reason the First of the Fifth had not yet requested the soldier bee army swoop in and sweep the newcomers away. Which was confusing. Did he not realize what had been said, so shocked that they would be so bold and arrogant? Or did he already know about the honey? Had he arranged it himself?

That in itself would be shocking, but the King saw much that she did not, so she would have no choice but to accept his wisdom. The last thing she wanted to do was defy the will of the King.

As such, she ordered her scouts to tail the dangerous one. The First of the Fifth was going to get to the bottom of this. The King and the hive of hives were depending on her.

The First of the Fifth's scouts followed them to the second-floor dirt tunnels, where the King had created new resources. There were the three new plants she had heard the dangerous one speak of, but also some rocks of some sort. The First of the Fifth wasn't sure about most of those, but one of them was made of salt. Salt could assist a hive's nutrition and cut down on the mana required to sustain them so that would be useful.

Which made it all the more aggravating that these potential honey-stealers were receiving such valuable gifts. But . . . if the King was rewarding them so highly, then surely they couldn't be stealing his honey? Maybe he was testing these things on them before gifting them to the bees?

Well, she had thought that last time when the flower meadow queens received flowers and she had turned out to be wrong then, so she couldn't say for sure. She would have to continue watching.

At that point, the King separated from the karnuq and returned to his rightful place by the hives, so the First of the Fifth could relax her stinger slightly. At the very least, he was once again out of the newcomers' immediate grasp. Now, she could focus all of her attention on the dangerous one.

The dangerous one returned to the karnuq hive, and to her own cell. Her cell was far larger than she, an inefficient use of space and a sign that the karnuq hive was poorly run. The dangerous one hummed an ominous tune as she rummaged through the corpses of once-beautiful flowers, the evidence of a callous and wasteful slaughter. She then moved back outside to a fire pit clearly copied from the King's own. She lit a fire as she hung some sort of hollowed black rock above.

So, she was not content to uproot the flowers that could have fed an entire generation, but now sought to burn them to ashes as well. The First of the Fifth couldn't even fathom the level of waste and malice required to do such a thing.

The dangerous and evil one filled the black rock with water, waiting until it began to bubble. Then she dumped some of the flower corpses inside. The First of the Fifth buzzed, but she bid her scouts to bide their time. She would see this until the end, no matter what horrors she would be forced to witness.

Soon, the dangerous and evil one nodded to herself and held her hand above the rock. She closed her eyes. The First of the Fifth considered having a scout sting her while she was distracted, to let her know that her deeds had not gone unseen.

But, before the First of the Fifth could give the command, something happened. Mana poured out of the dangerous and evil one's hand, forming into the shape of . . . a comb? A shape that looked exactly like when the King formed his own honey—but that couldn't be. That was impossible.

The First of the Fifth froze solid as she watched the pattern flash, and then golden mana honey dripped into the pot. The dangerous and evil one . . . made honey? With that magic of the King, granted to him by the Queen of All Bees herself?

Then . . . this dangerous and evil thing . . . was approved of by the Queen of All Bees?

The First of the Fifth couldn't comprehend what she had seen. At the very least, it was clear that the dangerous one had not stolen the honey she'd mentioned but had *made* it herself. That, at least, explained why the King hadn't been surprised when she mentioned honey.

But then, what exactly was she doing? And why had she slaughtered precious flowers when she didn't even need their nectar to make honey of her own? Would the Queen of All Bees approve of such waste and malice? Would the King?

Then, she noticed it. The flow of mana within the black rock had changed. Since she was sensing this through a communer's link to a worker, she couldn't get a completely accurate read on what was going on, but she could at least notice the mana of the flower and the mana of the honey mixing together. The dangerous one dropped the remaining flower corpses into the rock, and then filled it with her own mana. The mana mixed and swirled in ways the First of the Fifth had never seen, sparking and reacting and coming to life.

And then, the mana fell still, settling down within the contents of the rock. Inside was now some liquid that was like honey, but not, containing an entirely different kind of mana than any of the ingredients that had been placed inside of it.

The First of the Fifth stood completely still for a long time until her mind finally began to move again.

The mana of honey . . . could be changed? *After* it was made? Her mind was overwhelmed by the sheer implications of this discovery.

CHAPTER FORTY-FIVE

FUNK-BEE FUNGI

Belissar created some of the new options in the karnuq's dirt tunnels. In here, he could place the mineral nodes on the floor, walls, or even roof if he wanted to. Per Chief Rohsuak's request, he placed them on the walls of the cavern closest to the karnuq's settlement in the second-floor flower meadow for easy access. He also placed some glow cap nodes around . . . which were quite expensive at five mana a piece. He frowned at that.

Glowing mushrooms were certainly interesting, but were they really worth as much mana as a mana flower? Or was there something to them he didn't know? Juosiutik had mentioned something about a purifying effect, so maybe? They *did* have more mana flowing through them than the regular plants, though not as much as any of the mana flower types, so maybe they weren't entirely normal mushrooms?

Unfortunately, it turned out the other two options, the subterranean death caps and the shadow vines, were also five mana apiece. This was going to be an expensive day. But he wouldn't even have these options if not for the karnuq so there was nothing for it.

Belissar placed the shadow vines and death caps in a small cavern off to the side of a tunnel deeper in, where they'd be less accessible. Chief Rohsuak said she didn't want anyone but Juosiutik handling them.

After that, Belissar and the karnuq both thanked each other and Belissar left the second floor. Three new plants and mushrooms for his bees would be quite the boon. He grinned.

That is, until he checked his mana.

Mana: 23/485

He grimaced as he scratched out some math in the dirt. He could afford one each of the mushrooms and shadow vine. But then there were the minerals.

He wanted to at least offer salt to his bees, in case they needed that, but he wasn't certain about the others. Could his bees even interact with iron or copper? There *did* seem to be some mana flowing through the silver, but would that matter to the bees? Well, he wouldn't be able to afford it all today anyway.

And then there were the other two options: the thorned roses and lotus flowers. They were, perhaps, less impressive than super-deadly mushrooms or blinding vines, but they were guaranteed to have flowers and so guaranteed to be useful to the bees, unlike all these other options. Belissar groaned and rubbed his chin.

He shrugged and turned to Niobee. "Hey Niobee, can the bees do anything with rocks? Like, stone and iron and stuff?"

Niobee hovered in front of him, swaying side to side before slowly beginning to dance. "Sorry, not sure."

Belissar shook his head and gave her a smile. "It's fine, I didn't think so. Just wanted to make sure I didn't miss something, and that helps me decide, so thanks."

Well, if Niobee didn't know, then there was no reason for Belissar to continue pondering about it. He went ahead and tried to create a lotus flower node, moving it over the pond he had placed in the apiary. The node, which was red everywhere else, turned back to a transparent blue. Belissar let out a sigh of relief and confirmed the placement.

Then he moved on to the thorned roses. He figured he would place these by the bee barracks for some extra protection, plus some more flowers to boot. He brought up the option and a transparent rosebush appeared at the center of his sight. But as he moved it near the palisades that he and the karnuq had recently built, the roses changed. Instead of a bush, they turned into climbers wrapping around the wooden spikes rising from the ground. Belissar blinked for a moment before smiling. That seemed like a good option, as it would hamper anyone trying to climb over or through the barricade. He confirmed.

His mana was quickly dwindling, but he continued on. He added a glow cap node to the third-floor dirt tunnels for the bees to harvest. And then, he paused. He turned to Niobee. His face scrunched up as pain shot through his chest.

"King? King okay?"

Belissar took a deep breath and shut his eyes for a moment. "Niobee . . . would you mind testing a dangerous mushroom for me?"

It killed him to put Niobee, of all bees, in harm's way. But, logically speaking, she was the bee who could come back from death, so it was either ask her or potentially watch a bee die unnecessarily if it turned out the death caps were toxic to them as well. So, he had no choice.

Niobee, of course, responded immediately. "Okay! Will!"

Belissar sighed once more and then nodded. "Okay, let's move to the dirt tunnels then."

A short while later and Belissar had a subterranean death cap node in the third-floor dirt tunnels. For something of its name, the death caps were incredibly innocuous in their appearance. A plain white mushroom that Belissar wouldn't think twice of if he didn't know what they were. Or if he couldn't feel the slightly higher concentration of mana swirling through them.

He gulped as he watched Niobee land on the caps. He wanted to shut his eyes but he kept watching. It was the least he could do, since Niobee was risking herself for him. Niobee crawled over the cap until she found some liquid oozing out of the cap. She stuck her proboscis into it and drank. Belissar held his breath.

Niobee paused and retracted her proboscis. Her wings buzzed and then she started to pace around. Belissar's eyes widened.

"Niobee? Are you okay?!"

Niobee quickly began to dance. "Fine! Not hurt! Just . . ."

Her dance slowed down greatly.

". . . Tastes bad."

Belissar exhaled his breath. "As long as you're okay. How about we go get some honey to wash out the taste?"

". . . Okay."

Well, he didn't want his bees to have to drink bad-tasting mushrooms, but at least they wouldn't be seriously harmed by doing so, so he left the mushroom node as it was. If the bees decided they just didn't want to touch them, then maybe he'd get rid of them.

For now, Niobee definitely deserved something nice.

After retreating to the apiary's farmhouse and pulling out the best of the regular mana honeycomb for Niobee, Belissar considered what to do next.

Mana: 8/485

He had enough for a shadow vine node. So, he made one of those as well. The vines . . . were hard to see even with his tower sight. If anything, it felt like the dark tunnels somehow grew darker around them. Still, Belissar could faintly feel the mana flowing through them, and so figured out where the vines snaked across the ground. They were fascinating, but he had no idea how his bees were going to gather anything from them, or if they'd even make flowers in the first place.

With his last few points of mana, Belissar decided to create a salt node in the third-floor dirt tunnels. He wasn't sure if the bees needed it, but he'd let them check it out at the very least. None of the other minerals really made sense to offer to them, as far as he knew. Maybe the digging bees could dig them up, but what would they actually do with the ores afterward?

In any case, he had no available mana until the next purification. He decided to spend the rest of the day practicing his magic. Now that he had a combat spell, he felt it would be a good idea to learn how to defend himself.

At least, that was the plan until Niobee began to fly in front of him. "King . . . soldier doing something dangerous. Is okay?"

Belissar's eyes widened. "Wait, what?!"

Belissar practically ran down to the first-floor flower meadow, then dashed to the memorial. There, he found all of the wounded soldiers gathered around the very first. One of them had crawled forward while the first wounded soldier gathered her mana.

However, they all paused as they saw him approach, and began to salute.

"Yes, hi, thanks. Um, can I ask what you're doing?"

The first wounded soldier began to dance. "Giving lightning!"

Belissar blinked. "Giving . . . lightning?"

The wounded soldier saluted. "Got lightning from enemy, when King helped! Giving lightning now!"

Belissar's mind slowly turned as he processed that statement and thought back to when he had saved this particular soldier. His eyes went as wide as they could go.

"Wait, are you going to blast her with lightning?!"

The soldier confirmed. "Yes!"

Belissar groaned and was about to shut it down. But . . . he hesitated. Something about the soldier's complete lack of hesitation gave him pause. He grimaced but he held his tongue, turning to Niobee instead.

"Niobee . . . what do you think?"

Niobee flew slowly but did not hesitate. "Bees want to be useful. Hurt soldiers want to fight. Can't right now, but maybe can with lightning?"

Belissar rubbed his chin. He . . . honestly hadn't thought much about these soldiers. Of course he wanted every bee to survive if they could, but what happened afterward? The soldiers who had lost wings couldn't fly anymore, and a soldier bee who couldn't fly couldn't participate in a battle. They would be killed immediately as they wouldn't be able to dodge a shade's attacks.

But what then? Belissar hadn't seen any soldiers gather nectar from flowers, and he wasn't certain if they even could. He hadn't seen them making wax or cells, and they were too big to tend to the brood. Most could help carry things . . . but the inability to fly meant these ones couldn't. So . . . what, exactly, could these soldiers actually do?

He knew the answer in a normal hive would be . . . nothing. A bee that crippled would likely have been exiled by a normal hive. It was his own intervention that kept these bees around and fed. But then he had just, sort of, left them hanging around the memorial, didn't he?

So, was it any surprise they took matters into their own legs? And would it be right for him to stop them?

He continued to grimace, but slowly nodded. "Okay, but let's get some medicinal honey first. I'm going to go grab a tray . . . Niobee, could you see if . . . um . . . the medicinal one is the Second of the Sixth, right?"

"Yes!"

Belissar nodded again. "Good, okay, can you see if the Second of the Sixth could send some workers to help?"

"Okay!"

Belissar turned back to the wounded soldiers. "Just wait for us to get back, okay? Let's stay as safe as possible."

The wounded soldier bees all saluted as one. Belissar nodded, then turned to walk away, sighing once he was out of sight.

He just really hoped it would go well.

CHAPTER FORTY-SIX

A BEE-FICIENT DESIGNATION

Belissar stood before the memorial. The first wounded soldier with lightning stood before one of the others that was missing a leg along with a pair of wings. A pile of medicinal mana honeycomb was stacked nearby, medicinal workers hovered around, and Belissar stirred up his mana as well. All the bees were looking at him. He took a deep breath and nodded.

A crackle filled the air as the first wounded soldier's lightning wings began to speed up, surge, and surround the rest of her body. A moment later, the lightning arced forward and out, striking the five-legged soldier. She began to convulse as lightning surged across her body.

Belissar quickly formed his own magic honey and brought his hand to the five-legged soldier's face. Bits of lightning zapped his hand, causing sharp spikes of pain followed by numbness, but Belissar ignored the sensations. The five-legged soldier slowly extended her proboscis and began to drink while the first soldier adjusted the flow of the surge, toning it down a bit.

The five-legged soldier flared her mana as she drank the magical honey. She rubbed her legs and remaining wings against the hairs of her body, trying to generate some static of her own. The first soldier backed off and let go of the lightning. That would make it easier for the five-legged soldier to take control, but it also meant that no one was currently managing the lightning surging across her.

Belissar held his breath as the five-legged soldier continued to convulse.

But then, Niobee landed by her and began to dance. As she did, the tower's mana began to flow toward her. She then touched the five-legged soldier with an antenna and the mana flowed into the soldier. The five-legged soldier's convulsing calmed down a bit.

The five-legged soldier's mana flared as it was reinforced by both Belissar and Niobee. Her legs and wings moved faster as she began to generate lightning of her own.

And then . . . finally . . . the lightning across her body began to diminish, instead pulling back and gathering to a point on her back. It slowly began to extend and curl.

Until it formed a pair of wings, just like the first wounded soldier had. Belissar grinned and laughed a bit.

"You did it!"

The five-legged soldier was exhausted but began a salute and then a happy dance with as much strength as she could muster. The medicinal bees then began to pore over her, directing her to stop dancing and drink the medicinal honey.

Belissar then turned to Niobee and the first lightning soldier. "Nice work, and thanks for helping out too, Niobee."

"Yes! Bees always help King!"

Belissar shook his head. "It's me helping her this time." He then tilted his head. "Niobee, does the soldier have a name? Like the queens?"

Niobee's antennas twitched a bit as she danced. "No? Just called soldier. Why?"

Belissar rubbed his chin. "Well, there's more than one wounded soldier and more than one lightning soldier now, so I just thought it might get a bit confusing. Do bees not like names?"

"Don't mind!" Niobee danced.

Well, to be fair, it wasn't strictly necessary to name specific bees, as the tower's mana assisted there. Since Belissar could direct his mana toward a specific bee no matter where they were, the bees were never confused about who he was speaking to. And the bees themselves didn't seem to care about names. Even the queen's names were just their order of birth.

Still, after all this little soldier had been through and overcome, it felt wrong for her not to have some sort of name.

"Would you mind if I gave you one? How about I call you Beero?"

Belissar winced a bit even as the words left his mouth. Mashing *bee* and *hero* together wasn't exactly the most creative way to name her. But well . . . she was certainly a hero. She'd been wounded defending her home, but still fought even after being crippled, risking her life to save the tower yet again. And then she overcame the shade's lightning, and even now was crawling her way back to the fight.

Plus . . . Belissar never really had to name all that many things before.

The soldier bee, on the other hand, fell flat on the ground. But she quickly scrambled to her feet . . . and then began a salute dance. She continued repeating that dance over and over and over. It seemed the wounded soldier—or Beero, rather—liked the name. Belissar's cheeks flushed a bit, but he definitely couldn't take it back now.

"I'm glad you like it; it is well deserved. You've done well, Beero."

Her repeating salute dance continued until Belissar went to check on the new lightning bee. And then the shrine of bees off to the side began to subtly shine.

Fortunately, the five-legged bee wasn't seriously harmed by all that lightning she had been struck with, and the medicinal bees confirmed she would recover from the ordeal. And, well, the other wounded bees were practically scrambling over each other to be next. Belissar chuckled and shook his head.

"No need to rush, we'll take care of all of you."

They spent much of the rest of the day granting lightning to the wounded bees, until Beero's lightning wings grew dim and thin. Belissar topped her up with mana until he, too, started to run low. His head ached and his body grew sore as he tried to squeeze out more mana. He went back to the farmhouse and brought back some regular mana honeycomb, which managed to restore his and Beero's mana for a time . . . but the fatigue mounted even so. Soon, the mana from the mana honeycomb wouldn't even enter his body anymore, and trying to forcefully absorb it sent spikes of pain through his stomach and mind. Niobee and Beero were both equally exhausted from their own roles in the process.

Belissar sighed and his face fell as he turned to the remaining soldiers. "I'm sorry, it looks like we're out for today. But don't worry, we'll resume tomorrow, okay? We won't stop until we get all of you."

The wounded soldiers saluted and fell back.

Belissar could barely pay attention during that day's purification, which was a bit dangerous. Fortunately, the bees handled it without issue and he turned in for the night. The next morning, he went to welcome the fourth and final bumblebee queen, but his eyes widened as he arrived at the third-floor flower meadow.

The meadow was buzzing with bumblebees leisurely flying from flower to flower. There had to be at least a hundred of them.

"How . . . is this possible?"

The monster bumblebees weren't supposed to produce as many workers as the monster bees, right? Not to mention their workers flew slower than the monster bees as well, so they shouldn't have been gathering as much nectar. And yet, in just a few days they had grown to colonies of this size?

But Belissar soon discovered the answer as the First of the Fifth flew into the room, followed by workers and soldiers carrying honeycomb. She paused as she saw him, then flew over and began saluting. Belissar smiled.

"Have you been helping out the new queens this whole time?"

She slowly danced the affirmative. Belissar's smile grew. "Thank you for taking care of them.. You and the other apiary queens are helping a lot of bees now, right? Let me know if you need more flowers."

She froze for a second before breaking out into a happy dance, causing Belissar to chuckle. Soon, the bumblebees noticed the commotion and the three queens came out of their burrows to fly excitedly around both Belissar and the First of the Fifth.

Belissar grinned as wide as he could. Could this day get any better?

"Could this day get any worse?"

Tyhgak didn't respond to his fellow spearwoman's complaint, but he grunted his agreement. He grimaced as he thrust his spear forward, piercing through the shell of a giant beetle flying toward him. This beetle, like all the others they had slain, burst into an orange cloud. A cloud that made Tyhgak retch.

Monster stinkbugs were not his favorite thing to hunt. Not only were they filled to the brim with noxious gases, but they also only appeared in fields of rot cap, an orange mushroom that smelled exactly as its name implied.

But there was nothing for it. There was only a single Underway tunnel in this direction, so they had to pass through this way to scout the area. Besides, there were a handful of mushrooms and plants that only grew in rot cap fields which could be useful to Juosiutik . . . and perhaps to the sacred den master, too. It was just enough that it was generally worth fighting through the stinkbugs that fed on them.

Barely.

The stinkbugs themselves weren't that dangerous besides their smell, though, so Metsaitti and the other veteran hunters were letting a younger group handle the fight. These were the karnuq that Metsaitti had been challenging the dungeon with, and it would be good for them to practice fending for themselves. The fact that anyone fighting the bugs would be subjected to the full-strength smell of a digestive system specialized for rot cap *definitely* had nothing to do with it.

As Tyhgak was retching, another stinkbug jumped toward him. But just then, something moved in the corner of his eye. Noigakkuq stepped forward and thrust with a dagger. A black stinger made of mana formed around the blade and shot out as she thrust, stabbing into the stinkbug. Tyhgak gulped.

"T-Thanks . . ." he said.

And then Noigakkuq vomited. "Ugh, somehow, their mana smells even worse . . ."

Tyhgak's eyes widened and he pushed Noigakkuq to the side with one hand, thrusting his spear forward with his other. A third stinkbug had tried to pounce on her while she was retching. He barely managed to pierce through it.

Which, of course, bathed both him and Noigakkuq in another cloud of stink.

No, Tyhgak decided as he retched once more. This day could not, in fact, get any worse.

BEAR-ING YOUR GUILT

Tyhgak was hunched over and retching once more as the last stinkbug fell. It was weird—he had been exposed to more of the stink clouds than he cared to count, and yet each one still smelled as bad as the first. His nose absolutely refused to get used to it even a little.

But as he was hunched over and gagging, he caught sight of something. Once he had gathered himself enough to move again, he walked over to it and crouched down, trying to ignore the smell of the rot cap all around him.

Barely illuminated by the light crystal tied to the front of his clothes was a small patch of black flowers with the faintest hint of purple at the edges of their petals. They were short, shorter than the rot caps around them, which made them especially hard to spot as they blended with the shadows around them. If he hadn't been hunched over, he never would have caught it.

He didn't remember *exactly* what they were, but he did remember Juosiutik mentioning them, so he figured they were valuable. He nodded to himself and crouched down. He had *hoped* to hunt something a bit more substantial to offer to the sacred den master, but stinkbugs weren't great for . . . well, anything. Besides, bees liked flowers, so maybe the sacred den master would prefer this?

Tyhgak gathered a bunch of the flowers, wrapped them up, and stowed them, and then returned to the group. Metsaitti, with his face wrapped in a cloth doused in some sort of liquid, crossed his arms. His other companions were already there, and the spearwoman was nodding to Metsaitti.

"That's the last of them. At least, it better be."

Metsaitti shrugged. "There's never a last stinkbug."

They all groaned at that. Metsaitti turned to Noigakkuq. "Do you smell anything?"

Noigakkuq grimaced and held her nose. "Only one thing."

Metsaitti hummed and rubbed his chin. "In that case, we turn back for now. A rot cap field like this will keep most things from coming this way . . . and is a sign there's been significant death in the area. We should be fine leaving anything further than this alone, though we will need to be extra careful if we go in that direction."

Tyhgak and his companions gulped at that while the veteran hunters murmured their agreement. With that, Metsaitti turned around.

"In that case, let's get out of this field."

Tyhgak agreed wholeheartedly with that decision. The group turned around just before the end of the field, where the tunnel continued on into darkness.

Unknown to the group, two eyes opened in the darkness, watching their movements. They then slunk away, unnoticed by any of the karnuq . . .

Once the group got back to their base camp, Tyhgak asked Metsaitti if he could return to the sacred den. Metsaitti agreed and so off the young hunter went. His steps began to slow as he drew closer.

What, exactly, should he say to the sacred den master?

Tyhgak was many things, but a thinker was not one of them, so he pressed on even though he didn't know what he was going to say. He stepped inside the tower and took a deep breath.

"Um, Sacred Den Master? If you can hear me . . . would you mind meeting with me? I have something for you . . . and an apology to make."

He flared his mana a bit as he spoke. Metsaitti had said he would be able to speak to the sacred den master that way. Tyhgak wasn't sure how that was supposed to work, but sacred dens seemed to work however they wanted to in general, so that was nothing new. At first, he wasn't sure it had worked, but then . . . he heard something.

"Okay, I will meet you there."

A voice sounded out directly in his mind . . . or maybe through his mana? He wasn't sensitive enough to mana to tell. It was a little freaky, but he was the one who started the conversation, so he put his doubts aside and waited.

A short while later, the sacred den master came walking over, accompanied by the big bees as always. The sacred den master frowned and crossed his arms as he approached. Tyhgak began to sweat as his heartbeat picked up . . . but he guessed the sacred den master did have a reason to dislike him. That was why he was here, after all.

"Yes, you had something to show me?"

Tyhgak nodded and pulled out the bundle. He slowly unwrapped it to show the flowers inside. "I hoped to hunt something a little bigger, but I found these and figured you might like them. And, um, I wanted to apologize. I . . . didn't think much of you at first, and I was aggressive toward your bees. But you are brave and strong and have been kind to us all. You didn't deserve how I treated you."

The sacred den master took a step back, tilting his head with his eyes wide open. He opened and closed his mouth a few times without saying anything. Tyhgak wasn't sure what to make of that. He was about to try and say something when the sacred den master caught sight of one of the bees and his eyes narrowed. He took a deep breath before looking right at Tyhgak.

"I'm not the one you need to apologize to."

The sacred den master turned his gaze to the bees and Tyhgak followed. His eyes widened a bit. Ah, that was right. The bees could talk now, apparently. So, wouldn't it make sense to apologize to them, too?

Tyhgak lowered his head toward the bee. "I'm sorry. I shouldn't have wanted to steal your flowers."

The bee flew over to him and extended her abdomen. Tyhgak gasped as he felt a sharp pain in his arm. The bee had pricked him with the tip of her stinger but did not fully sting him. She then flew back and started to dance in the air.

"Is okay now. Don't do again, and don't hurt King, okay?"

Tyhgak nodded as quickly as he could. "Yes, I won't even think of that anymore!"

The bee paused, and then danced slowly. "Anymore?"

Tyhgak froze and began to sweat. "That's . . . I mean . . . I won't think of doing something like that ever!"

And honestly, he wouldn't. He hadn't been aware of how intelligent they were beforehand. Not that it would have made it right if they were just normal bees, but at the very least he knew now that they could understand his apology.

And then, to his surprise, the sacred den master began to chuckle. "That's enough, I think he got the message, Niobee."

The bee—Niobee, apparently—buzzed her wings but slowly fell back. The sacred den master then turned to him.

"Um, apology . . . accepted? As long as you don't hurt the bees. And, um, thanks for the flowers."

Tyhgak exhaled a sigh of relief and then nodded. "Of course, Sacred Den Master. I'll try to find something bigger on the next hunt."

The sacred den master smiled and shook his head. "This is plenty."

With that, Tyhgak took his leave. But just as he was about to step out of the tower, the shrine of bees began to glow. Tyhgak gasped as yellow light surrounded him and he was filled with mana. It wasn't a full blessing, but it did expand his reserves and strengthen his body slightly. He turned to the shrine of bees and bowed.

"Thank you. I'll bring him back something better next time."

The shrine's glow flashed brightly and then vanished.

Belissar crossed his arms and hummed. He . . . didn't really know what to think. No one had ever *apologized* to him before!

"*I'm sorry, Belissar . . .*"

He pushed aside the memories of his parents and Mrs. Imkomos on their deathbeds. That was . . . a different situation altogether.

Come to think of it, Juosiutik also apologized to him after the flame radish incident, but that had been an accident. This was the first time someone had apologized to him for something they had done intentionally.

Which . . . was strange. In Belissar's experience, no one who had ever treated him poorly had ever apologized for said behavior. So, Belissar had no idea how to react. Nor did he know if he should believe the karnuq. He had never considered a person like that changing their behavior. It was confusing.

But then he glanced down at the flowers in his hand and back up at Niobee. He took a deep breath. The karnuq had apologized to the bees, and Niobee was going to keep him in line. And he *had* done something nice for both Belissar and the bees. So . . . maybe he wasn't all bad?

Only time would tell. In the meantime, though, Belissar was not going to refuse the free flowers.

Absorb Underworld Phlox? Current samples: 0/5
Sufficient samples gathered. Underworld Phlox now available.
*Current Applications: Flower Meadow**

(=Near compatible features only)*

While Belissar still had plenty of things to spend mana on, these flowers only cost three mana per node. Besides, he still wasn't confident copper, iron, or silver ores would have any use for the bees, while he knew that a flower would. So, he went ahead and tried to make a node for this new flower.

Curiously, he could only make one in the first-floor flower meadow. But even when he tried to make one there, he found the transparent image was red. He frowned.

He tried moving it around to various places, but it continued to stay red. It wouldn't go in a pit trap, on a tree, or in the pond. He was beginning to groan when, finally, it turned normal.

Belissar blinked a bit. It seemed he could only place these flowers near the memorial. He wondered why that was but couldn't think of a reason, so he just made a node there without further questioning.

He was curious as to what a memorial-only flower would be . . .

CHAPTER FORTY-SEVEN

BEE-LICIOUS PREY?

A couple of days passed. Belissar continued to watch the karnuq as they swept through the way they had come. His eyes widened as he saw the mushrooms and the moss . . . and later a battle against the wolf-moles. The Underway was far livelier than Belissar had expected.

The hunting group was now making their way back with their spoils. Belissar went to welcome them back, along with Chief Rohsuak and the other karnuq . . . before remembering that the first-floor dirt tunnels hadn't been there when they left. He hastily swapped the tower's entrance back to the first-floor flower meadow so they wouldn't have to travel through the dirt tunnel maze.

Belissar wondered if there was an easier way to do that. Maybe some sort of room feature might work to bypass a room? But well, despite now having enough DP again for another room feature choice, Belissar was still staying away from those.

The hunting group arrived on the second floor to the sound of cheering. Meanwhile, the digging bee flew off of Metsaitti's shoulder, performing a salute dance in the air in front of Belissar. He smiled back at her.

"Welcome back, and great work."

Her salute dance only sped up. Belissar held out his hand. She paused for a second before landing on it. He then formed a bit of honey in his hand for her.

"Here, you must be hungry."

The worker bee stared up at him for a moment before gingerly starting to drink. In the meantime, Metsaitti walked up to Belissar, along with Tyhgak and one of the other young hunters. They were carrying a wolf-mole corpse.

"Sacred Den Master, thank you for sending your bee with us. She was incredibly helpful."

Belissar smiled and nodded. "I'm, um, just glad everyone's okay. Thank you for taking care of her."

Metsaitti nodded and then motioned to the two young hunters. They heaved with a collective grunt and placed the slain wolf-mole in front of Belissar. His eyes widened as he saw the sheer size of the corpse splayed out in front of him. Seeing one up close, they were a lot bigger than they had seemed while fighting the karnuq.

"We'd like to offer this to you, Sacred Den Master, if it pleases you."

Belissar slowly nodded. "Ah, yeah. That's . . . great?"

The question was what exactly he was going to do with—

Absorb wolf-mole corpse? Current samples: 0/1

Belissar's eyes slowly grew as wide as they could. He could . . . absorb animals? He thought about it for a second and then realized . . . why *wouldn't* he be able to absorb animals? The tower had never specifically stated what he could or couldn't absorb.

He shrugged and did just that.

Sufficient samples gathered.
Wolf-Mole Spawner is now available.

He just stared at the message for a bit. He expected something like that would happen when absorbing a living thing, but it was still a bit of a shock to have gained a completely new monster spawner just like that.

Place Wolf-Mole Spawner?
Mana Upkeep: 20 (40 with Blessing of Bees)

Belissar's face slowly fell as he looked over the message several times, particularly the numbers at the end.

Forty. *Forty* mana for *one* spawner? He hadn't noticed, since he didn't have any non-bee monsters before this, but the Blessing of Bees had that downside as well, didn't it? He *technically* had enough mana for that, but he could afford several monster bee or bumblebee queen spawners for that same price. He didn't even want to try and figure out how many mana flower nodes he could place for that much mana. And that was just for the spawner alone. What would wolf-moles need to eat? What would they need to make their homes? Belissar had no idea, but he imagined they'd need a bit more than a flower and a wooden box. This could end up very expensive indeed.

In any case, Belissar thanked the karnuq once more, and then left back for the third floor, thinking as he did. The wolf-mole was certainly an impressive sight . . . but how strong was it really? The karnuq hunters, who were already sworn to defend the tower, had no issue dealing with them from what Belissar had seen. In that regard, they did not seem worth the immense cost it would take to spawn them. Not to mention that they would receive no benefit from any of his tower's current perks.

They *did* have some value in that they were very large, and could add some much-needed bulk to his defenses. Likewise, they were optimized for digging and operating underground, so they would suit the dirt tunnels well. But . . . Belissar had the bumblebees who could grow to an admittedly uncertain but supposedly large size, and the digging bees who were now also optimized for subterranean environments. So . . . would the wolf-mole add something that the bees couldn't do themselves? Enough to justify such a heavy commitment of mana?

Maybe the karnuq could hunt them as a source of meat, but if the wolf-moles were like the monster bees and Belissar could communicate with them, would he be comfortable letting them be hunted? He shook his head. No, no he wouldn't.

So, all in all, he couldn't really think of a reason that justified the forty-mana upkeep. Especially not when he arrived back at the apiary and the First of the Fifth's workers signaled for his attention. He followed them to one of the hives, the same one the digging worker had come from. The First of the Fifth was waiting for him there, along with the hive's queen. A queen who had grown squatter and turned a dull shade of brown.

Digging Monster Bee Queen

Vitality:	*Minimal+*
Strength:	*Minimal+*
Speed:	*Below Average+*
Magic:	*Minor*
Defense:	*Minimal+*
Resistance:	*Minimal*
Special:	*Above Average*
Notable Skills:	*Dig, Poison Sting, Brood Mother, Command Offspring*

A monster bee queen raised or evolved on Ground Mana Honey.
Lays digging variant offspring by default. Builds a subterranean hive.

Belissar grinned. Well, now he definitely wouldn't need wolf-moles for digging. He was going to have a whole colony of digging bees to handle that task.

Then he paused and rubbed his chin as he read the last line of the description. "Would you like to move to the dirt tunnels? I can try to build you a new beehouse."

The queen froze, and then began a rapid salute dance. Belissar nodded. "Got it, let's talk about what you need."

Niobee came to assist, and they discussed what a digging monster bee hive should look like before moving to the third floor's dirt tunnels. They came to the large cavern that opened up into the apiary, where Belissar had placed most of the resource plant nodes for easy access. On the wall of this cavern, Belissar hollowed out a smaller cavern around the size of one of his beehouses. It turned out that the digging bee queen was now most comfortable when surrounded by dirt rather than wood, so Belissar had very little to do regarding the structure of the hive. All he ended up building was a single wooden wall to cover the entrance. However, the queen did still find his honeycomb frames useful, so he filled the cavern with those.

Belissar crossed his arms and hummed. It wasn't exactly a fancy beehouse. But it was what made this queen happy, and that was the important thing. He turned to the queen.

"How do you like it?"

"Amazing! Incredible! King is best king!"

He chuckled at the expected response. "Well, let me know if there's anything we can do to improve it."

"Okay!"

With that, Belissar tried to see if this beehouse would count as a beehive feature. And, fortunately, it did, despite the simplicity of its construction. The structure didn't change at all when Belissar applied the feature, but he could sense the mana flowing through the frames, so it seemed to work. The digging bee then happily left to begin moving her hive into their new home. It seemed that soon he would have digging bees in abundance . . . and Ground mana honey. He would give the queen a bit of time to get settled and convert her hive to the new type, and then arrange for deliveries of the honey to the first-floor queens.

He could only imagine what a digging soldier bee would look like. Maybe he'd end up getting wolf-moles of his own even without the spawner. And either way, the bee army would soon be able to take the fight to the dirt tunnels.

The only question was, should he wait for that before conducting the next expansion purification? He had long had enough mana to attempt an expansion. Between the karnuq, the first-floor dirt tunnels, the extra defenses they had added to the first-floor flower meadow, and the boost the communers were having on the soldier bee army, Belissar felt reasonably confident they could handle whatever the next purification could throw at them. On the other hand, digging soldier bees could be worth waiting for, now that he had a digging queen. Plus, the bumblebee hives were growing by the day, so maybe they'd be able to contribute as well if he gave them a bit of time.

However, it turned out that Belissar would not have to make a decision at all, as he suddenly began to quiver. His eyes went wide as a message passed across his vision.

Warning! Corruption levels surging! Emergency purification required!

CHAPTER FORTY-EIGHT

RAPID BEE-SPONSE

Belissar shivered as the chill of the Hunger assaulted him all over. He could feel the Hunger pushing in along the edges of the purified area around the tower, seeping into the flows of the tower's mana. But he had no time to sit and tremble. He *barely* managed to move the dirt tunnel room in front of the flower meadow again before the gates of his tower slammed open and the Hunger began to pour in, coalescing at the entrance. A massive foot crashed into the ground, digging deep into the dirt.

Belissar rushed to organize his defenses as the shade slowly emerged. He sent out a call to all his bees and the karnuq, informing them of the situation. Niobee had already moved to the soldier bee army, and the soldier bees and sprayers were now rushing to set up their formations by the first-floor flower meadow entrance. The karnuq cut their celebration short as hunters grabbed their spears and rushed for the staircase. Belissar was once again immensely glad he had put a dirt tunnel room between the entrance and the flower meadow, as it seemed they could set up in time.

Though, in this case, time was not the concern.

This time, there was no fast and lithe cat, nor a soaring bird. The shade vaguely resembled a turtle, though longer and squatter than any turtle Belissar had seen before. It sat low to the ground on six legs, though its sheer size was such that it was still as tall as Belissar. While the ever-present mist of the Hunger obscured the exact texture of its body, Belissar felt that its back seemed more solid than normal, like thick plates sealed together, with countless spikes growing out from them. Its head was squat and barely extended out of the plates, save for its massive beak, and its tail was tipped with several spikes the size of Belissar's arm. This was a solid, powerful shade that caused dirt to shake off the tunnel walls with each step it took. It seemed the Hunger was no longer attempting to outrun his bees.

The good news was that the shade was by no means fast. The bees and karnuq had all the time in the world to arrive at the flower meadow and set themselves up. Chief Rohsuak and Metsaitti came up to him.

"Sacred Den Master, what's the situation?"

Belissar was about to respond when he thought of something. He quickly called over Niobee and the bee queen in charge of the army today so they could hear as well.

"There's a massive shade moving through the dirt tunnels. Here's what it looks like . . ."

Belissar went on to describe the shade in as much detail as he could, then frowned. "I'm worried, to be honest. The past few shades have all attempted to run past the bee army. This one is not even going to try. It's got to be really powerful then, right?"

Chief Rohsuak crossed her arms. "Hm, that assessment is likely correct. The Hunger will adapt its approach if stopped."

Belissar gulped but shook his head. "Well, since it's slow, maybe it'll fall into one of the traps . . ."

Even as he spoke, the shade encountered the first pit trap in the dirt tunnels, one Belissar had moved near the entrance. One of its feet passed straight through the false ground.

The shade, however, did not fall, as it still had five feet on solid ground. It simply pulled its leg up and to the side, gripping onto the side of the pit with its claws. The Hunger seeped into the dirt wall of the pit and corrupted it . . . and turned it more solid than before. The shade then gripped the solid section with its middle two legs and extended out over the pit until its front legs touched the far side.

Belissar grimaced as he turned to the bee queen. So much for that plan. "Please, be careful. We don't know what it will do. It can bypass the pit traps, so we'll have to stop it ourselves."

The queen saluted. A communer came up to her and she began dancing out her orders, adjusting the soldier bees' formation. They took some distance from the entrance, with sprayers moving up to the front rows in order to engage at a distance.

Chief Rohsuak began to smile, though, and lifted a hand. "If it's as slow as you say, I should be able to help. I may need more mana, though."

Belissar nodded. "I have more mana honey upstairs. Let me grab it."

But Niobee flew in front of him. "King! Bees help!"

Belissar turned his attention to the apiary and found the bees already preparing to transport medicinal honey down to the first floor. He nodded and sent a message to the First of the Fifth, letting her know they needed regular mana honey and soon.

*

The First of the Fifth had heard the King and the Conduit's calls and was already organizing the supply run. The Second of the Sixth's workers were producing medicinal honey as fast as they could, while workers from the First of the Fifth and all the other hives were chewing through the wax, separating the honeycomb into chunks small enough for the apiary soldiers to carry. She then heard the King's command.

"King called!" she announced. "Wants regular mana honey first!"

Immediately her workers began flying back to her hive to prepare her own honey while the First of the Fifth organized the other queens. They had plenty of honey but they had not prepared the comb for transport, so it would take a bit of time to chew it into transportable size. Time that the King might not have. The First of the Fifth buzzed her wings, but there was only so much she could do.

Until she turned around in her dance and saw more bees on approach. The First of the Fifth paused her dance as the newcomer arrived.

"Fourth of Seventh? Why here?"

The Fourth of the Seventh danced happily. "Helping!"

The First of the Fifth's wings calmed a bit as she saw both the soldiers she had given to the Fourth of the Seventh along with new soldiers the Fourth of the Seventh had raised herself.

"Thanks, will help a lot. Please help carry—"

But the Fourth of the Seventh interrupted her. "One moment! Need to try something!"

The First of the Fifth was about to object, but it was then that she noticed the Fourth of the Seventh's soldiers were already carrying something. Vines made of flower stems woven together . . . much like those the King had woven for the soldiers to carry fire sticks with. Most of them were bundled up into bunches held by the soldiers' legs, but the ends of the vines appeared to be wrapped around the soldiers' thoraxes, abdomens, and back legs.

The First of the Fifth fell still. That . . . was the work of the King. So, either the Fourth of the Seventh was here on orders of the King . . . or she had replicated his work on her own. Either way, the First of the Fifth could not respond immediately.

While she tried to recover, the Fourth of the Seventh took her workers and soldiers to the First of the Fifth's own hive. The First of the Fifth's workers landed on top of the hive, tapping a glowing tray of honeycomb and causing it to remove itself from the beehouse as it did when the King came to gather his tribute. But, before the workers could start chewing it into chunks, the Fourth of the Seventh's soldiers landed. They let go of the vines in their legs, then picked up the ends with their mandibles. A soldier each traveled to the four corners of the square tray, and then chewed through the cell in the corner. They then pushed the vine through the hole and began wrapping it around the edge of the wooden frame.

Once they were done, the Fourth of the Seventh's workers moved in. They began adding wax and propolis to the vines wrapped around the frames, securing them in place.

A moment later, the soldiers began to beat their wings and rise into the air.

And the entire honeycomb tray lifted with them. The Fourth of the Seventh began dancing rapidly.

"It works!"

The First of the Fifth merely watched in stunned silence for a moment before breaking out into dance.

"Fourth of Seventh, have more of those vines?!"

"Yes!" the Fourth of the Seventh confirmed.

Her soldiers didn't only have the vines wrapped around themselves, but they also carried several bundles of different vines. The First of the Fifth quickly called over the apiary soldiers. Without further command, the Fourth of the Seventh told her workers to begin wrapping the vines around the apiary soldiers.

"Learned from King and karnuq! Stems help carry things! Thought could make moving honey easier!"

The First of the Fifth could only admire the wisdom of the King . . . and the Fourth of the Seventh for noticing his will. "You've done well, just like King wants. Let's move! King needs honey, let's bring whole trays!"

Every bee of the apiary saluted at that as the workers began to tie entire trays to the apiary soldiers.

Shortly after giving the command, Belissar was treated to the sight of soldier bees carrying entire trays of honeycomb by linen ropes wrapped around their bodies and looped through the trays. He simply stared for a moment. That . . . was an excellent idea. He should have thought of that after having the bees carry torches via the same method.

In any case, Belissar took the mana honeycomb tray while the bees chewed through the vines holding it. He then turned and handed it to Chief Rohsuak.

"Will this work?"

Chief Rohsuak licked her lips with a smile as a flame appeared and danced around her hand.

"Oh, that will do nicely. Thank you, Sacred Den Master."

CHAPTER FORTY-NINE

BEE-LAZING BATTLE!

Now that the honey had arrived, Belissar turned his attention back to the shade, trying to determine how long they had left to prepare.

It seemed they would have . . . quite a while. The turtle shade had barely passed the first section of the dirt tunnels . . . and had taken a wrong turn to boot. Belissar kept everyone updated as the turtle slowly reached the dead end and turned around.

And then, not so promptly proceeded down another wrong turn. And then another. And another . . .

Soon, the karnuq had begun to sit or even lie down around the field. Chief Rohsuak was just staring at the mana honeycomb tray in her hands. The soldier bees still maintained their formations, but their wings beat at a slower pace as they simply hovered in place. Belissar was mostly pacing about. On the one hand, more time to prepare was useful. On the other hand, Belissar could not calm down with the shade present and the feeling of the Hunger crashing against the tower's mana.

He glanced over to Chief Rohsuak and then began to rub his chin.

"Sacred Den Master? Do you need something?"

Belissar shook his head. "No, it's just . . . you're going to use fire, right?"

Chief Rohsuak nodded. Belissar then crossed his arms. "Hm, maybe I should reinforce the fire ditch, then."

"Ah, that would be wise."

Belissar began to add a second stretch of flower-less dirt across the flower meadow, this one in the middle of the room. And then a third, closer to the entrance. Anything he could do to keep a possible brush fire away from the bee barracks . . . and to give himself something to do in the meantime.

But then, finally, the shade approached the final stretch. Belissar's eyes narrowed. "Here it comes."

Metsaitti rose to his feet and barked a command to the karnuq hunters, who began to assemble once more. They escorted Chief Rohsuak close to the entrance of the flower meadow. The plan was still to let the bee army make the first attempt, but if the bees either could not bring the shade down or could not do so with acceptable casualties, then Chief Rohsuak would strike with her magic.

And if that failed?

Then the bees and karnuq hunters would have to do whatever was necessary. Belissar's chest tightened at that thought.

Soon, the shade lumbered past the final corner into the straight hallway at the end of the dirt tunnels. A sticky honey trap activated, spraying mad honey all over the shade, but the creature simply pulled its head back into its shell. Most of the honey covered the shell, where it did nothing. Some got onto the ground and the shade's feet, but with the shade's strength it could pull through the honey's grip on the floor. And since it was already moving slowly and carefully, the extra effort didn't slow it down in the slightest.

It then crossed over the final pit trap in the dirt tunnels and, a few minutes later, stepped out into the light of the flower meadow.

The queen in command immediately danced the attack signal.

Several squads of sprayers surrounded the shade and unleashed their toxic sprays. The shade, as it had done with the sticky honey trap, pulled its head back into its shell. The spray covered its back, but the shade didn't seem to mind. It continued to march forward without so much as a growl, even as the toxins bathed its shell.

But the queen noticed it protecting its head. She ordered a squad of sprayers to target the hole in its shell and they flew down to ground level, heading toward the shade.

The shade extended its head just to the edge of its shell and opened its beak. A cloud of black mist surged forward. The sprayers were still out of their own range, so they had plenty of time to evade. But the mist had forced them to break off their own attack.

The queen recalled the sprayers and ordered the soldier bees in next. They began to dive down toward the shade, targeting the gaps in the spikes on its back. But as they did, the spikes began to sway about, creating a shifting sea of deadly points that kept closing the gaps. The soldier bees were forced to break off to avoid impaling themselves.

One squad went for the tail on the shade's back. The tail was swinging about, complicating their approach, but the center section was both free of spikes and moving more slowly than the tip, so a couple of the bees were able to land on it. They thrust their stingers down . . . and then stopped. They had barely been able to get the tips into the shade, not deep enough to make a noticeable wound, nor to inject their venom. They still tried, but the venom just poured down the side of the shade's hide.

The soldiers let go and flew away from the tail so that another squad could attempt a diving attack. Most of them missed, since the targeted part of the tail was relatively thin, constantly moving, and covered by the shell's spikes and the tail's own on either end, leaving only a small stretch that the bees could attack safely. Others only managed glancing blows that failed to penetrate due to bad angles, bouncing off and away from the shade. The bees also tried targeting the legs, but the gap between the shell and the ground was small and partially covered by the shell's spikes, so none were able to make the full run.

One bee managed a direct hit on the tail and got her stinger maybe halfway into the shade. But the shade kept marching on without much response. If it had been damaged, it didn't show any sign of it.

Belissar gulped. It was clear that the bees weren't doing much to slow this shade down. Maybe they could hurt it through hits on the tail, but it seemed like it would take a long time to bring it down that way. More likely the bees would have to adopt a riskier approach . . . and even that might not do much to this shade.

He turned to Chief Rohsuak. She nodded, then began breaking off chunks of mana honeycomb and pouring the honey into her mouth, causing her mana to flare. Belissar let the queen know to pull back the army and they immediately broke off their attack. It took a moment for the one bee who had managed an actual sting to pull her stinger back out, but she managed and flew off to rejoin the formation.

In the meantime, Chief Rohsuak drank more and more of the honey and her mana flared brighter and brighter. Belissar felt the temperature begin to rise around her. The gray hair on her head turned red and spontaneously rose into the air, waving about like tongues of flame. Her eyes began to glow with red light and wisps of fire began to appear all around her. She soon set the tray down and wiped her mouth, grinning with a bright smile. She rose to her full height, straightening her back as she lifted a hand that burst into flames.

"Ah, I've missed this."

The other karnuq watched her in awe. Belissar's gaze was drawn to her as well. Metsaitti leaned over toward him.

"The chief was once called the Blazing Berserker. It's been a while since we've seen her at full strength."

Belissar just nodded as Chief Rohsuak stepped forward. The shade continued its slow and ponderous march, heedless of the karnuq woman approaching it. But that changed as she began to stir up the mana now surging within her and cupped her hands in front of her.

"God of Fire, grant me your flames to burn my enemies. Let them perish in the blazing inferno!"

She barked the words with a growl as the mana burst into flames all around her. The flames flowed down her arms and coalesced into a sphere between her hands. The sphere started out large and red, but then began to condense down and change colors. It shrank to slightly large and yellow, then to medium and orange, then to small and blue, and finally into a tiny white sphere too bright to look at directly.

The shade very much noticed the mass concentration of mana ahead of it now. It began to rush forward as quickly as its body would allow, which wasn't very. It extended its head and took a deep breath, unleashing as large a cloud of mist as it could toward the growing threat. But the bee army did not remain idle and the queen ordered the sprayers to react. They unleashed a wall of toxic spray that collided with the black mist, killing its momentum.

Chief Rohsuak then thrust her hands in front of her and the burning sphere shot forward, leaving a trail of white fire in its wake. The shade pulled its head into its shell, but the sphere shot right into its neck hole before it could turn away.

The shade exploded into flames. Fire burst out of every opening in its shell, creating a pillar of white and blue flames that reached for the skies. The shade screeched with a sound like grinding metal as its tail and spikes flailed about. The flowers all around caught fire, and a raging inferno surged across the field.

Chief Rohsuak collapsed as the mana faded from her body. Metsaitti had already stepped closer to her and caught her before she fell.

"Thank . . . you . . ."

Her breathing was heavy and labored. Metsaitti began to take her away, but she shook her head.

"Let me . . . see it through . . . to the end."

Metsaitti slowly nodded and instead propped her up as best as he could. Belissar, meanwhile, was staring wide-eyed. The inferno had grown such that the heat and the smoke had forced the soldier bee army to retreat. The shade was thrashing about as violently as it could, emitting as much black mist as possible, but nothing it did had any effect on the flames. Soon, it fell to the ground and black smoke began pouring out of its shell . . . until that, too, faded away and joined the smoke rising through the air.

Belissar was suddenly very glad the karnuq were on his side.

CHAPTER FIFTY

LOYAL-BEE

Belissar slowly began to smile as he watched the shade fade and a message pass before his eyes confirming they had succeeded. However, his smile quickly faded as he then realized the flower meadow was on fire. He first began moving toward the pond, hoping to try and do . . . something with the water there. But he soon realized that he would not be able to put out the roaring inferno on the other side of the flower meadow by hand. It was a blaze that reached up to the sky and sped across the field like lightning, rapidly engulfing the entire width of the flower meadow.

But then, it reached the first firebreak . . . and stopped. The fire halted, as there was nothing in the patch of empty dirt for it to burn. Some of the flowers on the other side of the break began to wilt from the heat, but none of them caught fire. And the inferno left as soon as it came, the meadow's flowers quickly burning up in the heat. The first quarter of the flower meadow was nothing but burnt and charred ashes . . . but the rest of the meadow was untouched. And Belissar hadn't even turned away before he saw small shoots already beginning to break through the ground in the aftermath. It seemed the flower meadow would be fine, and the fire had never even approached the bee barracks.

So, he turned his attention to the next object of his concern. Chief Rohsuak was still panting heavily, remaining upright only thanks to Metsaitti's support. Belissar frowned. The sight of an old woman struggling for breath brought back unpleasant memories, but he pushed them aside and stepped forward.

"Are you alright?"

Chief Rohsuak turned her head to him with effort. "I'll . . . be fine."

Belissar's frown grew. She certainly didn't look fine. "Can I help? We have some medicinal honey with a healing effect."

Chief Rohsuak slowly shook her head and chuckled a bit until she started to cough. "Thank you . . . but, unfortunately, I am not injured. My body isn't strong enough to handle that much power anymore. Just comes with age, I'm afraid."

Belissar's face turned dark. Chief Rohsuak blinked and then gave a gentle smile as best she could. "Ah, you don't have to worry about me, Sacred Den Master. This is nothing I haven't dealt with before. You won't get rid of me that easily."

Metsaitti smirked. "Indeed, didn't you *always* overuse your power even when you were young, Blazing Berserker?"

She smacked him on the head, though without much force. "One more word out of you and I'll show you a berserker."

Belissar took a deep breath and slowly exhaled. "Well, okay. Um, get some rest, then?"

Chief Rohsuak smiled at him and nodded. "Thank you, I will do just that, then. Metsaitti, help me back, will you?"

Belissar watched as Metsaitti and the karnuq escorted Chief Rohsuak home. Belissar then turned to the bees. "Ah, um, let's wait to celebrate until she's feeling better, okay? We should have her here for that."

The bees gave their salute and then dispersed, save for the queens. Niobee danced on their behalf. "King? Need talk?"

Belissar thought for a second before slowly nodding. "Yeah, we should."

Indeed, today could have been a disaster if it were not for Chief Rohsuak. The shade had been largely immune to the soldier bee army and to Belissar's traps. Without the Blazing Berserker's magic, the bee army would have had to resign itself to heavy casualties if it wanted to deal any meaningful blows to the shade . . . and given its defenses and its thick hide it was by no means guaranteed the bees could have actually stopped it even if they disregarded their own safety. Should that have been the case, they would have had little choice but to fall back and stay out of the way. Maybe they could have set the flower meadow on fire, but would a more normal fire have done the job? Belissar wasn't sure.

Worse still . . . today's purification had come without warning and without Belissar allowing it. And it had featured a shade perfectly designed to counter his tower's defenses. All of this reminded Belissar of a critical fact: the Hunger was not a passive threat. It would not sit back and wait for him to initiate purifications at his leisure; it would not let him just expand his tower at will. It would fight back, and it intended to win. It would not wait for him to be ready before doing so.

And, given Chief Rohsuak's current state, Belissar didn't think they could count on her repeating this feat every time. He would not want to ask that of her, either. Besides, who was to say the next shade would be vulnerable to fire at all? After he used pit traps to stop wolf-shades, a flying shade appeared. After his bees overwhelmed shades that tried to fight, fast-moving cat shades that could run right past them appeared. After speed and flight had failed, a shade immune to attack by his bees appeared. It seemed likely that the Hunger would not ignore what Chief Rohsuak had done today.

All of this meant that they could not neglect the tower's growth. They still needed more options and more defenses. And, fortunately, they had the opportunity to get some more right away. Belissar turned his attention to the messages he had brushed aside earlier.

All hostiles defeated.
Emergency purification successful.

Reward: Two random reward choices.
A non-patron god, the God of Fire, wishes to offer you a quest,
and will grant you a blessing should you succeed.
Accept?

Belissar froze as he read the last message, a new one that hadn't been there before. The . . . God of Fire . . . was reaching out? Was again offering a blessing if Belissar took on some sort of quest?

This . . . this was big, and equally concerning. On the one hand, the blessing of a god was a great boon, and it was being offered at a time when Belissar needed more power. It would be of great benefit to his tower to accept. But . . . on the other hand, Belissar had been taught that the gods were jealous. All mortals were to respect all gods, that much was true. But when a mortal had committed themselves to one god, such commitments should *not* be broken or disrespected. All stories of mortals who disregarded such commitments ended poorly for those involved, even when the gods involved were the ones with kind and gentle reputations.

The God of Fire was not such a god, according to the stories Belissar had heard about him. Sure, he could be as tender and comforting as a warm hearth to those he favored. He could also be passionate, tempestuous, and full of wrath, like the blazing inferno that had just raged through the flower meadow. Those who dealt with him carelessly could and would get burned, for fire was a dangerous thing even toward those whom it bore no malice. So, this offer, even considered by itself, needed to be thought over carefully.

But Belissar could not merely consider the offer by itself. Most importantly of all, Belissar had already made a commitment. The God of Bees was his patron, the god to whom he owed much of his success. Would she consider it an insult— or a full-on betrayal—if he entertained the God of Fire's offer? He would reject it out of hand if so, regardless of the consequences. Bees were what his tower was built upon and building toward. To gain fire but to lose the bees would be unacceptable. And, regardless of what the implications for his tower were, Belissar owed a great deal to the God of Bees. Ever since he had received her blessing, she had supported and encouraged him every step of the way. He did not want to hurt her, much less betray her.

But he did not know what she thought of the situation. There were no records on the God of Bees that the old beekeeper possessed, so Belissar knew nothing about her save what he could glean from his own interactions. Likewise, he didn't know receiving quests or blessings from additional gods was considered an insult to the original. So, Belissar did the only thing he could think of. He turned to the shrine of bees, intending to ask the God of Bees herself what she thought of the offer. If she was against it, he'd turn it down, regardless of the consequences . . .

But he never made it that far. The shrine of bees began to glow brightly.

New mission received: Earn the blessing of a secondary patron.

Belissar stood for a second, blinking repeatedly. Well, that answered that question. Apparently, not only would the God of Bees not be insulted by this, she actively desired it, to the point of offering him her own rewards for accepting it. In that case, there was no reason for Belissar to hesitate.

Offer accepted.
New mission received: Spawn or evolve one Fire attribute monster
of rare or better rarity.

The shrine of bees continued to glow and pull on the tower's mana. Belissar switched over to his tower sight and began to follow the pull. He followed the mana through the tower until it led him to a burning worker bee gathering nectar from a Fire mana flower.

"Ah, I see . . . I'll get right on it, then. Thank you for your guidance."

The shrine of bees flashed once and then the glow faded. Belissar turned back to his bees. Niobee was hovering in front of him, dancing rapidly.

"King! King okay?"

Belissar slowly nodded.

"Yes . . . and I know what we need to do next. The God of Bees and God of Fire both want us to evolve a fire queen."

His tower needed to grow stronger if he was to protect his bees, and now he had the means to do just that. Because at the end of the day, he was not alone. He had his bees, he had the karnuq, and he had the God of Bees herself on his side. And, if all went well, he might soon add another to that list.

One way or another, Belissar would do his best to prepare for the challenges sure to come . . .

THE NEGOTIATIONS

The sun shone down on a green and golden world. Fields of flowers blended right into hexagonal walls made of wax, like colorful jewels set against a golden background. Bees of all shapes and sizes filled the ground and skies, crawling out of neatly ordered hives, haphazardly placed wax pots, or out of burrows dug right into the ground. Honeybees and stingerless bees swarmed around bumblebees, carpenter bees crawled out of nests bored into trees, and digger bees pushed dirt out of their tunnels. The bees swarmed around newly blooming mana flowers and confronted one another for the best of the nectar, while cuckoo bees tried to steal honey and lay their eggs in the other bees' cells. Some bees even broke out into war, swarms colliding in the air as they fought to claim or defend their hives in turn.

Additionally, newly built wooden beehouses rose from the ground, and a large bee apartment expanded across several trees' canopies. New kinds of honey filled row after row of neat trays. Squads of soldier bees flew through the skies, training their formations, while communer bees spread out and gathered information. The edges of the world continued to grow, sprouting new flowers and new hives with each passing day.

And there were bees of other sorts, as well. Bees with blades for stingers, bees that could channel the elements, bees made of wood and metal. Bees without wings, bees without stingers, bees with claws, bees covered in spikes. Gargantuan bees that covered the sky and drank from flowers the size of the tallest trees. And bees that combined the forms of other creatures. Bees with more fur than normal, bees with scales and claws, bees with feathers and beaks. Any bee that did or could exist was here.

And in the center of it all was the largest bee to have ever existed, laying eggs of all shapes and sizes, watching as the brood tenders helped never-before-seen bees emerge from their cells before proceeding to lay yet another egg.

This was the Queen of All Bees, the God of Bees herself, as hard at work as any worker might be. Unfortunately, her work was about to be interrupted.

A fire burst into existence just before the God of Bees. The workers all around her began to swarm angrily, but she calmed them down with a short and graceful dance. Four of the swarms took a bit more convincing, for their queens burned with the desire to protect their second home after their failure to save their first. But the God of Bees convinced them that the fire was not a threat. Indeed, if it was as she expected, there was an opportunity to assist their first home even from here. The queens of the First Dynasty of the First Spawner of the First Bee Dungeon stopped and pulled back their armies at that.

A moment later, the flames expanded and formed into the shape of a man, with fire for his flesh and hot embers forming his clothes. Flames filled out his simple shorts and breastplate of embers. A bright blue fire formed the core of the man—his torso, limbs, and head—while yellow and red flames formed his hair, a great coat like the mane of a lion that surrounded his head and covered his arms and legs. His eyes were pure-white stars piercing through the blues and reds and yellows all around, causing even those flames to appear dim in comparison. He stood straight and tall with his arms crossed as his mere presence set the air around him ablaze.

And then the God of Fire . . . fell to his knees and clasped his hands together.

"Bee, you *gotta* let me into your tower!"

The God of Bees danced the same dance she had danced before.

"Come on, Bee! I know it's your only dungeon, but you have one of my favorite champions sworn to it now! Do you know how much stuff she's set on fire over the years, oh the great infernos she's unleashed upon the land?! She's called the Blazing Berserker, for fire's sake! You gotta let me bless my girl! She just saved your dungeon, you know?!"

The God of Bees buzzed her wings and then returned to laying her eggs. There was work to be done.

The fires around the God of Fire flared up. "Hey, come on! I know you're a busy bee, but listen to me! It's okay, right?! You even got a dungeon in an optimal position! Those are getting rarer thanks to that little human empire, you know?! You should be able to share a bit!"

The God of Bees paused her work, buzzing her wings again, and gave a short dance. "Need to work."

The God of Fire gritted his teeth and his eyes burned even brighter. "Work, what work?! You have all of one dungeon, Bee, and hardly any followers! You can't possibly have more work than the rest of us!"

The God of Bees laid another egg before dancing her reply. "Not me, you."

The God of Fire crackled as he gnashed his teeth. But then his flames died down and he exhaled a puff of smoke. "Okay, fine, let's work, then. Look, your little dungeon master is about to evolve some sort of fire bee, right, and he already uses a ton of fire. My blessing will really help him, you know?"

The God of Bees laid another egg.

"Of course, it'll be a mission from me, so I'll give him something too. How about a feature, since he's so fond of fire traps. That should help, right?"

The God of Bees checked on one of the larvae and conferred with the brood tenders before laying another egg.

". . . And once that fire bee evolves, our power should intersect enough for a cross-perk once he has my blessing too."

The God of Bees tasted the newest batch of honey, letting the hive in question know they had dried it just a bit too long. Though, the sudden rise in temperature may have had something to do with it, so she recommended they try the same method again once the environment was more stable. The God of Fire's colors turned toward dimmer reds, and he hung his shoulders.

". . . Okay. How about I give some of my dungeon masters a mission to earn your blessing on their dungeons in exchange? Let's say two?"

The God of Bees laid another egg.

". . . Three?"

The God of Bees ordered a hive to clean up the remains of the latest hive war. The bees would come back and do it all again tomorrow, so it was important not to let things pile up, after all.

The God of Fire burst into bright blues once again. "Okay, come on, Bee. I know you're protective of your first and only dungeon, and worried that my presence will distract from you, but that's why I'm giving you a good deal here, and an inroad to some broader recognition. I'll issue missions to *five* of my dungeon masters, including my biggest. That is my final offer!"

The God of Bees turned to the God of Fire as she danced, "Okay!"

The God of Fire exhaled another cloud of smoke and then shook his head. "Just where does a god on her first dungeon get that sort of confidence? But very well. By my name and authority as the God of Fire, let it be so."

The God of Fire snapped his fingers and a wave of power shot through the God of Bees' realm, raising the temperature throughout and causing all the bees to buzz. A reminder of his power, perhaps. But the God of Bees danced once more.

"Thanks, helps a lot."

And then she went back to work. The bees slowly calmed down and followed her example. The God of Fire chuckled.

"Well, I suppose we're both fond of our champions there. Let's stoke their fires together, shall we?"

And with that, the flames died down as the God of Fire departed. And the God of Bees couldn't help but break out into a happy dance once he did.

It was all coming together. She used to be one of the lowliest of gods, with no direct presence in the world below. Her only authority over the world was that given to her by the various plant gods in exchange for her services. None of the mortals knew of her existence, and individual bees rarely survived long enough to develop enough sapience to acknowledge her. Yes, a bee exposed to enough mana might evolve into a monster bee, but the bees who ventured outside of their hives to forage were normally the oldest and closest to death. Besides, mana-rich creatures attracted attention, so most of those on the brink of evolving ended up as prey.

Until one young boy decided to save a bee from a spiderweb. A bee that was on the verge of evolving into a monster bee with a far longer lifespan . . . and the chance to develop sapience. Just enough to give the God of Bees a direct hook onto the world.

It had taken her some years, but she eventually gathered enough authority to designate that bee as a conduit for a dungeon. It would be regrettable to lose her one direct hook, but every dungeon established would offer a trickle of authority to the god that created it, even if the dungeon master dedicated themself to another god. The God of Bees hoped to therefore establish a more enduring and permanent trickle of authority.

What she did not expect, however, was for the bee to take the boy, now grown into a man, along with her. Or for him to select bees as his first defender.

She rarely even got to offer her options, much less as a starting choice. While she knew the conduit would automatically give her a slot this time, she did not imagine anyone would actually pick it. Bee monsters could be powerful, but their strengths were their numbers and production, both of which required time and resources to build up. It was a risky choice for a starting defender.

But then the man, who happened to have been one of the most dedicated beekeepers she had ever seen, chose bees, and managed to pull off an initial purification with them. Then he chose *her* as his patron.

The trickle of authority she had hoped for suddenly became a stream. And, most of all, she now had a dungeon of her own. A direct presence in the world, and a place where she could gain recognition . . . and followers. And that was only the beginning of her dungeon master's devotion . . .

And now? Now the God of Fire, one of the most prevalent of the gods, with an established presence in nearly every world, was now negotiating with her as an equal, and letting her wring concessions out of him.

Yes, it was all coming together. The Queen of All Bees' queendom, the hive of hives, would grow beyond all recognition. The favor of the mortals and the respect of her peers would soon be hers.

But most of all? Most of all she now had the devotion of the most loyal follower. One who spared no effort in working for the bees. A follower who would be rewarded for his work.

And that's why the God of Bees danced one final dance before returning to her own.

"Belissar best dungeon master!"

The Glossar-Bee

Notable Non-Queens

Name	Other titles/ references	Current Location	Special Notes
Niobee	The Conduit	By Belissar's side!	Belissar's friend from before the tower!
Beero	The wounded soldier	The memorial	The first crippled soldier, personally saved by Belissar. Missing a pair of wings.
The Fourth of the Seventh's communer	The Fourth of the Seventh's worker	Orchard	The bee organizing the Fourth of the Seventh's hive . . . instead of her queen.

Notable Queens

Full Title	Common Shorthand	Other Names	Current Location	Special Notes
First Queen of the First Spawner's First Dynasty, the first of her line	First of the First		N/A	Gave her life in the first initial purification.
Second Queen of the First Spawner's First Dynasty, the first of her line	Second of the First		N/A	Gave her life in the first initial purification.
Third Queen of the First Spawner's First Dynasty, the first of her line	Third of the First		N/A	Gave her life in the first initial purification; prototyped the rotating squad-wave attack.
Fourth Queen of the First Spawner's First Dynasty, the first of her line	Fourth of the First		N/A	Gave her life in the first initial purification.

Full Title	Common Shorthand	Other Names	Current Location	Special Notes
First Queen of the First Spawner's Second Dynasty, the first of her line	Second First of the First	The Firstborn	Flower Meadow	Leader of the flower meadow queens and the soldier bee army.
First Queen of the Second Spawner's First Dynasty, the first of her line	First of the Second		Flower Meadow	Discovered that spreading her own soldiers among the army to pass on her commands improved response time.
First Queen of the Fourth Spawner's First Dynasty, the first of her line	First of the Fourth		Flower Meadow	Commanded the army against a bird shade in a minor+ purification.
First Queen of the Fifth Spawner's First Dynasty, the first of her line	First of the Fifth		Apiary	Leader of the apiary queens, top honey producer in both quality and quantity.
Second Queen of the Sixth Spawner's First Dynasty, the first of her line	Second of the Sixth		Apiary	Apiary queen who received access to a special flower by the First of the Fifth.
Third Queen of the Sixth Spawner's First Dynasty, the first of her line	Third of the Sixth		Apiary	First apiary queen not to get one of the initial apiary hives.
Fourth Queen of the First Dynasty of the Seventh Spawner	Fourth of the Seventh		Orchard	. . . What hasn't she done? Let's just say likes exploring and trying new things.
First Daughter of the First Queen of the Fifth Spawner's First Dynasty, the second of her line	First of the Fifth's First Daughter		Orchard	The first queen born from a queen rather than a spawner, currently running a joint hive with the Fourth of the Seventh.

Notable Non-Bees

Name	Description
Belissar	The dungeon master and king of the bees. Considered an honorary bee by the bees despite his lack of a bee-ish form.
Ruckanos	The tower lord's son who burned Belissar's village to the ground . . . and failed to acquire a tower of his own.
Chief Rohsuak	The leader of the karnuq, blessed by the God of Fire.
Metsaitti	The most skilled and experience hunter among the karnuq.
Tyhgak	A young karnuq hunter in training. Speaks faster than he thinks.
Juosiutik	A young karnuq aspiring to become an expert potion-maker.
Leijaliuk	The karnuq quartermaster.
Rakenliuk	Karnuq architect.
Noigakkuq	The runt of the karnuq clan. Has an exceptionally good nose.

FLOOR: 1F

FLOWER
MEADOW
ORCHARD
FLOWER NODES
BEE BARRACKS
PIT TRAP
TO 2ND FLOOR
GROVE
MEMORIAL
SHRINE
SHRINE
REGULAR
ENTRANCE
BEE-SIZED
ENTRANCE
TOWER
ENTRANCE
DIRT
TUNNELS

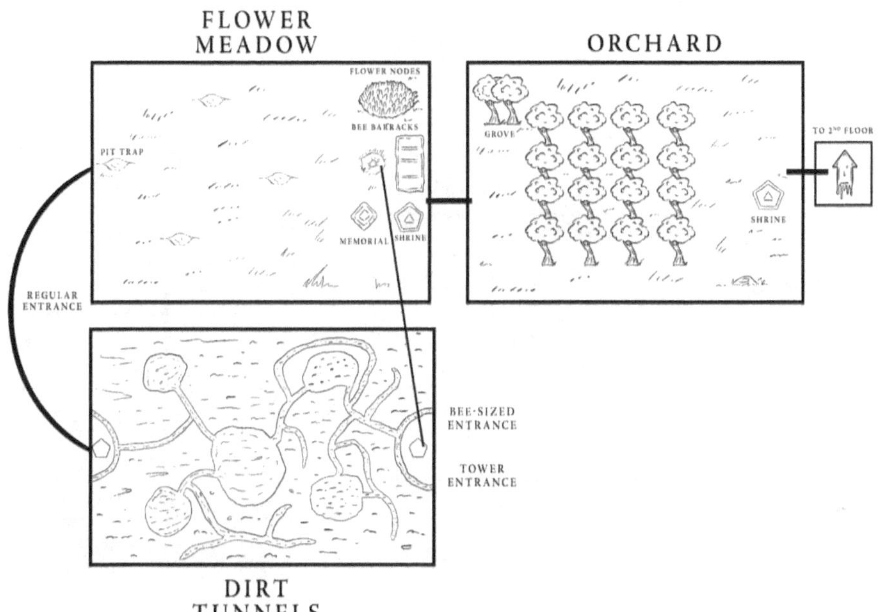

FLOOR: 2F

TO 3RD FLOOR
TO 1ST FLOOR
KARNUQ
FLOWER MEADOW
SHRINE
RESOURCES
KARNUQ
ORCHARD
SHRINE
SHRINE
KARNUQ
DIRT TUNNELS

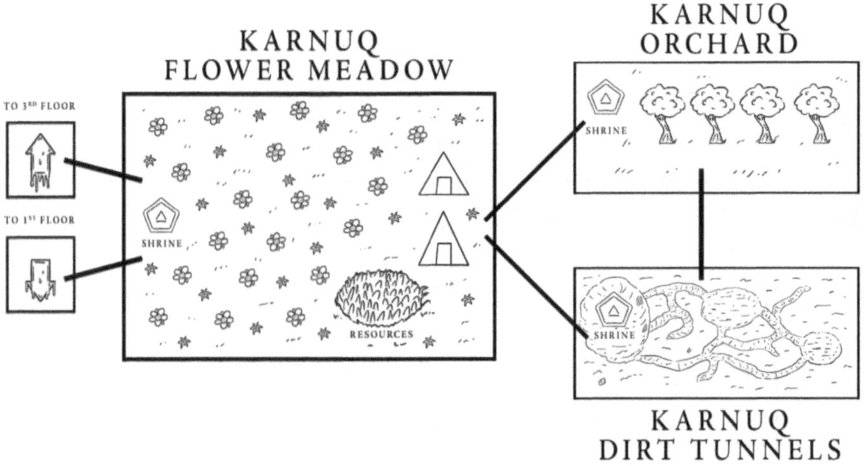

FLOOR: 3F

TO 2ND FLOOR
APIARY
CORE ROOM
FARMHOUSES
BEEHOUSES
SHRINE
SHRINE
FLOWER AND MUSHROOM NODES
SHRINE
BUMBLEBEE FLOWER MEADOW

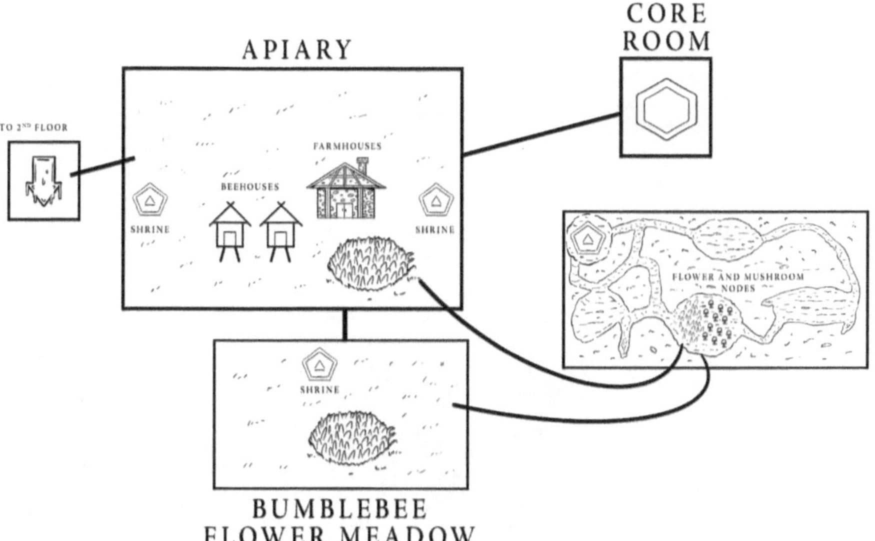

ABOUT THE AUTHOR

Icalos is a lifelong fan of sci-fi, fantasy, and video games, and the author of the Terminate the Other World! and Bee Dungeon series, which were originally released on Royal Road. To learn more, visit his website at icalosbooks.com.